Meaghan Wilson Anastasios spent her formative years in Melbourne before travelling and working as an archaeologist in the Mediterranean and Middle East. She holds a PhD in art history and cultural economics, has been a lecturer at the University of Melbourne and was a fine art auctioneer. More recently, Meaghan has been seduced by the dark side and now uses her expertise to write and research for film and TV. She lives in inner-city Melbourne with her husband and their two children. *The Water Diviner* was her first novel, which she co-wrote with her husband Andrew. The first Benedict Hitchens novel, *The Honourable Thief*, was her first solo novel.

Also by Meaghan Wilson Anastasios

The Honourable Thief

The Water Diviner
(with Andrew Anastasios)

THE
EMERALD
Tablet

MEAGHAN WILSON
ANASTASIOS

MACMILLAN
Pan Macmillan Australia

First published 2019 in Macmillan by Pan Macmillan Australia Pty Ltd
1 Market Street, Sydney, New South Wales, Australia, 2000

A catalogue record for this
book is available from the
National Library of Australia

Typeset in 13.5/16 pt Granjon LT by Midland Typesetters, Australia
Printed by McPherson's Printing Group

Cartographic art by Laurie Whiddon, Map Illustrations

The characters in this book are fictitious and any resemblance to real persons,
living or dead, is purely coincidental.

The paper in this book is FSC® certified.
FSC® promotes environmentally responsible,
socially beneficial and economically viable
management of the world's forests.

To Roman and Cleopatra. The finest things ever to come out of a dig romance.

Inset map

★ Istanbul

T U R K E Y

Kemerhisar ○ ○ Niğde

Mersin ○

S Y R I A

CYPRUS
Akrotiri ○

Mediterranean
Sea

LEBANON

ISRAEL
Jerusalem ★

○ Port Said   JORDAN

Alexandria ○

Cairo ★   ○ Port Suez

E G Y P T   SAUDI
ARABIA

Main map

LEBANON

Mediterranean
Sea

Palmachin ○   **Jerusalem** ★

Port Said ○

ISRAEL

Suez

E G Y P T

Negev
Desert

▲ *Har Karkom*

Timna ○

Canal

○ Port Suez

Sinai

Cairo ★

Peninsula

Aqaba ○

Jezirat Faraun ●

J O R D A N

Gulf of Suez

○ Serabit el-Khadim

SAUDI

Mt Serbal
▲

○ Monastery of St Catherine

ARABIA

▲
Mt Sinai

Gulf of Aqaba

The Sinai Peninsula
circa 1956

SCALE
0 ———————— 200
Kilometres

Prologue

He began the ascent before sunrise. Shards of cold desert air sliced through the rivulets of sweat streaming down his face and back. The shivering set him dancing like a marionette, teeth chattering and parched skin drawn tight across his bones. Before him loomed the mountain, its twin peaks slumbering black and beast-like against a dawn sky bruised violet at the approach of the sun. He'd spent long enough camped at its feet that he knew its every contour and shuddered at the thought of what lay ahead.

As the slope grew steeper he stumbled, chips of flint stabbing calloused feet through the worn soles of his shoes. He paused, heart pounding. Ragged breath scratched at his lungs and his vision blurred. The water in his flask was warm and muddy. There was barely enough left to get him to the summit, but it was sufficient. There would be no return journey.

The sun appeared above the horizon, a rosy disc piercing the haze of desert sand swept into the sky by the winds scouring the peninsula. Sunrise had always been his favourite time of day. A tight jab of nostalgia caused him to still his quaking body and shut his eyes. The warmth of the newborn sun brushed his skin, its light shining in starbursts through lids pressed shut over eyes burning from the poison in his veins.

He was decimated by fever and wearied by his labour here in this godless place at the ends of the earth. The ground beneath his feet seemed to buckle. Given a choice, he would stop and go no further. Sink to the earth, cross his hands at his chest, and succumb. But the heavy object strapped to his back like a tortoiseshell was an inescapable reminder of what he'd promised to do.

To have finally attained that which he'd sought his entire life, only to find that it was also the thing that would kill him, was a bittersweet revelation. Although he knew he should have been pleased, its power terrified him. When he first realised what he'd created he'd thought of casting it into the depths of the ocean, or smashing it to dust and scattering it to the winds. But his resolve wasn't strong enough. He needed to believe the time would come when an evolved world could benefit from this divine gift. Until then, it had to be hidden.

The desert air was thick and silent as the sun crept higher in the sky on white-hot fingertips. He was almost there. Everything was prepared. One final effort and the mountain would be conquered. He would retreat into the ancient sanctuary and heft shut the entrance behind him. Finding blessed peace at last, he would drop down into the dust, lay the stone in his lap and await oblivion.

As long as he remained undisturbed, the world and its creatures would be safe.

THE TIMES
28 July 1956
BRITAIN ACTS TO STOP SUEZ GRAB BY EGYPT

LONDON, Saturday (Reuters)

Before a wildly cheering audience of 100,000 people in Alexandria last night, Egyptian President, Colonel Nasser, declared the nationalisation of the Suez Canal Company.

Elsewhere, in the Sinai at Port Said, the Statue of Ferdinand de Lesseps, French builder of the Suez Canal, was stormed by hundreds of Egyptians calling for its destruction.

President Nasser declared that Egypt had no choice but to employ the income from the 103-mile canal in the construction of the proposed Aswan High Dam on the Nile River now that Britain and the United States have withdrawn their offers of financial aid. He said: 'We shall build the high dam on the skulls of the 120,000 Egyptian workmen who died in building the Suez Canal.'

The British Government today announced that it strongly opposed Egypt's move as a flagrant violation of international law. Prime Minister Sir Anthony Eden said Britain was consulting other governments on the canal shock. France, which retains a proprietary interest in the Suez Canal Company, is also expected to condemn the Egyptian action in the strongest terms.

Opened under French control in 1869, the canal passed into British hands in 1882 after Britain occupied Egypt and Sudan. The 1936 Anglo-Egyptian Treaty confirmed Britain's control of the canal. Today, Britain is the largest shareholder in the Suez Canal Company.

Sir Alexander Cadogan, a director of the Canal Company since 1951, said: 'There have been hints they might do this for two years, but no one thought the Egyptians would be so mad.'

The canal is the world's most vital oil artery. It forms a crucial link between the rich oil fields of the Middle East and European markets. Over half of Europe's oil passes through Suez. Experts say that any stoppage of the flow of oil through the canal would cast five million people out of work in Britain virtually overnight.

This comes as Anglo-Egyptian relations are strained by rising tensions in the Suez Canal Zone. Egypt has been pressuring Britain to quit its huge Middle East defence facility on the Suez Canal. The British base in Suez is one of the largest military installations in the world, housing a garrison of 80,000 troops.

Former Egyptian President General Naguib declared: 'We shall spare no effort, nor shrink from any sacrifice, however great, in taking such action as may lead to the achievement of our national rights. Twenty-two million Egyptians insist upon the evacuation of the British forces from their territory.'

In Paris, the general manager of the Suez Canal Company, M. Jacques Georges-Picot, commented: 'This is now a political matter. The next move must be made by our respective governments and all other governments who are interested in the running of the Suez Canal. It sets a dangerous precedent. We cannot take this lying down.'

An emergency summit of senior government figures has been convened in Istanbul. Representatives from Britain and France among other interested parties will meet for high-level talks in an attempt to avert military action.

I

Istanbul

'Well, here's to peace in our time . . .' Adam Penney raised a cut-crystal tumbler heavenward. 'Cheers!' He saluted his female companion. The expensive navy suit fitted him perfectly but despite its best efforts, it couldn't disguise the man's narrow shoulders and scrawny neck. For one so lacking in physical stature, he exuded a surprising air of self-confidence: that peculiar poise born of a lifetime spent at the right schools and in the best clubs.

He took a deep swig of his G&T and sighed with satisfaction. 'Essie, there's a drink you simply must try – it's a local favourite. I won't take no for an answer.' He leant forward conspiratorially. 'It's called *şerbet*. No idea what's in it, exactly. Spices, fruit. Plenty of sugar.' Clicking his fingers, he summoned the waiter. 'I'll ask the barkeep to add a good slug of vodka for you,' he added sotto voce. 'You'll thank me, I promise. This is one of the few things these bloody towelheads do well. Damned fine beverage.'

The woman in the chair by his side sat with ankles crossed demurely, her back straight and shoulders set. A powder-blue suit hugged her curves and highlighted the gleaming sheen of golden hair set in waves about her face. The ensemble would have made anyone else appear the very paragon of modesty, but although she made no effort to draw attention to herself, she still managed to attract the eye of every man in the Pera Palace Hotel's Orient Bar.

Her response to her companion's offer was restrained. 'Yes. I have tried *şerbet* before, Mr Penney. My husband and I travelled to Istanbul a number of times. On business. I thought I'd mentioned that already.'

'Oh, indeed?' Suddenly disinterested, the man's eyes flickered over her shoulder to scan the tightly clustered tables and chairs where diplomats, businessmen and tourists sipped icy drinks and tiny, tulip-shaped glasses filled with tea. A dull buzz of conversation filled air sticky with humid summer heat. 'What trade did you say your husband was in?'

'I didn't.' She took a deep breath. 'Import–export. Although if you don't mind, Mr Penney, I'd rather not speak about it. It's been a while now, but talk of my husband is still rather distressing.'

He leant over the marble tabletop and placed his hand gently on hers. 'Of course, Essie. Most insensitive of me.' He patted her fingers. 'You know, my door's open anytime you need to speak to someone. We may be work colleagues, but I'd like to think we're friends as well. And, please. I insist you call me Adam.'

She smiled tightly. 'Thank you. Adam.' His hand lingered on hers longer than absolutely necessary. The physical contact was inappropriate given the circumstances. But Estelle Peters had learnt very quickly that Mr Adam Penney gave little thought to propriety.

Withdrawing his hand reluctantly, the Englishman looked down at his watch. 'Now, where on earth is he? It's almost a quarter past the hour.'

The woman was pleased with the change of topic. 'With the traffic the way it is, it's little wonder he's late. It's not far to the docks, but those streets . . . they're mad. It's like a maze.'

'Well, he should have walked.'

'In this heat?' She laughed. 'I doubt Monsieur Josef Garvé would give up his air-conditioned limousine for the sake of punctuality. I'm sure he won't be long.'

Penney drummed his fingers on the tabletop. 'I can't for the life of me understand why he would go to the trouble of sailing his own yacht here to take up residence in the Bosphorus for such a short summit.'

'M. Garvé likes to have his own mode of transport on hand. Besides, have you seen his yacht? I wouldn't stay anywhere else either, if I had that as an option.'

'We're hardly slumming it here – I'm assured this is the best hotel in the city.'

'So you haven't seen his boat, then.'

'No. He hasn't seen fit to invite me yet. But you have had the honour, by the sounds. Should I be jealous?'

She ignored the question. 'If you had been on board, you wouldn't make the comparison.'

'Still.' Penney shook his head. 'Sometimes I wonder about that man.'

She pondered her long and complicated association with the Frenchman. *As do I, Mr Penney. As do I.*

She sensed his arrival before she saw him. There was no mistaking the frisson that sparked through the crowd gathered in the dimly lit bar as he stepped through the doorway. Conversations stopped mid-sentence and heads swivelled to watch as he passed between the tables. Such was the reaction to the arrival of one of the wealthiest men in the world.

His eyes were shielded behind tinted glasses, but she knew he would be scanning the crowd as he walked, taking the measure of the strangers around him. In his wake strode two broad-shouldered, black-suited bodyguards. He'd once explained to her that he didn't employ them because he feared kidnapping or extortion. He wanted to be attended by hired muscle at all times so he could do and say whatever he wished without fear of consequence.

Garvé approached Essie and Penney's table as his companions dropped back to take up position near the bar. 'I'm sorry to keep you waiting.' He reached across the table and took Penney's extended hand.

'Not a bother. Really.' In the presence of the Frenchman, Penney's bluster evaporated. 'We've been having a marvellous time here, drinking in the local culture. Haven't we, Essie?'

'Mrs Peters.' Garvé nodded. 'A pleasure, as always.'

It was a remote and impersonal greeting. She'd known Garvé for many years and although their relationship was strictly professional, it always struck her as peculiar that it hadn't evolved into a form of platonic friendship. But Garvé neither offered nor invited intimacy of any sort. And given the nature of their last transaction – also in Turkey but what felt a lifetime ago – she was not entirely unhappy about their personal distance. She'd never seen him express a sincere human emotion and as far as she could tell, he had no close friends or relationships – only connections with employees and business associates. Unusually for a man who wielded such power and had accumulated enormous wealth, he'd never married. Although she'd occasionally caught glimpses of very young women in his company over the years, it was a passing parade of changing faces. None of them stayed around for long.

In a rare moment of candour, he'd once shared with Essie the maxim by which he lived his life: 'My only rule is that I have no rules.' As she'd been exposed to some of the less savoury details of his business dealings, Essie realised that the less she knew, the better.

'So. Tell me.' The Frenchman lowered himself onto a seat offered with a flourish by an eager waiter no doubt anticipating a generous gratuity at the end of service. 'Have our illustrious leaders developed spines of steel yet?' He spoke in slightly accented, impeccable English.

'There are still some voices of dissent in the ranks,' Penney said beneath his breath. 'It's as we anticipated – those with closer ties to America are advising caution. They don't give a damn about the impact of military action on the bloody camel-jockeys, of course. They're just concerned about what our friends across the pond might do when we make our intentions clear. Word is Nasser's in the CIA's back pocket. And that gives the Yanks an advantage, considering they're looking for the same thing we are.'

'Adam, I can't overemphasise your importance at this stage of proceedings.' Garvé placed his splayed hands on the tabletop as the Englishman preened. 'You need to get in the right ears and make sure they understand that with the Egyptians in charge of the canal, it's not just oil that won't be getting through. We'll see a return to the days of rounding the Cape to get to the colonies. India . . . the Far East . . . to say nothing of Australia. Britain's passage to India will be a whole lot more complicated. And, of course, more expensive.'

'Don't worry, Josef. As you know better than most, we politicians are very easily swayed. I'll get them onside.'

'I believe you will, Adam. And what do the Jews have to say for themselves?'

'Same as always. Won't shut up about their Promised Land. And with the way the Egyptians have been harrying them across the border, we'd be hard-pressed to stop them crossing over into the Sinai even if we wanted to. No problem at all bringing them along for the ride.'

'Good,' Garvé responded. 'For our purposes we only need a brief diversion anyway.'

As the two men spoke, Essie Peters sat silently, hands cupped in her lap. It had been a long day of meetings during which she had played the part of Adam Penney's attentive secretary, taking notes and tending to his needs. The outcome of this conversation was irrelevant to her. She had a nuanced understanding of human nature and knew from the discussions she'd overheard at the summit that the die had already been cast.

Peachy-pink light seeped into the room through floor-to-ceiling windows as the sun set behind the arched domes and needle-thin minarets dotted along Istanbul's ancient skyline. Scarlet-red flags emblazoned with Turkey's white crescent moon fluttered in the warm dusk breeze. She half shut her eyes and gazed at the sunset through thick lashes, letting the soothing buzz of anonymous voices speaking in tongues from every corner of the globe wash over her. Essie lifted her drink to her lips and took a sip. Despite a churlish desire to prove him wrong, she couldn't disagree with Adam Penney's assessment; the şerbet was delicious. And the vodka was just what she needed to take the edge off the anxiety that had been building in her gut all day.

Outside, the haunting and melodic call to prayer rang out along Beyoğlu's tangled laneways, summoning the faithful to worship. Each muezzin's song was distinctive and dissonant. Just as Rome had its church bells, London had Big Ben and New York had its traffic, for Essie this would always be the sound of Istanbul.

'Bloody heathens with their caterwauling,' Penney lamented. 'About as musical as a flock of tomcats on the job, if you ask me.'

No one did, thought Essie.

The Englishman continued. 'Damned pity we had to traipse all the way to this goddamned outpost just to preserve the appearance of impartiality. Waste of time and money. Much rather we'd met up somewhere civilised. Paris. Rome. Anywhere but here.'

'I like it,' Essie countered.

'Well, I suppose the city itself does have its charms. Shame about all the Turks, though.'

Garvé changed the subject. 'And you, Essie? If what Adam tells us is right, then the countdown has begun. Have you everything we need?'

'Almost. I'm visiting the archives at Topkapı tomorrow. The document's there.'

'So you're going to leave me alone and defenceless, at the mercy of all my deathly dull colleagues?' Penney made like a petulant child, lower lip protruding and arms crossed at his chest. 'Who will I have to play with if you're not with me?'

'I'm sure you'll be fine, Mr Penney. It's the only chance I have to get the information we need. Without it, all this is a complete waste of time.' She smoothed her skirt down over her hips. 'On that note, if you'll excuse me, gentlemen, I need a good night's rest.'

Penney reached out and took Essie's wrist. Beneath the table his other hand brushed her thigh. It wasn't accidental.

'You won't join me for dinner, then? There's a market nearby with wonderful fish restaurants . . .'

'No.' She reclaimed her arm and stood. 'But thank you.'

'Well, remember what I said. Anytime you need a shoulder to cry on . . .'

'Thank you. But I find tissues do the trick nicely.'

'Fine.' Penney shrugged. '"*Yarın görüşürüz!*" . . . Turkish for "See you tomorrow!" I've quite the gift for languages. Doesn't take me long to pick up the lingo. Even this gibberish.'

Checking his watch, Garvé also took to his feet. 'I'll escort you out, Mrs Peters. I have another appointment to get to.'

'So, you're both leaving me?' Penney signalled the waiter. 'Well, I can't be held responsible for my behaviour if I'm left without a chaperone . . .'

Garvé paused. 'I'd recommend you keep your wits about you, Adam. This plan has been years in the making. You have an important part to play. Don't do anything foolish.'

His voice was measured and changed little in pitch or tone. Yet it still managed to chill Essie to the bone.

'What is he hiding from me?'

The domed ceiling soared above their heads as bellhops moved with muffled steps across the polished marble floors of the Pera Palace Hotel's grand foyer.

'Nothing,' Essie replied. 'He's too arrogant for that. And too stupid. He doesn't think he has anything to hide. Not from you, anyway.'

Garvé glanced into the bar where Penney had struck up a conversation with a group at an adjoining table. 'Can we trust him to keep quiet?'

She paused. 'From what I've seen, the only person he's genuinely concerned about displeasing is his uncle. Although he'd never admit it, Penney owes him his job in the Foreign Office. He'd be a joke without family backing, and he knows it. That's what will stop him talking. Besides, there's a limit to the damage he can do.'

'What's your reading of the meeting today?'

'The Americans are applying a great deal of pressure and it's having an impact. There are dents in the resolve of some of the people we need onside to push the British agenda.'

'The fuss the Yanks are making about backing Nasser – it's all just hot air, of course.' Garvé spoke below his breath. 'They're not interested in Arab emancipation. They just want to keep the British out so they can search for the tablet unimpeded. And British Intelligence informed me we've now got the Russians to worry about as well. They were privy to the same information all the Allies acquired after the fall of Berlin. I've spoken with associates in Moscow and Washington, and they confirmed that both nations have teams working to find it.'

'What's to say they haven't already beaten us to it?'

'Because they don't have you, Essie my dear. They may not know it themselves, but you're the real reason the British approached me for my help. An Englishman asking a Frenchman for assistance.' He laughed. 'Who would have imagined such a thing? But they need me. Such pride in the wealth of their museums, yet no idea how to furnish the cabinets that line their galleries. Their board members and curators have always known I can find them the impossible, not that they want to know the truth about what we're forced to do to get the treasures they seek. And in my hunt for ancient relics, you're my secret weapon.'

She smiled tightly. 'Well, there's no way anyone else is as close as we are to unearthing it. Once I've transcribed the document tomorrow, we'll be ready to go. The others may have some vague idea about where to start looking, but we'll have the exact location. If Adam manages to keep his colleagues on track, everything should go to plan.'

Garvé glanced once again at Penney holding court in the bar. 'And how are you handling the . . . personal . . . aspects of your relationship with him?'

'You've nothing to worry about. I'm more than capable of looking after myself.'

'Nonetheless, be careful. He's a man. Rumour is that he's not one to be trusted around beautiful women. Can't control himself. And despite your valiant efforts to project a respectable façade, he can smell your carnal soul.'

'What a charming way of putting it. I'll be fine.'

'Just the same. Handle him carefully. We need him. For the time being, anyway.'

'Was there anything else, Josef? Because if not, I really must . . .'

'No. That's all.' He took her hand and raised it primly to his lips, a strangely old-fashioned gesture. 'Please let me know as soon as you've returned from Topkapı tomorrow. A great deal depends upon what you find.'

'Good evening, Mrs Peters.' The lift attendant held open the wrought-iron gate and Essie stepped out into a lushly carpeted hallway.

Mrs Peters. Mrs Estelle 'Essie' Peters. Essie Peters. It had been an easy transition from the name by which Benedict Hitchens knew her – Eris Patras. She always ensured that her new name resembled the old when she adopted a fresh identity. It had been more than a year and she now wore her new persona like a close-fitting sheath. But answering to a name that resembled her former reduced the chance of slipping up as she transformed from one character to another.

She'd booked herself into one of the hotel's grandest suites overlooking the Golden Horn. Adam Penney had been rather taken aback when they'd booked in and he'd found that his secretary was staying in a better room than his own. Essie justified it by saying that she was paying the difference so she could stay in the same suite she and her husband had preferred when staying in the city. None of that was true, of course. But Essie could easily afford the astronomical price of the larger room, and had decided to make the most of her visit. The one personal failing she could not seem to shake despite an otherwise disciplined existence was a sybaritic appreciation of luxury. When required she could sleep anywhere, eat anything, and tolerate physical discomforts that would have broken most. But given the choice between a single bed in a pension and a down mattress with Irish linen sheets . . . well, there was no choice.

She kicked off her shoes and stepped out of her clothes, leaving on her stockings and slipping a silk gown over her shoulders, loosely tying the belt at her waist. A bottle of Spanish vermouth stood on the dresser – she poured herself a generous slug and turned the light out in the room. Crossing to the window, she took a seat in a high-backed armchair facing the world outside but invisible to anyone other than someone on the far side of the Golden Horn with a high-resolution telescope. If she was being watched by such a well-equipped pervert, she didn't care.

Framed by the heavy brocade curtains, the monolithic rose-madder buttresses of Hagia Sophia dominated the ancient district of Sultanahmet on the opposite shore. Corpulent clouds of smoke billowed from the chimneys of ferries idling by the Galata Bridge, awaiting commuters seeking passage across the Bosphorus to the Asian side of the city.

Benedict. As the reflection of sulphurous night lights sparkled on the velvety waters below, she thought of him treading the city's cobblestoned streets. She sipped her drink. He was out there – she could feel his presence. Her throat constricted with desire.

She slipped her hand between her legs and her knees dropped apart as she recalled the feeling of his lips against hers. Stroking herself, she played with him in her mind – her full breasts pressed against his broad chest as her back arched and she slid her groin along his body, his legs clamped between hers. She was wet and swollen beneath her fingertips as she remembered him, strong and pulsing, sliding inside her. A warm breeze blew into her room and teased her naked body, exposed as the silk gown fell open. Fingers moving faster, she reached climax as she imagined him bucking and groaning above her, his head dropping forward onto her shoulder and his teeth digging into her flesh.

Taking a deep swig from the vermouth sitting on the table beside her, she exhaled deeply, relieved yet bereft. When Eris had become Essie, a woman whose husband had been tragically lost in an automobile accident, she had imagined Benedict Hitchens. It allowed her to mourn the loss of their relationship publicly and hold on to the feelings she had for him.

Returning to Istanbul had been a risk. But now that she was in the city, the hot rush of excitement at his proximity was tempered by a deathly wash of fear that he would somehow unmask her. It was unlikely – her appearance had changed so dramatically that he would scarcely recognise her – but the consequences of being discovered were grave.

She'd toyed with the idea of excusing herself from the trip. Although there was no denying that it was best that she visited the archives in person, there were many valid reasons Essie could have used for not wanting to leave London. If she'd briefed Garvé fully about what it was she was looking for, he could have gone in her place. But the thought that she would once again be near Ben scratched at her insides with hungry claws. She couldn't stay away.

Like a bee to honey, or a moth to a flame, she thought to herself. *Let's just hope it's not like a lemming to a cliff.*

THE TIMES
25 October 1956
INCREASED BRITISH AND FRENCH NAVAL ACTIVITY IN THE MEDITERRANEAN

LONDON, Thursday (Reuters)

Attempts to negotiate a peaceful resolution to the dispute with Egypt appear headed for failure today. Britain and France remain committed to military action in Suez, a Reuters correspondent reports.

In recent speeches to the House of Commons, the British Prime Minister, Sir Anthony Eden, stated the government's intentions and defined the issues with regards to the Suez Crisis. Declaring that the world's commerce depends upon the Suez Canal, he stated that: 'it carries goods of all kinds for Europe and America, for Australia and New Zealand, and for Eastern countries like Pakistan, India and Ceylon. It is, in fact, the greatest international waterway in the world.'

The Prime Minister's condemnation of President Nasser's actions was unequivocal. 'This is how fascist governments behave; the world knows what it costs to give way to fascism. With dictators you always have to pay a higher price later on – their appetite grows with feeding. We have too much at risk not to take precautions. That is the meaning of the movements by land, sea and air of which you have heard.'

The Soviet Communist Party chief, Mr Nikita Khrushchev, was reported to have warned Britain and France about the consequences of becoming involved in a war with Egypt. He said if war were waged against Egypt it would be seen as a 'just or holy war' from the Egyptian perspective. If this were the case, Egypt would not stand alone, but would be bolstered by the assistance of volunteers from other Moslem nations elsewhere in the Arab world.

2

Istanbul

'You're certain it's her? It's not a very clear picture.' Superintendent Hasan Demir handed over the small black and white photograph.

Benedict Hitchens' fingertips gripped the sticky corner of the picture, crushing and creasing the paper. His heart was pounding.

'Yes. No doubt at all.' Recognise her? Despite his best efforts, he knew he'd never be able to forget her. The scars she'd left were still too raw. Yes, her hair was different – blonde, not the raven tresses he remembered. The light makeup, stockings, kitten-heeled shoes and tailored outfit were unlike anything he'd ever seen her wearing. But still, he knew. There was something in her carriage that was unmistakable – the knowing glint in her eyes and proud tilt of her head. Goose bumps prickled his skin and adrenalin surged through his veins – the Pavlovian response of a fieldmouse passed over by a falcon's shadow.

The day had started with such promise. As the rising sun had filtered through the gauzy curtains in his first-floor bedroom, the low moan of a passing freighter sounding its horn had woken him from a deep and satisfying slumber. Ben had squinted his sea-green eyes against the encroaching sunlight and stretched his arms above his head until his back cracked. A delicate hand had slipped around his waist and he'd felt the yielding warmth of a body tucked behind his, her breath fluttering on his shoulder.

The news of his discovery of Achilles' tomb on Mt Ida had galvanised public attention and attracted the interest of the most prominent practitioners in the field. When he'd opened the excavation he'd sought to employ the best professionals available. Fiona Melville was easily the most accomplished archaeological illustrator working in the Middle East, and Ben was relieved to know when she applied for a position on site that they had no personal history he had to worry about. With the emotional battery he'd endured in recent years, he'd sworn off 'dig' romances.

That resolution was tested once Fi – as she preferred to be called – made it clear she had other ideas. She was brilliant, fierce and beautiful, and just the type of woman Ben found irresistible. He didn't stand a chance. Determined pursuit on her part eventually paid off and at the tail end of a long formal reception at the British Embassy to celebrate the conclusion of the excavation season, Ben invited her to his home. That had been three months ago, and Fi had showed no desire to move on. If Ben were honest with himself, when he wasn't chafing against the unfamiliar cloak of domesticity, he enjoyed her company and was beginning to imagine a future quite different from the one he'd always pictured. Where once he'd imagined himself dying old, decrepit and alone, on the good days, he could now see the appeal of conjugal bliss.

So it had been on this morning before Hasan arrived to stir up the malignant ghosts from Ben's past. Languid lovemaking was followed by breakfast served at a table set on the cracked and mossy tiles of the terrace overlooking the Bosphorus' treacly waters. Like Ben himself, his newly acquired house was a handsome edifice that had seen better days. But it was a significant improvement on the dingy one-bedroom Beyoğlu apartment he used to call home.

When she'd first seen his waterside mansion, Fi hadn't said a word. She knew, of course, about Ben's chequered past, because who didn't? But she hadn't asked whether or not he'd acquired the house from the proceeds of the illicit trade in antiquities that had caused his downfall and he was happy to avoid explaining his reversal of fortunes. Although Ben was learning that Fi's enthusiastic embrace of a bohemian lifestyle meant she was open to experiences many frowned upon, he suspected she was unlikely to look too favourably upon his involvement in antiquities fraud on a grand scale.

Beneath a chestnut tree in the hazy autumn air, they were silent as they'd devoured their breakfast: fresh *simit* – the sesame-crusted bread rings synonymous with Istanbul mornings – crumbly white cheese, pucker-inducing dried olives cured in salt, boiled eggs, slices of fresh cucumber and the last of the season's tomatoes. As the dappled light fell on Fi's bare arms and the cries of gulls pierced the air, Ben had felt an unfamiliar but very welcome wave of tranquillity wash over him.

It had been short-lived. Hasan's arrival was impeccably timed to cast a pall on his day.

'So that's her, is it?' Fi leant over Ben's shoulder and took the photograph from his grasp. 'Hard to understand the appeal, really,' she added. Her response was too quick; too defensive. When they'd first met, Fi had quizzed him about his romantic history, and although Ben knew better than to discuss historical entanglements with new lovers, one evening after a night of drinking and dancing in Galata's jazz bars she'd caught him off guard. As he told her everything about the woman he'd fallen in love with and who'd twice betrayed him, Fi had comforted and consoled him. But regret for his lack of discretion wasn't long coming. Her compassion for his failed romance soon waned and anytime Ben shied away from an expression of affection or commitment, she'd bring up 'that bloody woman'.

'After everything you've told me about her, I was expecting more,' she said curtly.

Ben turned to Hasan, shielding his eyes from the morning sunlight with a raised hand and struggling to feign disinterest. 'So why was she in Istanbul? And why should I care?'

'I was hoping you might be able to help me shed some light on that.'

'As you'd know better than anybody, Hasan, my track record when it comes to second-guessing that woman is unimpressive.'

'That may be, Benedict. But you still know more about her than anyone else in my phone book. And if she's been here, sniffing around my city, I want to know why.'

'You're the detective, Hasan *Bey*, not me. It's been a long time since I gave her a moment's thought.' The lie burnt his tongue like bile.

'She was here three months ago as a member of a British delegation attempting to negotiate a way out of the mess in Egypt. It was just good luck that we managed to identify her. I wanted to confirm my suspicions with you.'

'So she's branched out into politics now, has she? One thing she could never be accused of is a lack of ambition.'

'We're presuming that's just a front. She's going by the name of Mrs Estelle Peters these days. Widowed, according to her travel documents.'

'Black widow, more like.' Ben laughed wryly. The last time he'd tangled with her he'd been lucky to escape with his life. 'But why would this be of any interest to you, Hasan? Political intrigue isn't your thing, is it? Or have you moved on from the Antiquities Bureau?'

The policeman tilted his chin up and clicked his tongue against his teeth, meaning 'no' – a gesture peculiar to eastern Mediterranean populations. 'It wouldn't have crossed my desk if she hadn't also arranged a visit to the Topkapı archives during her stay.'

Ben sat bolt upright. 'Topkapı?' *What was she looking for there?* he wondered. The archives stored in the library at Topkapı Palace dated from the earliest years of the Ottoman Empire. Since Mehmet the Conqueror drove the Byzantine Emperors from the city of Constantinople in 1453 and established his palace on Seraglio Point, the archives had become a repository for books and documents from across the known world, many of them unique and all of them historically significant.

'Yes. Thankfully, one of my overzealous underlings who harbours an exaggerated mistrust of foreigners noticed the entry in the museum's ledgers. We've learnt from experience to take note anytime a visitor to our country demonstrates an unseemly interest in our cultural heritage without going through official channels.' Hasan cast a sharp glance in Ben's direction.

It had been several years since the woman now going by the name of Estelle Peters had seduced a gullible Ben and implicated him in the antiquities smuggling ring that had tarnished his reputation. His name was now as clear as it would ever be, but he suspected Hasan would always have doubts about him. *Not that it's undeserved*, he reminded himself.

The Turk continued. 'She put herself in a great deal of jeopardy by coming here. Whatever she's after, it's important enough for her to risk a lifetime in prison. But fortunately for her – and unfortunately for me – I wasn't made aware of her presence in Istanbul until long after she'd left.' He pulled a notebook out of his pocket. 'So. The *Kitab sirr al-khaliqa wa san`at al-tabi`a*. Any thoughts?'

'Only that my Arabic is a little rusty.'

'It's also known as the *Kitab Balaniyus al-hakim fi'l-i`llal*.'

'Thank you . . . but still not helpful.'

'*Book of Balinas the Wise on Causes*?'

Ben smiled. 'Ah, yes. Now you're talking my language. The venerable Balinas. Also known as Apollonius of Tyana. Scribe of the most sacred of all alchemical texts – the Emerald Tablet. And through that, the patron saint of every crackpot who thinks they'll one day find a way to fabricate pure gold from pure bulldust.'

Fi laughed. 'It's lead. Alchemists make gold from lead.'

'Lead. Bulldust. Same thing.' He paused, puzzled. 'But why would she bother coming all the way here to see a document she could see in any number of other libraries? Why take the risk?'

'That's a question I'm hoping you can answer, Dr Hitchens. Trouble sticks to that woman like flies to rotten meat.' Hasan slipped his notebook back inside his jacket. 'And I'm less than thrilled to hear she's set her sights on Topkapı. Who knows what's caught her eye? The Spoonmaker's diamond . . . The Topkapı dagger. And, of course, Moses' staff and the Prophet's mantle. Priceless and irreplaceable relics.'

'Don't forget Muhammad's beard hairs and broken tooth. Though, let's be honest, who'd want to handle those?' Ben feigned a shudder of disgust. 'Thirteen-hundred-year-old body parts. Nasty.'

Hasan shook his head at Ben's irreverence. 'You seem to forget your own faith's obsession with the worship of saintly relics, Benedict. But I'll ignore your insult to the Prophet – only because I want your help. I need you to visit the archive and see if you can work out why she was so interested in this edition of Balinas. I've spoken to the staff – they're expecting you.'

'That was a little presumptuous, wasn't it?' For Fi's benefit, he tried to project an air of indifference. But it was a wholesale sham. Adrenalin coursed through his veins at the thought of the woman he'd known as Eris Patras. After all she'd done to him, the knowledge that he was still in thrall to her filled him with self-loathing. Every instinct told him to decline the Turkish officer's request. He was under no obligation to help him, and he had more than enough things to occupy him without embarking on a wild-goose chase after the woman who'd made such a complete mess of his life. But he couldn't resist. He was still consumed by her.

'Fine. On one condition. I'll need to take someone with me to help with the Arabic. The modern script gives me enough trouble – I won't stand a chance with the Classical variant.'

'Yes, yes. Whatever you need.' The Turk flicked his hand impatiently.

'Don't be too hasty, Hasan. You're not going to like this – there's only one man in the city whose knowledge of Classical Arabic exceeds that of most scholars, and who'll drop everything to help me.' He paused. 'Ilhan Aslan.'

Hasan looked up, mouth hanging open in disbelief. 'Is this a joke, Benedict? The only reason he knows so much about ancient languages is because he makes a living stealing and selling antiquities. And you're asking me to give that man permission to have unrestricted access to the museum? I'd more likely trust a fox in a henhouse.'

'Yes. Thought that might be your reaction. But you don't know him as I do, Hasan. And our visit will hardly be "unrestricted", will it? Presumably there'll be staff with us in the archive. I'll vouch for Ilhan's behaviour. If anything goes wrong, you can hold me personally responsible.'

'There's a saying in English, isn't there, about shutting the gate after the horse has bolted? He won't be able to help himself. And after he's gone, the damage will be done. How can I trust him not to take advantage of being there?'

'If you want me to help, Hasan, you've got no choice.'

Looking into the distance, the Turk's eyes were stormy. He nodded tightly. 'All right. I'll speak with the chief librarian. But you warn Ilhan *Bey* – they will be watching his every move. And if anything goes missing, yours will be the door I'll be knocking on.'

Ben nodded with more confidence than he felt. Confronted with a collection of precious documents so extensive that it was largely uncatalogued, he hoped his friend could resist the temptation to liberate a book or two from the archive on the assumption they wouldn't be missed. The American had spent the past year working hard to redeem himself in the eyes of his peers and the authorities. The last thing he needed on his report card was another scandal.

Hasan turned to leave, then halted mid-stride. 'I almost forgot. Your old friend Josef Garvé was here at the same time as her.'

Ben's hands balled into fists instinctively, fingernails digging into his palms. Unless pushed, he generally couldn't be bothered wasting energy on grudges. But Garvé was a special case. 'That malignant bastard . . .' he hissed through his teeth.

'It was a group of foreign politicians, so of course the delegates at the meeting were under police surveillance. When I found out she was there, I looked through the notes made by our agents. She met with Garvé at the Pera Palace. There's no record of what they discussed.'

Ben's head buzzed. 'You can bet that whatever it was, it's bad news for you.'

'That's what I thought, too. Anyway, Benedict. It's something to bear in mind as you think about the document's significance.'

If he'd been in two minds about whether or not to pursue her, news of Garvé's involvement was the nail in the proverbial coffin. He'd dreamt of destroying both of them. And if he had the opportunity to sabotage their scheme – whatever that may be – there was no way Benedict Hitchens was going to pass it up.

3

Istanbul

'You need to explain it to me again, Benedict.' Ilhan Aslan walked with his head hanging down and arms crossed angrily in front of his chest.

The Turk was dressed in one of the meticulously tailored and expensive suits that always made Ben's favoured costume of weathered chinos and corduroy jacket look even more down-at-heel than usual. To those who didn't know them, the two men appeared an unlikely couple. Despite his recent reversal of fortune, to his friend's disgust, Ben hadn't been tempted to invest any of his windfall in a new wardrobe. His indifferent approach to personal styling had never seemed to work against him when it came to the things that counted, and he had no plans to change now.

Beneath a furrowed brow, Ilhan's golden eyes flashed. 'Explain to me why I'm helping a man who'd happily throw me into jail if I ever fell out of favour with his superiors?'

'"Fell out of favour"?' Ben laughed. 'Stopped paying them,

you mean! I never understood – why don't you just put Hasan on your payroll as well?'

'He's the worst type of policeman – fancies himself as incorruptible. And he's doing everything he can to destroy my business.'

'In his defence, that is his job. In case you hadn't noticed, your business is built upon the breaking of laws he's trying to enforce.'

'Not the point.'

Soaring branches arched above their heads like the vaulted ceiling of a medieval cathedral as the two men strode in dappled autumn sunlight across Topkapı Palace's First Courtyard. Ahead of them rose the distinctive pointed turrets of the twin towers on either side of the Gate of Salutation.

Ilhan had been less than pleased by Ben's call. Although he'd begrudgingly agreed to accompany him to the Topkapı archive, the Yeni Kütüphane, it had taken some persuading on Ben's part. The dealer had been anticipating the arrival of a wealthy German collector who wanted to purchase a first century AD Roman statue of Eros and Psyche that Ilhan had 'sourced' from Ephesus. Over the phone, the German had used the magic words: 'money is no object'. By succumbing to Ben's entreaties, Ilhan had been forced to entrust the sale to his well-meaning and diligent assistant, Yilmaz. The young man's intentions were always good, but his ability to close a major sale was yet to be tested. Ilhan feared this could be an expensive excursion.

Ben understood he was putting a great deal of pressure on Ilhan by asking for his assistance – in Turkey, the bonds of friendship carried a much higher burden of obligation than they did in the West and he was duty-bound to help when asked. But that didn't mean Ilhan was particularly happy about it, and his irritation had been plain to see when the two men met beneath the chestnut trees in Divan Yolu and began their walk towards the palace library. Ben tried to pour oil on the waters by changing the subject. 'You know, only the Sultan was permitted to ride his horse through the Gate of Salutation. Everyone else – even visiting heads of state – had to dismount.'

Ilhan ignored him. 'Superintendent Demir is the last person I should be helping,' he grumbled.

'Think of it less as helping him, and more as helping me. Besides, it does mean you'll have one positive mark in your ledger with the department of antiquities.'

'I doubt he'll see it that way.'

'Well, then – it's the only way you'll ever be able to see inside the archives. Countless priceless books and manuscripts. Uncatalogued. There's no other way of getting to see the treasures housed in the library.'

'Uncatalogued, you say?' Despite himself, Ilhan laughed. 'Demir must be really desperate if he's letting me in there.'

'Come on, Ilhan. Behave.'

His friend glanced at Ben through narrowed eyes. 'Me? Of course. I won't put a foot wrong. I promise.'

A long timber table stretched out before them, its surface pitted from centuries of use. Golden sunlight streamed through rippled panes of handmade glass, illuminating the turquoise and cobalt-blue Iznik tiles covering the four walls of the reading room. The air was filled with the dusty smell of ancient vellum and parchment and the intoxicating scent of leather bindings.

When Ben had introduced himself to the librarian at the Yeni Kütüphane, the elderly man's white eyebrows shot skyward.

Fatih Alkan's spindly spine poked against the fabric of his ancient but well-pressed cotton shirt as he ducked his head deferentially, impressed to be in the presence of the noted archaeologist, Dr Benedict Hitchens. His reaction when he made the acquaintance of Ilhan Aslan was less sanguine. Tut-tutting and shaking the misty cloud of hair atop his head, Fatih shuffled into the archive to retrieve the book Ben had requested.

'Do you think he's heard of me, then?' Ilhan asked beneath his breath in English, stifling a laugh.

'Yeah. Your reputation precedes you,' Ben responded. 'Hasan did say they'd be keeping an eye on you.'

'Please. They can't stop me. I can deceive them in ways they wouldn't even imagine.' Ilhan paused and drew a deep breath. 'That aside – Ben, it may not be my business, but I have to ask. Why are you doing this?'

'Doing what?'

'Doing the bidding of a man who should mean nothing to you.'

'I do owe him, Ilhan. If he hadn't lobbied the Ministry on my behalf, I wouldn't have been given permission to open my excavation on Mt Ida. More likely I'd have been kicked out of the country.'

'He was just looking after himself. That discovery made him. As for that woman and the Frenchman, they're just shadows who should be left to live in the dark place you found them. Why can't you just leave them be?'

'What can I say?' Ben whispered. 'I'll never be done with them.'

The scuff of leather soles on the library's cold flagstones heralded Fatih Alkan's return. He shuffled towards the two men clutching a worn volume.

As he drew closer, Fatih fixed Ilhan with a baleful gaze. 'Here you are, gentlemen. The *Kitab Balaniyus al-hakim fi'l-i'llal.*'

He placed it reverentially on the reading table before Ben. As Ilhan slid his chair closer to the book, the old man tapped the desktop with an arthritic forefinger.

'I'd prefer you remain where you are, Ilhan *Bey*. This is an extremely early and valuable edition of Jabir ibn Hayyan's text and I do not want it to be damaged. Or – heaven forbid – lost.' He glared at him.

Ilhan leant back in his chair, brows arched above flashing eyes. 'Fatih *Bey*, I'm here at the invitation of Dr Hitchens and Superintendent Hasan Demir. I've nothing but good intentions.'

The old Turk looked sceptical. Ben attempted to distract him as he gestured to Ilhan to move closer, his hand beneath the table's edge and out of the librarian's line of vision. Without Ilhan's participation, the visit to the archive would be a futile exercise. 'I'd be grateful if you could tell me all you know about this book, Fatih.'

Preening, the old man was delighted to flaunt his expertise to a respected peer. Somehow, news of Ben's fall from grace didn't seem to have reached his aged ears. 'Well, as I'm sure you know, Dr Hitchens, we have the foresight and genius of the early Arabic philosophers to thank for the preservation of Balinas' writings – and that of many other important Western thinkers. While the early Christians were busy burning books, Islamic scholars were transcribing and studying the great works of Graeco-Roman thought. Without their efforts, all the greatest writers of the pre-Christian era would have been forgotten.'

'There's a Christian monk or two who may have something to say about that revisionist history,' mumbled Ilhan in English under his breath. Ben nudged him beneath the table.

As Fatih warmed to the task and began to pace up and down before the table, he seemed to forget his reservations about Ilhan. The librarian didn't notice the Turk as he moved to sit

by Ben's elbow. 'Jabir was Persian . . . an extraordinary man –
astronomer, physician, engineer, physicist. This was during
the first century of the Hijri calendar – or the eighth century
by your Gregorian calendar. But he was also an alchemist. In
this book, he translated the texts Balinas composed while he
was in Alexandria, although by then, of course, Balinas was
known by the name Apollonius.

'Alchemy is an art – a pursuit – that has obsessed humankind
for thousands of years. And this –' The old man leant over
Ben's shoulder and carefully peeled open the fragile pages of
the volume lying on the desk. 'This is the most important
alchemical text Balinas left us. Or, more accurately, a transcription of that document. The *Tabula Smaragdina*. The
Emerald Tablet. After Balinas discovered the tablet, he copied
down the text that had been written upon it many thousands
of years ago.'

Fatih left the book lying open on a densely packed page
of text and indicated it with a flourish. 'Here, it's said, lie the
secrets of the universe. And, for those who believe such things,
the instructions for transforming base metals into gold. Jabir's
translation is the oldest surviving version of Balinas' work.
Islamic scholars regarded Balinas as being gifted with one
of the greatest minds of all time, and when the Moors took
Spain in 771 AD, they carried copies of Jabir's translation
with them. From there, Balinas' words spread across Europe,
eventually reaching the ears of influential Christian thinkers –
St Thomas Aquinas, Francis Bacon, St Albert the Great.'

Ben cast his eyes over the opened book. The ancient
parchment was brittle and riddled with hairline fractures. 'And
this was the page of the book the Englishwoman was studying?'

'Yes. She didn't examine any other part of the volume. I was
watching her very closely.' The librarian dropped his voice.
'The scholars and academics who come here . . . well, within

these walls, most of the beauty is found in the pages of books, not in the visitors themselves.'

Ben examined the fragile parchment before him. There was nothing that immediately distinguished it from any other manuscript of the period. He ran his eyes over the ornate and – to him – largely incomprehensible but exquisitely drafted Arabic script and made a silent prayer of thanks that he'd insisted on bringing Ilhan with him. 'Remind me – where did Balinas discover the tablet? I studied under Ethan Cohn for many years. But it's been quite a while since I gave much thought to hermetic history.'

Fatih's eyes widened, impressed. 'Ah, if you studied with Professor Cohn, your knowledge of the subject matter will be a hundred times my own.'

'I doubt that. It was during my period of callow youth. I never paid his pet subject the attention it deserved. After that . . . well, we haven't spoken for years.' As a mentor, Ethan had been a steadfast and generous patron. But the older man was incapable of making the transition from patron to peer and as Ben's reputation grew and he began to enjoy independent success, Ethan set about undermining his student every chance he had. To lose the counsel of a man he admired and considered a friend had confused Ben, and their relationship had begun to fray. Any chance of salvaging their association was shattered when Ethan led the phalanx of detractors who came after him when his reputation was under siege. The betrayal still smarted.

'It's a shame you've lost contact with him. He's the foremost expert in the field. Much of what I know I learnt from his research.'

'Just the same – if you could refresh my memory . . .'

Fatih resumed his sermon. 'The tablet itself was reputedly created by the founder of Hermetic wisdom, Hermes

Trismegistus. Most of what we know about the great Hermes is conjecture. Some believe he was a prophet who lived during Ancient Egyptian times and that he was a contemporary of Moses. Others think he was a mystical figure in the pre-Egyptian era.'

'Yes, and there are even those who think he was an extraterrestrial being from outer space,' Ben interjected.

'No one with any good sense,' Fatih countered. 'Either way, the great Hermetic texts – including the Emerald Tablet – were discovered by Alexander the Great when he conquered Egypt. Deep in the desert at the Siwa Oasis, he found them inside the Pillars of Hermes – two columns, one solid gold and the other an emerald green that glowed brilliantly at night. When Alexander left Egypt in 331 BC, he brought the contents of the pillars with him to Cappadocia and hid them in an underground cavern. Balinas was a young boy living in the village of Tyana early in the first century AD and doing what young boys do – exploring caves – when he stumbled on Alexander's hiding place.'

'What happened to the tablet itself?'

'Nobody knows. After a life of service, Balinas died. But no trace of his body was found. Some of his followers believed his mortal remains ascended to heaven after he died. Others claimed his disciples entombed him in a secret cave with the Emerald Tablet held in his arms.'

'Let's hope there's something unusual about the inscription,' Ben said hopefully, taking his notebook and pen from his breast pocket. 'Ilhan, would you mind? What I'm confused about is that it's not difficult to find copies of the text. She could have laid her hands on that at her local library. There's got to be something about this copy that's important enough for Eris – or Estelle, or whatever name she's going by now – to have put her own head on the chopping block. If you could translate the text for me . . .'

'So this will tell me how to conjure up gold, you say? How can I refuse?' Under Fatih's watchful eye, the Turk leant over the book and began to read.

It's true without lying, certain and most true.

That which is below is the same as that which is above. That which is above is like that which is below. To make the miracle of the one and the only thing.

And as all things have been and arose from the contemplation of the one, so all things are born from this one adaptation.

The sun is its father, the moon is its mother, the wind carried it in its belly, and the earth is its nurse.

It is the father of all perfection in the world.

Its force or power is entire if it is cast towards earth. It separates the earth from the fire, the subtle from the gross, sweetly with great industry.

It ascends from earth to heaven and again it descends to earth and receives the power of things above and below.

By this means you shall have the glory of the whole world and then you shall drive away all shadows and blindness.

Its force is above all force, for it overcomes every subtle thing and penetrates every solid thing.

So it was that the world was created.

From this are and do come admirable adaptations where all means are here in this.

I am called Hermes Trismegistus, having the three parts of the wisdom of the whole world.

That which I have said of the operation of the sun is accomplished and ended.

Ilhan looked up. 'Am I missing something?'

'No. That's it. You wouldn't expect them to give it up that easily, would you? Alchemical wisdom is always couched in deliberately obscure terminology – hidden in plain sight. Deciphering it is as complex as cracking military codes. More so, even, because it requires expert knowledge of an arcane and obscure world.' Ben was puzzled. 'OK. So that sounds like every other translation of the tablet I've read. What makes this one so special?'

He passed Ilhan his notebook and pen. 'Be a friend and transcribe the Arabic for me, would you?'

'Friend, you say? Secretary, more like,' the Turk grumbled.

Ben ignored Ilhan's bellyaching and took a jewellers' loupe from his satchel. Running the magnifying glass over the manuscript, he looked for anything out of the ordinary. Other than patches on the parchment that had a strange, glossy sheen attributable to wear and handling over many centuries, there was nothing unusual about the page. He dropped his head into his hands, frustrated.

What had been a balmy autumn day outside had begun to turn wintry. Through the reading room's windows a dense bank of clouds came scudding across the Bosphorus towards the emerald-green gardens of Topkapı. Ben's gaze was focused on the ancient manuscript as the approaching storm bled across the face of the sun and cast the room into darkness. Then he saw it; a slight luminescence on the parchment. Doubting his own eyes, his heart began to pound as he ducked his head closer to the page and cupped his hands around his eyes to block out as much light as he could. There was no mistaking it. The patches of glossy texture he'd dismissed as patina were glowing.

He leapt to his feet. 'Fatih! The woman who was here – did she examine the book in the dark?'

'Well, yes, now you mention it. It did seem a little odd. She said she wanted to look at it under torchlight. I didn't think it would do any harm.'

'Where? Where did she take it?'

The old man gestured to a doorway set in the reading room's wall. 'There. It's one of our archive rooms. No windows in there.'

'What did she find?'

'I don't know. I took the book in there for her, but left her alone. It wouldn't be proper to be in there alone with her in the dark. A foreign woman? And one so beautiful? Not proper at all.'

'Fatih, may I . . .?'

The librarian shrugged. 'I don't see why not.'

'What is it?' Ilhan stood at his friend's shoulder.

'I don't know. But we're about to find out.'

Hands trembling, he placed the open book carefully on the desktop. 'Ilhan, shut the door, would you?'

As the room was cast into pitch black, his eyes adjusted slowly to the dark.

There was no mistaking it. Markings on the ancient page seemed to hover in midair, glowing an eerie, phosphorescent green.

'*Maşallah*!' Ilhan exclaimed.

The entire page had been over-painted with delicate ink brushstrokes that were invisible in daylight, but which gleamed in the dark with the same luminosity as the markings on the dial of Ben's Omega watch. Twin mountain peaks stood side by side, the one on the left surmounted by an erect phallus pointing skyward, the other breached by a stylised vulva. In the sky above the twin mountains hung a solar disc and a crescent moon. A constellation of stars shone above the mountain on the right.

'Orion,' Ben mumbled, dumbstruck by the hidden tableau the darkness had revealed to them.

His friend stood at his shoulder, his fast-paced breathing betraying his excitement. 'What?'

'The stars. There . . .' He pointed, his finger a black shadow against the gleaming inscription. 'It's the Hunter. Those three stars there, in a diagonal row above the mountain? That's Orion's Belt.'

'Have you ever seen anything like this?'

Heart pounding, he shook his head. 'Never.'

In the space immediately beneath the mountain on the right-hand side of the composition was a pyramidal mound of what looked like small, round stones covering a crescent-shaped object. At the apex of the mound sat a raven, wings outstretched and holding one of the stones in his beak.

Above the summit of the mountain, in line with the three stars of Orion's Belt, was a black-eyed skull.

'A warning?' Ilhan asked.

'Don't take it literally. Alchemical symbolism is always obscure. A skull doesn't necessarily mean "death".'

'What does it mean, then?'

'Rebirth . . . renewal. A process – the death of one thing to give birth to another . . .'

'I thought you said your recollections of alchemical lore were hazy.'

'It's coming back to me.' Ben flicked the switch by the door, and the room was flooded with light. The luminescent drawing disappeared. 'That ink, though – that's bloody interesting. I've never seen anything like it. The Romans added uranium to glass for mosaics to make them glow – same as the decorative glassware you can buy now. But I've never heard of it being used for something like this – if that is what they've done here. Most peculiar. And ingenious.'

'Excuse me? Are you done?' The ancient hinges of the door behind them groaned as the librarian inched into the room. 'Did you find anything?'

'No, nothing unusual.' Ben tried to control the excitement in his voice. 'But can you tell me, Fatih – do you know where this book came from?'

'The Englishwoman asked the same thing. Most of the books in the archive aren't catalogued. Truth be told, we don't know what's in here, much less how the books got here. The Ottoman Sultans gathered treasures from across the known world, and foreign dignitaries sent gifts to swell the royal archives. But it wasn't like nowadays – back then where books came from wasn't deemed important. Most times, they didn't keep any records. But there is this . . .' The old man reached for the volume and carefully turned to its flyleaf, indicating a faded stamp in the top corner about the size of a small coin.

'A collector's stamp?'

'Yes. So it seems. But you don't usually see them in books. And I've never seen that one before. The combination of symbols is very unusual.' The motif comprised an oval line encircling a collection of apparently unrelated forms: a circle, a crescent, a horned staff and a serpent.

Ilhan leant forward to examine the page. 'That doesn't seem right. I've seen these on prints and drawings from major collectors, but they usually used their own initials, or an identifiable family crest.' He peered closer. 'I've never seen an abstract one like this. It's very peculiar.'

Ben opened the book again at the Emerald Tablet inscription. They had been conversing in Turkish, but now he switched to English. 'Ilhan, I've no idea what this is about, but the only way I'll work it out is if I borrow this document from the book and study it in more detail.'

'Borrow?'

'OK. Steal. I don't see Hasan – much less Fatih – letting me take it out of the archive. So this is my only chance.'

He glanced up at the librarian, who was frowning, oblivious to the purpose of their conversation. 'How about you take a stroll among the collection? I only need a short distraction.'

Ilhan didn't need to be asked twice. Spinning on his heel, he wandered aimlessly over to the teetering bookshelves. Fatih watched him suspiciously. 'Where are you going, Ilhan *Bey*?'

'I've heard much about the Topkapı Koran. I'd really like to see it. Is it back here?'

'The Qur'ān of 'Uthmān? It is almost one-and-a-half thousand years old, and the work of 'Uthmān ibn 'Affān . . . the companion of the Prophet,' the librarian said, voice quavering. 'It is a sacred manuscript, and you're to stay well away from it!'

'So . . . you mentioned that most of these books are uncatalogued.' As he spoke, Ilhan strode purposefully into the stacks, his fingers trailing along the spines of a row of ancient books. 'That's fairly risky, isn't it? Would you even notice if one or two of them went missing?'

Without a backward glance, Fatih rushed after Ilhan into the dimly lit corridor between bookshelves that reached to the ceiling.

Ben acted swiftly. He knew he didn't have long. The stitch-binding of the book was loose, and it didn't take much to tease the page away from the spine. *What on earth am I doing? If Hasan gets wind of this, I'm finished . . . again,* he thought ruefully as he carefully slipped the sheet into his journal.

'Ilhan?' he called. 'If you've done tormenting Fatih, we need to go.'

His friend emerged from the stacks, eyes sparkling. 'All finished, then?'

'Yes. Time we were off.' He closed the book and handed it back to the librarian, willing him to keep it shut, at least until they'd had time to escape the palace grounds.

'It's quite remarkable, you know,' the librarian said, clutching the ancient tome in breadstick-brittle arms. 'I may as well put this out on permanent display with the interest it's been getting. This book has been here for hundreds of years. I can't think of a single time I've had to bring it out of storage until recently. But now? A constant stream of visitors. The Englishwoman. An American diplomat. Two visiting Soviet scholars – they were here just yesterday. And now you!'

It would have been comforting to dismiss it as coincidence, but that was something in which Benedict Hitchens put little stock.

Despite the autumnal chill in the air, a sheen of perspiration sat in a slick across Ben's back as he and Ilhan walked briskly away from the archive, heels clicking on the courtyard's worn paving stones.

A beetle-browed man with a linebacker's shoulders fixed them with a leery glare as he strode towards them from the Gate of Salutation's shadowy entrance. *Well, that was quicker than I expected*, Ben thought helplessly. He'd expected the librarian to put the book back in the archive without opening it again. Not for the first time in his life, he'd taken a bet on long odds, and it seemed he'd lost.

'A guard?' Ilhan murmured.

'Looks like it.' His muscles tensed and he greedily sucked air deep into his lungs, readying for a fight. 'Keep walking.'

'Should we run for it?'

'No point.' *I'm a goddamned idiot.*

As the man approached, Ben steeled himself. The sensible thing to do would be to surrender to the inevitable. But as the events of the preceding half-hour confirmed, common sense wasn't one of Ben's strongest character traits.

The man narrowed his eyes as he was forced to walk off the path and onto the grass to pass them. He shot a sullen glance back at them and then was gone, walking towards the library building.

Relieved, Ben exhaled. 'Jesus. That had me worried.'

'Had *you* worried?' Ilhan elbowed his friend. 'I've spent most of my adult life avoiding arrest, Benedict. Give me a little warning next time you plan to do something so foolhardy. That was an amateur job. If you'd let me help, I'd have made sure it wasn't so damned obvious.'

The library door groaned. A gust of wind blew in as it opened, causing the pages of the manuscript to flutter like a moth's wings.

Fatih sighed as he turned to face the entrance. 'I'm sorry, but you need to make an arrangement with the museum to visit the archives. I have no record of any more appointments today.'

'Appointment?' The man slammed the door behind him and slid the lock shut with fat, blunt-ended fingers. 'I don't make appointments.' In two strides he crossed the room and, before the librarian could utter a word, wrenched the old man's arms behind him and frogmarched him into the airless archive. Fatih struggled weakly as he was cuffed to a chair, but was in such shock he didn't make a sound as his mouth gaped like a hooked fish.

'Who were those men?'

The librarian's breath came in ragged gasps. Drawing back a fist the size of a baseball mitt, the man slammed it into Fatih's thin-bridged nose. The cartilage snapped and a vermillion stream of blood ran in rivulets down his chin, gore dripping onto the front of his white shirt.

'I'll ask you again. Who were those men?'

'Two men . . .' The librarian stammered through the blood bubbling from between his lips. 'An American – an archaeologist. Dr Hitchens. Dr Benedict Hitchens. And Ilhan . . . Aslan. Ilhan Aslan . . . antiquities dealer . . .' He dropped his head. 'Please . . .'

'What were they looking at?'

'A book.'

'Do I look like an idiot?' With an open hand, the man slapped Fatih in the side of the head. The librarian collapsed against the weight of the blow. 'Of course they were looking at a book, you stupid old man. Which book?'

'Out there. On the desk. It has a page . . . the Emerald Tablet.'

'And has anyone else been here to see it?'

'No . . . I mean, yes . . . two . . . three. No – four people. I don't . . .' The librarian was panting, his eyes clouded with fear.

'I was always a terrible student,' the man said in a conversational tone. 'Didn't have the patience for it. But there's one field of research that has always fascinated me: the countless – very creative – ways people have found to hurt each other. For me, history is one great lesson after another in how to inflict pain. I've become something of an expert . . . a student of suffering, you might say.'

He took something out of his pocket. 'I'm also not a very patient man. So the quicker you tell me what I want to know, the happier I'll be. And, believe me . . . if you don't like me now, you don't want to see me unhappy.' He held an object in Fatih's line of sight. 'Do you know what this is?'

'Shell . . .? A . . . a . . . a . . . mussel shell?'

'Correct. '*A . . . a . . . a . . . mussel shell*,' the stranger mimicked the old man. 'When the Christians murdered Hypatia in Alexandria in 415 AD, they scraped the flesh from her body with oyster shells while she was still alive. She was a librarian too, you know?' He turned the inky-black mollusc in his hand. 'I couldn't find any oysters. But inspiration struck as I was eating lunch. Those stuffed mussels in the Spice Bazaar – fucking delicious. And I figured their shells'd do the same trick as oysters.' The man inspected Fatih as if he were a corpse on a slab. 'Guess I'll find out soon enough, won't I?'

The old man began to weep. 'I have a wife. Grandchildren. Please. I'll tell you anything.'

'Yes.' The man smiled grimly as he pressed the scimitar-sharp edge of the shell against Fatih's rheumy eyelid. 'I know you will.'

4

Istanbul

'So. What do we do now?' Ben took a bottle and two glasses out of the top drawer of Ilhan's oak desk.

'"We"? There's no "we" in this, my friend.' Ilhan raised an eyebrow and shook his head at the offered glass. 'Isn't it a bit early in the day for that?'

'Never.' Ben poured himself a measure of raki, the potent aniseed-flavoured Turkish spirit. Throwing his head back, he savoured the warm rush as the alcohol hit the pit of his stomach.

'You've a stronger constitution than me, then. But you should water it down with some tea. Yilmaz?' Ilhan summoned his assistant. '*İki çaylar, lütfen.*'

The young man nodded and retrieved an ornate brass tea tray from beside the front door. '*Tabii, efendim.*'

Yilmaz darted out onto the narrow street, dodging the compliant groups of tourists snaking along the pavement behind tour guides who regaled their charges with the history

42

of the Grand Bazaar, Istanbul's Kapalıçarşı – the 'Covered Market'. Founded as a market for textiles in 1455 by Mehmet the Conqueror soon after the Ottomans seized the city from its Byzantine rulers, by the early 1600s it was home to three thousand stores and was the centre for trade in the Mediterranean, bringing together goods from Asia, Africa and the Near East. Ben had heard the same tale a thousand times before, told in a hundred tongues.

The tourists peered through the front window of Ilhan's store where the two men sat like mannequins among the Aladdin's Cave display of oriental treasures: hand-painted ceramic figurines of Ottoman sultans, belly dancers and whirling dervishes; gleaming copper *hamam* bowls and shimmering silk carpets.

'Well?'

'Well, what?'

'What's your plan, Dr Hitchens?'

'Plan? Ha! What plan? I'm just making it up as I go along.'

'It was a stupid thing to do . . . you know Hasan will find out. What good's the manuscript to you, anyway?'

'No idea at all. Not yet, anyway.'

'So why take it?'

'Seemed like a good idea at the time. Whatever this means – whatever message it contains . . . well, it's going to require a fair bit of effort on my part to decipher it. It'll certainly require more than an hour or two in the Yeni Kütüphane. The poisonous Frenchman and that damned woman have quite a head start on me already. I have to get moving if I'm going to position myself as the fly in their ointment. And unfortunately I'd rather die than ask the only person I know who could decipher this nonsense without breaking a sweat. Ethan Cohn. I'll never give that old bastard the satisfaction of turning up on his doorstep, cap in hand.'

'Your pride will be the end of you, Ben.'

'There's a good twenty candidates ahead of pride in the race to finish me off.' He paused. 'Niğde – have you ever been there?'

'Of course. There aren't many corners of the country that have escaped my attention.'

The tiny bell above the door to Ilhan's store jangled as Yilmaz returned from the tea vendor carrying two tiny, waisted glasses of toffee-coloured Turkish *çay*.

'It wasn't that far from my dig at Eskitepe, but I never had the chance to visit – other things on my mind at the time.' Ben dropped a small sugar cube into his glass and stirred it with a silver spoon. The tannin-rich aroma made his mouth water. 'Nice place?'

Ilhan shrugged. 'Unremarkable. Why?'

'The town of Tyana in Cappadocia is where Balinas is supposed to have discovered the Emerald Tablet. It's also where he lived in the first century AD after finding the path to enlightenment and took the name Apollonius of Tyana. Discovering the secret of eternal life had quite an impact on him – as you can imagine. He spurned worldly possessions, cured the ill, raised the dead, took to the road as an itinerant preacher with a devoted band of followers, and was persecuted by the Romans.'

'That story sounds familiar.'

'Yes, I've always suspected the early Christians plagiarised the best bits of Apollonius' life story for their Messiah.'

'That sounds like blasphemy, Dr Hitchens.'

'I'm a historian, not a Christian, Ilhan.' He swirled the dregs of his tea in the bottom of the glass, crystalline fragments of sugar accumulating in the curved base. 'So – Niğde. Or its museum, anyway. That's where all the archaeological material from Tyana ended up. If my memory of Ethan's ranting and raving serves me correctly, it's also where I might be able to get my hands on the scant remains of Balinas' life. Care to join me?'

'Take time out from my business at the tail end of the tourist season for a pointless journey into the Anatolian hinterland? Not a chance.' Ilhan dropped his voice. 'Yilmaz messed up the sale this morning royally. There's that saying you people have about running before you can walk. It will be some time before I'll trust him with such an important customer again.'

Ben shrugged. 'Suit yourself. I don't have the luxury of choice, and it gives me a good excuse to leave the city. Hasan'll be on my heels, so the quicker I can interpret this bloody document and its hidden message, the better. If I can return it to him with the sweetener of Eris' head on a platter, he might find it in his heart to forgive me. If you change your mind . . .'

'I won't.'

'Well, there's one thing you can do for me if you're not going to join me on the road.' Ben took the notebook out of his pocket and carefully removed its priceless cargo. 'If I actually had any beliefs, I'd say this goes against all of them,' he said as he reached for a pair of scissors and carefully snipped a tiny piece of parchment from along the manuscript's bound edge. 'I need you to get this to Raphael Donazetti.'

'Donazetti? That degenerate Italian . . . why get him involved?' Ilhan snapped. The Italian was a master of the art of deception – skills he put to good use lining Ilhan's coffers by crafting the forgeries the dealer sold to unsuspecting tourists on the black market. The collaboration between Ben, Ilhan and Raphael the previous year had resulted in the sale at auction of three spectacular, and exquisitely fake, antiquities that had earned the three men a windfall and financed the acquisition of Ben's waterside mansion. Not that it eased the tension between the Turk and the Italian. The two men couldn't have been more different; Ilhan was urbane, dignified and charming while Raphael was raffish, foul-mouthed and an unapologetic opium addict.

'I need to know what's been used to make this ink,' Ben responded. Raphael had acquired a working knowledge of chemistry that could have landed him employment in a professional laboratory if he'd had either the desire or the ambition. Ben also knew he'd analyse the ink used on the document without asking any questions.

Ilhan looked at Ben quizzically. 'So . . . what do you plan to tell Fiona? She can't be too pleased that you're chasing off after that woman.'

'It's not like that.' Guilt made his stomach clench. As always, Ben hadn't given Fi a moment's thought. 'This is about getting some of my own back . . . She'll understand,' he said hopefully.

'Are you the eternal optimist, or just delusional?'

'It'll be fine. I haven't made any promises. We're just having some fun.'

'Does she know that?'

'I suppose so. We haven't really spoken about it. But she knew what she was getting herself into.'

'Really?' His friend laughed and shook his head. 'Good luck with that.'

5

Istanbul

Fat raindrops spattered on the slow-moving waters of the Bosphorus as Ben manoeuvred his decrepit motor launch between the bulky hulls of ferries crisscrossing between continents. His boat dipped and bobbed in the choppy swell and the motor roared as it plunged in and out of rank water scented with seaweed and sump oil.

He didn't regret the substantial investment in his run-down seaside *yalı*. The roof leaked and the floors creaked, and he loved it. But he was less enthusiastic about the spur-of-the-moment decision to acquire a boat to get about town. Unfortunately he very quickly realised he was born a landlubber. He'd never really had the chance to sample recreational boating during the war when every occasion he found himself at sea had had an operational purpose and meant his mind was on something other than the movement of the boat beneath his feet. Now, he found that the persistent lurching made him queasy, and the salt spray on his face wasn't bracing or refreshing, just irritating. Ilhan had warned him about the potential pitfalls of his house's location, but, true to form, Ben had ignored him. Now he was damned if he was going to admit defeat.

At the time, the decision to move from his home base in the crowded streets and lanes of Beyoğlu on the city's European shore to the gentrified surrounds of Üsküdar in Asia seemed intrepid and audacious. He had also figured that removing himself from temptation would force him to reform. But the move had come at a cost. Nowadays, when he felt the urge to socialise in the *meyhane*s and restaurants at the foot of the Galata Tower, the commute was murderous. He'd been on his best behaviour in the months after he'd opened the excavation on Mt Ida. But now the sirens' call of the clubs and bars across the water was irresistible. He'd lost count of the number of times he'd ended the night passed out on the sofa in Ilhan's apartment, only to wake and face a gruelling boat ride across the Bosphorus fighting the symptoms of a noxious hangover.

Ahead lay the salt-bleached timbers of a dilapidated jetty. Beyond that his two-storeyed home was set back from the water's edge amid a lush and overgrown garden. He cut the motor as the launch eased towards shore. Through the arched window in the morning room, he could see Fi bent over a table, sorting through her portfolio of drawings.

His heart sank at the thought of what was to come.

Think of it as tearing off a bandage, he counselled himself. *Just rip it off. Besides, you're doing her a favour.*

She looked up as she heard him docking the boat. The door out to the terrace opened and she flitted, barefoot, towards him through the ankle-deep grass, a newspaper held aloft to shield her head from the autumn shower.

'Fi, do you have a minute?'

Shushing him with an upraised finger, she interrupted. 'Later, Ben. You've got a visitor.'

'Visitor?' His muscles tensed as he feared the worst.

'Superintendent Demir. And he doesn't look happy.'

For a moment, he entertained the thought of jumping back into his boat and fleeing. But his infirm water vessel would be hard-pressed to outpace an arthritic turtle, let alone the Turkish water police. Besides which, he had nowhere to run.

With a rueful sigh, he turned towards the house.

The door to his study was open. Hasan barely seemed to register Ben's entrance. He stood with his back to the door, deep in thought as he gazed out at the picture-perfect view of boats steaming along the Bosphorus; one hand rested on his hip, and the other absent-mindedly flicked a set of amber *tesbih* beads about his fingers.

'Playing with your worry beads, eh?' Ben tried to be flippant. 'Never seen you with those before. Must be serious.'

The Turk turned, his expression dire. 'Benedict. Something has happened at Topkapı –'

'I can explain –'

'Explain?' Hasan's face blanched. 'Please tell me you had nothing to do with this – deceiving tourists, forgeries, that's one thing. But murder . . .?'

'Wait . . . what? Murder? What are you talking about?'

'Fatih Alkan. The Head Librarian. He's dead.'

Ben's mind whirred. 'That's . . . I can't believe it! . . . Murder? No! An accident, surely.'

'Unfortunately not. One of the gardeners heard him screaming. He had to break the door down, and then he found . . .' The Turk paused and drew a deep breath, crossing his arms in front of his chest. 'Well, it was ghastly. Both his eyes scooped out of his skull and chunks of flesh torn from his bones. Like he'd been picked over by carrion birds. He died of blood loss before they could get him to a hospital.'

'Jesus . . .'

'When did you leave the library?'

'It's hard to say exactly – early afternoon. Do you know who did it?'

'Not yet. But it's not my case. The investigating detectives only contacted me because the appointment I arranged for you was in the librarian's diary. And given the coincidence between your visit to the archive and his death, they're very keen to speak to you.'

'Why? I had nothing to do with it!' Ben's stomach dropped. 'I don't know anything! Christ! He was alive when we left. Ilhan can confirm that!'

'Well, with the reputation Ilhan has acquired over the years, he's probably not the best corroborating witness.'

'Wait . . . there was a man . . . he passed us as we were leaving the library. At first I thought he was Turkish. But when I think about it, I'm not so sure. About my age. Not too tall. Heavy-set. Dark hair. It could have been him.' His heart was racing. 'Hell . . . what should I do?'

'I don't know that there's much you can do. And that should concern you.'

'Are you here to warn me?'

'Despite our history, well, let's just say I don't want to see you blamed for something you didn't do. You might find it hard to believe, but there are far more belligerent police in the force than me. The men who'll be knocking at your door are a different breed. The death of such a revered public servant in such a horrible manner – they're very eager to find someone to blame.' He paused and locked Ben in a meaningful gaze. 'Finding the truth is less important to them than arresting somebody. Whether or not they accuse the right suspect is irrelevant. And a high-profile perpetrator of a high-profile crime – it would be quite the feather in the cap.'

'Looks like I owe you a debt of thanks.'

'Yes. It's getting to be a habit. One day I may need to call in the favour.' Hasan paused. 'There's one other thing. The book.'

Ben flinched. 'What about it?'

'It was the only thing out of place – other than that poor man's death, of course.' Hasan looked Ben in the eye. 'The edition of Balinas – it's gone. Any idea what happened to it?'

'I left it with Fatih. I don't know where it went after that.' Ben was relieved that he didn't have to lie. It also didn't hurt to know that if the book had disappeared, then nobody would notice it had a page missing.

'And did you notice anything unusual about it that might suggest why Mrs Estelle Peters was so keen to examine it?'

'No. Nothing. Just a run-of-the-mill transcription of the Emerald Tablet as far as I could tell.' He winced. *Now, that was a lie.* 'Sorry I can't help, Hasan.'

'No matter. So whoever killed Fatih took that book.' He shook his head. 'As I said, wherever that woman goes, trouble follows.'

Ben and Fi stood in uncomfortable silence by the road, waiting for the Kadiköy *dolmuş* that would transport her to the Eminönü ferry.

The rain had passed, leaving the air humid and heavy with the scent of damp earth and asphalt steaming in the sun's hot rays. Ben's fine cotton shirt stuck to his back and he could feel perspiration beading on his forehead. He rammed his fists deep into the pockets of his chinos and scuffed at the gravel by the side of the road with the heels of his worn work boots.

When he'd told Fi about the librarian's death, he'd spared no details, hoping that it would stimulate her sense of self-preservation and prompt her to leave voluntarily. Most importantly, he thought the shock would make her forget Estelle's involvement in the events of the past twenty-four hours. He was wrong.

'It's that bloody woman again, isn't it?'

'No. Well, not exactly.'

'And you're choosing to dive headfirst into this god-awful mess ... for what reason, exactly?' She'd thrown her arms in the air, frustrated. 'Look – it's not that I mind for myself. Honestly. But I could slap you silly for getting sucked into her vortex again. Look at what happened last time, for Christ's sake!' She spun away from him, fighting the fury in her voice. 'Things are so good for you right now. Why can't you just be happy with what you've got?'

She had a point, and he knew it. 'After what the Frenchman – and what she – did to me, I can't just pass this up. The opportunity to get back at them for all they put me through ... I can't ignore it.' He'd reached out and rested his hand gently on her shoulder. 'I'm sorry, Fi. I really am.'

She smacked his hand away. 'Don't touch me!'

Cramming clothes into her duffel bag, she'd kept her back to him but there was no hiding the tears in her voice. 'Don't worry, Ben. I'll be fine. Sure – the pride's a little injured. But if I'm honest with myself, you're not really my type.'

She'd turned, hands on hips, and appraised him with cold eyes. 'Look at you. There's no denying it – the packaging's great. But there's no getting past the fact that you're a self-destructive narcissist. Every woman's dream ... ha! I should be thanking you. I've already invested too much time in this bullshit.'

When she'd finished packing, he'd insisted on escorting her on the walk up to the coast road to wait for a ride to the port. She very wisely declined his offer of a lift across the Bosphorus in his clapped-out boat. Until that moment he hadn't really thought that Fiona might actually feel strongly enough about what he planned to do to leave him, so when the inevitable happened, he was forced to acknowledge an unfortunate truth. When he was with her, he could believe – if only for a moment – that he could aspire to an ordinary life. But the surge of adrenalin in his blood at the thought of what now lay ahead of him confirmed his worst fears. He wasn't built for ordinary.

A dusty black Chevrolet Deluxe approached along the potholed road. The front and rear bench seats were crammed with passengers. Ben stepped onto the asphalt and flagged it down.

The *dolmuş* slowed and pulled to the side of the road. He reached for the handle and hefted the door open.

'It's good that you're leaving. You'll be much safer.'

'Safer? Yes, I'm sure you're right. But not in the way you mean it.'

'Well ... bye, then.'

'Yep.' She clambered into the back seat of the lumbering Chevrolet and slammed the door. As the car pulled away, she leant out the window and waved cheerlessly.

The car's rear tyres spun a fog of dust into the air as the vehicle accelerated. He stood and watched it lurch along the road until it turned a corner and disappeared from sight. His breathing was shallow and his heart thumped loudly in his ears. But any lingering regret evaporated in the hot afternoon sun as he contemplated the path he'd chosen. His gut reaction told him he was on to something – that pursuing this was worthwhile, even if he had no idea where it might lead him. On the hunt for ancient treasures, his instincts rarely failed him. It was only in the present that he always seemed to land himself in trouble.

People often threw around the hyperbolic statement that something or another was worth killing for. Proof of that willingness was another thing altogether. If the tragedy at Topkapı was anything to go by, whatever it was that Garvé and the woman were searching for would be worth the effort. But it also meant Ben had a great deal to be concerned about.

Trudging down the drive towards his home, Ben was preoccupied. With Fi gone, his mind had switched from the immediate to the strategic, running through a checklist of what needed to be done next. A sudden and unfamiliar sound broke his concentration and made him flinch.

A telephone. *His* telephone. When Ben had first bought his house, he'd taken Ilhan up on his insistent offer to arrange a private phone line through his personal – and undoubtedly shady – connections in the upper echelons of government. Ben estimated it to have rung no more than a handful of times since – not surprising given the scarcity of privately owned telephones in Turkey. The persistent trilling from inside the house suggested that what had become little more than an expensive paperweight was, for once, fulfilling its intended purpose.

'Ah . . . yes? . . . Hello . . . Good day . . . May I ask who is calling? It is Benedict Hitchens speaking . . .' Ben still struggled with the etiquette of telephone ownership.

'Who else would it be, other than you, Ben? Unless you've recently hired yourself a housekeeper.'

'Ilhan? Is that you? Me . . . a housekeeper? Not likely. Now what's so urgent? Have you any idea how much these calls cost?'

'Yes, I do. Which is why I never ring. But this time, it was necessary. I'm glad I caught you. I've changed my mind. I will join you on your travels.'

'Really? You seemed so certain. What's changed?'

'Does it matter?' Ilhan snapped.

'Of course not. I'll be happy for the company.'

'Fine. Train?'

'Yes – I was planning to head off tonight.'

'Can't it wait till tomorrow?'

'No. I've just spoken with Hasan –'

'Ben! I warned you!'

'It's not what you think. But the sooner I leave the city, the better. And, come to think of it, it might be a good time for you to be out of town as well.' Ben had only just realised that if the police planned to arrest him for involvement in Fatih's murder, Ilhan would be in their sights as well.

'Why? What's happened?'

'Can't explain now. Operators listening in and all that.'

His friend sighed. 'I'll meet you at the station, then.' Ilhan hung up.

What's up his nose? Ben wondered. His normally affable and even-tempered friend was clearly out of sorts. *And why the change of heart?*

6

Niğde, Turkey

Ben stood beneath the elaborate pointed archway at the entrance to the Niğde Akmedresi and waited. Three attempts to elicit a response from the other side of the bolted door had amounted to nothing. He could hear no movement inside and there was nothing to indicate when – if ever – the museum would open.

When Ben and Ilhan had arrived in Niğde, they'd gone in different directions – Ben to the museum, and Ilhan to meet with a dealer who in the past had proved to be a good source of black market goods. Ilhan was planning to join Ben once he'd wrapped up his business, though at this rate it looked like Ben would be finished long before his friend.

Again, he pounded the heavy oak with a bunched-up fist. Hands on his waist, his eyes drifted to the ornate honeycomb ornamentation in the archway above his head.

'A masterful example of Seljuk design.' A voice at his shoulder made him start. 'Muqarnas vaulting – intended to replicate stalactites and inspire in the faithful thoughts of the cave on Jabal al-Nour where Allah visited the Prophet Muhammad with the first of his revelations. But you'd already know that.'

Ben spun on his heel. A slight figure stood before him, head tilted to one side and blue eyes peering out from beneath a mop of hair cut unfashionably long. A timid smile spread beneath a neatly trimmed moustache. 'Dr Hitchens. I *knew* it was you.'

'I don't believe it . . . Cem?' The last time he'd seen Cem Yıldız was the day Ben departed the excavation at Eskitepe, bound for a fateful meeting with the Director of the British School of Archaeology in Ankara. As the most senior Turkish archaeologist on site, Ben had put Cem in charge while he took what he assured his deputy would only be a brief sojourn in the capital. He had been wrong.

'Yes, it is I, Dr Hitchens. These days I'm dedicating most of my time to institutional work – I find it suits my constitution better than on-site excavation. I have oversight of the collection here. And you? I've been reading all about your discoveries on Mt Ida. Remarkable. Quite remarkable.' As he spoke, Cem fussed with the hair that fell over the left side of his face, grown long to cover what Ben knew to be extensive scarring from a burn suffered in childhood.

'I'm researching something else at the moment, Cem. And I was hoping to have access to the museum's collection.'

'Of course. It would be my pleasure to assist you. We keep the front door shut outside hours. Come round the side – we'll use the staff entrance.'

Dim light filtered down into a central courtyard through a filthy glass roof. Ben could only assume the building's shabby exterior must fall outside Cem's purview, given the meticulous and well-maintained condition of the museum collection contained within its walls.

The madrasah had been built in the early fifteenth century on the four-*iwan* floorplan, with four vaulted rooms opening onto the courtyard. The largest of these was framed by a single stone arch that Ben assumed faced Mecca and would contain the *mihrab* the Muslim students would have faced to pray when the building still operated as a Koran school. Within the alcoves these days, conscientious religious scholars had been replaced by dust-free stacks of documents and tidy boxes of artefacts lined up neatly on shelves in chronological and alphabetical order. Cem obviously took pride in his work and showed great reverence for the ancient treasures entrusted to his custodianship.

'What is it you're here to see, Dr Hitchens?'

'I'm looking for whatever material you have from Tyana. More specifically – anything relating to Balinas, or Apollonius – whichever of his names you prefer.'

'Either's fine with me. Most of the museum's Tyana collection dates from the Graeco-Roman period, which is the right time frame. Emperor Caracalla established a shrine dedicated to Apollonius in the city, and it was the centre of Apollonius' cult. But not much has been salvaged – most of what we have are surface finds rather than things unearthed in a proper excavation.' He paused. 'There is one thing that was brought in to us recently, though . . .' The young man walked over to a row of shelves.

'Come . . . here it is . . .' He pointed to a piece of marble, its top edge squared off with the remains of a lip that suggested it had once formed a lintel above a door or an architrave running between columns on a sizeable building. Ancient Greek script had been chiselled into its surface.

Ben ran his forefinger along the inscription as he translated it. '". . . This man, named after Apollo, and shining forth from Tyana, extinguished the faults of men. The tomb in Tyana received his body but in truth heaven received him so that he might drive out the pains of men." Do you think it came from the shrine? Though judging by the text, it sounds like it may have been used on a tomb. Where did you get it?' He stepped back, rocking on his heels. 'Looks like third or fourth century BC. What do you think?'

'Judging by the lettering and punctuation, that's probably about right. Although it's hard to tell without seeing it in context. This was carted in by a well-meaning local who uncovered it, so there's no way of dating it by what was found around it.'

'But still – shouldn't you look into it? Might be that your well-meaning local can show you where it was found and that would tell you more.'

'I'm sure you're right.' Cem's voice was clipped. 'It's something the department will pursue. Eventually. But for now, it's just one more thing to add to the ever-growing list of artefacts we need to research without the manpower to do it. I do the best I can and look after these precious things until we have the money and the people to examine it. Will that time ever come?' Cem shrugged. 'Who knows? But I remain optimistic.'

'Look, this is too good for me to ignore, Cem. Would you be willing to tell me where it came from? It might amount to nothing, but you never know. Of course, in the spirit of collegiality, I'd share any information that came my way with you. How does that sound?'

'Have someone with your qualifications investigate one of my artefacts? How could I refuse? But . . .' Cem lowered himself into a desk chair and found a sheet of writing paper.

'. . . If you're going to visit *Bayan* Sebile, I should write you a letter of introduction.'

'*Bayan* Sebile?'

'The woman who brought this in to us. She lives in Tyana and fancies herself the guardian of Balinas' legacy. And she's also likely to disappear into thin air if a stranger turns up on her doorstep without warning. She's . . .' Cem paused and looked into the distance, struggling to find the right words, '. . . rather peculiar.' He signed the letter with a flourish, slipped it into an envelope and scribbled an address onto the outside.

Ben took it with a nod of thanks.

'I never had the chance to thank you, Dr Hitchens. You know, many of us Turks were quietly very pleased you undermined the British School as you did.'

'Undermined?' Of the many reasons he'd come up with to justify to himself the theft of material from his own excavation to sell to Ilhan and fund the new trenches he'd wanted to open, 'undermining' the institute had never been one of them.

'Yes. The arrogance and high-handed manner in which we're treated in our own country by these people who think they know so much more than we do about our own heritage . . . the day will soon come when we'll be excavating our own past and writing our own history. You were never like the others.'

'Me – like them?' Ben laughed. 'Well, that's one thing you're right about, Cem.'

Ilhan was waiting for Ben at a small table set beneath the arching limbs of an ancient plane tree that cast the tiny tea garden outside the museum's entry in dappled shade.

He stood as Ben approached. 'So, did you get what you needed?'

'Kind of. I've been pointed in another direction, anyway. Feel like a trip to Kemerhisar?'

'Sure. My business here is done, at any rate. I was in luck – Metin had just had a truckload of new artefacts arrive from the mountains. Unbelievable Hittite material. Worth a small fortune. If my luck keeps up, maybe I'll be able to sniff something out in Kemerhisar as well. Though I've been there before, and to say it's an unexceptional place would be over-stating things.'

Ben was happy to see Ilhan in a cheerful mood. 'You're back to your old self,' he observed.

'It's just getting out of the city. Sometimes Istanbul makes me feel like I'm going insane.' The two men walked towards the street, raking autumn sunlight warming their backs. 'Speaking of insane, my mother . . .' Ilhan sighed. 'I need to find a phone before we go. She was expecting me tonight for dinner. Yet another doomed attempt to set me up with a good Turkish girl.'

Ben laughed and elbowed his friend in the side. 'Ah . . . so *that* was your problem? Why didn't you mention it earlier? Barely got two words out of you on the train.'

'A man of my age still under his mother's thumb? It's not something I'm proud of.'

'So. She's on a mission again . . . she'll never learn, will she? It explains your change of heart, anyway. I *was* wondering . . .'

'Don't be smug, Benedict. It doesn't suit you.'

7

Kemerhisar, Turkey

'**C**ursed little monsters!'

Ben and Ilhan ducked to avoid a volley of horse turds flung through the air as a cluster of rough-headed young boys shouldered their way past them, cackling maniacally. One of them clutched at his head, blood oozing from between fingers pressed hard against his scalp.

As with so many Anatolian towns and villages, the once-important city of Tyana had been through a series of name changes as the territory in which it lay passed from one conqueror to the next. So it was that Ben and Ilhan had found their way from Niğde to the outskirts of the place now known as Kemerhisar aboard a tiny local bus.

It hadn't been difficult to find *Bayan* Sebile's residence. Walking beneath the vaulted remains of the Roman aqueduct that was – as far as Ben could see – the town's only redeeming feature, the two men approached a shepherd who'd stopped by the road to gawk at the new arrivals in town, goats milling about his legs. An enquiry about where they might find the address they were looking for had prompted a string of muttered curses and theatrical hand gestures that left no doubt that the woman they were seeking wasn't considered a pillar of the community.

That impression wasn't helped by the greeting they received when they arrived at a stone fence encircling an outcrop of soft, white volcanic rock that had been fashioned into one of the many thousands of cave homes scattered across Cappadocia's lunar landscape.

A surprisingly tall figure whipped around the corner of the house, a ball of horse shit brandished above her head.

'*Eşek herif*! And don't come back, you little demons!'

Ben and Ilhan both reflexively threw their hands in the air. The woman was straight-backed and broad-shouldered, her silver hair arranged beneath a delicately embroidered black scarf. Fierce blue eyes peered out from beneath a brow creased with fury. Realising her quarry had fled, she dropped her foul missile.

'*Bayan* Sebile? My name is Dr Ben Hitchens. This is my friend, Ilhan Aslan. I've been sent by Cem Yıldız from the Niğde Akmedresi . . .' He held out the letter Cem had written for him.

Sebile shook her head as she approached, muttering as she brushed her hands on her apron. 'Evil children. Not that their parents are any better. They're just doing what the adults wish they had the spine to do themselves. Today it was stealing my apricots – last week, a dog's corpse dumped in my well.' She took the letter and opened it.

'You can read?' Ben blurted out without thinking. To find anyone literate living in a small Turkish town was unusual enough, but for that person to be a woman was almost inconceivable.

'I may be a flawed human being, but ignorance is not one of my failings.' She ran her eyes over the paper. 'So. You're an archaeologist, then? An archaeologist who's going to do what that lazy man should have done himself.'

'Lazy man?'

'Cem Yıldız. Couldn't even be bothered levering himself out of his desk chair to come down here and pay me a visit after I hauled that piece of marble into his museum.' She shrugged. 'He might have cause to regret his action someday soon.'

She turned and walked towards a wooden door set beneath a lintel carved from the porous white tuff stone that Ben knew was as friable as honeycomb. 'Well, you'd better come in, then.'

The door opened into a small room with an earth-toned kilim rug covering the floor. A timber-framed bed, a table and four rush-bottomed chairs were the only pieces of furniture in the tiny space. But what struck Ben most were the books. Carved into the soft stone walls from floor to ceiling were alcoves, stuffed to overflowing with books, newspapers, pamphlets and manuscripts.

Pulling out three chairs from where they sat against the wall, Sebile indicated that Ben and Ilhan should take a seat. 'You will have tea.' It was a statement, not a question. By then, she was already at the *çaydanlık* that simmered atop the wood-fired stove and before Ben and Ilhan had the opportunity to respond, three small glasses of tea were full to the brim.

'So – you like to read, then . . .' Ben observed. *Jesus. That's the best you can do?* he berated himself. There was something about the woman that made him feel like a guileless fool.

Sebile threw him a withering glance. 'Well, aren't *you* blessed with razor-sharp powers of observation.'

Ben tried another angle. 'You seem to have a French accent when speaking Turkish . . .'

'I was born there. But I left many years ago.' She took a seat and stared fixedly at the American. 'Now – why are you here?'

'Balinas . . . Apollonius. I'm trying to find out more about the *Tabula Smaragdina* . . . the –'

'The Emerald Tablet.'

'You know of it?'

The woman scoffed. 'Know of it? Balinas is my life. How could I not?'

'Well, the inscription you took to Cem . . . I'd like to see where you found it.'

'You would, would you?'

Ben hesitated. She wasn't young, but she was seething with a ferocity and vigour that would have put most women half her age to shame. 'I'm not sure what to say, *Bayan* Sebile. You're not what I was expecting.'

'Well, I'm terribly sorry to disappoint you.'

'It's not a bad thing.'

'What *were* you expecting?'

'I was told you were an old woman.'

'You don't have eyes? That's exactly what I am.'

'Yes . . . but you're not the sort of old woman I'm familiar with.'

'Which would that be?'

'Quiet. Reserved. Kindly. Not the sort who flings about balls of horse dung.'

'Yes. Well, I apologise for that. You caught me at a bad moment. So, you'd like to see where I found the inscription?'

'I would.'

'First, we'll talk for a bit. We'll talk, and we'll drink tea.' She took a deep draught of the steaming hot drink. As she savoured it, her eyelids dropped and she inhaled deeply. All was silent as sunlight streamed through windows punched through the volcanic tuff. Ilhan looked at Ben quizzically. The American shook his head. He knew there was no point in pushing.

'You know, this is where he found it.' She broke the silence.

'Where who found what?' Ben asked.

'Balinas – or Apollonius. Whatever you want to call him. This is where the Emerald Tablet was revealed to him. In the caverns beneath this room. Why do you want to find it?'

Ben paused. 'I'm not trying to find it. I just want to know more about it.'

'Well, it's said that when Balinas was a young boy seeking wisdom, he was transfixed by a statue of a man standing in what today is my *patlıcan* patch . . . eggplant. You know it?'

'Know what?'

'Eggplant.'

'Of course.'

'Well, my *patlıcan* marks a very important site. It was early in the first century after the birth of your Christ when Balinas was inspired to dedicate his life to the study of Hermetic wisdom by words engraved on a gilt plaque on the statue that was in my eggplant bushes – though, of course, the plants are a recent addition to the landscape. It read: "Behold! I am Hermes Trismegistus, he who is threefold in wisdom. I once placed these marvellous signs openly before all eyes; but now I have veiled them by my wisdom, so none should attain them unless he become a sage like myself. Let him who would learn and know the secrets of creation and nature, enquire beneath my feet." Eventually, this led Balinas to discover the cavern beneath the statue that contained the cache of treasures brought to Tyana by Alexander the Great from deep in the

Egyptian desert. "Enquire beneath my feet." Wasn't very subtle, was he?' She finished her tea.

'We're very near the Cilician Gates here,' Ben pondered. 'When Alexander travelled north from Egypt, that was how he made it through to the Anatolian plateau. Tyana was the most important city in the region at the time. So it's quite possible he came here.' The Taurus Mountains formed an impenetrable barrier between the heart of Anatolia and the fertile southern coastline fringing the Mediterranean. The Cilician Gates formed a natural pass through the massif that had been used by humans for thousands of years.

'Possible?' Sebile scoffed. 'It's not a question of being "possible". It's a statement of fact. Would you like to see it?'

Ben had the sensation of being an autumn leaf buffeted along in an unseasonal gale. 'See what?'

'The cavern. It's also where I found the carving I gave the lazy man.'

'Yes. I'd definitely like to see that.'

Sebile stood. 'Fine. Finish your tea. Then follow me.'

Sickly yellow light from a kerosene lantern flickered on the undulating walls of a tunnel that had probably been carved into the tuff almost four thousand years before and had since been reused and extended by countless generations seeking refuge from persecution.

Ben shone the light of his torch deep into the velvety black shadows of the arched entrances and passageways that branched off the tunnel. Sebile raised the lamp as they passed a series of long sepulchres, their lintels carved with Greek crosses. 'Without these hidden cities, your early Church wouldn't have survived.'

'It's not my Church. Not anymore.' Whatever flimsy belief Ben had once possessed had been destroyed during the war. The things he'd seen on the island of Crete – the horrors he'd perpetrated himself – would have been enough to shatter his faith. But the death of his wife and their unborn child had destroyed any sense that there was a benevolent force overseeing the day-to-day workings of humankind.

'I see.' She gazed at him, eyebrows raised. 'You're a student of history and you don't believe there to be an underlying order to the universe? Curious.'

'What I've seen just confirms that life is governed by chaos and driven by a string of random phenomena.'

'Balinas wouldn't have agreed with you.' Sebile turned to Ilhan. 'What about you? Follower of Islam, I presume?'

Ilhan laughed. 'On paper, yes. But I'm not a very good Muslim. Any observances I follow are just to keep my mother happy.'

'So, two faithless men. Interesting that you should find your way here.' She ducked her head to pass through a small entrance partially blocked by a massive stone disc that once would have been used as a defensive barrier to roll across the doorway and protect those hidden within from attackers.

Inside, the space opened out into a surprisingly large room with a vaulted ceiling and columns carved into the volcanic stone. At the apex of the rectangular cave was a rough-hewn altar surrounded by niches that would have contained religious icons when it was used for Christian worship. Remnants of paint showed that the walls of the room had once been decorated with scenes from the New Testament to communicate Biblical stories to the illiterate faithful at a time when the only people who could read the Bible were the priests.

Sebile placed the lantern on the altar, its light casting flickering shadows across the walls. 'When his life story became known, the early Christians accused the followers of Balinas – or Apollonius as he was then known – of fabricating a pagan alternative to their own Christ. It was no accident that they chose to refashion the cavern in which he discovered the Emerald Tablet into a place of Christian worship.'

'So this is where you found the inscription?'

'Yes.' She gestured towards a depression in the dirt floor. 'Right there.'

Ben inspected the shallow pit. He took a small trowel from his satchel and scraped away the densely packed soil from its sides. The cavern's floor was covered in fill that had accumulated over thousands of years – an agglomeration of dust and finely ground tuff that had fallen to the floor as the room had been expanded and transformed over the millennia. As far as he could tell, it was clean fill – there was nothing that told him why the inscription had been there.

'When I'm bored I come down here and dig around a bit to see what I might find,' Sebile said. 'The tunnels go on for miles. I've never found the end of them.'

'Dig around?' Ilhan's ears pricked up. 'So, do you find much?'

She shrugged. 'A bit. Why?'

'Let's just say I'm always interested in acquiring interesting old things.'

'I don't know whether or not you'll find them interesting, but I can assure you they're old.' She gestured towards Ben. 'When your friend finishes what he's doing, I'll show you.'

The depression in the floor yielded nothing. Frustrated, Ben sat back on his haunches, playing the light of his torch across the wall. As he panned the beam across the flakes of paint clinging to the pitted stone surface, something caught his eye. He fell forward onto his knees and crawled towards the wall, torch held awkwardly in front of him.

'Ben . . . what is it?' Ilhan walked to his friend's side.

'Maybe nothing.' The closer he got to the wall, the less certain he was that what he'd seen was something deliberate and not just an accidental play of light on the uneven stone. He stood and handed Ilhan the torch. 'Do us a favour, would you? Shine the torch here . . .' He showed Ilhan how to rake the beam of light along the wall on an angle to emphasise the shadows.

Ben stepped back. 'Well, I'll be damned.' Carved into the wall but later painted over by the Christian chapel builders was what looked like an Ancient Egyptian cartouche. When writing the pharaoh's name, Ancient Egyptian scribes enclosed it within an oval line with a horizontal or vertical line at one end. It was the only time the motif was ever used in hieroglyphics. But here, the oval line surrounded a collection of abstract forms. The outline was abraded and indistinct but unmistakable.

'What is it?' Ilhan made to move to Ben's side.

'Stay right there!' Ben insisted as he fossicked in his satchel and withdrew his notebook. He wasn't imagining things. The circle, crescent, horned staff and serpent were an exact replica of the collector's stamp inside the book in the Topkapı archive.

He turned to Sebile and pointed at the wall. 'This engraving. Have you noticed it before?'

Sebile shrugged. 'There are so many things carved into the walls down here. It doesn't look very interesting. Just some random scribblings someone made here a very long time ago.'

'You say you know all there is to know about Balinas –'

'I didn't say that.'

'So, do these symbols have anything to do with the Emerald Tablet?'

'I wouldn't know.'

He paused and drew a deep breath. 'You said you found some other things . . . I have to see them.'

Her eyes, hooded in shadow, were inscrutable. 'Fine. Don't know how they'll be of any use to you, though.'

Sebile led the two men up the ladder that had given them access to the underground labyrinth through a hatch hidden beneath the kilim on the floor of her home. Once back inside, she hefted a large wooden box from a niche in the wall, and handed it to Ben. 'Here you go.'

Inside was a jumble of ancient artefacts: palm-sized terracotta oil lanterns, their necks charred with use; crudely carved votive figurines and bronze and silver coins; small flasks and tiny Roman glass bottles; a scatter of iron spears and arrowheads.

Ilhan reached into the box and began to rummage around in the collection. 'Some good touristy stuff here,' he murmured. 'Won't retire on it. But decent just the same . . .'

'Wait!' Ben exclaimed. Something glittered in the depths of the box, buried beneath the dull baked surfaces of the ancient pottery and tarnished metalwork. He pushed the other objects aside.

At the very bottom was a dark-green stone that had been carved into the form of a stylised beetle about three inches long. Mounted onto its flat base was a gold plate inscribed with hieroglyphics. Ben picked it up and turned it in his hands, its dense weight cold and heavy against his skin.

Ilhan's eyes lit up. 'A scarab!'

Ben studied its base. 'More than that. It's a heart scarab. Third Intermediate Period, by the looks of it . . . seventh century BC. Egyptian. Doesn't make any sense.' He turned to Sebile. 'You found this here? Really?'

She shrugged. 'Of course I found it here. What business would I have in Egypt?'

'These things, well, they were placed under a mummy's linen wrappings on the chest – the Ancient Egyptians thought the heart was where the mind resided. The jackal-headed god, Anubis, would weigh the dead person's heart against a feather. If it was lighter, the deceased would pass into the afterlife. But if it was heavier, weighed down by mortal sin, they'd be devoured by a carnivorous hippopotamus waiting on the sidelines. Why would it be here in a cave in the middle of Anatolia?'

She looked at him intently. 'Well, you're the one claiming to be an archaeologist. So maybe it's your job to work it out. One thing I can tell you is that Balinas travelled to the Alexandrian Library in Egypt to study the Hermetic texts housed there. He was greeted by the learned people in the city as a wise sage. In the biography Philostratus wrote about him, he says that as Balinas left his ship and walked through the city, the people of Alexandria hailed him as if he were a god, making way for him as they would a priest carrying the holy sacraments. And it was in Egypt that he found what he'd been looking for . . . it was the birthplace of alchemy. "Al-khem" – that was the ancient name for Egypt . . . the black land. And that . . .' She pointed at the amulet in his hand. 'That was buried beside the marble piece I sent to the museum. How it got there . . . well, that I can't tell you. Perhaps Balinas brought it back here with him.'

During his linguistic studies at Oxford University, Ben had mastered Egyptian hieroglyphics. Scanning the ancient text inscribed onto the gold plate on the scarab's base, he saw that, as would be expected, much of it was a recitation of a spell from the *Book of the Dead* giving the deceased instructions on how to pass Anubis' heart-weighing ceremony. But it was the name of the dead person upon whose chest the scarab had once been placed that caught his attention. 'That name . . . I know it. "Psamtik" . . . and his title, "overseer of sealers in the city of Jezirat Faraun" . . . now *where* have I seen that before?'

As Ben attempted to retrieve a long-buried memory, Ilhan began to pick things out of the box. 'So, *Bayan* Sebile – would you be willing to part with any of these things?' He shifted gear, slipping effortlessly into dealer mode and jockeying for a bargain. 'Of course, other than the scarab, there's not much here that I haven't seen before. If I'm honest, there's nothing too special.'

She looked up at him, eyes glittering. 'Is that a fact? Well, then. If it's not of any interest to you, I'd just as soon hold on to it all. We do get the odd visitor to these parts. Might set up a little business of my own selling these knick-knacks to the tourists.'

Ilhan raised his hands in protest. 'Now, now! I didn't say I wasn't interested. It all just comes down to the price . . .'

'As it so often does.' She smiled. 'Nothing but things to gather dust, if you ask me. This will be my own attempt at mastering the science of alchemy – transforming base materials into gold.'

Ilhan laughed. 'So even a disciple of Balinas has her price.'

'Unfortunately, yes. Enlightenment doesn't put food on the table. Take whatever you wish. Other than the scarab. That, I'll keep.'

As Ilhan and Sebile embarked on a bout of good-natured haggling, Ben walked to the window and placed the scarab on the sill, gazing out over an arid landscape softened only by the emerald-green foliage of Sebile's apricot orchard and the gnarled, grey limbs of ancient olive trees.

Ben's photographic, if also selective, memory was both a blessing and a curse. When introduced to a person he had no interest in getting to know, their name slipped from his mind within seconds. In contrast, anything relating to his passions was locked away in a formidable mental filing cabinet. And buried somewhere in there was the name engraved on the stone that lay in his hand. But despite his best efforts, as Ilhan and Sebile concluded their business, his mind remained blank.

Plumes of dust kicked up into the air from their heels as the two men walked along a chalky laneway covered in ancient volcanic ash towards the bus stop outside Kemerhisar. The sun was low in the sky, casting dusky shadows across the barren landscape.

'Well, I don't know if that did us any good other than to confirm there's a connection between Balinas and the map from Topkapı,' Ben grumbled, his fists crammed down into his pockets. 'And we knew that already. Wasted trip, really.'

Ilhan brandished the bundle of artefacts he'd acquired from Sebile. 'Speak for yourself!'

The crunch of cloven hooves behind them heralded the passing of a farmer and his cows as he herded them across the road towards a distant river pasture. It was the prompt Ben's memory needed. He came to an abrupt halt and slapped his hands together. 'Jesus! That's it . . . *That's* how I know that name. *Hathor Protecting Psamtik* . . . it was a sculpture in the Met Museum, or, at least, a plaster cast in the Met Museum. The original's in Cairo . . . I was *obsessed* with that thing when I was a kid.'

'What are you talking about?' Ilhan asked.

'Over there – the cows. Hathor was an Egyptian goddess usually depicted as a cow. She symbolised rebirth and renewal . . . the statue is exquisite – the figure of Psamtik is escorted by Hathor as his protector. That scarab – the one Sebile was so desperate to hold on to – that would've been placed on Psamtik's mummified corpse before he was interred in his sarcophagus.' He spun on his heel. 'Come on! I need to look at that thing again. Besides. I'm fairly sure there's something she's not telling us.'

8

Niğde, Turkey

In the tiled courtyard outside the Niğde madrasah where whispering drifts of autumn leaves eddied in deserted corners, a stream of spring water spurted from an ornate tap into a deep marble basin once used by the faithful to cleanse themselves before worship.

A rusty stain spread through the pool as the man immersed his hands and forearms, sleeves rolled above his elbows.

When he'd first learnt that the saying 'death by a thousand cuts' was more than just a pithy turn of phrase, it was a revelation to him. But despite his best efforts, he'd yet to find any subject who could endure more than two hundred and forty-seven. Granted, the Chinese torturers who had invented and perfected the art were not operating under the conditions he was forced to endure. He rarely, if ever, had the opportunity to work in an environment where he could exercise his skills without fear of interruption.

As soon as he'd laid eyes on the slope-shouldered, timid-eyed curator at the Niğde Museum, he'd known the man's pain threshold would be low. He didn't bother counting how many cuts the Turk endured before he fell unconscious and received the final, mercy stroke that slashed his jugular vein and ended his life. But as predicted, his levels of endurance had not been worthy of note.

As for the old woman in Kemerhisar the young man had spoken of as his blood pooled on the white stone floor . . . well, she was a woman. He suspected that just the threat of slicing her aged skin from her body would be enough to encourage her to tell him what he wanted to know.

9

Kemerhisar

Even before they caught sight of Sebile's house beyond the rise of the low hills surrounding it, Ben and Ilhan knew something was wrong. The sound of voices raised, one ringing in fear and the other a threatening baritone, carried through the heavy dusk air.

Ben picked up his pace and broke into a trot, turning to Ilhan to raise a finger to his lips. Whatever might confront them when they crested the hill, it wouldn't be wise to telegraph their arrival.

A baying pack of men surrounded the old woman. Her back was pressed up against the wall of her house while the leader of the lynch mob pressed towards her, his neck craning forward and bulky shoulders flexing as he jabbed at her chest with his finger. In his other hand he wielded a rough-hewn wooden club. Sebile had removed her head scarf and held it pressed against her forehead. Blood from a wound was smeared across her cheek and her eyes were wide with shock.

'My son!' the man screamed. 'You attacked my son! You're a curse on this village, witch!' He raised the club above his head.

'You!' Ben shouted as he ran down the hill. 'Get away from her!'

He heard the crunch of footsteps as Ilhan joined him. 'Do you know what you're doing here?' the Turk panted in English. 'I'm useless in a fight.'

'There's only five of them. We're fine. Just try to look the part,' Ben replied.

Faces swollen purple with fury spun round to face the intruders. The ringleader looked the two men up and down. 'Not your business, foreigners. You should fuck off if you know what's good for you.'

'This woman.' Ben shouldered his way into the group and put himself between Sebile and her attackers. 'She's my friend.'

Most of the men just stared, slack-jawed. But the leader's eyes flashed with malicious intent. 'Want to be more careful who you're friends with, then. This one's poison.' He raised his club again. 'Get out of the fucking way! Or do you want a taste of this, too?'

'I'm not moving.'

'Don't do this,' Sebile whispered. 'I can look after myself.'

'Really? Doesn't look like it. We're here now, anyway. And we're not leaving.'

'OK, then.' The man laughed and braced himself. Hefting the club back over his shoulder like a baseball bat, he swung it towards Ben's head.

As the wood arced through the air, Ben dropped down into a crouch to dodge the blow and swivelled, the side of his body facing his attacker. He thrust out his right leg and caught the man below the knees, throwing him off balance as his weight shifted with the club's movement.

As the Turk fell back and landed heavily on the ground, the club fell from his hands. Ben leapt to his feet and grabbed it. Before any of his comrades could help, Ben had pressed his boot into the soft spot in the man's throat, wielding the club against his temple.

The man's friends pressed forward. 'All of you!' Ben shouted. 'Stop right there! Or I'll smash his skull in.'

They looked doubtful but stopped just the same. 'Now, I tried to warn you. This woman is my friend, and if anything happens to her after I leave, every man in this dismal place will be thrown into jail. Superintendent Hasan Demir in Istanbul is an old friend of mine. And if I command it, he'll destroy this village.' Ben dropped the club by the man's side and removed his boot from his windpipe. 'Now, get out of here!'

Cursing beneath their breath but with their fury deflated, the men gathered themselves and disappeared back over the hill towards the town.

'You're going to "command" Hasan? To destroy the village?' said Ilhan, who'd managed to stay well clear of the mob. 'Good luck with that.'

'The threat alone should be enough,' Ben responded. He turned to Sebile. 'Silly question, but are you all right?'

She winced as she dabbed at the wound on her forehead. 'Nothing time and a good shot of raki won't fix,' she replied. 'Care to join me? Seems it's the least I can do.'

'Şerefe!' Sebile hailed her companions as she raised her drink into the air.

The two men raised their glasses in response. 'So what brought the mob to your door?' Ben asked.

'Ah, it's always one thing or another. Today, it was that man's little piglet – the child you saw leaving with his tail between his legs when you first arrived, and a lump on his head for his trouble. He's a little demon – always leading the other children in their pathetic war against the unmarried old woman living at the end of the lane. Easy pickings, the way they see it.' She sighed. 'I'd leave, if I had any choice. But I can't. It's my duty to stay here.' She indicated the bottle of raki. 'Another?'

Ben and Ilhan both threw back the remnants of their drinks. 'Certainly. Thank you,' Ben replied.

She stood and retrieved the bottle, filling the men's tiny glasses to the brim. Golden late-afternoon sunlight shone into the room, reflecting off motes of dust spiralling in the air. Sebile brushed the dirt from her baggy black *şalvar* pants and lowered herself into a chair. 'So. Tell me.'

'Tell you what?'

'Why you're here. I suppose I should thank you. But I'm curious . . . why did you come back?'

'The scarab. Or, at least, the name on the scarab. I remember now where I've seen it before.'

'I see.' She paused. 'So you'd like to see it again?'

'Very much.'

'First, you must tell me why you're here. The real reason.'

As Ben saw it, he had nothing to lose. The coincidence of the wall engraving in the catacombs was too great to ignore. And the appearance of an Ancient Egyptian artefact in a spot where it had no reason to be needed explanation. The more he thought about it, the more certain he was that Sebile would be able to give him some insight into its meaning.

He took his journal out of his satchel and opened it to the page where he'd transcribed the inscription he'd removed from the book in Topkapı so he could study it without needing to find himself a darkened room every time he wanted to examine it. 'This was in an edition of Jabir ibn Hayyan's *Book of Balinas the Wise on Causes*.'

Leaning forward, Sebile squinted to see the detail in Ben's drawing. She started and pulled back as if burnt. 'It was hidden?'

'Yes – painted in ink that was invisible in the light.'

Her face blanched and she clenched her lips into a thin line. 'You've found it . . . you've found *him*.'

'What do you mean?'

'Here . . .' She pointed with a spindly finger to the stylised skull above the mountain peak. 'The *caput mortuum* . . . the death's head. It signifies the alchemist's *nigredo* experience – the blackening that occurs when the soul withdraws from the physical world and exits the body. Balinas' death.' Sebile drew a deep breath. 'I'd heard of an ancient map that revealed his final resting place. I never dreamt I'd one day see it. His remains were never found – some of his disciples have said it was because he had physically transformed himself into the Philosopher's Stone . . . the perfect marriage of the One Mind and the One Thing and ascended to the firmament. But the less romantic among us believed his body was entombed in a hidden cave with the Emerald Tablet and that a map was kept to record its location for the day his disciples decided the world was ready to receive his gift. So why do you want to find it?'

'I didn't know I did.'

'More fool you.' She shook her head. '"As the wise man points to the moon, the idiot looks at the finger." Either way, you seem to know more about the esoteric arts than you care to admit. Those symbols you found in the cave beneath us. Let's assume they have alchemical significance. What do they mean to you?'

'So you *had* noticed them before.'

'Of course! I may be old, but I'm not blind. Now, answer my question.'

'Well, the crescent and the circle could represent the sun and the moon – the chemical marriage of the Red King and White Queen. Am I on the right track?'

'What on earth are you talking about?' Ilhan was getting impatient.

'Doesn't matter. I'll explain later,' Ben replied. 'So, is it the union of opposites?' he continued.

'That's right,' Sebile said. 'And the serpent and staff?'

'If the snake had been eating its own tail it would have meant something to me.' Ben knew that Gnostics and alchemists used the circular symbol of a serpent devouring the tip of its tail, a motif called the 'ouroboros', to represent the infinite cycle of life. The oldest depiction he'd seen had been found in Tutankhamun's tomb, where two ouroboroi encircled the boy king's head and feet.

'This one, though . . . it's different,' he continued. 'This snake is prone. As for the staff . . . well, it could mean many things.'

'So what would you say if I told you that Balinas was a healer, an adept of Asclepius –'

'Christ!' Ben exclaimed.

'No,' she said with a wry smile, 'he doesn't have anything to do with this.'

'I'm sure he doesn't. A staff . . . a snake . . . you're talking about the caduceus!'

'Really, Dr Hitchens. I expected more of you.'

He rapped his head with his knuckles. 'You're right. I'm an idiot. There's only one snake here. It's not the caduceus . . . it's the Rod of Asclepius.'

'Easy mistake to make. The caduceus is the symbol for Hermes Trismegistus, adopted from the Greek symbol for their messenger god, Hermes. But it has two snakes and was topped with wings. The Rod of Asclepius is the attribute of healers and doctors. It's wingless and has only one snake. But here, the snake isn't entwining the staff. Why not? Here, it's showing us that the rod of healing is fractured. This is the promise of what might have been if Balinas had deemed humankind worthy of the Emerald Tablet's healing gifts. To discover the tablet would be to unite the rod and the serpent.'

'Excuse me for interrupting again,' Ilhan said. 'But what, exactly, are those "gifts"? What's the Tablet supposed to do?'

'I suppose you could call it a shortcut. Those master alchemists who study their entire lives and manage to attain the "Great Work" may, if they are blessed, learn the art of transforming matter. The Emerald Tablet was made using that sacred knowledge. If it fell into the hands of men of science, it wouldn't take them long to decipher the processes used to create it. They could then replicate alchemical trans-formation, but would do so without any understanding of its true meaning and power. To put it bluntly, it would be like putting a machine gun in the hands of an infant.'

'I've heard all this before,' said Ben, hands clamped on his hips. 'Science has moved well beyond what it was even half a century ago. I think it's damned insulting to suggest that we're not responsible enough to handle some "magical" artefact created thousands of years ago. Civilisation has progressed.'

'That it has, Dr Hitchens. But not always in the right direction. Alchemists wish to achieve salvation through perfecting the soul within. And although very few people recognise the fact, every human being is trying to do the same thing. That's the tablet's true gift. Not showing scientists how to turn one thing into another. It's a path to spiritual purifica-tion. But most of those who seek to find the tablet see it only as something to be exploited.'

'But, alchemy . . .' Ilhan said. 'I'm sorry if I'm being obtuse, but it's just about making gold, isn't it?'

'If only,' Ben retorted. 'But it's not that simple. Once the alchemist learns how to transform matter, and could – technically – turn lead to gold, apparently he or she no longer wishes to do so.'

'Really? If I got to that point, I think I'd still have a try.' Ilhan laughed.

'You're sceptical,' Sebile said. 'Why is that, Dr Hitchens? You've spent your entire life searching for things of this earth. But perhaps you should ask yourself what you're really trying to find?'

She walked over to one of the alcoves lining her walls. 'The Emerald Tablet is only a tiny piece of the puzzle, you see – the key that lets us into the endless life cycle of matter . . . birth, life, death and decay. It can show us how to shift around the building blocks and transform them into something else.' Running her finger along the rows of books, she withdrew one. 'But true alchemical wisdom is the pursuit of the divine spark of life. It's in every living thing. Even those beastly men who attacked me and their ghastly children.'

Sebile resumed her seat. 'Stop, listen, and think. You both seem to have been blessed with good minds. This shouldn't be too challenging for you . . . Your heart beats, pumping blood around your body. But what made it jump to life the first time it throbbed in your chest? Who teaches a newborn lamb how to stand? How does a dormant seed fall to the ground and decide to grow? Even those idiots' children knew to suckle their mothers' teats the minute they slithered out of the womb. Why? *How*?'

'You don't need magic to explain any of those things,' responded Ben, frustrated. 'If I have any religion at all, it's science. Everything you mentioned can be attributed to natural instinct. And the seed? Give it dirt, water and sun – and it grows.'

'Yes, but *why*? Where does that "instinct" dwell? Where in a seed are the instructions that tell it to sprout when it encounters the base elements – earth, air, water and fire from the sun? Isn't that enough to hint at the existence of the divine in every living thing? Alchemy isn't magic. It doesn't stand in opposition to scientific theory – it *is* the consummate science. It shows us that we're ignoring the most important aspects of existence by never looking past the material.'

Sebile opened the book she'd selected and read a passage aloud. '"When the body is exhausted, the soul ascends, full of contempt for the brutal, miserable slavery it has suffered. So it is for everything in the world below. When it is defined by matter we can see it, but when it sheds matter, it becomes invisible. So why do we carry this false notion of birth and death? A human being is brought to birth *through* his parents, not *by* them. Authentic transformation is not caused by an individual being's visible surroundings but by a change in the One Thing contained in every man." Balinas' words, of course. He spent his life searching for the unseen force that exists within every human being – the soul, as Christianity would have it. It's an immortal presence, and one that evolves and is reborn many times over as it seeks perfect expression. The human body is only a vessel for something much more important. You speak of science – did you know that Isaac Newton was also an alchemist? A translation of the Emerald Tablet was found in his papers after his death.'

'Yes, I was aware of that.' Ben clenched his fists. He'd heard all this before and thought it no more sensible today than when he'd been studying under Ethan Cohn. He responded through gritted teeth. 'And I don't see anything contradictory in it. It always made sense to me that one of the greatest scientific thinkers would have been interested in the foundational documents of the tradition that gave birth to one of the major branches of science . . . al*chem*y . . . *chem*istry. While the alchemists were on their misguided quest, one thing they did do was pave the way for the very rational discipline that grew in their wake.'

Sebile shook her head. 'The metaphysical dimension of the study of matter was forced underground in the Christian era only because it contradicted the ambitions of a Church that wanted to keep its flock under its thumb and profit from humanity's search for salvation. The solitary pursuit of enlightenment advocated by Balinas was a threat to Christian dogma, so alchemists had to hide the spiritual aspects of their studies in arcane language for fear of persecution. That map,' Sebile said, gesturing towards Ben's journal, 'was drawn to protect the hiding place of what is – for want of a better point of comparison – our Holy Grail. It is physical proof of the truth of alchemical wisdom.'

She opened the book on her lap again and extended it towards the two men. 'Here. This is what it looks like, apparently.'

A seventeenth-century engraving showed a slab of rough-edged stone covered in Greek text. 'It was no fairytale – like the two Pillars of Hermes that once housed it, the tablet was seen and described by ancient travellers. After Alexander the Great discovered it in the Siwa Oasis, he put it on display in the Temple of Ra in Heliopolis. A Greek visitor to Egypt described it . . .' She read aloud from the printed page. '"It is a precious stone, like an emerald. On it, the characters are represented in relief, not engraved into the stone. It is estimated to be more than two thousand years old. The emerald must once have been in a liquid state like melted glass, that it might be cast in a mould."'

'So, forgive me for sounding like a simpleton, but is everyone looking for it because it's an enormous emerald?' Ilhan asked.

'You're missing the point,' Sebile snapped, slamming the book shut. 'It's not literally an emerald. In the right hands, it could do much good for the world. A handful of sand could be used to generate enough energy to power a city. But if used with ill intent, it could destroy the planet.'

'A handful of sand?' Ben had been puzzling over what it was about the tablet that would drive somebody to kill. Now he had his answer.

'Yes. That's why some people will go to the ends of the earth to protect it. And why others will do anything to steal it.' Sebile held out her hand. 'Show me your drawing . . .'

Ben handed her his journal. 'Here.' She pointed at the page. 'It's a mountain with two summits – one male, the other female. The signs – the stars and the *caput mortuum* – are leading you to the female summit. It's a cave, of course. I'd expect to find a phallus marker on the twin summit. This is the union of opposites recorded in the land itself – the divine marriage or *hieros gamos* you mentioned before, where male and female unite to become whole. This is a literal depiction of an actual place. Where did you find it?'

'It was . . . well, it was a woman. She led me there. Or, should I say, I followed her there.' Ben cringed.

Sebile paused. 'You love this woman.' It wasn't a question.

'Love?' He could tell there was no point denying his feelings. 'It's complicated.'

'You know, many of the most powerful alchemists were women – Mary the Jewess, Cleopatra –'

'*Cleopatra*?' interjected Ilhan.

'Not *that* Cleopatra. Cleopatra the Alchemist. Your woman, Dr Hitchens . . . Is she a good woman?'

'I don't know if I'd call her "good",' Ben responded.

'Is she searching for Balinas as well?'

'Yes, I think she is. And now I know why.'

'Do you trust her?'

'Trust? No.'

'Then you must stop her.'

'My problem is that even if this is a map, I've no idea where it's leading me. This mountain? Could be anywhere.'

'Psamtik. You recognise his name.'

'Yes. From a statue I saw when I was a child.'

She raised her eyebrows. 'Really? You know it? Well, that's most interesting.' She fanned through the pages of the book in her lap again. 'Is this the one you saw?' She held the book open for Ben.

A skilfully rendered drawing filled the page. Ben recognised it immediately. 'How the . . .?' He couldn't believe it. The noble figure of Psamtik strode forward beneath the protective dewlap of the cow-goddess, Hathor.

'I suppose the coincidence isn't so great,' she replied. 'I wouldn't for a minute claim that my knowledge of Ancient Egyptian art is exhaustive. But as far as I know, this is the only depiction of Psamtik in existence.' She passed the journal into Ben's hands.

'There's an inscription here. In Ancient Greek,' he observed.

'Can you read it?' Sebile asked.

'Almost better than I can English,' he responded as he ran his finger along the line of carefully drawn ancient text. '"From Jezirat Faraun where Psamtik the keeper of His tribute laboured under Hathor's watchful eye, Thuban will guide you past riches revealed to mankind by angels to the mountain where Apollonius finally achieved the Great Work."' He glanced up. 'Mountain. Again with the nameless mountain.'

'Not that I'd assume to tell you your job. But it seems that Psamtik here might be a good starting point.'

'He's in Cairo.'

'From Mersin on the ferry, it's not such a difficult journey across the sea to Alexandria.'

'What makes you think I should pay any attention to what's in this book? Where did you get it?' Ben leafed through the pages. At the front were scribbled notes in French and drawings such as the one Sebile had shown him depicting Psamtik and Hathor. But the pages in the second half of the book were pasted with fragments of scorched paper covered in partial passages and sentences written in French.

'It was given to me. In France. Many years ago . . . before I came here. I moved in circles where these things were studied. And I was told that it's all that remains of the writings of the French alchemist, Fulcanelli.'

'Fulcanelli? Sounds Italian.'

'It was a pseudonym. "Fulcan", "Vulcan" – the Roman god of fire and the forge. A most appropriate namesake. Ever since Balinas accepted a young man as his disciple – Damis of the city of Hierapolis – an unbroken lineage of master and adept has continued for thousands of years. It's through this line of descent that the secrets he discovered have been kept alive – and the resting place of the Emerald Tablet kept hidden. Fulcanelli is – or was – the latest in that long line.'

'So he was an alchemist, then?'

'Yes. But his research wasn't all arcane. The man who gave this to me told me that he'd shown these pages to a scientist at the Sorbonne. The experiments and theories show Fulcanelli had an understanding of nuclear physics that exceeded the knowledge of most experts in the field.'

'Where is he now?'

'Nobody knows. Against his wishes, the nature of his research was publicised, and during the war the Nazis pursued him, desperate to tap into his knowledge. For them, of course, it was always about gold . . .'

'Bloody Himmler,' Ben scoffed. 'Gold teeth ripped from Jewish jaws weren't enough for him. I did hear a rumour he had an alchemy lab set up at Dachau.'

'That he did. And after the fall of Berlin, the Americans and Russians seized the Nazi archives. It was there they learnt of Fulcanelli's research. And so, the race began. Fulcanelli disappeared and there was an attack on his laboratory. Much of his work was lost in a fire. All that survived is in here. They were hunting for him then, and are still hunting for him now.'

Something didn't add up for Ben. 'You mentioned an adept . . .'

'Yes. There was a young man who had promise. Fulcanelli accepted him as his apprentice and initiated him into the sacred arts. But he betrayed his master. He was seduced by an evil man. He told him everything. If your woman is following the same trail you are, it's possible that's how she knew where to find the map. And if that's the case, under no circumstances should the tablet fall into her hands.'

'I have my own reasons for wanting to do this,' Ben responded. 'But why is it so important to you?'

Sebile knotted her hands together in her lap, her brow furrowed. 'Humankind is so close to stumbling onto the truth . . . about the power that creates – and destroys – life. But most of us are little more than sentient chimpanzees. Very few people understand how dangerous this knowledge is. The bombs over Japan were a twitch in the corner of the eye compared to the apocalyptic destruction that could be released if the secrets of the tablet are revealed. Because just as it can lead us on a path to the purest light in the universe, so too can it evoke the dimmest corners of hell. The sun is our only source of life. It burns in our heavens – a gift. And it costs us nothing. We've been blessed with all the elements we need to live – the sun, water, wind and earth . . . creative forces that generate light and life. Yet we burrow in the soil to dig up ancient corpses to fuel our hunger for energy. The world today – motors . . . engines . . . artificial light – it's all powered by death; the decayed shells of things that once lived. We're ignoring light and life and choosing death.'

'Oil . . . you're talking about oil.'

'Of course I am. And Balinas discovered an alternative that outshines that coarsest of fuels – it could be human-kind's salvation. But it could also bring about its end. Even your Isaac Newton knew this. He lived during the Age of Reason. Magic, superstition and religion were forced into the shadows cast by the bright light of scientific logic. It seemed that every natural phenomenon had a rational explanation. But when it appeared that the purest truth – the secret of the Emerald Tablet – might be revealed, Newton wrote a letter to his fellow alchemist, Robert Boyle, urging him to remain silent about his discoveries, to protect the world from itself. He knew that the infinite power that could be unleashed through the alchemical transmutation of matter could be cataclysmic. And that's why you must pursue this. You will find the tablet, and you'll bring it to me.'

'Why do you trust me?'

She gazed at him. 'A lifetime's experience observing human nature. You're an honourable man.'

Ben laughed. 'Many would disagree with you.'

The tiny bus back to Niğde bounced and swerved across the potholed road, the only other passenger a toothless old man with two well-trussed chickens resting on his lap.

Weighing heavily in Ben's pocket was the scarab, which Sebile had pressed into his palm without a word when they were leaving.

'Ever been to Egypt?' he asked Ilhan.

'Egypt? Never.'

'Want to come with me?'

Ilhan said nothing, the crunch of gravel beneath tyres the only sound in the cabin.

'Well?'

'With all you've got going on, Ben — what do you think you'll gain by pursuing this?'

'The excavation season at Mt Ida's finished for the year. The only thing I should be doing at the moment is writing up the findings . . . and there's still plenty of time for that. Not to mention, unless they've already decided I didn't have anything to do with the librarian's death, from what Hasan told me I think it's best I stay away from Istanbul for a bit. Spending some time out of the country is probably a good idea. That's if they haven't already moved to stop me leaving. Besides . . . Cairo? It'll be fun. I promise.'

'Fun?' Ilhan shook his head. 'The history you have with those people . . . I just don't see how any good will come of it.'

'Shame . . . I'd imagine Cairo's ripe for the picking for a man with your interests.'

'So there's no talking you out of it?'

Ben shut his eyes for a moment and took a deep breath. Pass up the opportunity to upset the plans of the woman who had destroyed his life and played him for a fool? 'Not a chance.'

'Fine. I'll come. I guess I'll be able to find a way to make it worth my while.'

Glancing at his friend sitting by his side, his arms crossed tightly at his chest, Ben could see Ilhan was anything but thrilled at the thought.

THE TIMES
29 October 1956
INCREASED BRITISH AND FRENCH NAVAL ACTIVITY IN THE MEDITERRANEAN

LONDON, Monday (Reuters)
British and French naval activity in the Eastern Mediterranean and the massing of troops in Algeria and on Malta and Cyprus suggest the inevitability of a military response to the looming crisis, a Reuters correspondent reports.

Amid condemnation by the eleven-member United Nations Security Council and the U.S., reports of mounting military activity in the Mediterranean continue to emerge. The U.S. Secretary of Defence, Mr Charles Wilson, has said that any military action in Suez would be 'regrettable'.

America is alarmed by Communist attempts to find a foothold in the Middle East, and is seeking to collaborate with President Nasser in an alliance to fight Communism in the region. This requires Washington to maintain neutrality in the ongoing conflict between Israel and its Arab neighbours. To be seen to be supporting the British and French military build-up would damage Washington's relationship with the Egyptian Government.

Washington has also distanced itself from Israel amid suspicions that Israeli actions along its borders with Egypt and Jordan are backed by covert French military support.

In a frank discussion, U.S. Secretary of State, John Foster Dulles, expressed his concerns, noting the 'danger of our being drawn into the hostilities as we were in World Wars I and II – with the difference this time that it appears in the eyes of the world that the British and French might well be considered the aggressors in an anti-Arab, anti-Asian war. I've been greatly worried for two or three years over our identification with countries pursuing colonial policies not compatible with our own.'

10

London

'We shall fight them on the beaches ... and we shall *nevah* surrender!' Adam Penney spun in the cracked leather office chair, hand raised to mimic Sir Winston Churchill's famous victory salute. 'Hard to imagine the portly old bugger jammed in here – always thought this place would be bigger, for some reason. The way Daddy described it, I thought it must have been an underground city.' He leant back and put his feet on the table. 'But it's little more than a rabbit warren, after all.'

The Cabinet War Rooms were oppressive and stalked by ghosts. Essie looked up. Although she knew it was nothing more than an optical illusion, the low-slung, bulky steel girders supporting the room seemed to be sagging towards the floor, weighed down by the men and women rushing by on the London streets above and oblivious to the hidden world beneath their feet. Completed a week before Britain declared war on Germany in 1939, the War Rooms were built as a bunker in which the Prime Minister and his Cabinet could convene in safety when Hitler sent his bombers across the English Channel. These days, it served as a meeting place that was private and perfectly situated for those who were attempting to avoid scrutiny.

Although the antique table they were seated at had been buffed and polished recently in anticipation of their arrival, much of the furniture in the room – filing cabinets, bookshelves, side tables – was covered in a thick layer of grey dust. Essie had determined long ago that she didn't have the luxury of acknowledging any significant psychological weaknesses, but if she were to grant herself one, it would be claustrophobia. And this stifling and confined space below ground pushed her to her limits.

Josef Garvé leant back in his chair and checked his wristwatch. 'Mind what you say, Adam. Your uncle's due at any moment, and given his long association with that "portly old bugger", I imagine he'd hope you were a little more respectful.'

'Respectful? Let's talk about "respect", shall we? Where's the "respect" for the man whose work I'm continuing, eh? You *do* realise where the "V" salute came from, don't you? Not Churchill, that pompous old prig. Aleister Crowley, believe it or not. And if Churchill and his bunch of spineless lackeys had stolen a little more from Crowley than just a hand gesture, we'd all be a hell of a lot better off today. The world's going to shit, and those idiots are the ones to blame!' Adam was ranting. 'If they'd paused for just one moment to absorb Crowley's teaching and revelations, to open their minds to the gifts he offered the human race instead of treating him as a pariah –'

'Adam?' Essie assumed her most mollifying tone of voice. 'Josef's right. We *do* need to be careful. That doesn't mean you don't have a point – though you must admit that your former master is hardly "in favour" with those in power. So it's probably best to keep all mention of him out of this discussion . . . don't you think?'

Adam stood, walked behind Essie's chair and began to knead her shoulders. 'Seeing as you asked so nicely, it'd be churlish of me to refuse, wouldn't it?' She felt the pincer-like grasp of his fingers on her skin and squirmed. The physical contact was uninvited and inappropriate; worse still was his undisguised ogling of her deep cleavage. She fought her natural instinct to slap his hands away.

'Speaking of Crowley, Adam,' Essie said through gritted teeth. 'I need to examine your papers again before we leave London.'

'Always so serious, aren't you, Mrs Peters?' He sighed and released his grip. 'Well, all work and no play makes for a very dull boy . . . How about we mix our business with a little pleasure? The journal's at my home in Knightsbridge. I'll send my car for you tonight . . . we'll have supper afterwards. I have some friends joining me for a study group – you'll enjoy it.'

'I'd rather you just brought it in to the office tomorrow, if you wouldn't mind.'

'Well, I *do* mind, as it happens. Those documents are priceless – I shan't be shuttling them about town and putting them at risk of loss or damage. Like it or not, you'll need to come to me if you want to see them again.'

Essie saw Garvé shoot her a quizzical glance.

'Fine.' She had no choice. Now she had all the other references on hand, she needed to double-check she'd interpreted the notes in Aleister Crowley's diary correctly. 'Get your driver to pick me up at seven. I'll be at –'

Adam winked and tapped his forehead. 'No need . . . I've got your home address committed to memory.'

Essie didn't doubt it for a minute.

Shuffling footsteps down the corridor signalled the approach of a visitor. The door creaked open. 'Ah...hello...?' Peering through heavy, horn-rimmed spectacles, William Penney caught sight of the trio awaiting him inside and removed his grey felt fedora, holding it awkwardly by his side. 'Monsieur Garvé ... delightful, delightful ... and Mrs Peters ...' The Deputy Chairman of the Atomic Energy Authority shook the Frenchman's extended hand vigorously and raised Essie's to his lips for a chaste kiss. 'Young Adam ... keeping out of trouble, are you?' For his nephew, a chummy double handshake.

'Uncle Bill. How *are* you?'

'Good. Good. Well, as good as can be expected ... as you're all no doubt aware, internationally things are getting terribly grim.' William Penney drew breath. 'A situation which we know far more about than we possibly should, don't we?' Penney grimaced. 'I'm still unconvinced military action is necessary ...'

Garvé indicated a seat and the group resumed their places at the conference table. 'I understand your concerns, and share them, William. But I assure you, it's a necessary evil so we can enter the peninsula without detection, and convince the monks to do what we need them to. But you can put your mind at ease – the incursion will be very short-lived – we won't need long.'

Penney raised a finger, its nail chewed to the quick, and tapped his dimpled chin. 'Still ... as much as we're just stirring a pot that was already well on the boil, I can't help thinking there must be another way ...'

Leaning forward, Essie spoke forcefully. 'If what we've learnt since my visit to the archives in Topkapı is correct, Mr Penney, there are others looking for the tablet as well. Russians and Americans, by all reports –'

'That's correct,' Garvé interjected. 'I have reason to believe there are advance teams from both nations in Cairo. As far as I know, they don't have the information Adam brought us, which would make it difficult for them to decipher the geographic references in the hidden map. But they'll be watching us. And it's hard to know how much they've seen. We must be extremely careful.'

'The Reds . . .?' Penney shook his head. 'God help us, then. We always suspected they got their hands on the Nazi files on Fulcanelli. If they've worked out what the tablet can do to accelerate nuclear fission they'll be as keen to get hold of it as we are. And although it pains me to say it after the time I spent at Los Alamos working on their nuclear development program, we can't trust the Yanks anymore either. They're determined to dominate the Muslim world, regardless of the cost. When I was a young chap, we scientists all worked together. Collegiality and all that. Sadly, those days are long gone. To protect the motherland, we need to find the tablet and we can't depend on any external assistance, I'm afraid.'

He reached into his pocket and withdrew a tiny, stoppered glass flask. 'Here . . .' He handed it to Essie. 'I've never shown you the thing that convinced me you know what you're talking about. In 1905, Flinders Petrie – the archaeologist – excavated a temple dedicated to the Ancient Egyptian goddess, Hathor, at Serabit el-Khadim in the Sinai. There were many singular features about the place, but there were two things in particular that interested him . . . a crucible of the sort used by metallurgists, and a massive deposit of that material in there. He unearthed it beneath the temple's foundations. Petrie called it white wood ash. He excavated vast quantities of it and transported it dutifully to London, but he had no idea whatsoever what it was. And the truth is, neither do we.'

Essie held the flask to the light. The powder inside was as white as sifted cornflour, but insubstantial – as she turned the glass, it swirled and eddied like mist.

'When our scientists examined it,' Penney continued, 'they couldn't determine its physical properties. You see, it seems to be powdered stone of some sort, but it's inherently unstable. When it's cooled – it seems to enter a state where it has a negative mass. To put it in layman's terms, when you push something, you expect it to accelerate away from you. With negative mass, a push will send something back towards you. We've no idea why it acts as it does, but we've long suspected from the hieroglyphic inscriptions Petrie found in the temple that this is the substance the Egyptians called "white bread" and the Mesopotamians, "fire stone". The reason we're so interested in it, though, is that under the right conditions, we've found that it's also capable of transforming matter. The promise of synthesising gold may not be as much of a pipe dream as we once believed, particularly given what you, Monsieur Garvé, told us you witnessed at Dachau . . . and that would make our Prime Minister very happy, given the parlous state of the British Treasury.'

Penney pointed at the bottle in Essie's hand. 'But what excites me most of all is this material's extreme volatility. There's no telling what we might make of it if we were able to fabricate it ourselves. But, of course, we can't. Not without the Emerald Tablet. If what you've found in that old deviant's notes can be believed, an analysis of the tablet itself will allow us to master the processes used to make it. And with that knowledge, anything's possible. That's why we need it for Mother England. Can't have it falling into anyone else's hands.'

Leaning across the table, his hands interlocked before him, Josef Garvé considered William Penney with a clinical gaze.

'As I explained to you on the telephone, we're poised to go, Mr Penney. We'll be in Egypt at the assigned time; all we need is information from you about the military options for transporting us into the desert. Once we find the tablet, as negotiated, we'll hand it over to you.'

'Yes, yes. Quite.' Penney stood and walked to the door. 'Which is, of course, why we're here . . . I've invited Captain Knight to join us. He'll be escorting you into the Sinai. He's a good man, but he's straight as a die – he knows only that this is a secret mission and that it's of the utmost importance to the nation's security.'

'Well, that's hardly an exaggeration, is it?' interrupted Adam.

'You're quite right, Adam. But see here . . .' Penney spoke below his breath to his nephew as he would to a dull child. 'It's very important that nobody outside our immediate circle knows what we're really looking for. We're in luck that the PM is a vain man who developed an impressive chip on his shoulder after having to serve as Winston's sidekick for so many years. The Benzedrine he's on has made him more suggestible than ever. It didn't take much for me to convince him that it was a good idea to take a trip into the desert to find a recipe to replace the gold that the Americans are threatening to take away from us. But if he was in his right mind, he would have laughed me out of his office. If Macmillan – or any of the others who'd be quite happy to send Eden packing – got wind of what we have going on here . . . well, for one thing, they'd likely lock us all up in the madhouse. And – to be frank – that's not where I want to spend my retirement. So best we tread carefully and keep this to ourselves, yes?'

Chastened, the young man just nodded in response.

'Captain . . .?' Penney opened the door and summoned someone waiting outside.

Captain Matthew Knight was tall and lanky with carefully coifed auburn hair, a man who'd clearly cultivated the studied expression of focused intensity he seemed to believe was expected of a celebrated war hero. Knight ducked his head instinctively as he walked through the door into the cramped room, his peaked hat tucked beneath his arm and Royal Air Force uniform embellished with a reassuring array of military awards and decorations. Penney introduced him.

'So I'm to brief you. Seems we're going to be flying you in with the troops.' Eyebrow raised, Knight cast a dubious eye over his charges. 'Which of you will be on board?'

'All three of us,' Garvé replied.

Knight was sceptical as he took in Essie in her snugly fitting suit. 'War's no place for a woman, if you don't mind me saying, ma'am.'

Essie bristled. 'Don't you worry about me, sir. I'll be fine.'

'That's as may be. But on the frontline? Doesn't seem right to take a lady into combat.'

'She's essential to the mission, Captain Knight,' Garvé responded.

'Essential, you say? They didn't warn me I was leading a ladies' brigade into battle. Fair enough. I'd better make sure I wear my Sunday best.' He winked at Essie.

She smiled thinly. She'd once imagined that the day would come when the endless condescending barbs shot in her direction as she went about her work would eventually bounce off and leave her unscathed. But she now knew that had just been wishful thinking. If anything, it irritated her more than ever.

'Well, there'll be plenty of room for you to make yourself comfortable, anyway, Mrs Peters – plenty of space for your luggage and whatnot. We've got a Wessex Whirlwind lined up to get us across the battlefront and back. It's quite something.

We'll be heading to shore from the HMS *Theseus*. It's the first helicopter assault the RN has ever launched. History in the making, if you don't mind . . .'

'Not that we'll ever be able to talk about it, though, isn't that right, Captain?' William Penney reminded him.

'Yes. Quite. Of course,' Knight responded tightly. 'Anyway . . . by my calculations, our journey'll take about an hour. Though that doesn't account for any hostile fire we might encounter. Once we clear the coastline, we should be right. None of it is without its dangers, of course – if we *do* get into trouble . . . well, there's not much in the way of roads or settlements in the desert, just tribes of Bedouin, and I don't see them being too keen to help us, given the circumstances.'

The phone on the desk rang, cutting though the room's oppressive silence. 'Excuse me . . .' William Penney fumbled for the receiver. 'Yes . . .?' As he listened, his brow creased and the colour fled his cheeks. 'I see . . . thank you for letting me know.' He placed the handset gently back into its cradle.

'Well, gentlemen – and Mrs Peters – the orders have been signed and the countdown has begun. The Israelis are poised to launch their initial foray and the main attack will commence in the days that follow. It's time.'

After William Penney took the phone call, the meeting dispersed quickly. Taking the first opportunity to flee the cloying environment, Essie had made her way to the street above and hailed a cab.

It shouldn't have come as any surprise to learn that British and French convoys were already assembling in Malta and Cyprus, with troops and supplies landed in Marseilles and Toulon. Penney's assessment had been blunt: 'They're certainly not gathering in the Mediterranean for a regatta.' But still, Essie always found it felt strangely surreal when plans that had been gestating for so long came to fruition.

The countdown had begun. Israel would cross the Sinai border to attack Egypt, which would have no choice but to retaliate. Britain and France would then use the justification that the continuing operation of the Suez Canal was a matter of global importance, and warn both parties to withdraw their troops. When Egypt refused, as was inevitable, France and Britain would take that as an excuse to attack. Essie, Garvé and Penney would then take advantage of the large-scale distraction to go into the Sinai without detection.

Essie settled back against the cab's unyielding vinyl upholstery and watched the passing parade of Londoners bustling by along the footpath, cast in silhouette by golden autumn light. The cab pulled up at an intersection where a mother watched on indulgently as her three children kicked at a pile of crumpled brown leaves fallen from the plane trees lining the street.

She felt a sharp stab of guilt at the thought that she was playing an instrumental role in the tempest brewing just beyond the horizon – the dangers of which these people were blissfully unaware. Yes, they'd set all the safeguards in place to ensure the smouldering embers of war were snuffed out before they burst into flame. But she'd seen enough of history and human nature to know how quickly events could spiral out of control.

II

London

As the hand on the clock in her kitchen ticked towards the hour, Essie sipped from a cup of strong black tea. The day outside the bay window was fading and streetlamps were lighting up as blackbirds serenaded dusk's arrival.

A grim sense of trepidation sprouted in her gut. She'd stemmed her hunger with a chicken sandwich and tomato salad in anticipation of turning down the expected invitation to share a meal with Adam Penney and his companions. She had no intention of succumbing to whatever his plans were for her evening, but suspected negotiating her way around him this time wasn't going to be easy.

The time was fast approaching when the doorbell would ring, announcing the arrival of his driver. She retreated to her bathroom where she ran warm water onto a facecloth and worked up a soapy lather to wash away any lingering traces of makeup. She looked at herself in the mirror. Clad in the most modest outfit in her wardrobe, and with clean, bare skin and her blonde hair pulled back tightly into a chignon, she looked young enough to be a schoolgirl. The black woollen turtleneck and tweedy skirt were working hard to disguise her physical assets, but there was no hiding the fact that cloaked beneath the houndstooth were undeniably womanly curves.

It was the best she could do to divert Adam's unwanted advances, short of defending herself physically, which she'd have no qualms about doing if she was left with no other choice. The art of jujitsu wasn't generally regarded as a pursuit that was suitable for a respectable lady. But Essie considered herself neither respectable, nor a lady. And working in the world she did – consorting with people operating outside the bounds of common law – she'd always assumed that eventually she'd be forced to confront a bodily assault of some sort or another and she fully intended to be prepared. Her instincts and wiles were sharp enough that she'd so far managed to avoid using the skills she'd acquired under the tutelage of her jujitsu trainer, May Whitley. Though if she were honest, the thought of testing her skills on someone other than a sparring partner was wickedly tempting.

Outside, she heard the distinctive squeal of her wrought-iron front gate. The knot of anxiety tightened as Essie gathered up her bag and headed for the entrance. As she reached for the handle, the shiny brass mail slot set into her front door clattered and a handful of letters popped through.

Not a chauffeur – the postman. Relieved at the temporary reprieve, she rifled through the mail and cast all aside other than the distinctive blue aerogramme envelope embossed with an instantly recognisable stamp – an olive-green backdrop graced with the noble profile of a woman acclaimed as one of the most beautiful ever born – Nefertiti – the wife of the heretic Egyptian king, Akhenaten. Instinctively, Essie shut her eyes and raised the letter to her nose, sniffing to see whether the whispery blue paper carried with it the exotic aroma of the place she'd called home for so many years. She knew it was most likely just her imagination, but she thought she caught a hint of cinnamon sticks, cardamom and peppercorns – the scents of her stepmother's kitchen.

The message the letter contained was short and to the point. Written by her half-sister in words shaved of any sentiment, it informed her that the woman who'd done her best to love her and raise her as her own after the death of Essie's mother was, herself, dying.

Essie looked at the postmark. Cairo, dated a week prior. Meera had sent it as a formality . . . a courtesy. She'd written it to inform Essie of an impending event, not in the expectation that she would – or could – do anything about it. On the many occasions she'd relocated over the years, Essie had always made sure her family had her address. She also periodically sent them money – though whether to help them or assuage her own guilt she could never be sure. But she'd never received any acknowledgement of any sort from them – this was the first and only communication she could recall in many years.

The doorbell rang. Essie had thought she'd successfully amputated and cauterised all emotional links to her past. But the surge of grief and regret that swamped her as she opened the door to greet Penney's driver suggested otherwise.

Any vague hopes she'd harboured that Penney may have had something on his mind other than seduction were shattered when he opened his front door clad in a maroon silk dressing-gown belted loosely enough to show that he wasn't wearing a shirt beneath it to match his black dinner pants.

'Answering the door yourself now, Adam?'

'I gave Basil the night off.'

That does not bode well for my evening, thought Essie. She'd much rather have known that Adam's butler was on duty, if only because it meant he was – at the very least – mindful of the appearance of propriety.

'I'm disappointed.' Penney's eyes skimmed her shapely form. 'You didn't dress for the occasion.'

'No.' She smiled tightly. She'd already been dubious enough about spending the evening beneath Adam Penney's roof. The unexpected news from Egypt only heightened her apprehension. 'Just here to look at the documents. Then I'll be going. I've already eaten.' *Might as well knock that one on the head right off the bat.*

'Fine, fine.' He stood back and Essie passed beneath the porticoed entranceway, edging past him as her olfactory senses were assaulted by a nauseating fog of citrusy aftershave. The corridor inside the terrace house was dimly lit and a low murmur of conversation and muted laughter came through double doors left partially ajar and leading into what Essie guessed would be the main reception room.

'Let's go through to the library then ...' Penney strode towards the back of the house, the click of his well-polished brogues resounding on the black and white chequerboard tiles. He paused as they passed the entrance to the room that was – judging by the sound levels from within – hosting a gathering of a reasonably large group of people. 'Now, what we're doing here ... the group I've gathered ... I'm *sure* what we're discussing will be of great interest to you.'

She shook her head. 'Really, I've a great deal to do. I'd much rather get straight onto it.'

'Fine. Though it's a shame. My uncle and your Monsieur Garvé – even you, I'm sorry to say – you're all missing the point. You've no idea what we're really searching for.' He opened a door leading off the corridor and ushered Essie into a wood-panelled room lined with bookshelves and leather-bound volumes she was sure were there strictly for show. Penney continued, 'Aleister knew. The power trapped inside the Emerald Tablet is so much more than a way to transform one thing into another. It's how we can break the bonds that enslave all forms of life. Preparing ourselves to receive that wisdom . . . readying ourselves for the new world order . . . that's what we're here to do. The tablet's the most sacred of all magical objects.'

'So tell me, Adam,' Essie said. 'I'm curious. Why are you insisting on coming into the desert with us? It's going to be the most ghastly slog. Surely it would be much easier if you were to let us go and fetch it for you? We've got all the information we need . . . you could just stay back here in comfort and wait for us to deliver it to you.' And she could think of nothing better.

'And miss the chance to be one of the first people to see it in thousands of years? Not on your life. Besides, don't take it the wrong way, but without me, none of this would be happening. Without me, you wouldn't be getting your helicopter and military escort. So I fully intend to be there at the end. Before I give it to my uncle and it's desecrated by his microscopes and test tubes, I will commit myself to worshiping the tablet, and through mediation, ritual and incantations, I will discover the path to eternal life. I need to be there to make sure that happens.'

Essie sighed heavily. She'd heard it all before and it never sounded like anything other than the half-baked ravings of a lunatic. 'The thing is, Adam, I'm just here to find the tablet for your uncle. And for England, of course. What happens to it after that doesn't concern me at all. Couldn't care less.'

111

'I'll open your eyes to it one day, like it or not.' He turned to a heavy floor safe sitting in the corner of the room and fiddled with the lock. 'Just you wait.'

He reverently placed a large book bound in brittle vellum on the oak desk that dominated the room. 'Here. The words of the Master, as dictated to me before he crossed the Abyss. As you read it, remember that Aleister was the one true prophet. Apollonius . . . Jesus . . . the Buddha . . . Mohammad . . . all false prophets. They were given small pieces of the secret. Only Aleister understood all. The Master taught us that life isn't about a search for spiritual perfection. That's the lie we're told from the cradle to the grave. The truth is – we're all born perfect. There is no judgement for wrongdoing because we can do no wrong. "Do what thou wilt shall be the whole of the Law . . ."'

'Yes, quite. You'll recall I have seen it already.' *More times than I'd prefer, if you really want to know.* 'Thank you, Adam. Now, if you wouldn't mind . . .?'

'I'll bring you round. A piece at a time.' He smirked. 'Drink?'

'Certainly. Thank you.' *Anything to get you out of here.*

Essie shuddered as she placed her hand on the reptilian-like casing of the book Penney had placed on the table. She knew vellum was nothing more sinister than treated calfskin, but its colour and the way it preserved the hair follicles and shadows of the network of veins that had once crisscrossed a living creature's body were so like mummified human skin that it had always unsettled her. Her response was amplified by what she knew of the contents of the book.

Her flesh crawled as she flicked past the pages she'd been forced to plough through when Adam first showed her Aleister Crowley's deathbed confessions. Determined not to give Adam the satisfaction of seeing her cringe, she'd attempted to hide her distaste as she trawled through page after page of vivid descriptions of the ghastliest accounts of physical and mental degradation imposed on both men and women – his 'Scarlet Women' and 'Divine Whores' – by the man who'd declared himself Baphomet – the Beast. His words had burnt themselves into her soul . . . 'Send spouting the tide of your sizzling piss in my mouth . . . splutter out shit from the bottomless pit . . . chew it with me, whore . . . vomit it, spew it and lick it once more . . . I'll bugger your grin into a shriek.'

Crowley offered his 'sex magick' as the cure-all that would liberate the spiritual being from the deception of the material world, and it demanded the rejection of all social and cultural constraints. There were no taboos. Sodomy, bestiality, pederasty, orgies, coprophilia . . . all lubricated with boundless quantities of every intoxicant known to man, and all in the name of becoming one with the higher self. Crowley's followers saw him as a messiah. Essie just saw an odious snake-oil salesman who'd struck upon a gimmick that lured the damaged and gullible into a snare where they could become proxies for his most perverted desires.

One of those damaged souls was a man named Gerome Cushman, and in a roundabout way, it was thanks to him that Essie found herself hunched over a desk in Penney's home. Born to a wealthy family of merchants in the port of Marseilles, Gerome had lived a childhood of pampered neglect. Knowing he'd never want for any material comforts, once Gerome reached adulthood, he'd embarked upon a lifelong search for the sense of purpose and belonging he'd never managed to find with the long line of nannies and paid carers who'd raised him.

Gerome's quest led him to Paris where he fell under the sway of the master alchemist, Fulcanelli. The alchemist saw great potential in the young man and recruited him as his adept, schooling him in the ancient philosophy and its secrets and expecting of him resolute attention to his studies. But Gerome was unaccustomed to abstinence and restraint and chafed under Fulcanelli's strict discipline. Curiosity drew him to the Parisian esoteric society, the Ordo Templi Orientis, to hear Aleister Crowley speak. Gerome's conversion was immediate. He was seduced by the older man's promise that his new world order would break the repressive bonds of Judeo-Christian society. His future was set when he heard Crowley declare before a transfixed audience: 'the hell with Christianity, Rationalism, Buddhism, all the lumber of the centuries! I will build me a new Heaven and a new Earth. I want none of your faint approval or faint disrespect; I want blasphemy, murder, rape, revolution, anything, bad or good, but strong.'

The pages that lay beneath Essie's hands documented Gerome's descent to the depths of debasement and eventual death while under Crowley's sway, and the sacred secret he'd revealed to his master before he died. It had been a rapid decline. When Cushman learnt that the charismatic older man had journeyed to the island of Sicily to set up a spiritual centre, the young man abandoned his studies with Fulcanelli and joined his new master at the place that would become known as the Abbey of Thelema until Crowley was banished from Italy by no less than Benito Mussolini. When she'd first read his account, it had struck Essie as more than a little astounding that details of the goings-on in Sicily were disturbing enough that once they reached the ears of one of the most corrupt and evil men of the twentieth century he'd immediately expelled the foreigners from Italian shores.

Cushman became one of Crowley's many sexual partners and quickly surrendered to the same crippling addiction to heroin and cocaine that plagued his master. Released from inhibitions, Cushman performed sadomasochistic sexual rituals with Crowley. Judging by the relish with which he recalled their encounters, their union brought Crowley great pleasure. 'Even his mouth remains in a somewhat greasy condition after it has achieved the holy task, and we have no hesitation in plumping for the anus as the one vase into which the perfumed oil of manhood may best be poured. I found myself naked in his naked arms, his giant member still throbbing and beating in my flooded bowels,' he said of one of their couplings.

From what Essie read of the months Cushman spent on Sicily, she knew the sepsis that entered his bloodstream and ended his life might have come from any one of the many unsanitary practices common to the residents of the Abbey of Thelema. Anyone who dared utter the word 'I' was compelled to slice themselves with a razor. Animals were sacrificed, and the blood of the dying creature consumed, and stinking drinking water was drawn from a creek behind the building that also served as the abbey's sewer.

Before he died, Cushman stripped his soul bare before his master. To completely break with his former life, Gerome Cushman thought the ultimate demonstration of his slavish loyalty to Aleister Crowley would be to betray the oaths he'd made to Fulcanelli and reveal the secrets of the Emerald Tablet and its final resting place.

Crowley cared little for Cushman's claims. He had no interest in pursuing another man's spiritual vision. In Cairo in 1904 on a honeymoon for his short-lived marriage, Crowley had reputedly experienced his own divine revelation. An entity sent by the Egyptian god, Horus, transmitted to him the foundations of Thelema, the esoteric faith he began to preach to followers around the world. It was only later in life that he began to question whether he'd too readily dismissed the gift he'd been given by his dying disciple, but by then Crowley was a crippled man living in a hospice as war raged across Europe. He no longer had the means or the capacity to travel into the desert in pursuit of a dream. So he relayed the story to the young man who'd been appointed his personal secretary during his last days at the Netherwood boarding house in Sussex. Adam Penney had been sent to Crowley's side by a government concerned that the dying man might have been divulging national secrets on his deathbed. At first, Essie had been horrified to learn that a man like Crowley had been recruited to spy for the British Government during both World Wars. But when she gave the matter more thought, it made sense. Given his well-documented and very public personal failings, no reasonable enemy counterintelligence agency would suspect him of being capable of, far less entrusted with, espionage duties.

Although at first Penney had given little thought to the possible importance of the Emerald Tablet, he was seduced by the dying occultist, whose magnetism had not waned, even in his last days. As Penney had described it to Essie, after he was sent to transcribe Crowley's account so the government could ensure its secrets were safe, he had become Crowley's last convert. It came as no surprise to her that Penney would happily throw in his lot with anyone who could justify his taste for debauchery.

She'd already spent far longer between the pages of this poisonous book than she'd have preferred. Flipping to the passages where Crowley had dictated to Penney the coded instructions for finding Balinas' tomb, Essie compared the transcription with the notes she'd taken on her last visit. Now that she had the map from the Topkapı archives, she wanted to be sure she hadn't misinterpreted or overlooked anything important.

As she scanned the pages, she couldn't see anything she'd missed. She had everything she needed.

The library door groaned as it opened, and Penney stepped in holding a tray bearing two cups of what Essie assumed from the fragrance was mulled wine. 'Sorry it took me a while . . . got held up with my guests.' He handed her one.

'Thank you, Adam.' Figuring there was little chance that Penney had resisted the temptation to slip something into her drink, she feigned a stumble and spilt the wine across the floor. 'Oh, God!' she exclaimed, grabbing the cloth from the tray and mopping up the sticky mess. 'How very clumsy of me. So sorry.'

'No matter,' he replied, handing her his cup. 'Plenty more where that came from. Here. Have mine. I haven't even raised it to my lips yet.'

She took it reluctantly and edged towards the door.

Adam smiled. 'As the Master said, "Magick is the science and art of realising the divine self by changing the human self."'

Essie had no idea what he was talking about. But with what she now knew of Aleister Crowley's 'Magick', if that was what was required to realise the divine, then she was very happy to remain earth-bound.

Counting the minutes until she could escape Penney's lair, she downed the wine in a single draught.

The cloying taste of nutmeg and orange rind stuck to the roof of her mouth as she turned into the hallway, Penney following uncomfortably close behind her. Something was wrong. A warm kernel had lodged itself deep in Essie's belly, sending tendrils of heat through her body, seductive fronds that began to encase her brain. It wasn't an unpleasant sensation, but it was eroding her focus in a way that sounded an alarm bell. To dissolve in a puddle of euphoria was one thing if it were to happen in a place of refuge. For it to occur here was terrifying.

She felt every beat of her heart reverberating against her ribcage as she tried to find her way to a front door that seemed to be fleeing from her. Penney had obviously put whatever narcotic he had planned to slip her in his own cup as well. She cursed herself for not second-guessing him as she fought to regain control of her limbs, if only so she could smash his solar plexus with a roundhouse kick. Her stomach clenched with impotent rage as she struggled to stay upright. Leaden feet betrayed her, sending her stumbling against the wall.

Adam caught her around her waist. 'Essie . . . you look pale. What's wrong?'

Even through a fast-approaching narcotic stupor, she knew it was a rhetorical question.

He guided her towards the double doors she'd seen when she arrived. 'I think you could do with a seat.' He pushed the doors open.

Inside was a room dimly lit by candles dripping wax in stalactites from rows of tall candelabra. Chaise longues and banquettes arranged around the walls hosted myriad couplings and groupings of naked and near-naked figures in every imaginable combination of age and gender, writhing in an obscene dance of limbs and bare flesh. The air was thick with the scent of sweat and body fluids.

Essie's consciousness was split in two. While one part of her mind was panicking and struggling to take control of a body that no longer seemed to be hers, the other half was drawn in an almost clinical way to a tall man standing at the centre of the room, his chest bared. A naked and voluptuous woman with golden curls gyrated around him, her hair cascading over his olive skin. He'd watched as they entered the room.

'Here . . .' Adam guided her towards an empty settee, a hand slipping deliberately beneath her jumper to cup her breast. 'I think we'll forgo introductions.' She felt only disgust towards him. The smell of stale red wine on his breath made her feel sick, and although she willed herself to fight back, her limbs were frozen.

Pulling her down to sit beside him on the velvet-upholstered seat, Adam moved his other hand to the gap between her thighs and began to slide it towards the top of her stockings. He kissed her neck, his saliva sticky on her skin, and whispered what she assumed were endearments but sounded to her ears like curses.

Despite herself, as she recoiled from Adam's determined groping and thick-fingered fumbling, Essie was transfixed by the spectacle around her. In one corner of the room, a hirsute man seated in an ornate chair had his head thrown back in ecstasy as a youth sucked hungrily at his swollen cock and an audience of two women stood by watching them, mouths agape with fingers slipping and thrusting inside each other until their knees gave way and they fell to the floor, one woman dropping her face down to bury it between her partner's legs. On the floor in front of a blazing fire, a buxom woman lay prone while a rotund, white-bellied man frantically stuffed his cock inside her, his cheeks purple with effort, while her face was straddled by another woman riding her tongue as a group of men stood around the group in a circle, tugging their cocks and splattering the two women with their seed.

The tall man at the centre of the room had disentangled the woman from about his limbs and was moving towards where Essie and Adam sat. His dark hair was unusually long, falling in waves to his broad shoulders. She was mesmerised. A sense of abandon took hold, and she felt herself losing her grip.

Dragging what remained of her consciousness to a needle-sharp point behind her eyes, Essie tried to ignore Adam's probing fingers as she fought to awaken her senses. She flexed her fingers and toes, and craned her neck, shutting her eyes and focusing on her limbs as she reconnected her mind with her body.

Adam nibbled and licked her ears wetly, murmuring beneath his breath. 'This is my gift, Essie. All beings contain a spark of life. The only way to liberate that spark is by setting your will free.' His fingers found the top of her stockings and began to fiddle with the buttons that held them to her suspender belt. Feeling as if she was dragging her arm through wet concrete, Essie lifted her hand and swatted at Adam's wrist. He caught her hand in his and raised it to his lips.

'When two people join in fornication, it is the purest form of worship . . .' Having managed to undo both stockings, Adam's hand moved to the mound between her legs. Fighting back, she clamped her thighs shut while he tried to lever them apart. As she struggled, she felt her body begin to stir from its narcotic slumber. Whatever he'd given her, its effect seemed to be short-lived.

'I'll show you another life,' he continued in a low-pitched voice she presumed was meant to be seductive but just turned her stomach. 'I will carry you to the point of exhaustion — carry you to the brink . . . and when I bring you back from the abyss, the visions you'll have —'

'No!' A screaming wraith from the depths of Essie's soul broke free and drove her to her feet. She'd seized back control of her body, and now knew exactly what she wanted. She shoved Adam away and stumbled towards the tall stranger, falling into his outstretched arms and pressing her lips against his, her mouth wide and probing to find his tongue. Tearing her jumper over her head and kicking off her skirt, she felt for his cock, which was long and hard against the fabric of his pants. Fumbling with his fly, she shoved his pants down beneath his knees. As he lifted her, digging his fingers into her thighs, she wrapped her legs about his waist and impaled herself on him. Their teeth clashed together as he stumbled to the wall and she felt his broad chest heaving against hers. All eyes in the room were on them as Essie felt the cold plaster against her back and he grabbed her breasts and drove himself deep within her again and again, their groins slamming against each other. She heard someone screaming in ecstasy and barely recognised her own voice.

From the corner of her eye, she caught a glimpse of Adam Penney yanking himself into a frenzy. She shut the image out and succumbed to a blinding release.

THE TIMES
30 October 1956
AMERICAN ANGER AT ISRAELI MILITARY ACTION

LONDON, Tuesday (Reuters)

American leaders warn that Israeli action along the Egyptian border will be the spark that will ignite the Middle East, a Reuters correspondent reports.

World fears of a Middle East war grew tonight as Egypt announced she had moved against Israeli troops that had crossed into her sovereign territory in the Sinai Peninsula. A government spokesman refused to confirm or deny whether Israeli objectives included occupation of the Canal Zone.

America responded by immediately calling a meeting at the United Nations and issued a warning to Israel that in the event of a war, it would support Egypt.

The U.S. is unequivocal in its condemnation of Israel's aggression. Although it is widely acknowledged that Egypt and its Arab neighbours have deliberately provoked Israel, the United States was reported to favour the sternest of measures to halt Israel's sabre-rattling in the Sinai Peninsula.

Egypt announced that Israel was signing its own death warrant as Arab leaders rushed to support their Moslem neighbour. Iraq told Egypt: 'Our army is ready to help you crush the invaders.'

This came as former friends become foes, with the U.S. Secretary of State John Foster Dulles warning Britain and France that if they went to war over the Suez Canal they would no longer receive any military or financial aid from the U.S.

It is suspected in many quarters that France is secretly encouraging Israel. Reliable reports indicate that Israeli armed forces are equipped with far more French weaponry than U.S. authorities believed they had.

The British and French governments strongly object to the American alliance with Egypt, which they see as under-mining their centuries-old dominance of the region.

An unnamed source in the British Government said: 'The Americans have not only undermined British prestige in the Middle East, but the prestige of all white men; they have created a power vacuum in the Middle East which is rapidly being filled by the Communists. Russia, meanwhile, has done nothing to facilitate a solution of the Suez crisis. Russian misrepresentations about alleged Western colonialism have sharpened and their attitude creates the impression that it pays the Soviet Union to foster ill-will between the peoples of Asia and Africa and the peoples of the West.'

12

Cairo, Egypt

The sight of the pyramids looming above the chaotic city skyline took Ben's breath away, as it did every time he visited the ancient city on the Nile.

'Well, just when I thought my sense of wonder had been tapped dry . . . They really are remarkable, aren't they?' Ilhan observed, unnecessarily.

Ben just nodded.

As a child trying to find space for himself in a life knotted up in his parents' rigid rules and expectations, the world of history had provided the young Benedict Hitchens with an escape route. Tucked in one corner of the library in his palatial Boston childhood home had been an antique stereoscope with a polished ebony box full of slides showing archaeological wonders of the world. If Ben was to ascribe his career choice to one thing, it would have been the countless hours he spent escaping into the three-dimensional photographs of places he knew he would one day visit. And the one image that found its way into the viewer more than any other, until its corners frayed through handling and the lettering in its margins faded to almost nothing, showed the monumental Egyptian tombs rising from the desert. Fascination grew into that singular obsession peculiar to childhood. He'd taught himself everything there was to know about the pyramids – their scale, their form, their composition, and the many conflicting theories about how they'd been built.

He'd been an adult when he'd first visited Cairo, and had experienced enough of life to know that things that are highly anticipated rarely live up to expectation. He'd approached Giza with no small amount of trepidation, carried through Cairo in the back of a decrepit taxi along streetscapes that might have been sets from a Cecil B. DeMille movie. But the tombs built for the pharaohs Khufu, Khafre and Menkaure in the middle of the third millennium BC didn't disappoint. The pyramids appeared without warning – ethereal in the golden desert air, but still massive; a surreal apparition hovering above Cairo's slums and dwarfing even the tallest buildings in the city. The towering stone edifices trumpeted an unassailable challenge to mortality and stood as proof of his own inconsequentiality. It was a realisation that gave Ben a peculiar sense of solace.

Now, outside the car's grimy windows, Cairo was as frenetic as he remembered it and the passage along the city's narrow streets torturous. The driver Ben had hired in Alexandria to transport them to the city idled behind a ridge-backed donkey hauling a cart overladen with building materials. Ahead, a camel train led by a bow-legged cameleer ambled along, the animals' skinny rumps dipping and swaying in a mesmerising dance.

The air in the car was stifling, its roof scorched by the Saharan sun, but Ben kept the windows firmly shut – the air outside was no cooler, and carried with it the fetid stench of the street and swarms of flies that kept pace with the beasts of burden. As the car passed over the rough road it shuddered and rocked, lulling Ben into a pleasant stupor.

Their journey from the heart of Turkey to Egypt had been uneventful but protracted. It had been easy enough to find two seats aboard a cramped *dolmuş* that wound its way south across the Taurus Mountains through the same Cilician Gates that had once admitted Alexander the Great's army to the Cappadocian plateau. At Mersin's port, Ben and Ilhan had booked two berths on a virtually empty overnight boat to Alexandria. Any concerns Ben might have had about being stopped at the border amounted to nothing. As the two men had joined the scant gathering of passengers waiting to pass customs, the only thing the Turkish official who stamped their travel papers had seemed worried about was ensuring Ben and Ilhan understood they were travelling into what would soon be a war zone. Although there had seemed to be heightened activity in Alexandria's port when they'd arrived, they'd engaged a driver without any difficulty and the journey south through the Nile Delta to Cairo had been unremarkable.

Edging round the livestock, the driver honked his horn and forced his way forward. The traffic was at a standstill. He shook his head. 'No good. Something wrong.' A cloud of dust appeared, billowing along the street. Cars jack-knifed as they tried to reverse, honking horns as they encountered the dense jumble of animals and vehicles jammed behind them. A fierce chanting cut through the air. The driver wound down his window and listened. He spun in his seat, eyes wide with fear. 'You, sir!' He flapped his hand at Ben. 'Hat . . . you have hat?'

'Yes.' Ben fumbled around behind him and found his Stetson on the rear sill.

'Hair . . .' The driver pointed at Ben's head. 'You hair . . . is English . . . very English . . . Cover. Men come. They angry.'

'And me?' Ilhan asked.

'You OK. Good. Brown skin. No problem. Like me.' He pointed at Ben again. 'But you? You problem. Head down! Please, sir!'

The car's floor vibrated with the stamping of hundreds of feet pounding along the narrow laneway. A press of bodies surged along the street, fists slamming on car roofs and hands slapping in unison to the fearsome chanting that drove the mob forward.

As faces purple with rage pressed past the windows, Ben kept his head tilted down with his elbow lodged in the window and hand shielding his brow in what he hoped appeared to those outside to be the casual stance of a disinterested bystander. He couldn't understand exactly what was being said, but he didn't need to. The protestors certainly weren't screaming terms of endearment. It was a lynch mob baying for British blood, and if anyone caught sight of him and twigged to his Anglo-Saxon heritage, he was finished.

'So, the time has finally come when to be British is a disadvantage,' murmured Ilhan beneath his breath. 'I was wondering if we'd live to see the day . . .'

'Shut up,' Ben snapped. 'And I'm not British.'

The car was buffeted by the angry Egyptians charging past. The sound of their fists on the roof was like thunder.

'Good luck explaining that to them,' Ilhan responded.

The storm passed quickly. Crowds began to thin and the traffic snarl unfurled.

Ben leant forward to the driver. 'Thank you for helping me.'

The driver sighed heavily. 'Is big shame. England friends. During war, I fight . . . England and me, we fight together. Brothers. Now . . .' He waved his hand at the last stragglers joining their brethren on their rampage through the city. 'This? Is big shame.'

The street opened out onto a wide promenade. Ahead, a bridge arced over one half of the most famous river in the world, terminating on an island blanketed in manicured gardens dominated by grand mansions. Bright green lawns swept down to the waterfront where pontoon jetties swayed in the eddying river as feluccas bobbed along the Nile like toy boats in a bathtub, their white sails blinding in the midday sun.

The car crossed onto the island and passed into the cool shade cast by a double row of fat-trunked trees, which formed a grand avenue past wrought-iron gateways with guard-houses stationed to ward off any unwanted intrusions into the residences and embassies beyond. Cairo was a city distinguished by a sudden and very distinct geographic division between most of its populace, who lived in unimaginable poverty, and the minority who wanted for nothing. Gezira Island was a sanctuary in the heart of the city that was the exclusive enclave of the latter group of Cairenes.

'When you said you knew someone who'd put us up here, Ben, you didn't mention we'd be living in such palatial surrounds,' said Ilhan. 'I'd have packed my dinner jacket.'

Ben laughed. 'Don't get too excited.' In the immaculate row of estates, one stood out – and for all the wrong reasons. They approached twin pillars of roughly painted stone flanking a potholed dirt driveway. 'Hold on . . .! That's it,' Ben instructed the driver.

'This? You go here?' The man looked doubtful.

'Yes.'

Through the overgrown remnants of what would once have been a grand and imposing garden, a two-storeyed house loomed like a peculiar fungus, its whitewashed walls flaking and shutters hanging by the hinges. The car swept round the leaf litter–strewn circular driveway and pulled up beneath the still-grand porticoed entrance.

Ben smiled. It had been many years, but it was exactly as he remembered it.

13

Cairo, Egypt

The weatherworn front doors were open before the car lurched to a stop. A tiny man with a neatly trimmed and very black moustache at odds with his powdery eyebrows darted forward, a faded red fez atop his bald head. He reached for the rear door handle and stepped back, head bowed in greeting.

'Mr Hitchens, sir. Welcome to Arcadia. It is being a pleasure to be seeing you again.'

'Farouk.' Ben felt his hand gripped between the old man's spindly fingers. 'You haven't changed a bit.'

Ilhan stepped out of the car behind him. 'Farouk, this is my dear friend, Ilhan Aslan. Ilhan, Farouk. Farouk is . . .' Ben struggled to find a word to describe the man who – as far as he could tell – had taken care of everything that needed doing when he'd spent time recuperating at Arcadia during the war.

'I would say I am being Madam's butler, sir.'

'And – if memory serves me correctly – her chauffeur. And plumber. And cook.'

Farouk smiled. 'You are surely too kind, sir. Your bags?'

Ilhan hefted their two small satchels out of the back seat. 'Thank you, Farouk. We're fine. Travelling light.'

'If you come with me, you will be finding Madam awaiting your arrival inside.'

'Would you mind telling me who "Madam" is, Farouk? Mr Hitchens has been very coy about telling me anything about our host.'

'Countess Katerina Anastasia Orlova, Mr Aslan. Mr Hitchens, she is saying she is very happy to be seeing you.'

Ben gazed at the familiar façade of the mansion that had been his sanctuary during some of the darkest years of his life. 'As am I, Farouk. As am I.'

'Benedict Hitchens.' A slender figure moved through the dusty haze permeating Arcadia's grand ballroom. Backlit by the sun streaming through the windows and clad in a diaphanous white gown, Countess Orlova appeared as insubstantial as a wraith.

'Katerina.' He moved to take her hand. Instead, she wrapped him in her arms and warmly kissed both his cheeks. Drawing back, she placed her hands on his shoulders. 'You're still handsome. But you have aged.'

He laughed. 'Haven't we all? But not you. You're as beautiful as ever.'

'Always so smooth with your words.' She spoke perfect English flavoured by her Slavic heritage. Turning, she fixed her pensive, ice-blue eyes upon Ben's companion. 'And you are . . .?'

Ilhan stepped forward and dipped his head. 'Ilhan Aslan, ma'am.'

'Delighted to meet you, Mr Aslan.' She dropped her voice and tilted her head. 'Ben, when you told me you were gracing me with your presence, you didn't mention that you were travelling with such a charming Turkish gentleman.'

'May I ask how you know my friend, countess? He hasn't been at all forthcoming,' asked Ilhan.

'You really must call me Katerina.' She fluttered her eyelashes. 'Ben and I met during the war, Mr Aslan –'

'Ilhan, please.'

'Well, Ilhan . . . it was during the war when I opened my home to officers from the British Special Operations who needed to convalesce in pleasant surroundings.'

Ben laughed. 'Pleasant? That's not the word I'd use to describe the parties you hosted here.'

'Perhaps not. But you were hardly blameless in what went on, Dr Hitchens. That sofa you set alight – it was a priceless heirloom. My parents dragged it all the way here on their flight from the Bolsheviks, only for it to end up as firewood, thanks to you.'

'Well, I was hardly the worst offender. As I recall, it was the King of Egypt who pushed your grand piano through the front window.'

'Sixteen windows broken that night. I haven't forgotten.'

Ilhan was transfixed. 'It sounds as if I missed out on a very memorable moment. It could be that you're a woman after my own heart, Countess Katerina.'

'Many more than just the one moment, I can promise you.' She looked at him through thick lashes. 'You should know – I'm at least as old as your friend here, Ilhan. Surely you prefer a younger girl?'

'I prefer a woman.'

'Ah. I see. Farouk?'

The butler appeared from the shadows.

'Madam?'

'We will have aperitifs now.'

Farouk nodded. 'Certainly. Mr Hitchens – what would you be liking to drink?'

'Anything but the rocket fuel your mistress used to concoct. What was it you put in it, Katerina Anastasia? Plums and lemon?'

'Peaches, if I could find them. I was attempting to replicate peach schnapps. I did my best. It was the war – what choice did I have? I was raised to be a good hostess and maintain a well-stocked bar. But with the alcohol I was using as an ingredient . . . well, it needed all the help I could give it – it came from the officers' garage at the Gezira Sporting Club. They used it to clean out the fuel lines. I can't believe I didn't kill one of you boys with it. And it was one of the reasons I was delighted when the King accepted my invitation to our soirees. I tolerated him only because he came with cases of French champagne from the royal cellars.'

'As well-meaning as it was of you to create your own cocktails, I'm too old to take a trip down that particular memory lane. I doubt my liver could survive it. So what else is on offer, Farouk?'

'Are you still liking to be drinking the Bowmore single malt?' the butler asked.

'Bowmore . . . You remembered! And you found some? In Cairo?'

Farouk nodded, pleased with himself. 'Yes, sir. I do still have the people to be asking when I am looking to find something special. Even now, with all the troubles in the city.' The old man shook his head and tut-tutted. 'And for you, Mr Aslan?'

'Do you have any raki?'

'I certainly have arak. But it is –'

'– virtually the same thing. I know. I'd like that, thank you, Farouk. With ice and water, please.'

The countess led the two men to a conservatory. On the way she bent and picked something up from the floor. 'Oh, Ben – look. You remember little Vladimir Ilyich . . .?' A brilliant green lizard with a scarlet collar climbed Katerina's arm to solemnly take up residence on her shoulder. Katerina turned to Ilhan. 'He is named for the bald and pencil-necked little bureaucrat with the silly beard who drove my parents from our ancestral lands.' Tickling the reptile beneath his chin, she smiled indulgently. 'But you're far sweeter than that monster, aren't you, my little man?'

Katerina lowered herself onto a settee and crossed her legs demurely at her ankles as Farouk poured and served the drinks in lead-crystal tumblers. 'So . . . how was your journey?'

'Generally good.' Ben took a seat. 'Though our reception once we arrived in Cairo was . . . heated. There was a protest.'

'Those animals.' Katerina pursed her lips. 'The city you knew is gone, Ben. The Gezira Sporting Club? You remember it?'

'How could I forget?' Constructed as a leisure facility for the British military establishment, the club occupied one hundred and fifty acres of open land on Gezira Island and was graced with polo fields, a golf course and swimming facilities. For the gentlemen of Arcadia and their hostess, it had felt like their own private playground.

'Well, now – that *dreadful* man has nationalised it. Nasser. Beastly, beastly man. He's admitted the public! It's a tragedy. The golf club? Nine of its eighteen holes given over to a "youth club" . . . whatever that means. The club was a perfectly wonderful establishment for adults. The "youth" have more than enough to do without needing to take over our places.'

'A travesty. What does your venerable Great Aunt Natalia have to say about this dire state of affairs?' Ben began sniggering. 'Speaking of which, how *is* her health?'

Ben and Katerina laughed out loud.

'I must be missing something,' interjected Ilhan.

'Great Aunt Natalia ...' The countess wiped tears of laughter from her eyes. 'She was a fiction ...' Another guffaw escaped her lips. '... A fiction invented to defend my reputation from neighbours who might have thought it indecent that a young woman was entertaining battalions of British officers in her home without a chaperone.'

Ben fought back another fit of giggles. 'The elaborate tales we had to come up with to excuse her always being indisposed ... never has there been a sicklier human being. Remember when Signora Castegli sent her personal physician around to attend to her? What excuse did we come up with that time?'

'I think she'd gone to take the waters at Hammam Musa – the mineral waters did wonders for her health ...'

'But the effects were very short-lived ...' Ben burst out laughing again.

The hilarity subsided. 'So, Ben.' Katerina was serious now. 'Why are you here? It's not just to share memories with me.'

'No. As delightful as that is. I'm chasing something ... someone.'

'Always so mysterious, Benedict.'

'I'm not trying to be. It's just that I'm not entirely sure yet myself. But there's an ancient artefact two people are searching for – and if they want it, then it's something important. And you can help me. Do you still have contacts at the museum?'

'Of course.'

'I'm looking for a particular statue in the collection.'

'I'll speak to the director. He's a dear friend.'

Ilhan leant forward. 'Countess, I've never been to this city, and although I've arranged to meet some antiquities dealers tomorrow to see if I can turn what would otherwise be a waste of time into a profitable journey, I certainly don't want to miss the chance to look around. It seems that Ben's going to be preoccupied with his dusty research, so might I beg the pleasure of your company to escort me to Cairo's best sights?'

'It's a charming invitation. And one I'd be happy to accept – on the understanding that we do so only as friends.' She smiled sadly and placed a hand on his sleeve. 'Perhaps Benedict might explain . . .'

Hand cupped theatrically over his mouth, Ben spoke sotto voce. 'The countess has had many lovers. Many, many lovers. But most of them have been women. Which is why her virtue was largely left intact even though she was living in a house full of horny Allied officers.'

'Ah, I see.' Ilhan smiled.

'Not *entirely* intact, though.' She glanced knowingly at Ben.

'No. Not quite.'

'I think we both introduced each other to new things that night,' she said. 'The French embrace – it has been useful to you in your relations with women, I'm sure. But it was just a brief, passing moment between you and I . . .'

'. . . Facilitated by more than our fair share of "peach schnapps".'

'Ah, yes. There is no doubt about that. Though I regret nothing.'

'That's your motto for life, isn't it, countess?'

'Yes, you could say that.'

Ben drained the last of his drink and stood. 'Now, if you will permit it, Katerina, might I make use of your telephone?'

'. . . Just transferring your call now, sir.'

The operator flicked a switch and Ben listened to the crackling and buzzing of the long-distance line. A muffled voice speaking Turkish with an unmistakably Italian accent broke through the background noise.

'Yes? Benedict? Is you, *faccia di cazzo*?'

'Yes, it's me, Raphael. You do realise the operator can listen in on the call, don't you? So keep it decent.'

'You think the *zoccola* understand Italian? *Va fan culo*! If she can, then to her, I say good luck. Now, Benedict. This paper. Where you find it?'

'In a book.'

'You think I stupid? Of course I know is from a book. What book?'

'A medieval manuscript in the Topkapı archives.'

'Is interesting, then. The ink you ask me to check? Is made with uranium – as you think. But is strange – it make no sense. I never see in this form. Chemical makeup is very different from normal.'

Uranium . . . is that what Sebile was talking about? Ben wondered. 'The power that creates – and destroys – life', she'd called it.

During the ferry ride between Mersin and Alexandria, he'd pored over the journal Sebile had given him in Kemerhisar. Much of what it contained were obscure and – to him – incomprehensible strings of formulae and calculations. But what he could decipher was written in French and included a fragmentary account of Fulcanelli's life. It recounted a visit the alchemist had paid to a Russian-born chemical engineer in 1937, where Fulcanelli had warned the scientist about the nature of his work, claiming that alchemists had long ago mastered the manipulation of matter and energy to create a force field that put the alchemist in what he described as a 'privileged position', where realities of the universe that were hidden by time and space, matter and energy were revealed. By purifying certain materials, geometric arrangements of subatomic particles were produced that would create an explosive force powerful enough to level entire cities.

According to the journal, when the Nazis heard about Fulcanelli's research, they arrested him in France and brought him to Berlin where he was to be questioned by Hitler's Minister for Propaganda, Joseph Goebbels. When Goebbels entered the prisoner's cell and pulled up a chair opposite Fulcanelli, he asked him if he would answer some questions. Rising to his feet, the Frenchman replied, 'No. I will not,' then exited the room by walking through a solid concrete wall. Minutes later, the alchemist dined with his friends in Paris.

Ben assumed that account was allegorical, but had no idea what it represented. Allegorical or not, whatever was recorded in Goebbels' report of the incident was compelling enough to pique the interest of the KGB, into whose hands it fell at the close of the Second World War. In August 1945, when American Army Intelligence was seeking information on German research into atomic energy, they also joined the hunt for Fulcanelli in France.

Wherever this was heading, Ben suspected it would be no garden-variety hunt for ancient treasures.

He thought of Essie and his gut clenched with a strange mix of dread and desire. She was brilliant and she was dangerous, and she had a hold over him he could not explain. *Where are you leading me this time?* he wondered. Whatever else was going on, Ben was beginning to suspect he was joining the last lap of an arms race.

14

Cairo, Egypt

If she'd been in any doubt about how long it had been since she'd turned her back on her family, the feathery top of the date palm that had barely been visible above the tall whitewashed front wall when Essie left now rustled and swayed well above the rooftop.

Running from one mess into another, she thought.

Her departure from London had been abrupt and the explanation she'd given to Garvé wasn't only plausible, it was also true – she had a family emergency she needed to attend to in Cairo. The other reason – which was that she couldn't bear to face Adam Penney after the evening she'd spent at his home – she kept to herself. With the Sinai invasion imminent and her presence at Penney's side no longer necessary, there was no reason she couldn't meet Garvé and Penney at the staging post for the operation once final arrangements were confirmed. And given what had occurred in London, she had no desire to spend any more time with Adam Penney than was absolutely necessary.

She had no regrets about her encounter with the stranger at Adam's gathering. But the fact that she'd been so compromised and had only narrowly escaped physical assault at Adam's hands was deeply disturbing. That he'd witnessed her at such an unguarded moment made it even worse. With so much feverish sexual activity preoccupying the other men and women in the room that evening, she'd been able to slip out without attracting any attention other than an attempt by her lover to extricate her name and a promise to see him again. Knowing that some relationships are best consigned to the realm of fond memories, she'd said nothing; just smiled and kissed him on the lips. It was the first time she'd been with a man since her last, brief encounter with Ben on the island of Lesvos – a union that, for her, had been tarnished by a messy inner conflict at the knowledge that she was going to betray him. If she was honest with herself, the physical and mental release in London had been liberating and immensely enjoyable. But that didn't change the fact that Adam had tried to rape her. Acknowledging that, and breathing the same air as him without succumbing to a desire to tear his throat out, was going to be a challenge.

She paid the cab and stepped out onto the dusty street. The parade of children that had kept pace with the vehicle as it crawled along the potholed laneways, shrieking and gawking at the well-dressed foreign woman within, had now transformed into an impenetrable human barrier between her and the blue-painted front door of her stepmother's home. She was surrounded by a gaggle of waist-high, nut brown–faced boys, their heads shaved bare to keep lice at bay. They tugged at her skirt and leered up at Essie with bright eyes, babbling the only English they knew: 'My name is . . .? My name is . . .?'

'Don't touch!' she snapped in perfect Arabic, slapping their hands away. 'Your behaviour is deeply shameful! Now, go home to your mothers!'

Her cheeky assailants withdrew, eyes wide with shock. That this glamorous woman, so clearly European with her blonde hair and contemporary, foreign clothing, spoke their language, was inconceivable to them. They turned and fled, laughing and chattering. The news that the widow Shadid had a most unusual visitor would spread like the plague in the lanes and alleyways of Al-Azbakiyya.

Essie took a deep breath and held it in – a feeble attempt to quell the anxiety that rose in the back of her throat. Her heart lurched in her chest as she glanced up at the perforated dark timber *mashrabiya* screen projecting above the street on the first floor of the eighteenth-century Ottoman building. *Are you watching me, old woman?* she wondered.

No more avoiding it. She grasped the heavy iron knocker and hammered it against the door. She heard it echo around the internal courtyard which she knew opened to the sky above.

Nothing. She raised the knocker again. Then came footsteps inside, the sound of slippers on wooden stairs, now shuffling across the tiled floor. A smaller entrance set into the large, double timber doors opened a crack. Black eyes framed by a white headscarf peered out. 'You? What are you doing here?'

'Meera. You've grown.'

'Shouldn't come as any surprise. It's what people do.' Essie's half-sister's voice was brusque, the guttural Arabic words clipped and angry. 'And it's been twenty years.'

'But you still recognise me. You were barely five when I left.'

Meera looked Essie up and down, lips thin with disapproval. 'Your time in the West has changed you. But your face is the same. A face I've had to look at every day – she still has your photograph hanging in her room . . . a rod for her own back. If I had my way, I'd throw it out. Why are you here? And why didn't you use the side entrance to the *haramlik*? You know how she feels about that. Women upstairs in the *haramlik* apartments. Reception rooms down here in the *salamlik* are for men only. What will the neighbours think with you arriving, bare-faced, at the front door?'

'They won't care because they won't recognise me. They'll think you're being visited by a Westerner. And what would an infidel know about *haramlik*s and *salamlik*s? Please, Meera. May I come in?'

'I'll get you some tea, but then you'll have to leave. She won't agree to see you, you know. And, you'll need to come upstairs. The last thing she needs before Allah calls her is to be upset by you flouting her rules. Again.'

'There are men here?'

'No, there most certainly are not. That's not the point.'

'Meera – you're not happy to see me. And I understand why. But I thought you and I could speak –'

'Speak about what? I've nothing to say to you. But if you insist, meet me at the *haramlik* door.'

Essie lurched back, startled, as her sister slammed the front door in her face.

The room was exactly as she remembered it. Low benches surrounded the walls, topped with kilim-covered cushions upon which guests were expected to recline. As was the custom, she'd left her shoes at the door before she entered and climbed the narrow, timber stairs that led up to the *haramlik*. She sat down, breathing in the aromas of decades of family meals shared in the communal living and dining area – the distinctive signature of browned onions, cumin, bay leaves and coriander seeds. A Bedouin table with a collapsible timber base and blindingly polished brass top stood at the centre of a finely woven red Baluchi carpet Essie knew had been a gift to her father from a British officer in Palestine in the years before the troubles.

The thought of her father made her gut clench with guilt and regret.

Her sister returned to the room carrying a tray bearing gilded glass teacups filled with steaming, absinthe-green mint tea and a small dish of *lokum* dotted with pistachio nuts and dusted with icing sugar.

'Thank you. You shouldn't have gone to any trouble.' Essie took a glass of tea, its delicate aroma awakening many bittersweet memories.

'I didn't. The tea was already made.' Meera lowered herself onto the cushions on the opposite side of the room. An awkward silence descended.

'So, what has been happening in your life . . . since . . . well, since I left?' Essie knew it was a ridiculous question the minute it left her lips.

Meera raised her eyebrows. 'Twenty years you'd like me to recount, would you? How about we start with more recent events?' She picked at the delicate red and orange embroidery on the skirt of her *thobe*, the traditional dress worn by Palestinian women from Yafa, their father's birthplace. 'Well, as you can see, I'm unmarried. Without a father to arrange my dowry, and with my obligation to care for my mother –'

'*Our* mother,' Essie corrected her.

'She stopped being *your* mother the day you left,' Meera snapped. 'She tried so hard with you. But you were always Father's favourite. The daughter she gave him could never measure up to the offspring of the sainted dead wife.' Long-harboured bitterness had carved lines around Meera's mouth and eyes that belonged on a much older face. 'And then you left in disgrace and made her an object of scorn and mockery. Not even Father's martyrdom could lift her in the eyes of our neighbours after you left as you did. What do you want here? Is it money? You think you're due something after she dies? Because this house is all there is.'

'No. Of course not. I don't want anything. Just her . . . and your . . . forgiveness. Please.'

'As I told you. She won't want to see you. Not now. Her last days shouldn't be troubled by your demands.'

'Could you please do me this one favour, sister? Just ask?'

Brow furrowed, Meera rose to her feet. 'Fine. If it will hurry along your departure.'

Her sister's rage was incandescent. Essie couldn't say she blamed her.

'She'll see you.' Meera stood at the door with hands on her hips. 'Come.'

The door into Fatima's bedroom stood ajar at the end of the long corridor. The old woman sat propped up against a pile of cushions, her frail shoulders rising and falling with her laboured breaths. Once-proud features were drawn and gaunt and framed by a halo of whispery white hair.

'Why are you here?'

Essie was shocked by how much she'd aged. 'To say I'm sorry. I didn't want you to leave this world without hearing it from my own lips.'

Fatima's dark eyes were set in sunken sockets, but they flashed with fury. 'You have said it. And I have heard it. Now leave.'

'If there's anything I can do . . . I have money now, more than enough . . .' Essie stumbled over the words. 'I can help you with doctors . . . anything you need.'

'Help?' the old woman wheezed, her body racked with a rattling cough that seemed to crackle from between her ribs. 'The time for you to help me is long past.' She glared at Essie. 'It was because of you, you know. It was because of you that he died.'

'But I wasn't here, Mother.'

'Don't call me that. And if you'd been here rather than running off with that Greek boy, he might have stayed in Cairo. Stayed to care for his precious daughter, instead of going back to Palestine to fight. She –' The old woman extended a spindly finger to where Meera stood in the doorway. '– She and I, we were never enough for him. You were his pearl. And when you left, he had no desire to stay.'

The shocking realisation that her stepmother was speaking the truth made Essie's knees feel as though they were giving way.

'So why are you here?' Fatima asked again. 'Why did you come to bother a dying woman with black memories?'

Essie no longer knew the answer.

Essie and Meera were both silent as they found their way downstairs. There was nothing left to be said.

Tears clouded Essie's vision as she took her father's dusty fez from where it still sat upon its stand near the entrance. 'Sister – would you mind, if it's not too much to ask . . . I've nothing of his. Might I . . .?'

'His hat . . . you want his hat? That's all?' Meera opened the door to the street. 'Fine. Take it. And get out. *Sister*.'

Essie leant back against the taxi's stiff upholstery and dabbed her tears with a handkerchief as Cairo's familiar streets rushed past the window. The failed attempt to make peace with her stepmother and half-sister had broken her.

She lifted her father's fez to her nose. It had been many years since it had last rested on his head, but it still bore his gentle scent – a warm blend of talcum powder and hair pomade. Despite the passage of time, it was still comforting.

The last time she could remember feeling truly safe was when she'd felt her father's arms wrapped around her. Her early childhood in Palestine had been idyllic. Before the fall of the Ottoman Empire at the close of the Great War, her father had been a government official, and although the imposition of British rule over their lands disrupted the status quo, Omar Shadid retained his standing within the Arab community and was called upon as an advisor by the administrators of the British Mandate.

As the daughter of a community leader, she'd been enrolled in a school along with her two older sisters. Each day she passed through the tiny entrance set into the monumental brass-studded door that opened into a vast interior courtyard where the sound of chattering girls resounded off the ancient stone walls of the building that had once been a Mameluke palace. After the principal inspected their uniforms to make sure they were observing the school's strict standards, the girls peeled off to their classes, where they were taught English and French, mathematics, geography and history. At the end of each day, she and her sisters bolted home between fragrant rows of citrus trees to share their newfound knowledge with their parents.

Her teachers identified her as a student of precocious intellect with a remarkable capacity for learning. When informed of his daughter's talents, it went some way towards salving her father's lingering disappointment, never voiced but always acknowledged, that he'd not yet sired a son. Essie suspected that was why she'd been inspired to conjure up an imaginary twin brother when she'd used her own childhood to furnish a life story for Eris Patras, the woman she was when she met Benedict Hitchens. It was as if she could give her father in death what he'd secretly wished for in life.

Occupied as she had been with childish things, she'd never been fully aware of the terminal fractures that were developing in the fabric of her homeland. But as the worry lines inscribed into her father's forehead and around his mouth deepened, and she overheard snatches of impassioned adult conversations from the groups of men who periodically gathered in the *salamlik*, she understood that something was terribly wrong. Her mother, never one to involve herself in political debate, joined what she'd called the 'women's movement', marching in protest to the British High Commissioner's headquarters in Jerusalem. Essie was never certain what, exactly, her mother was protesting against; her parents were determined to shield their daughters from the festering political unrest and never explained what it was that was beginning to cause such disruption in their lives.

Omar could never have imagined how absolute that disruption would be. With the bitter wisdom of hindsight, he wished he'd opened his daughter's eyes a little so she might have been able to brace herself for what was to come. But Essie knew there was nothing that could have prepared her for the horrors she would have to endure. From the dark memories of what followed, the only recollection she could bear was the talcumy scent still preserved in her father's fez. It was the smell that had saved her sanity the day so long ago when a mob of settlers inflamed with rage by an Arab assault on a Jewish homestead attacked her village, baying for blood.

Fighting in the streets to help defend his neighbours, a phalanx of Jewish fighters had blocked Omar from his own home. By the time he broke through the line of attackers, he found his world destroyed. She was the only survivor, hurried into a hiding place by her mother as they heard the mob battering down the front door. Her father discovered her cowering beneath winter rugs in her mother's dowry chest, white faced and struck dumb with fear. While he carried her to safety through their house, she'd buried her head in the crook of his neck, blocking out the stench of blood and bad things with the smell of him. She never saw her mother or two sisters again.

The local leaders of the Jewish paramilitary organisation, Haganah, had offered an unconditional apology to Omar Shadid for what they attributed to the undisciplined actions of a fringe group of extremists within the organisation, men who would eventually join the radical Zionist group, Irgun. But their words were meaningless to a man who'd lost everything. 'An eye for an eye, and the whole world goes blind,' she'd once heard her father say to his more militant-minded friends while he was arguing for a peaceful resolution with their Jewish neighbours. But that was before. Omar took his only surviving child to Cairo and swore vengeance on the people who'd murdered his family.

Determined that Essie's education should continue in Cairo, he enrolled her in the American College for Girls. She decided the only way she could make any sense of the loss of the people she loved, whose absence left a raw-edged and hollow place in her heart, was to immerse herself in schoolwork. If she could understand the world, she reasoned, perhaps she could find a larger purpose to a tragedy that – to her nine-year-old way of thinking – seemed pointless.

In time Omar remarried, in part because he believed his daughter needed a mother. Fatima was a far more observant Muslim than the mother Essie grieved for every waking hour, and she'd tried her best to care for the pensive and serious-minded girl who wanted nothing more than to be left alone. But by the time Meera was born, Essie was becoming a woman, and tiring of the strictures placed on her life by a conservative guardian who disapproved of her ambition to become something other than a respectable Muslim wife and mother.

As her curves began to blossom, Essie secretly altered her *thobe* – a modest gown designed to hide the wearer's physical assets – so it clung to her breasts and hips. She began to highlight her almond-shaped eyes with kohl to bring out their coppery gleam. It wasn't long before she was attracting the eye of every eligible young man in Al-Azbakiyya. But the boy who most interested Essie was living with his cousin in the Greek quarter and reminded her of the movie posters she'd seen of Gary Cooper. He was, of course, a completely unsuitable match.

Word of Essie's furtive liaisons with the dark-haired and dashing young man reached Omar's ears. Her now grim and stern-faced father beat her and warned her never to be seen with him again. Pride and back stinging, Essie made sure she was never *seen* with him again – instead, she concocted more cunning means of meeting up with her young lover. She never dared venture out to meet him when her father was home. But when Omar embarked on one of his regular expeditions to Palestine, where he continued his fight against the Jewish settlers in his homeland, Essie had no qualms about defying her stepmother's wishes and would leave the house for hours at a time.

The last time she was caught by Fatima trying to sneak out of the house, it was Essie's seventeenth birthday. With her father absent again, she ran from the Ottoman mansion she'd called home for almost ten years, and fled to Xander's side. Vowing their undying love for each other and likening their plight to that of the teenaged star-crossed lovers, Romeo and Juliet, the couple left the city together and embarked on a ferry to Xander's home in Cyprus.

Docking at the harbour in Paphos, Essie received a wordless and chilly reception from Xander's Orthodox Christian family. She wasn't surprised and knew it was as warm as the one Xander might have expected from her own Muslim family in Cairo if the situation had been reversed.

To explain her sudden arrival, Xander's family told their neighbours that Essie was the disgraced daughter of a Muslim housekeeper who worked for their wealthy relatives in Cairo. According to the elaborate – and implausible – lie, she'd been sent to Cyprus to work for them as a servant and to escape public shame. It didn't matter that the story was utterly unbelievable, because it was nothing more than a face-saving exercise for the family.

The young foreigner became the favourite topic of conversation for the gossips who gathered each morning around the village well, but none dared confront the matriarch of Xander's family about what was such an obvious lie. And so the deception worked. It also gave Xander and Essie an excuse to be seen together – nobody in the village cared if one of their sons had a dalliance with a non-Christian girl, provided he eventually married one of the flock.

It was a month before any of his family members said a single word to Essie, and that was only when Xander approached his father about marrying his young lover. A marriage between their good Christian son and a Muslim girl was condemned as an abomination, even if it had not been impossible under the strict rules of the Church. Essie half-heartedly suggested converting – as far as she was concerned, it made no difference whether you were a woman under the watchful eye of the Christian or the Muslim god, it was a dismal existence either way. But of course, the marriage was never going to happen. And as it turned out, it was just as well.

During that time, there were many occasions when Essie had watched mournfully as the ferry between Paphos and Alexandria pulled away from the shore, and wished she was on board and headed back to Egypt. But the overinflated and easily wounded pride peculiar to youth could never allow her to admit that she'd erred. The thought of begging her father and stepmother's forgiveness was inconceivable. So she stayed by Xander's side.

Xander, who spoke Arabic, taught Essie Greek. He also introduced her to the family's stock in trade: ripping antiquities from tombs and lost cities on Cyprus to sell to international dealers, who sold the purloined treasures to collectors and institutions in Europe and America. Essie proved to be an able student, mastering ancient languages and demonstrating a natural instinct for finding things buried beneath the soil. Her reluctant new family begrudgingly began to acknowledge her skills and entertain the thought that perhaps she wouldn't be the burden they'd anticipated when she first appeared on their doorstep.

Essie spent every spare moment she had at the Cyprus Museum in Nicosia, learning about long-dead civilisations and the artefacts they'd left behind. It became a sanctuary for her, and even today, there was nowhere she felt more at peace than buried in the mausoleum-like surrounds of a museum with the remnants of ancient worlds around her.

It was there that she retreated the day she thought a return to Cairo was inevitable. She should have guessed that Xander's family would conspire to end their relationship. With crocodile tears in his eyes, he'd announced to Essie that he'd been forced to carry through with the betrothal that had been arranged for him since birth. Adrift and shame-faced, she'd fled to the museum, where she'd hidden behind a teetering glass cabinet of turquoise-blue faïence *ushabti* figurines and sobbed, the rows of tiny sarcophagi making her feel lost and homesick.

Although Essie was devastated, she suspected her distress was caused as much by humiliation as anything else, and so it was a blessedly short-lived period of mourning. The truth was that after arriving on Cyprus, she'd soon realised the swarthy young Greek was deliciously pretty, but not blessed with much of a mind – and certainly not one that could keep pace with her own fierce intellect.

She mourned the loss of his body for a moment or two, then set about establishing her own business doing what she'd learnt from Xander and his family. But she had much bigger ambitions than those of her estranged Cypriot family. Recruiting workers from Xander's team wasn't difficult. Loyalty was easily bought, and in the time they'd worked with Essie, they quickly realised the young Arab woman was ten times the businessman Xander was. Not to mention, she had an uncanny knack for the craft – they knew she'd lead them to far greater riches than he ever had. And they were right. Despite her youth, she used her multilingual skills to form relationships with other outfits working across the Aegean and became a central point of contact with the inter-national trade, arranging shipments and sales for a cut of the profits while also conducting her own illicit excavations. She tried not to enjoy it too much when Xander appeared at her door begging her for help re-negotiating a sale with a Dutch dealer that had fallen through. Though she did make him pay for the privilege.

Her past was a wraith that always followed close on her heels, surprising her on occasion during the infrequent moments she had time to reflect on anything other than her work. She saw the news from Palestine while she was nursing a cup of thick, sweet Greek coffee and waiting for the arrival of a boat from Crete at a *kafeneion* by the harbour in Limassol. Ignoring the disapproving glares of the white-whiskered old men who were already discomfited enough to find a woman in their midst, she stood and took the newspaper from where it sat on the counter. A series of photographs on the front page depicted three Palestinian rebel leaders executed by the British. Her father's features were unmistakable – unrepentant and proud. She caught herself as a surge of grief rose in her chest. Throwing a handful of coins onto the table, she squeezed the newspaper into a ball and stumbled out to the water's edge.

The sea was placid and seemed to dissolve at the horizon, bleeding into the pale blue sky. She was, now, truly alone. She'd loved her father dearly. And there had been many moments when she'd regretted the pain she knew she must have caused him when she left. That guilt was amplified by the sorrow that welled from the marrow of her soul at the knowledge that she would never see him again.

Her solution had been to throw herself into her work. For most of Europe, the coming of the second great war was apocalyptic. But for Essie, it was a godsend. It made her job easier as Europe turned its attention to the wholesale slaughter of its population rather than the defence of its cultural heritage, leaving archaeological sites untended and unguarded. And the war brought her other opportunities. It was on the island of Crete that she'd met Josef Garvé and formed a professional relationship that had enriched them both. It was also thanks to Josef Garvé's machinations that she'd crossed paths with Benedict Hitchens.

Essie sighed heavily and placed her father's fez in her lap. It was only ever meant to have been another job – entrap the American and convince him to authenticate a priceless collection of antiquities. But it hadn't quite worked out that way. Of the many men she'd known, he was the only one she'd ever continued to think of with deep longing. Her peculiar relationship with Ben had given her the only moments of joy and meaning she'd experienced since her father's death. But he was gone. And she was alone. Again.

Steeling herself, she pushed to one side the memories that hurt. Life had taught her many things; the futility of floundering about in self-pity foremost among them. Her reason for visiting the city hadn't resulted in the outcome she'd planned, or hoped for. But that didn't mean she couldn't make the most of what might otherwise be a wasted trip. With the expedition into the Sinai Desert just days away, she'd take the opportunity to revisit the Egyptian Museum and double-check the inscription on the statue, just to be certain she hadn't missed anything when she last visited.

Essie couldn't afford to fail. If she was correct in her interpretation of the clues they'd found that seemed to point towards the Emerald Tablet's hiding place, the financial rewards would be substantial enough that she could step back into semi-retirement. She'd spent much of her life running and was tired and empty. All she really wanted was a chance to stop for a moment to gather the pieces of her life together again.

She was fairly sure she could find the tablet, but had no idea whether or not it would do all the things it promised. She didn't really care, either way – all that mattered to her was that the material benefits of finding it would buy her the luxury of time. But she couldn't imagine the consequences if she'd made an error. An elaborate and extremely complex plan that placed a great many people's lives at risk had been put in motion on the basis of her research. She was comfortable playing with people's money; but lives were another matter altogether, and the responsibility she bore weighed heavily upon her shoulders.

She could only hope her instincts were right.

15

Cairo, Egypt

'*Old*' *has a smell*, Ben thought as he passed by the monumental statues of the pharaoh Amenhotep the Magnificent and his queen, Tiye, that towered over the inner courtyard entranceway of the Egyptian Museum.

It wasn't an unpleasant aroma – and it was something more than just the dusty remains of mummified Egyptians, unceremoniously lifted from their protective sarcophagi and put on display in the public viewing galleries, their withered limbs protruding from yellowing linen wrapping and shedding musty particles into the air. It wasn't just the scent of the ancient cedars brought to earth in the mountains of Lebanon and traded by the Phoenicians to the pharaohs, the timber used to line their burial chambers and the oil used for embalming the dead. It was also the scent of ancient leather; of dust, soil and charcoal; of papyrus and parchment; stale air, baked mudbricks and wood-fired kilns; rusted ironwork and broken, sun-bleached clay. It was a smell Ben was certain had permeated his own skin over his years spent in the field, and one he always found comforting.

'Dr Hitchens, I presume?' A tall and barrel-chested man stood at the top of the stairs, his heavy black eyebrows arched quizzically above deep-set black eyes. A coif of silvery hair was swept back in shiny waves from a high forehead, and his pale linen suit and white shirt were immaculate. Whatever his other personality traits, there was no overestimating the depth of Professor Hosni Zahir's vanity. The pristine state of his clothing also confirmed that the Director of the Egyptian Museum wasn't a man who liked to get his hands dirty. He took in Ben's comparatively shabby presentation with barely veiled disdain.

Always heard you were a show pony, Ben thought rather uncharitably. Zahir had acquired a reputation as being very quick to claim others' discoveries while demonstrating an impressive capacity to curry favour with social and political powerbrokers around the world, who rushed to invest their capital in worthy cultural projects that made them feel they were 'doing good'. As the custodian of the remains of one of the three civilisations that were, to moneyed patrons, the marquee stars of the ancient world – the other two being Greece and Rome – Hosni Zahir knew exactly how good the hand was that he'd been dealt. And he had no hesitation playing it when he felt it would work to his advantage. Which apparently was most of the time.

Ben extended his hand. 'Professor. Delighted to meet you. And thank you so much for lending me some of your time.'

'The countess is a dear friend . . .'

'. . . the exact words she used to describe you.'

'Well, she has always been a great supporter of the museum. Her contacts in Europe have been invaluable to us.' The heels of his brown brogues clicked on the tiled floor as he ushered Ben inside. 'I'm terribly busy at the moment, trying to arrange safe passage of some antiquities for a long-standing loan overseas. And with the political trouble . . . well, as you'd imagine, it complicates things. So your choice of timing was less than convenient . . . But I'd never turn down a request from the countess.'

He led Ben towards a door tucked behind a display of mummified heads lined up like a macabre row of carnival clowns, their empty eye sockets glaring and desiccated lips pulled back from bared teeth. 'It's good you had her call me before your visit. The statue you want to see is in storage.' Hosni opened the door and ushered Ben through, pulling a switch to illuminate a row of fluorescent lights set into a ceiling far above their heads.

It was a shock, even to Ben, who'd spent more time than most in the bowels of the world's major museums. This was an overwhelmingly enormous repository of ancient material. Beneath the chilly artificial light, ranks of granite statues were stacked like dominoes beside metal storage units stretching to the roof, their shelves packed with boxes crammed full of ancient artefacts sifted from Egypt's archaeologically fertile soil. It was a warehouse of treasures that extended so far into the distance that the back wall of the facility was invisible.

'This way . . .' Hosni indicated a path between twin ram-headed sphinxes, like the ones Ben remembered from his visit to the Temple of Luxor. Winding past the knees of nameless pharaohs, seated on their stone thrones with arms crossed before them and clutching the crook and flail of Egyptian kingship, Hosni directed Ben to a bay located about twenty feet along the double row of statues.

It was just as beautiful as he remembered it. The gentle-eyed cow goddess, Hathor, rested her chin protectively on the crown of Psamtik's head, who stood beneath her dewlap.

Between her arching horns sat the disc of the sun with twin feathers and a rearing cobra – the *uraeus* – that was the Ancient Egyptian symbol of divine authority.

'Our statue of Hathor and Psamtik,' announced Hosni. 'It's a marvel, and should, of course, be on display. But with the wealth of material we have here . . .' He indicated the warehouse with a flourish. '. . . Not everything can fit in the public galleries. It's something I'm attempting to raise with the new government – we need another, more modern, gallery.'

Ben laughed. 'Sounds like the battle cry of every gallery director I've ever known.' He put his satchel down on the ground and took out his notebook, pen and torch.

'Tell me, why are you so interested in our friend Psamtik, Dr Hitchens?'

'I want to study the text. Relates to some research I'm doing.'

'It's been decades since the statue was discovered in Saqqara. Its inscription has been published many, many times since then. The work of other academics wasn't good enough for you?' Hosni responded archly.

Ben gritted his teeth. 'Not at all. I just want to see if there's anything unusual about the inscription.'

'I can assure you, if there was, we'd have noticed it. And it would have been reported.'

Positioned as they were in a storehouse the size of an aeroplane hangar, Ben refrained from pointing out that the staff of the museum would be hard-pressed to keep track of all the antiquities they had in storage, let alone indulge in any detailed examination of the treasures under their care.

Ben went to work, attempting to ignore the hovering presence of the director, who exhaled theatrically to emphasise the fact that he was there under sufferance. Although the fluorescent lights overhead were bright, they were so far above the floor that the illumination was dim and quite inadequate for deciphering the intricate hieroglyphic inscription on the front panel of the carved ceremonial apron that fell to Psamtik's ankle. The additional band of text running around the statue's base would be invisible without the light provided by Ben's torch.

Switching it on, he ran it over the pictograms cut into the highly polished grey stone. He could recall every swell in the cow goddess' finely wrought flanks and the soft curves of her muzzle. It surprised him that something he hadn't seen for many decades had managed to leave such a mark upon him.

While knotted up in his boyhood obsession with Ancient Egypt, he'd managed to convince his father to let him accompany him on a business trip to New York. Any hope his father may have harboured that Ben was eager to learn something of the family trade was quashed when his young son revealed what had motivated his wish to visit the city. Instead of joining his father at his business meetings, Ben elected to spend entire days in the Ancient Egyptian rooms of the Metropolitan Museum. It was there that he'd first seen the statue of Hathor and Psamtik – or, as he found out many years later, a plaster replica of the original, just one of many in the Met's cast collection.

It was on his third day that the curator of the collection sought him out, intrigued by the child who was so transfixed by the ancient world that he would resist the temptation of fine spring weather and the vast lawns and lakes of Central Park and choose instead to take up residence in a museum. He told Ben of Hathor, who held dominion over the sky and stars and was the goddess of love, joy and mirth, and of Psamtik – the high state official in the sixth century BC known as an 'overseer of sealers' and responsible for supervising the sealing of the containers packed with precious goods and destined for the king's treasury. To discourage tampering by any light-fingered workers, the overseer would check the contents then seal the mouth of the storage vessel with wet clay and stamp it with his personal seal. If it arrived at the treasury unbroken, then the contents were assumed to be intact. Psamtik had been entrusted with a great responsibility – he had oversight of the precious materials coming from the pharaoh's mines in the Sinai and Negev deserts. But what any of this had to do with Balinas and the Emerald Tablet, Ben had no idea.

He turned his torch back onto the inscription on Psamtik's kilt. There was nothing he could see that was particularly edifying – it described his titles and achievements in the impersonal clerical language characteristic of monuments of this type. The statue would have been made for the Egyptian official's tomb, carrying the goddess' patronage with him into the afterlife, and there was nothing Ben could see that distinguished it from hundreds of other similar dedications he'd studied over the years.

A line of hieroglyphics ran around the statue's base. Ben dropped to his knees and began to crawl around the granite block. Nothing he could see was out of place. The long-dead artisan who'd laboured over the stone so many thousands of years ago had carved prayers and exaltations to the pantheon of Egyptian gods in an earnest attempt to win favour for Psamtik, and recorded his achievements to preserve his status in the afterlife.

The statue's far corner was wedged up against a timber crate. Ben forced his wide-shouldered frame into the gap and attempted to heft the barrier to one side.

'What are you doing back there?' Hosni exclaimed.

'Just trying to get a proper look at the back of the statue.'

'There's nothing there you won't find in our documentation, I can assure you,' the director responded impatiently. 'I have a very busy day before me, Dr Hitchens. I'd appreciate it if you could please conclude your examination. Quickly.'

'Just give me one minute!' Ben shouted as he braced his back against the crate, shining the thin beam of light down into the crack between the timber planking and the statue's base. He craned to see the line of text.

'If you come with me, I'll give you a copy of our report on the statue. It's all in there. But for now, I really need to go. So I'll have to ask you to accompany me. Now!'

'Christ almighty!' Ben exclaimed under his breath. 'Be right there!' *Need to buy some more time*. As he saw it, he only had one option. He placed his journal on top of the crate.

'Here.' Hosni Zahir handed Ben a sheaf of papers. 'You'll find what you're looking for in here.' The director had taken up residence behind an enormous French Empire desk, its marble top resting on plinths in the form of gilded lotus columns with gleaming sphinx heads set on each corner. It was so imposing, it managed to dwarf even the director's impressive frame.

'Magnificent desk,' Ben observed.

'Yes. Napoleonic, of course, 1806. Rumoured to have been used by the Emperor himself. A gift to me from one of our French patrons.'

'It suits you.'

Uncertain whether he was being flattered or insulted, Hosni's brow furrowed. 'You've everything you need, then?'

'Yes – I think so.' Ben rummaged around in his satchel and feigned shock. 'Dammit! My notebook! Must have left it in there.'

'Oh, for –!' Hosni stood and reached for the great ring of keys stashed in the top drawer of his desk, clearly unimpressed. 'I'll let you back into the storeroom. You'll be able to open the door yourself from the inside – just make sure it shuts behind you when you're finished. And come and tell me when you're leaving.'

Liberated from the director's oppressive presence, Ben set to work shifting the timber crate away from the statue, relieved that whatever it contained, it wasn't too heavy for him to move by himself. Once he'd made enough space to be able to see the rest of the inscription, he switched on his torch and knelt down in the eddies of dust and stone chips on the concrete floor.

Right, he thought. *What, exactly, am I looking for here?*

He opened his notebook and examined the extract he'd copied from Fulcanelli's journal: 'From Jezirat Faraun where Psamtik the keeper of His tribute laboured under Hathor's watchful eye, Thuban will guide you past riches revealed to mankind by angels to the mountain where Apollonius finally achieved the Great Work.'

Elements of the message made sense to him. Thuban was the star used by the Ancient Egyptians as the Pole Star, so from the island of Jezirat Faraun in the Gulf of Aqaba, he was expected to travel north. Given the ancient belief that humans were directed to valuable mineral deposits by benevolent gods or angels, Ben assumed the 'riches revealed to mankind by angels' referred to a working mine. It also made sense, given Psamtik's occupation. But there were an infinite number of mountains in the desert region. Without more clues to narrow the search, he'd be trying to find a needle in a very sandy haystack.

Frustrated, he began crawling on his knees around the statue. Shining his torch along the band of hieroglyphics now revealed from behind the timber crate, he saw nothing unremarkable until he reached the very end of the inscription.

What he saw stopped him in his tracks. Any doubts he'd had disappeared in an instant.

16

Cairo, Egypt

Carved unobtrusively into the inscription, and appearing to the casual observer as if it was an intentional inclusion on the part of the sculptor, was the symbol Ben recognised from the Topkapı archives and the wall of the chapel in the underground city in Cappadocia. The horned staff, circle, crescent and serpent were unmistakable.

He dug his fingers into the engraving. The edges were too rough-edged to be contemporary with the original inscription that dated to the sixth century BC, showing none of the abrasion or smoothing that occurs over time when carved stone is exposed to the elements. It would have passed a superficial examination, though, which was probably why – as far as he knew – no scholars had noted the recent addition, but the patina and wear didn't match the texture of the older carvings on the same statue.

This is a message. Written recently . . . relatively speaking. Ben's heart raced as he shone the torch on the symbol. *But what're you trying to tell me?* His eyes scanned the adjacent hieroglyphics.

A sharp sound made him jump. *The door!* He turned off his torch and jammed his body behind the timber crate.

'Dr Hitchens?' Hosni Zahir's voice echoed in the vast space. 'Are you still here?'

Ben held his breath.

The director flicked off the light switch and plunged the warehouse into darkness, closing the door behind him with a loud clang.

Waiting a beat before he turned his torch back on, Ben refocused on the engraving.

What the hell? Something was out of place.

The only time cartouches were ever used in hieroglyphics was to encircle the name of the pharoah. But on the band of text around the base of Psamtik's statue and right next to the foreign symbol he'd identified, someone had chipped away the stone and engraved a cartouche around pictograms that were not a regal name.

He bent closer and translated the inscription enclosed within it, murmuring beneath his breath.

'The unpleasant mountain where the Asiatic sand-dwellers worshipped the moon god Sin before the coming of the *remetch en kemet* who took the copper buried in their lands.'

Remetch en kemet he knew to be the name Egyptians used to refer to themselves. It meant the people from the 'black land', 'black' being the fertile and rich soil of the Nile Valley. As for the 'Asiatic sand-dwellers', he assumed they were the Semitic people who occupied the vast deserts to the east of Egypt where the pharaohs discovered the rich copper mines that contributed to their enormous wealth. And the 'unpleasant mountain' where the moon god Sin was worshipped?

Ben rocked back on his heels. 'Sinai . . . It's Mt Sinai!' he exclaimed.

But something was wrong. He opened his notebook, flipping back to the text he'd transcribed from Fulcanelli's journal. 'From Jezirat Faraun . . . Thuban will guide you.'

The tiny island of Jezirat Faraun was a port used by the Ancient Egyptians to ship the fruits of their labour to their homeland on the Nile from the oldest copper mines in the world at the tiny settlement of Timna in the Negev Desert.

Ben shone his torch onto the dusty floor and used his finger to trace a rough triangular outline. The Sinai Peninsula with its flanking waterways, the Gulf of Suez on the west and the Gulf of Aqaba on the east. He picked up three pebbles and placed them on his makeshift map: one where he knew Jezirat Faraun was located at the apex of the Gulf of Aqaba, the other at the site of Mt St Catherine, or Jebel Musa – biblical Mt Sinai – in the southern quadrant of the peninsula, and the third on the site of the mines at Timna.

'If I'm meant to follow the north star from Jezirat Faraun, I'd be heading *away* from Mt Sinai,' he murmured.

There had been copper mines in the region other than those at Timna, of course. One of the richest of those was discovered at Serabit el-Khadim in the peninsula, ten miles north of Mt Sinai. The temple complex near the mine had been excavated by Flinders Petrie in the late nineteenth century. But the metal ore and turquoise from that area was ferried from the peninsula's western coast across the gulf to the Eastern Desert on Egypt's Suez coastline, not from Jezirat Faraun.

He traced his finger northward from the tiny island in the Gulf of Aqaba into the desolate wastelands of the Negev Desert. If his interpretation of the clues was correct, and it was a very big 'if', then the Emerald Tablet was hidden on a mountain that could not be the Mt Sinai marked on every map Ben had ever seen. He also knew there was only one man who could help him find it.

He sighed. As much as he hated it, he knew he had no choice.

'You win, Ethan.' He laughed wryly.

Hosni looked up from his desk as Ben entered his office. 'All done, thank you! On my way out now. I just wanted to have a quick look around the collection while I was here,' Ben explained, lying through his teeth.

'Oh?' the director responded, startled. 'I thought you'd already gone. No matter. Did you find your journal?'

'Yes. Thanks again for your help.'

'No bother, really. Please do pass on my kindest regards to the countess.' Hosni had once again assumed his cloak of unctuous charm. 'I'm sorry I couldn't entertain you any longer. But it seems I'm in for a busier day than even I expected. Surprising as it sounds, my secretary just told me there's another person coming in to examine Psamtik. And they should be arriving any minute.'

'Someone else?' Ben froze. 'Do you know the name of the person visiting? I've some old acquaintances in town – it'd be quite a coincidence if it was one of them.' *Coincidence?* Ben thought. *Unlikely.*

'It's someone from the British Government.' Hosni glanced down at his appointment book. His eyebrows shot up. 'Well, there's a surprise. It's a woman. One "Mrs Estelle Peters".' He looked up. 'Friend of yours?'

'Friend?' Ben smiled thinly. 'No.'

Trying, and failing, to make it look as if he were there simply to examine the workmanship of the monumental seated statue of King Ramses II in the museum's forecourt, Ben's eyes were anywhere but on the polished stone statue of the monarch.

The sun scorched his head and neck and sent a trickle of sweat running between his shoulder blades and down his back.

He knew it was idiotic. But the thought of seeing her again had taken hold of his mind like a delirium.

What do you plan to do, you moron? he chastised himself. *Pretend it's a chance encounter? You just happened to be wandering about the Egyptian Museum when she passed by? You're not that good an actor. And she'd never believe it, anyway.*

Ben moved to the side of the statue that was shielded from the forecourt's entranceway and sat on its base, his back to the front entrance. His heart was pounding. He'd never been able to work out what it was about her that was so different. But the woman who'd managed to deceive him twice had a hold over him that was incomprehensible and also – apparently – unshakeable.

His heel tapped nervously on the crushed quartz beneath his feet. From a distance, he heard the click of high heels. Fingernails digging painful welts into his palms, he glanced around the edge of the statue to see a shapely figure striding towards the entrance.

It's her.

The blood pounding in his head made him dizzy as he watched her step up the short flight of marble stairs to the museum's bronze doorway.

What do I do? What do I do? Even as he thought it, and knowing that to confront her was lunacy, Ben rose to his feet. *Why? What do you think she's going to say?*

He had no idea of the answer to that question. But he didn't plan to miss the opportunity.

He began to walk towards the entrance.

A crunch of gravel behind him alerted him just as a forceful hand took hold of his elbow.

Ben spun around.

17

Cairo, Egypt

As Essie approached, it appeared as if the museum director's already well-filled shirt had been inflated with a tyre pump, his chest puffing up and shoulders squaring. She knew the effect she had on most men, and had no qualms about using it to her advantage. Not that she thought it would be necessary here.

Hosni Zahir primped and preened, adjusting his lapels and smoothing the front of his suit jacket before extending his hand in greeting.

'Mrs Peters, I presume?' He raised her hand to his lips. 'I'm Professor Hosni Zahir, director of this establishment.' He looked her up and down appreciatively. 'Charmed. Really . . . quite charmed. Might I offer you some tea – or coffee – before I show you the statue?'

'You really needn't bother, professor.'

'It wouldn't be a bother at all. My man brews a lovely coffee. Can I tempt you with a slice of cake? All women adore cake ... and you're a woman – and quite a lovely one, if I may be so bold. So, surely it's an offer you can't refuse?'

You'd be surprised, Essie thought. 'Thank you, no. It's very kind of you. But I'm in quite a hurry. If you could please just show me the statue of Psamtik, I won't take up any more of your time. I shan't be long – I was here to examine it many months ago; but then I met with your assistant. I just need to check my translation of the inscription.'

'Of course. Of course.' He smiled and nodded benevolently, guiding her towards the entrance to the warehouse.

Hosni opened the door and ushered her through. 'It's been like Waterloo Station in here this morning.'

'You don't say.'

'Just before you – you probably passed the man on your way out. He was here to look at the exact same statue you're interested in. What are the chances of that?'

Essie's blood ran cold. 'A man, you say. What was his name?'

'An archaeologist. Got himself in a bit of trouble with the authorities a while ago, I've been told. But it seems he's back in the good books now. You might have heard of him – Dr Benedict Hitchens.'

Essie's heart leapt in her chest. She froze in the doorway.

Hosni took Essie's hand when he saw the pallor of her face, his brow creased with concern. 'Are you all right, my dear lady? You look pale. Do you need to sit down?'

'No ...' Essie struggled to gather herself. 'No, really. I'm fine. Thank you. It's just the heat.'

'Ah, yes. You English roses aren't made for a desert climate, are you? Are you sure you don't need a moment to recover in my office?'

'I'm absolutely fine,' she said, hoping she delivered it with enough bravado to disguise the roiling turmoil within her.

'Fine. If you're sure. We'll go on, then. But, remember, my offer stands – that coffee will be waiting for you.'

Although a decent shot of caffeine was probably exactly what she needed right now, if Benedict Hitchens was on the hunt for the same thing she was, Essie knew she had no time to spare.

But how did he find out? she wondered. *And – most of all – what does he know that I don't? Because if there's anything I've missed, he'll find it.*

18

Cairo, Egypt

'Hitchens? It *is* you. I'd know that damned ugly mug anywhere, pardon the French!'

A tall man wearing a well-cut double-breasted suit and a grey, narrow-brimmed Stetson filled Ben's field of vision, his square-jawed and suntanned face split with a beaming smile featuring the unnaturally perfect teeth that seemed to be a defining characteristic of the American race.

He released Ben's elbow and grabbed his hand, pumping it enthusiastically as his other hand slapped Ben's shoulder. 'You don't remember me, do you? It's Harry. Harry Martin. We met at Arcadia. Been a while, though!'

Harry Martin? Ben's recollections were of a grim-faced American officer recovering from a leg shattered by machine-gun fire, whose disapproval of the riotous behaviour that reigned at the countess' home found expression in regularly spouted Bible verses. His memories of the man didn't match the exhausting vigour of the person standing before him.

174

'Ah . . . Harry. Of course I remember you. It's just that . . . well, you've changed.'

'Yep, yep. You'd be right there. The good Lord's been kind to me. Got myself a fine lady wife. Been blessed with three kids. And I'm working at the US Embassy here.'

Another man of similar build and with the same generic, lantern-jawed American-quarterback good looks had been hovering a few feet away. Harry summoned him over. 'Hey – Roger! Get over here. This guy here – you'd never guess it to look at him now, but he was a maniac, back in the day. Roger Ford . . . Ben Hitchens. One of the craziest men I've ever met.'

Roger stepped forward and shook Ben's hand.

'Nice to meet you.'

'Likewise.' Ben glanced at the entrance to the museum. Essie was gone. *Dammit!* She'd be in there a while if she was going to view the statue. But he couldn't afford to lose sight of her once she left the building.

'So, how've you been, Ben? Got yourself hitched yet?'

Ben flinched. 'I was married . . .'

'Damn! I knew that. She passed, didn't she?'

'Yes. During the war.'

'Nobody since then?'

'No one I wanted to marry, anyway.' It wasn't a lie.

'Well, gotta say, there are days when the rugrats are squalling fit to burst and – between you and me – I miss the bachelor's life. Bet you've got some stories to tell.'

'Don't know about that, Harry.'

'Sure, sure. Nothing to see here, right? I don't buy it for a minute – seem to remember you swatting the ladies away like ants at a picnic. Nudge, nudge. Wink, wink! Still, it'd be just super to hear what you've been up to. Say – we were just headed for lunch at Café Riche. How about you join us? Take a trip down memory lane.'

'It's a kind offer, Harry.' Ben's eyes were fixed on the museum. 'But I'm waiting for someone.'

'Ah, I see. So, what brings you to Cairo then, Ben? You still into that archaeology caper?'

Ben laughed. 'Caper? I suppose you could call it that. Yes, I am.'

'That's why you're here then, is it? What're you looking for?'

'Why would you think I was looking for something?'

The American's eyes narrowed and he shrugged. 'Well, this place is going to hell in a handbasket. Why else would you be here? You'd hardly come to a battlefront to do a bit of sightseeing, now, would you?'

Ben focused his attention on Harry's expression. The jocular façade was intact, but the American's eyes were icy. 'You said you're working at the embassy. What exactly do you do there?'

'A bit of this. A bit of that.' Harry cocked his head. 'We just keep an eye on what's going on around town. Looking out for Uncle Sam's interests.'

A flock of pigeons burst into the air and flew overhead, the sudden clapping of their wings making Ben start. Sensing danger, his muscles tensed reflexively. *So. CIA, then. Great. Just great.* 'Well, this reunion has been delightful. But if you don't mind, I really must be going.'

Harry grabbed Ben's upper arm. 'Whatever you Brits are doing here – whatever it is you're trying to get your hands on – well, we're not just going to let you take it, you can bet on that. Not without a fight.'

'I've no idea what you're talking about, Harry.' Ben pulled his arm away. 'You've really got the wrong end of the stick. And don't you remember? I'm not a Brit. I'm an American.'

'Well, as a patriotic citizen, then, you'll be wanting to help out these United States of ours, won't you? How about you come with us for a little chat about what it is that so many people seem to be running about trying to find?'

'I'm no help to you. Really. I've no idea what's going on.'

'You think we're not listening in to the phone calls that come out of Arcadia? You know, all your dear countess cares about now is getting back to her damned "old country". Forget it's swarming with Commies now. Nothing goes on in her house that we don't know about. And there aren't any secrets from the Reds, either. What she doesn't tell them herself they pick up from the bugs they've planted in that dump she calls a house.'

'Katerina? In with Stalin and his crowd? You're lying. She's a White Russian – she wouldn't piss on a Communist if he was on fire.'

'Trust me. Your dear countess just wants her family estates back. She'll sell anything and anybody to the Reds to make that happen – even you. And she's desperate enough to believe the promises they've made her.' Harry signalled to his partner. 'Sorry about getting physical here, but if you won't come with us willingly, well, I'll have to insist.' The two men began to frogmarch Ben towards the museum's gatehouse and a car that idled at the kerb, its rear door open. 'It was a mistake to trust her, you know.'

'Here's the thing, Harry.' Ben wrenched his arms out of the men's grip and spun on his heels, readying to fight. 'I make it a rule not to trust anyone these days.'

'Let's not make this a public fight, Ben. It won't end well for you.'

Ben sized Harry up and raised his fists. The other man was in fighting form and moved with a physical grace that showed him to be an intimidating adversary.

This is going to hurt . . . me, not him, Ben thought as he drew his fist back and Harry prepared to defend himself.

Ben felt it before he heard it – a movement of air above and past his right temple. A grim, black hole appeared at the centre of Harry's brow as his head jerked back, the whites of his eyes exposed as his pupils rolled in their sockets. It was only then that Ben heard the shot, nearly deafening him. The American's jaw dropped open as the back of his head was blown off in an explosion that left a halo of arterial red fog in the air, and blindingly white shards of skull and grey flecks of brain matter splattered into the air in a grisly starburst. Harry's body hit the pavement with a wet thud.

Harry's legs were still twitching as Roger reached for the holster hidden beneath his pinstriped suit jacket. He was taken down by a second shot before he could withdraw his own gun.

It felt as if time was on a loop as the thunder of the gunshots ricocheted around the stone walls and monuments, the museum's forecourt silent but for the sound of death.

Run. Ben's survival instinct kicked in. *Run, Ben. Get out of here.*

As the Americans' blood seeped out of their now empty brain cases and pooled on the pavement, Ben ran. Nobody tried to stop him.

19

Cairo, Egypt

As he watched the first man's head disintegrate, Ricard Schubert thought it was probably the first time he'd killed someone with the intention of saving another. Killing was what he did – but it was usually a means to an end. It rarely came with any collateral benefits to any of the people involved. He killed to get information, as he had in Cappadocia and at Topkapı. He killed to get rid of people who got in the way. And he killed just for the hell of it. But he couldn't remember a time he'd done it to help someone else.

The spent casing spat onto the paving and Schubert set the other man's skull in the sights of his Luger pistol as the target's head swivelled round, searching for the shooter and fumbling for his holster. Before he had a chance to take hold of his own gun, Schubert squeezed the trigger and saw him fall to the ground, a cascade of gore exploding from his skull. Neither of the men twitching on the pavement would be posing a threat to anyone again.

Hidden behind the fragmentary torso of an ancient statue, Schubert steadied his hand on the crook of the neck of a pharaoh whose head was as large as Schubert was tall. He watched as the archaeologist took a moment to recover from the shock of what had just occurred. But this was a man Schubert knew had been acclimatised to the brutal sensory assault of war. For Hitchens, violence was an old – and most likely loathed – acquaintance. As the German had anticipated, it took only a fraction of a second before the American's well-honed reflexes responded and he was bolting across the museum's forecourt and out onto Cairo's streets like a hare pursued by hounds. Finger hovering over his pistol's trigger, Schubert feigned a shot.

Whether or not the other man knew how easily Schubert could have brought him down didn't matter. It was enough for the German to know that he could have, if he'd wanted to.

Unlike the Turks he'd murdered in Istanbul and Cappadocia, he didn't bear the archaeologist any real malice – or the two Americans he'd just shot, either. That was just a job that needed doing. The Turks had been another matter. Although he'd been acting under instructions to get information from them, there'd been no real need to kill them. But he'd just gone with the mood in the room at the time. And he'd enjoyed every minute of it.

Ricard Schubert had been born in Smyrna to a German railway engineer and a Turkish mother. His fiercely patriotic father had forbidden him from speaking anything but German when he was growing up, casting his son in the role of pariah in the cosmopolitan Aegean city where Turkish and Greek were the languages spoken on the streets. As a skinny and knock-kneed child, he was tormented by schoolyard bullies. But as he grew, he began to fight back, and his poisonous contempt for his Greek and Turkish schoolmates found expression in fists that became calloused through the beatings he distributed. Antipathy spread like a tumour inside him, and he relished any opportunity to revisit his childhood grudges. The people he'd tortured and killed in Turkey had been the unfortunate targets of those urges.

When he'd told his employers what he'd learnt at Topkapı and Niğde, they'd instructed him to keep watching the archaeologist and make sure nobody got in his way. Whether that meant he was to eliminate anyone who looked like they were giving Hitchens trouble hadn't been made clear. They hadn't gone into specifics, which to Schubert meant he could do whatever he deemed necessary. Nobody who asked him to do a job would be in any doubt about the lengths to which he'd go and the methods he'd employ to make sure he did what was required. And although he didn't know exactly who the people were who'd been intent on bustling Hitchens into the car that was waiting outside the museum's grounds, he could make a fair guess; the vehicle had American diplomatic plates, which to Schubert's way of thinking meant trouble.

Even now, the driver of the sedan and the other man who'd been sitting in the passenger seat jumped out of the car and ran towards where their colleagues lay dead on the pavement. It was Schubert's signal to move. Once they confirmed their countrymen were dead – and one glance at the state of their skulls would tell them that – they'd start looking for the gun that had brought them down. And he had no intention of being found.

He already knew where the archaeologist was headed, so he didn't need to follow him. Schubert ducked below the level of the raised garden bed to keep out of sight of the men now scoping the forecourt, and took the same route out of the side service entry to the museum grounds he'd taken when he'd arrived on the American's heels earlier that day.

Schubert didn't know why it was so important to make sure Hitchens was allowed to keep doing whatever it was that he was doing unhindered. More to the point, he didn't care.

20

Cairo, Egypt

'Mrs Peters?' The museum director's voice echoed about the walls of the enormous warehouse.

Essie stood from where she'd been kneeling beside the statue of Hathor and Psamtik to re-examine the inscription. *What the hell is it now?* she thought, brushing the dust from her knees. 'Yes, professor?'

He edged between the statues and took her benevolently by the elbow. 'Now, you mustn't be alarmed, my dear. But I'm afraid you'll need to take me up on my offer of a coffee whether you wish to or not. Something terrible's happened . . . outside. A shooting.'

She drew in her breath sharply. *Ben . . . Please, no. Don't let it be him.*

Interpreting her response as fear, Hosni patted her hand. 'You really need not concern yourself, Mrs Peters. You're quite safe in here with me. Apparently two men from the American embassy were shot. But it would be most unwise of you to go outside now while the police are hunting for the shooter.'

Men from the embassy . . . not Ben. Thank God. The intensity of the reflexive response to the thought that something might have happened to him surprised her.

The director shook his head disapprovingly. 'This unrest . . . people are just losing their minds. It's all quite irrational, of course. It will be the end of us all. Now . . . your coffee . . . or would you prefer tea? And don't forget that cake!'

Essie clenched her fists. She needed to call Garvé from the privacy of her hotel to tell him that Ben was on their tail. *But if I'm stuck here . . .* She had another idea. 'Professor, now that I think of it, a mint tea would be wonderful. And a slice of cake, of course.' She smiled sweetly at the director. 'But I must ask you a favour. A colleague from the government is expecting a call from me about a very important matter. Might I use your telephone? I'll also need to trouble you for some privacy while we speak – it's a rather sensitive matter.'

'But of course, good lady.'

'We might have a problem.'

She heard the intake of breath at the other end of the line. 'What?! What is it?'

'Benedict Hitchens. He's been here at the museum. Looking at the inscription.'

'Oh. Is that all? Nothing to worry about, I can assure you.' Josef Garvé's relief was palpable.

'The fact he's been here doesn't bother you at all?'

'No. I'd heard he was sniffing around. We suspected the Americans and Russians would be hunting for this damned thing. So I've had someone keeping an eye on the archive in

Topkapı to find out who paid the manuscript a visit. And it seems Dr Hitchens is one of the interested parties. I'm surprised he found his way to Cairo so quickly, though. I may have underestimated him.'

'And you didn't think it worth sharing that information with me?' Essie snapped.

There was a moment's silence before Garvé responded. 'Well, considering the way things ended with the two of you . . . I felt it might cloud your reason if you knew he was involved.'

'That's an insult to my professionalism, Josef.'

'It's not intended to be taken that way. I did it out of concern for you.'

Bullshit, she thought. *The day you do something for anyone other than yourself will be the day I go skiing off-piste in Hades.*

'Anyway,' Garvé continued. 'Even if he's worked out where the tablet is, within a matter of days, the place he needs to be will be inaccessible to anyone. Other than us, of course. You've nothing to worry about. I promise.'

Essie placed the phone back in its cradle. A deep sense of unease had worked its way into her bones. It may have been caused by the knowledge that she was in a race against the one other person she knew had the skills to find the tablet. Or it might have been the corrosive and all too familiar sense of regret she felt any time she thought of Ben. Perhaps it was a bit of both.

Either way, she wished she shared Garvé's confidence in their ability to outwit the American. She knew what he was capable of, and it worried her.

21

Cairo, Egypt

As he darted between the donkey carts and buses zigzagging along the Nile Corniche, Ben thought that if there was any positive benefit to Cairo's chaotic traffic, it was that it made it very easy to disappear.

Heart pounding, he passed between the twin lions and obelisks at the easternmost end of the Qasr El Nil Bridge, conscious of anyone following him. Other than the obligatory stares – many of them scornful – at the sight of a European walking the streets, Ben didn't detect any untoward interest in his passing. But he hadn't been able to spot the shooter at the Egyptian Museum, either before or after the attack, so if he was still being followed, he doubted that whoever it was who'd killed Harry and Roger would be careless enough to let Ben see him now.

He was still processing what had just occurred and what it meant. The shooter at the museum had put a bullet in the brains of two men from what must have been a reasonable distance. That meant they'd known exactly what they were doing, and Ben assumed that if they'd wanted him dead, he'd be lying cold on the pavement beside the two Americans. He might have found some comfort in that realisation if he had any idea why the shooter had allowed him to live. But he hadn't put in an order for a guardian angel, and without knowing the motivations of whoever had intervened in his confrontation with Harry and his friend, the niggling fatalism underpinning Ben's world view assured him that whatever the reason, it was unlikely to be good news for him.

The screaming wail of sirens tearing through Tahrir Square towards the museum spurred him to action.

Time to put a little distance between me and the dead bodies, he thought. And if he was to follow this trail to its logical endpoint, he needed to see Ethan Cohn. If anyone could help him unravel the clues he'd just discovered, it would be him. And that meant he and Ilhan needed to go to Jerusalem.

Hailing a passing taxi, he gave the driver directions to Arcadia.

He found Ilhan stretched out on a deckchair on the tiled patio beside the slow-moving waters of the Nile, eyes closed and breathing heavily as he indulged in a nap in the warm sunshine.

Ben shook his shoulder. 'Ilhan? We need to go. Now.'

Starting awake, his friend shielded his eyes from the sun as he looked up at Ben. 'That was a very pleasant dream you just interrupted, Ben. What's the hurry?'

'Someone's been shot.'

Startled, Ilhan stumbled to his feet. 'Shot? Who?'

'Nobody you know. But I was there. And I don't want to get caught up here by the police.'

Ilhan shook his head. 'Ben, this isn't a game. I don't understand why you're persisting. Let's just go back to Istanbul.'

'I can't, Ilhan. The more I'm finding out about what they're up to, the more convinced I am that this is something pretty serious. Besides, I made a promise to Sebile.'

'And what would that be?'

'I promised her I'd make sure the tablet didn't find its way into the wrong hands.'

'I thought your life's work was breaking the promises you make to women,' Ilhan mumbled.

'Don't be an idiot. We're getting close. I can't stop now.'

'Well, your friend will be happy to hear we're leaving.'

'Who?'

'The countess. She's suddenly quite desperate to push us out the door.'

'What do you mean?'

'We had an afternoon of sightseeing planned, but she took a phone call and had to postpone our trip while she went out. Ever since she returned, she's been on edge. Keeps asking when I think you'll be back and trying to convince me we'd be much happier staying in a hotel.'

'Ah, Christ!' Ben exclaimed.

'What's wrong?'

'Nothing. I'll tell you later. Can you get our things together?' he asked. 'Meet me downstairs. Meantime, I'll see what's going on.'

Countess Katerina met Ben in Arcadia's grand entrance foyer, the dusty crystal chandelier hanging above their heads casting rainbows on the marble-tiled floor.

'Benedict. You *are* here. I'm so relieved. I thought I heard you return.' She grasped his wrist and Ben could feel her hand quivering. 'I must warn you – in the city, things are getting dangerous. Terrible things are happening.'

'I've noticed.'

'You know I'd happily have you stay here for as long as you like . . .'

'You always were the most gracious host.' Ben smiled cautiously. *Bloody hell*, he cursed. *Fucking Harry was right. I hate that.*

'. . . but I fear you may end up in trouble if you stay.'

'You know me, darling lady. I've spent a lifetime getting myself into trouble. I'm sure it's nothing I can't handle. But, as a matter of fact, something's come up. We're going to have to leave, anyway.'

The nervous tension in her body evaporated. 'I am *so* glad to hear that. But might I insist you make it sooner rather than later?'

Footsteps on the marble behind Ben heralded Ilhan's arrival. 'All packed.'

'Great. I'll just need to go and arrange a driver to take us to Alexandria. I won't be long.'

'A driver? No – you should go now. There's no time to waste. Farouk will take you in my car.'

'Farouk? Really, that won't be necessary . . .'

She ushered the two men towards the rear of the house. 'I insist. You'll find him in the garage.'

As she heard the sound of gravel crushed beneath the tyres of more than one vehicle in the front driveway, Katerina's movements took on a renewed sense of urgency. She glanced frantically over her shoulder at the front door. 'No! They're here already! Ben, you must go! Now! Farouk can take you out the service entrance. It leads to the bridge. They won't even know you were here.'

'"They"? Who're "they"?'

Katerina embraced him, her head barely reaching his shoulder. 'Please forgive me. I just tell the Soviets about the movements of foreign nationals in the city. I didn't think it would do any harm – they're never particularly interested in what I have to say. But when I told them about where you were going and what you were looking for . . .'

'Don't apologise, countess. I understand. But what will they do when they find we've gone? Will you be safe?'

She laughed scornfully. 'From those boors? They wouldn't presume to lay a hand on me.'

He kissed the crown of her head. 'Thank you, Katerina. I'll return another time and we'll laugh about this.'

Countess Katerina Anastasia Orlova bent and scooped Vladimir Ilyich into her arms. The lizard took up his perch on her shoulder.

She stood in the foyer and listened to the heavy footsteps outside her front door, followed by an impatient pummelling of fists on the heavy oak. Stepping forward, she released the latch.

'Comrade Orlova . . .' trumpeted the bull-headed man who pushed past her into her home.

'Don't call me that.'

'You'd rather we use your title, would you?' the man sneered. 'Never again. Not if I have anything to do with it. Where is he?'

'Who?'

'Who do you think? Your house guest.'

'He's gone.' She held her head high on her noble neck, fixing the Russian with a haughty glare born of generations of aristocratic breeding.

'Did you warn him we were coming?' He glared at her from beneath an incongruously angelic mop of golden curls.

She laughed dismissively. 'What if I did?'

The Russian looked up at the men who'd followed him into the entrance. 'Search the house.'

'You won't find anything. They're long gone.'

The man's hand flashed out, slapping her hard on the cheek.

She pulled back, shocked. 'How *dare* you!' she snapped.

'How dare I?' He pulled a gun from a holster strapped to his side, chambered a round and shot her between the eyes. 'How dare *you*!'

She slumped back onto the floor, lifeless. Vladimir Ilyich, who'd clung to her shoulder as she fell, scrambled onto her chest and sat stock-still, staring at his mistress' murderer with an unblinking gaze.

The Russian poked her with the toe of his shoe. 'Fool.'

22

Alexandria, Egypt

'No! No more ferries! No ferries going and no ferries coming, sir!' The man at the port office in Alexandria looked at Ben and waved his hand frantically at the military vehicles jamming the roads into the harbour. 'How is there ferries? War is coming! No boats in or out. Only navy! Only soldiers!' The black telephone on his desk jangled insistently and the Egyptian grabbed the handset and started yammering into the mouthpiece in Arabic, his visitors already forgotten.

Ben and Ilhan walked down the short flight of steps from the office. 'Well, that's going to make getting to Jerusalem fairly challenging, isn't it?' observed Ilhan unnecessarily.

The autumn sun beat down on Ben's shoulders and he slipped his sunglasses back on to shield the glare reflecting off the asphalt road. 'Not going to give up that easily, my friend.'

Dodging past ranks of troops marching in line and buffeted by the salty winds blowing across the bay, Ben and Ilhan made their way towards the Corniche that ran in an elegant curve along Alexandria's Mediterranean waterfront and was fringed by grand, tiered edifices housing fashionable clubs and hotels.

The sight of a tall, blond-headed European man walking side by side with someone who looked like an Arab attracted many curious – and contemptuous – glances. Ben barely noticed. 'When I was here during the war, you could hardly move for all the smugglers plying their trade between Africa and Europe,' he said. 'I doubt it's any different today. Can't tell me we won't be able to find someone willing to scoot us over to Tel Aviv if we pay them enough. Come on, Ilhan. This is your area of expertise. Surely you'll be able to sort something out!'

'I'm sure I could, Ben. But don't you think it's about time we admitted defeat?' He indicated the jumble of soldiers and military vehicles tearing along the streets. 'Look – it's hardly a good time to be heading east. You know what I think is a much better idea? Let's find ourselves a nice little pension on a beach outside the city and put our feet up for a bit. Have a holiday while we wait out the troubles. Swim. Fish. Play some cards. And if you're still keen to pursue it when this political mess cools off, you can continue your search then.'

Ben laughed. 'Wait? Thought you knew me better than that. Come on, Ilhan. You know I'm not giving up on this. Everything I've learnt over the past few days just confirms something deadly serious is going on. Three people killed? Whatever it is, it's big. If I was still only motivated by nothing more than my rather petty desire for revenge, I might agree with you. But now I'm worried. And if you don't help me, I'll go down to the port and start asking around myself. It might take a little longer, but you know I'll eventually find someone. Wouldn't you rather it was someone you know we can trust? It'd certainly be my preference.'

'There's really no talking you out of this, then?'

'Not a chance.'

'Fine. I'll see what I can do.'

'Great! Where should we start looking?'

'There's no "we" in this, Ben. In case you hadn't noticed, at the moment, you're *persona non grata* round here. I'll have a much better chance if I do this by myself.'

Ben knew he was right. 'Fine. There's a café on the ground floor of the Cecil Hotel. I'll wait for you there.'

Speaking over his shoulder as he strode back towards the port, Ilhan tried one last time. 'Are you sure this is what you want, Ben?'

'Absolutely.'

The warm smell of cloves and cardamom made Ben's mouth water as he sipped from a small, gilt-edged cup filled with freshly brewed Arabic coffee.

Outside the Cecil Hotel's arched windows, he watched the wind whip across the Mediterranean, setting aflutter the feathery tops of the colonnade of palms planted along the Corniche.

The city had been established by and named for the man whose presence in this part of the world had left more of a mark than almost any other – Alexander the Great. In his wake came the great Ptolemaic queen, Cleopatra, whose palace had since been lost in one of the many earthquakes that had ravaged the city.

At the far end of the promenade that edged the bay on the easternmost end of Pharos Island was the now-abandoned Citadel of Qaitbay, built by the Mamelukes in the fifteenth century on the site of the ancient Lighthouse of Alexandria, one of the seven wonders of the world, whose light could once be seen thirty miles out to sea.

They were her last words to me . . . 'We will meet at the base of the famous lighthouse of Alexandria . . . I have always wanted to see it.' The thought erupted, unbidden, into Ben's mind. *Karina.*

It had been here that Ben had waited for the arrival of the British frigate that was to have brought his Greek wife to meet him after he'd arrived in the city on a faster launch from Crete to deliver the captured Nazi collaborator, Josef Garvé, to British authorities. A shadow of the same hollow sense of disbelief and icy chill of dread assaulted him as he recalled the moment he'd heard of the German capture of the ship that had been carrying Karina to him and his grim but frantic efforts to get back to the island to save her.

Cleopatra and Mark Antony . . . that's who we are . . . Cleopatra and Mark Antony. That had been his only thought as the launch he'd managed to commandeer cut through the waves towards Crete. And like those star-crossed ancient lovers, theirs was not to be a happy ending. He'd arrived too late. Karina had died in German hands, along with the child she'd been carrying. His child.

'Waiter?' He summoned the liveried bartender. 'Double scotch, please.'

Being alone with his thoughts for too long never served Ben well. It was why he tried to stay in perpetual motion.

The sun was setting in a blaze of colour when Ilhan returned.

'I've found someone. A good man. He'll take us tonight.' He took in Ben's slightly glazed expression and the half-finished drink sitting on the table in front of him. 'I see. Everything all right, Ben?'

He looked up. 'Absolutely. Just memories. You know how it is.'

'Well, I'd put those memories to one side and switch to coffee if I were you.' Ilhan called the waiter over. 'It's going to be a long journey. You'll need to have your wits about you.' He ordered coffee and sandwiches. 'Are you still sure you want to go ahead, Ben? It's not too late to pull out.'

Ben shook his head. 'Not on your life. I'm doing this. I have to.'

23

Akrotiri, Cyprus

The sun was low in the sky over the mountains of Cyprus as the open jeep jolted along the dirt road towards the British military base at Akrotiri, its wheels jarring in potholes and ditches and spinning dust and gravel into the air. The metal bench seat slammed into Essie's rear as she tried and failed to ignore the bare-faced ogling of the two young soldiers sitting opposite her who were transfixed by the movement of her breasts beneath her clothes each time the vehicle moved. It seemed the heavy-duty khaki military canvas shirt she'd buttoned to beneath her chin in an attempt to draw less attention to herself did nothing to discourage the ardour of the two men, who were barely out of adolescence.

Oh, for Christ's sake, she cursed inwardly. *Not today. I'm not in the mood*. Returning to the place she'd once called home had put her on edge. She leant forward and tapped one of the young soldiers on the knee. 'Excuse me?' she asked in her sweetest voice.

197

He started and his eyes snapped northward to meet her gaze. 'Ah, yes, miss?'

'It's Mrs. And I just wanted to thank you.'

The young soldier looked confused. 'Thank me, ma'am? For what?'

'For reminding me that at least one of us has something worth drooling over.' She offered him a handkerchief from her purse. 'Here – I think you've got some on your chin. Drool, I mean.'

The soldier's face flushed a colour that rivalled the scarlet gleam of the setting sun. Shamefaced, the two men set their eyes firmly on the road ahead.

It was unlike Essie to make a fuss about such commonplace – and common – behaviour. But she was on edge, dreading the reunion with Adam Penney. She'd spoken with Josef Garvé and arranged to meet the two men at the military base, where they were readying to embark on the aircraft carrier, HMS *Theseus*. From there, a helicopter would transport them into the Sinai as an advance on the general British air assault on Port Said that would occur in a matter of days. When they'd spoken on the phone, Garvé had made no reference to the reason for Essie's sudden departure from London, other than a polite enquiry after the health of her stepmother. She'd been relieved to know that Penney might have kept the events that had occurred at his home on her last evening in London to himself. But the thought of looking him in the eye again made her feel physically ill.

She had no doubt at all that he'd put something in her drink that night with the intention of raping her. And that knowledge made her burn with a blinding rage. Most women had men to fight their battles for them – fathers; brothers; husbands. She had nobody. If she wanted someone punished for mistreating her, the only avenging angel she had to call on was herself. But she was also a pragmatist. Although every instinct urged her to strike out at Adam Penney, she knew that if she did want to get her hands on the Emerald Tablet and the financial windfall it would deliver – not to mention the freedom she now so desperately wanted – she'd have to find some way of stomaching being around the man. As difficult as she knew it was going to be, she was damned if she was going to let him strip her of her prize.

Watching through the windscreen as they approached the intimidating defensive measures protecting the headquarters of Britain's Middle East armed forces, Essie braced herself.

It won't be long. And once this is over, you'll never have to look at that pig of a man again.

Notified by the guardhouse of Essie's impending arrival, Josef Garvé and Adam Penney were waiting for her by the mess hall. Garvé stepped forward as the jeep came to a halt and opened the door for her, extending a hand to help her down from the tray. She didn't need any assistance but accepted it anyway.

The chagrined soldier took her case from the back of the vehicle. 'There's quarters set up for you in the estate with the airmen's families, ma'am. I'll take your gear there.' He couldn't bring himself to meet her eye.

'Fine. Thank you,' she snapped.

'Difficult trip?' asked Garvé, sensing her discomfort.

'No worse than usual,' she responded. 'At least – nothing I can't handle.' She couldn't bear to look at Adam, who she sensed hovering just behind the Frenchman like a mosquito waiting to strike. *No more avoiding it*, she thought as he took a step towards her.

'Essie!' Penney gripped her firmly by the upper arms and planted a wet kiss on each cheek. 'Darling lady.' He dropped his voice and looked at her from beneath hooded lids. 'I was *so* delighted you decided to join our party the other night. And you seemed to be having *so* much fun!' he purred. 'Then you left in such a hurry . . . well, I was concerned.'

She squirmed and extricated herself from his grasp. 'No need to worry about me, Adam. You shouldn't have wasted the energy. I was tired. Bed was calling.'

'Bed? Yes – I noticed,' he smirked.

She glared at him.

Penney turned to Garvé. 'I saw a different side to our Mrs Peters the night she visited my home. I doubt I'll ever be able to look at her the same way again.'

'Is that a fact?' The Frenchman glanced at Essie. 'Well, she is quite the woman of mystery.'

'That she is.' Adam chortled coarsely. 'That she is.'

Garvé raised an eyebrow. Essie responded with a curt and furtive shake of her head. She knew he wouldn't care what had happened unless it was relevant to the business at hand, which it wasn't.

'I've had news from Cairo,' Garvé said. 'Both the Americans and Russians have stepped up their activities. Seems they're closing in on your Dr Hitchens. If you'd like to join me for dinner on my yacht, Essie, I can let you know what's been happening.' He pointedly excluded Penney from the invitation.

'Thank you, but no. The only thing I need to catch up on is some sleep.'

'I'll just look after myself then, shall I?' grumbled Penney.

'It would be a fine gesture to show some support to the men in uniform, Adam,' Garvé said in a conciliatory tone. 'They're about to go into battle, after all, and I'm sure it'd bolster their morale no end to have someone from Whitehall join them for their evening meal.'

'Yes . . . well, now that you mention it . . . yes, of course. Fine idea. Fly the old Union Jack and all that,' he preened. Essie recoiled.

'Now, Essie,' continued Garvé. 'The orders to move out may come at any moment. Unfortunately, we don't have any control over the timing. We're just waiting for our friends in London to give the go-ahead. Operation Musketeer is what the military have called the invasion, apparently. The three musketeers – Britain, France and Israel. Has there ever been a less likely alliance? Anyway, you'll need to be ready to leave.'

'I'm ready now. If it was up to me, we wouldn't be waiting.' *Anything to avoid hanging around a military base populated by lecherous soldiers and a would-be rapist.*

24

Jerusalem

The rosy stones of Jerusalem's Ottoman city wall gleamed in the sun's white glare as blinding shafts of light shot in beams from the Dome of the Rock's golden cupola. Ben and Ilhan travelled in silence, slumped back onto the taxi's rear seat. They were both exhausted after the long passage across the rough seas between Alexandria and the remote beach of Palmachim on the Israeli coastline, where they'd disembarked in the shadows of a ruined fortress on a promontory overlooking the Mediterranean.

The taxi flashed by ancient walls whose worn and weathered surfaces were blemished by bullet holes and divots gouged out by shrapnel. Ahead loomed the multistoreyed splendour of the King David Hotel, the fresh limestone bricks in the south-western corner of its façade dazzling next to the older stonework on the rest of the building – a scar left by the 1946 bombing attack on the hotel by a Zionist paramilitary group that had killed ninety-one people. Not that Ben needed it, but it was a grim reminder of how troubled the region was that they'd just entered.

Sweeping into the hotel's circular driveway, the cab pulled up beneath the grand porte-cochère. 'Decided we deserved a treat, did you?' asked Ilhan, clearly impressed as a solemn doorman wearing a peaked cap and a long coat with gold braid and buttons opened the taxi's door.

'Always wanted to stay here,' said Ben. 'Last time I was in Jerusalem, I was a student. Didn't feel comfortable with the grandeur. But these days . . . hell, why not, I say?'

Ilhan caught sight of the healthy wad of US banknotes Ben handed the concierge, who accepted his offering with a nod and a tip of his cap. 'A bit excessive?' the Turk murmured.

'My rule of thumb is to always look after the man who'll be looking after me,' Ben responded. 'Just wait. Bet my generosity will buy us one of their best rooms overlooking the old city.'

Ben leant back in an armchair and took in the hotel's imposing decor as he waited for the hotel manager to connect his call to the Hebrew University of Jerusalem. Ilhan had already left to explore the tiny antique shops lining the narrow laneways they'd seen on their taxi ride into the city. 'You can waste your time with your pointless search,' he had cried as he disappeared around a corner. 'Just watch! I'll make something out of this yet!'

The hotel's interior was a theatrical confection of historical details. A finely woven red carpet stretched through the hotel's monumental lobby, where the walls had been embellished with richly coloured icons including Solomon's shield and abstract representations of the 'seven species' – the seven agricultural products described in the Tanakh as Israel's natural bounty and the only sacrificial gifts that could be brought to the altar of the Holy Temple. With Egyptian revival and Phoenician architectural features interpreted in an Art Deco style, it was a mishmash of cultural references that Ben assumed were meant to carry the viewer back to a time when King David ruled the city.

'Excuse me, sir?' The manager summoned him from the front desk. 'Your call is connected.' He indicated a bank of telephone booths against the wall in the hotel's foyer.

Ben levered his broad-shouldered frame through the narrow cedar doorway, ducking his head to avoid hitting it on the roof. He picked up the handset. 'Hello?'

'Yes.' It was a female voice. 'How may I help you?'

'I'm calling to speak with Professor Cohn. I was a student of his . . . many years ago.'

'I'm his secretary. I'll see if he's available. Your name?'

'Dr Benedict Hitchens.'

'Give me a moment.' Ben heard the clack of heels on a timber floor and a murmured conversation. There was a clatter as the woman picked up the phone again. 'I'm afraid he's too busy to take your call. You'll need to try again another time.'

'Well, what I'd really like is to meet with him. I'm here in Jerusalem. It's a matter of some urgency. Could you please ask him if I might come in to see him – perhaps some time this afternoon or this evening?'

'I'm terribly sorry, Dr Hitchens, but he's a very busy man –'

'Please. Could you please ask him again? Tell him it's about Balinas . . . Balinas and the Emerald Tablet.'

The woman on the other end of the line let out an exasperated sigh. 'Fine.' The sound was muffled as she covered the mouthpiece of the phone with her hand. After a few seconds, her voice came back on the line. 'He said you can come in the afternoon. Late. Do you know where we are?'

'Yes. Yes, I do. Thank you.'

'My pleasure.' The woman hung up with a force that showed it was anything but.

25

Jerusalem

*I*f *ever a building embodied the contradictions of this city, this would be it,* Ben thought as he walked towards the temporary accommodation of the Hebrew University of Jerusalem's humanities department.

In the most contested city on earth, Christians, Jews and Muslims had done everything they could to make a mark. That urge found its expression in construction as well as destruction. In the Terra Sancta building, the monks of St Francis had conceived an edifice that established an enduring presence in the Holy City, but the building's destiny had proved to be as chequered as the city itself, and part of it had been requisitioned as a campus of the Hebrew University. From the summit of the four-storeyed building that had been constructed in the Italianate style from rough-hewn limestone blocks, echoing the construction of Jerusalem's great walls, a haloed statue of the Madonna stood on the belltower's cupola, her hand raised in blessing over the serious-faced Jewish students flooding out of the front entrance at the day's end.

Ben hailed a young man passing by, a pile of books clamped beneath his arm.

'Excuse me? Where's Professor Ethan Cohn's office?'

The student's forehead crinkled above black-rimmed glasses. 'Professor Cohn . . . what does he teach?'

'Archaeology.'

'Ah – that's why I haven't heard the name. I'm in philosophy. Archaeology . . . take the stairs to the third floor and head towards the back of the building.'

Finding his way to the Department of Archaeology was, appropriately enough, like negotiating a labyrinth. The hallways were stacked with books and boxes hemmed in by clusters of gesticulating students squabbling over the volumes they wanted to take home to study that evening.

He pushed past the sparring students and caught the attention of one boy standing on the fringe of the group. 'Ah . . . Professor Cohn's office?'

'Cohn?' He indicated an office door further down the corridor. 'That's him.'

The frosted glass door was shut and Ben could see no movement within. Raising a hand, he rapped on the glass.

A shadow passed before the door, then another. It opened a crack and a flinty-faced woman wearing tortoiseshell spectacles on the end of her nose looked out. 'Yes?' she snapped.

'Ah – I'm Dr Hitchens. I think we spoke earlier. I've an appointment with Professor Cohn.'

Her chin tilted back and eyebrows shot skyward. 'Dr Benedict Hitchens, you say?' She looked him up and down. 'Well. I've heard a fair bit about you over the years . . . Not how I imagined you. Give me a moment.' She slammed the door and retreated into the room.

Ben waited, tapping his foot. *Curmudgeonly old bastard*, he thought. *Looks like you got yourself a secretary after your own heart.*

The door swung open again. 'Come in.' The woman took an overcoat from a stand beside the door and slipped it on, swinging a purse onto her shoulder. She addressed someone, unseen, in the corner of the room. 'If there's nothing else you need, professor, I'll be going home now.'

A familiar voice rang out, stern and sonorous. 'Fine. Thank you, Mrs Levin. See you tomorrow.'

Ben entered the room. It was high-ceilinged and spacious with windows overlooking the busy promenade below. Glass display cabinets filled with ceramic vessels, terracotta figurines and stone tools lined the walls. Hanging in a tiered display by the door was a collection of what Ben recognised as Roman weaponry – swords, daggers and javelins. But the floor was stacked with so many piles of paperwork and storage boxes full of ancient artefacts that it was difficult to see a way into the room. He caught a movement out of the corner of his eye.

'Well. Benedict Hitchens. What brings you here?'

With his prematurely silver hair, grizzled brow and sternly set lips, Ethan Cohn had always looked older than his years. Looking at him now, Ben realised his age had finally caught up with his appearance.

'Ethan. It's . . . it's been a while . . .'

Cohn said nothing, just stared at Ben with a detached expression on his face.

'How's everything? How're Esther . . . and the children?' Ben stumbled over his words.

Ben's former mentor took a deep breath. '"How's everything?" you ask? Even you, in your self-absorbed world, would have heard what's been going on here. How do *you* think "everything" is, Benedict? Esther and I moved here from Crete during the war. The university campus on Mt Scopus was a sanctuary – a beacon for us as we fought for the liberation of Israel from the British. And today? The road to the mountain is in Arab hands. Seventy-eight of my colleagues and students were slaughtered in a medical convoy on that road. Our classrooms . . . the books . . . everything we fought for. Gone.'

Ethan gestured to the streets outside. 'Out there, along that street, there's a wall. You probably walked past it to get here. Well, six months ago, that wall wasn't there. You would've been taking your life into your own hands if you'd walked that street. Arab snipers from the battlements of the old city made no distinction – old men; women; children. Anyone they could get their sights on. But Jews will never again be victims. In one night, we built that wall . . .' Ethan held his gnarled hands out before him. 'These hands – they know dirt and they know stones. Perhaps they're doing something useful at last.' He dropped them back to his side. 'So. That's how "everything" is. Now, why are you here?'

'Ethan, I'm sorry we lost touch. I'm not even sure how or why it happened.' Though that was anything but the truth. Any desire Ben might have had to keep in touch had evaporated once he learnt that Ethan had been bad-mouthing him to anyone who'd listen. He gritted his teeth. Conflict had always brought out Ethan Cohn's bull-headed and intractable side. Ben knew the only way he'd convince him to help would be if he took a conciliatory stance.

'I can tell you exactly why it happened,' the older man scoffed. 'You lost direction – lost sight of the noble purpose of the work you were doing. Instead of searching for truth and fulfilling your promise – making the most of the gifts you were given – you were more concerned with getting your face in the papers.'

And that's the crux of it, isn't it, old man? You were just bitter that I was getting the attention you thought should have been yours. But Ben knew there would be no benefit in pointing out that fact.

Two leather armchairs were jammed beneath the sills of the room's two windows. Ben gestured towards them. 'Could we sit down for a moment, Ethan?'

'Yes – if you would please stop wasting my time and tell me why you're here. Esther's waiting dinner for me . . . the only reason I managed to find time in my very busy schedule is that you mentioned you had something to tell me about Balinas.'

The two men took up defensive positions facing each other.

'So. Tell me,' Ethan said curtly.

Ben took out his transcription of the hidden manuscript from the Topkapı Palace archives and held it in front of the older man.

Peering through his spectacles, Ethan studied the document intently. Startled, he pulled back. 'Where did you find this?'

'Topkapı archives. In a copy of Balinas' *Book of Causes.*'

'You know what it is, I presume?'

'Yes. And there's more.' He opened the journal to the notes he'd taken in the Egyptian Museum. 'I was led to an inscription in Cairo. It directs me towards the mountain where the moon god Sin was worshipped –'

'Mt Sinai!' Ethan interrupted.

'Yes. But there's a problem. The description has me heading north from the island of Jezirat Faraun.'

'In the Gulf of Aqaba . . .'

'Which means it can't be Jebel Musa. Whichever Mt Sinai is hosting Balinas' tomb, it isn't the one in the Sinai Peninsula.'

'The Negev!' Ethan exclaimed. 'I *knew* it! It's what I've always said. I *knew* that's where I'd find him. It was the only place that made sense.'

Ben flipped to the page where he'd transcribed the enigmatic mark that appeared in the book in Topkapı and which he'd found again in Kemerhisar and Cairo. 'Does this mean anything to you?'

Ethan's face blanched. He leapt to his feet and scrambled through a maze of cardboard boxes to a stack of artefact drawers set against the wall. He opened one and lifted out a storage container the size of a shoebox which he carried back and handed to Ben. 'Open it,' he said, voice quavering.

Lifting the lid, it took Ben's eyes a moment to adjust in the late-afternoon light. It was Ben's turn to be shocked. The box was full of flat, black stones, each of which had been roughly engraved with the same symbols in the enigmatic design Ben had been pursuing: a crescent moon, a sun, a staff and a snake. He lifted one out of the box and felt its cold, heavy weight in the palm of his hand. 'Petroglyphs! Where'd they come from?' he asked.

'It's a long story.'

'I've nowhere else to be.'

'Fine. We've known here in Israel about the Emerald Tablet and its power since the war. Here, nobody laughs at my obsession with alchemy. Not since Daniel Zable arrived here after escaping the camp at Dachau. He's a physicist who was put to work in Himmler's laboratories. The Nazis had learnt of the research of a man named Fulcanelli –'

'I've heard about him,' Ben interjected.

Ethan looked up, surprised. 'Is that a fact? Well, you'll know, then, about his findings relating to nuclear physics. When they saw the potential for transforming matter, the only thing the Nazi morons were interested in doing was working out how to make gold, of course. Which they did manage to do, in small quantities. But Daniel saw the potential of the research. Fulcanelli's notes pointed him towards the Emerald Tablet. As for trying to find where the tablet itself is hidden – well, that's what I've been trying to do. I knew from Balinas' biography as written by Philostratus that I was looking for a cave . . . and everything I found pointed me in the direction of the Negev Desert.' He leant over and took one of the stones out of the box on Ben's lap. 'So ever since 1948, along with their myriad other responsibilities, the Israeli Defence Force has been tasked with searching the desert for caves in the Negev and Jordanian territory. It's become something of an initiation for the new troops – they call it the "run to red rock". Much of what they bring back is useless. But these . . .' he said, turning the petroglyph in his hand, '. . . I knew they were important the instant I saw them. And I was right.'

'So where are they from?'

Ethan stood and retrieved a map from a shelf which he spread out on his desk, jabbing the centre of it with a stubby forefinger. 'Here.'

Ben joined him. 'Har Karkom?'

'That's right. The Bedouin call it Jebel Ideid – the Mountain of Celebrations. It's a major Palaeolithic and Bronze Age cult centre.' Ethan slammed the engraved stone down on the map. 'Petroglyphs like this are thick on the ground. The area's covered with ancient shrines and altars. Har Karkom may well be your Mt Sinai. Where's your map?' Ben handed Ethan his journal. 'See here?' The older man pointed at the twin summits depicted in the Topkapı manuscript. 'Har Karkom has two peaks and the summits are surrounded by *gal`ed*s – tumuli of stones erected as dedicatory monuments over altars or sacred stones. Some of them are twenty feet high. Stones have always been focal points of worship for Semitic people. Long before it became sacred to the Muslim faith, the Nabateans made annual pilgrimages from Petra to worship the black stone that's now embedded in the Kaaba at Mecca.'

'So that –' Ben pointed a finger shaking with excitement at the curious mound shown in his drawing. '– That could well be a *gal`ed*! What better place could Balinas have chosen than somewhere hidden deep in the desert that had been a centre for worship in ancient times, not to mention the spot God reputedly handed down the Ten Commandments to Moses? Would that make sense to you?'

Ethan nodded, looking at Ben thoughtfully. 'Your only problem? It depends on when the clues you're following were written.'

'Well, the book the map came from was eighth century, so the map itself can't be any older than that. But it could also have been written in later than that.'

'Of course. A Muslim text . . . so it post-dates Muhammad's appearance in the sixth century. Well, in that case, it mightn't be so easy.'

'Why? Seems pretty straightforward to me.'

'If the clues belong to an older tradition and somebody's just transcribed them into the book at a later time, you might be all right. Har Karkom was such an important cult centre for the worship of the god Sin that it would make sense for that to be the place referred to in your clues if they have a very ancient origin. However, if they were drawing from seventh-century knowledge, well then – that was when

Jebel Musa began to be popularly identified as Mt Sinai. And that didn't start until the Byzantine Emperor, Justinian, ordered the construction of the Monastery of St Catherine on the spot where Constantine's mother Helena decided she'd found Moses' burning bush. But there's also a third possible candidate. If the alchemists who constructed the trail you're following lived in the fourth or fifth centuries AD, the Mt Sinai they would have known would have been the place now called Mt Serbal, which is also in the Sinai Peninsula . . . right there.' He jabbed at a point well to the north of the Mt Sinai marked on the map.

'Dammit.' Ben's heart sank. 'And Mt Serbal is also pretty close to the Ancient Egyptian mines at Serabit el-Khadim. Which would make it a plausible alternative.'

'Do you have any way of knowing when this trail of clues to Balinas' tomb was originally devised?'

Ben thought of Sebile. She might know, but he had no way of contacting her. Without her help, he could only guess. He shook his head. 'No. Unfortunately not.'

The two men were silent for a moment.

'So, there are three possibilities, then.' Ben tapped his finger on the desk. 'But I can't overlook the reference to the island of Jezirat Faurun and the north star,' he said. 'Mt Serbal might be further north than Jebel Musa, but it's still a long way from being north of the island. The only one of the three that could be described as north of the Gulf of Aqaba is Har Karkom. Don't you think?' He said it with more certainty than he felt.

Ethan nodded. 'Yes. I think you're probably right. What do you have to lose, anyway? With all the troubles there, there's no way you'll be able to get into the Sinai Peninsula. The Negev will be difficult enough. And the petroglyphs . . .' He picked up the stone. 'They're also pretty difficult to ignore.'

He looked at Ben intently. 'One thing I don't really understand; why are you doing this? You were always so scornful of my research.'

'At the start, it was just about stirring up some trouble. But the more I look into it, the bigger it gets. There've been people killed. And now I know the Russians and Americans are trying to get the tablet as well.'

'Wouldn't surprise me. After Germany collapsed, they would've had access to the research from Dachau. But why would you care? This isn't your fight.'

Ben thought for a moment. 'Maybe not. But even if only some of the things I've learnt about the Emerald Tablet and its powers are true, there are some hands I'd rather not see it fall into. And if what you're saying is right, we might be the only ones who know that there's a Mt Sinai other than the one everybody knows in the peninsula.' *Will you have worked that one out, Essie? You're good ... but are you that good?* he wondered.

'Well, if you're determined to go into the Negev, you'll need an escort. With the military build-up in the Sinai, you can't go wandering around on your own. It'll attract the attention of all the wrong people. Let me see if I can arrange you some transport.'

'You'd do that for me?'

'All self-interest, I can assure you. I'm too old to go in there myself, and if the tablet *is* entombed at Har Karkom, I'd rather be involved in its discovery than have someone else get there first. Go back to your hotel. I'll call you there.'

26

Jerusalem

Ricard Schubert watched the American leave. A soft, mauve twilight had fallen over the city and the Terra Sancta Building had been deserted by the students and teachers. One light still burned in the building's façade, and Schubert knew whose office it was.

He'd been told everything he needed to know about the man he was following. Whatever his other failings, Schubert had a memory that stored away details as efficiently as a library card system. A call he'd made from a payphone to the university when he realised that was where Hitchens was headed confirmed it was the workplace of the man the American had worked with in Crete: Professor Ethan Cohn. But what Hitchens hoped to learn from him was unclear.

Once the American was safely out of sight, Schubert slipped from behind the barricade he'd been using as a vantage point and strode towards the university's front door.

He had no idea what it was that Hitchens had discussed with the old man. But whatever it was, Schubert had every intention of finding out.

The evening was warm and fragrant as Ben strode back towards the King David Hotel. It would have been bucolic if not for the sporadic crack of gunfire and wail of sirens echoing along the city's streets.

The hotel's floodlit façade loomed ahead and Ben was relishing the prospect of a celebratory Scotch when he stopped in the middle of the street and cursed aloud. He'd left behind the map and petroglyph Ethan had given him.

Although he had no reason to doubt Ethan, Ben knew that if the promised military escort to take them to Har Karkom didn't materialise, with Ilhan's assistance he was sure they'd be able to find themselves another vehicle. But he'd spent enough time in deserts over the years to have a healthy respect for what he knew were confusing and disorienting regions. To wander into the Negev without a map would be suicide. And given that Jerusalem was a city on a war footing, Ben doubted he'd be able to just pick up a topographic map at a corner store with the level of detail of the one Ethan had handed him.

Cursing his oversight, Ben turned back towards the Terra Sancta Building.

He was halfway down the hallway when he heard the scream.

Ben's breath caught in his throat. The sound had been muffled but it was unmistakable. It was the cry of someone in tremendous pain, and it had come from the only room in the hallway that was still illuminated – Ethan's office. Heart pounding, he took stock of the situation.

Need to find out what I'm up against here. His only advantage was that whoever was in the room with Ethan wouldn't know he was there. Because there was minimal light in the hallway, he could approach the doorway without detection. But he was unarmed, and once he opened the door, he'd be exposed.

Dropping to a crouch so his head was below the level of the frosted glass panel set in the door, Ben scuttled towards the entrance to Ethan's room. Silently rising to his feet, he sidled up beside the doorjamb and peeked into the room. He caught sight of an imposing silhouette against the backdrop of a blind now shut to shield the sight of whatever was going on in the room from passers-by in the street below.

Light streamed into the corridor through a wide gap beneath the door; Ben lowered himself down and rested his cheek on the stony-cold floor, peering through the opening. What he saw inside made his blood freeze.

Ethan had been bound in one of the chairs, his arms and legs strapped down, with another bond holding him so tightly against the chair's back that the old man was struggling to breathe. A cloth gag was tied tightly around his mouth, digging into his cheeks and distorting the skin on his face. His eyes were stark white against the pupils of eyes dilated black with terror.

A heavy-set man paced in front of Ethan, sleeves rolled above his elbows, holding a murderously sharp stiletto blade between blunt fingers. His jacket had been removed and hung on the back of the other chair, exposing a holster containing what looked to Ben like a Luger pistol.

Great. Unarmed hand-to-hand combat against a man with a knife was bad enough. But those odds worsened exponentially when the other combatant had a gun as well.

The knife had already made a mark; a gash in Ethan's left cheek ran with blood that dripped onto the front of his white shirt. As the man paced back and forth in front of Ethan like a caged lion, Ben could hear him speaking, but in tones so quiet and conversational it was impossible to hear what was being said. And it didn't matter. Whatever his reasons for punishing Ethan, Ben had to stop it.

Without anything to fight with, he had limited options. A sense of desperation took hold as he tried to figure out the best way to intervene without getting both himself and Ethan killed. Then, he remembered: *Ethan's collection of weapons.* He shut his eyes and visualised the room. *They're just inside . . . on the left.* Ben glanced at the door. It opened to the right. *If I'm fast enough, I can get in, grab something off the wall, then roll down behind the piles of boxes Ethan's crammed into his room.*

Now . . . just have to pick my moment . . . Ben dug his fingernails into his palms, controlling his breathing and focusing his mind on what he was about to do as he watched and waited. Inside the room, the man stopped his pacing and leant forward, shoving his face within inches of Ethan's own. For the first time, he raised his voice. 'Where's he going?' he asked, tearing the gag out of the old man's mouth.

Ethan sputtered and coughed, spitting out droplets of blood that freckled his chin. 'You think I'm afraid? I'm not telling you anything.'

The other man just shook his head. 'You're all so damned predictable. That's what everyone says . . . at first.' He yanked the gag back into place.

Ben readied himself as the man leant forward and ran the blade of his knife across Ethan's other cheek. He clenched his teeth as he heard the old man's muffled scream while rivulets of bright blood ran down the cloth and soaked it scarlet.

Taking advantage of the assailant's temporary distraction, Ben pushed the handle down and shoved the door with his shoulder, dropping as he entered the room and grabbing at the weapons hanging from the wall. Startled, the other man spun on his heel as Ben got his hands on a spear and rolled down beneath the fortress of cardboard boxes that filled much of Ethan's study. He scurried along the makeshift corridor. *A spear?* Ben cursed himself. *Really?! You had to choose the most impractical weapon there, didn't you?*

'Dr Hitchens?' The other man's voice rang out. 'Is that you?'

Ben was shocked that the man knew his name. But he didn't respond as he focused on his next move. A pathway led round the edge of the room, protected from the intruder by the wall of boxes. If he could make it to the windows, it'd be close to where Ethan was confined.

'Not going to speak with me, then? Fine.' Ben heard the sound of the safety catch on the man's pistol. 'This should slow you down a bit.'

He quietened his breathing and lay as still as he could. A round blasted from the gun, the bullet shattering the cabinet above Ben's head, showering him in broken glass and the fist-sized chunks of obsidian that had been housed in the cabinet. Without thinking, he grabbed one of the sharp-edged lumps of black volcanic glass and slipped it into his pocket. As the man squeezed off another shot, Ben was fairly sure that the thunderous sound would hide the noise, so he grabbed the lid off a file box and used it to sweep aside the largest pieces of glass from the carpet in front of him. Glittering shards embedded in the carpet were an unavoidable hazard – but if he wanted to move forward, he'd have to do so on his hands and knees or risk showing his head above his cardboard battlements.

Another bullet whizzed through the air, smashing into a cabinet further back towards the door. *Good – he doesn't know I've made it this far into the room*, Ben thought. Using the cardboard to protect his hands, he scuttled towards the windows with the Roman spear held under one arm. Sharp pieces of glass pierced the knees of his pants and embedded themselves painfully into his flesh. Ben's reflexes caused him to start as more shots rang out, thudding into the boxes that were his temporary refuge as the man peppered the room with bullets.

Ben leant back against a box and looked in the glass cabinet in front of him for the other man's reflection. He could see him moving cautiously towards the door. As the man did so, Ben turned the corner and crawled to a point where he could see Ethan. The old man caught sight of him and his eyes widened. Ben held his finger to his mouth, urging him to be still. He hazarded a glimpse between two boxes and saw his assailant with his back to him.

Now or never. He stood and flung the Roman javelin at the same instant the other man caught sight of the movement in the corner of his eye and spun around, pulling the trigger of his raised pistol.

Ben dropped to the floor as the bullet whizzed by his head, embedding itself in the wall. He heard the sickening thud of his spear hitting its mark and a sudden expulsion of air and a grunt as Ethan's attacker was struck. A fecal stench filled the room.

Cautiously edging around the row of boxes, Ben looked for the other man. The instant he saw him, Ben knew he no longer posed a threat. The five-inch iron blade of the short javelin had pierced his abdomen and pinned him to the door. Poisonous dark ooze was seeping through the man's shirt where the wooden shaft protruded from the soft flesh of his belly. The pistol had fallen from his grip. The man fumbled and tugged at the javelin with hands now sticky with the gore pulsing from his gut with every beat of his heart.

Ben pushed his way through the mess of boxes and confronted him. 'Who the hell are you?'

The man's face was doughy and white as he struggled to overcome the pain. 'Schubert. Ricard Schubert.'

'What are you doing here? Why are you doing this?'

'Not going to tell you that. Already did you one favour . . . in Cairo . . .'

Ben thought for a moment. 'The Americans?'

'Yes. But that's it. Nothing more,' Schubert wheezed. 'It's usually me standing where you are. Always wondered how I'd go if the situation was reversed . . . I suppose I'm about to find out. Sure my name means nothing to you? Schubert.'

'Why the hell would I know you?'

'Crete. I thought you might remember me from Crete.' He winced.

Schubert . . . a German . . . that'd be right. 'You're a Nazi? Is that what you're doing here?'

Schubert looked confused for a moment. 'Here – in Israel? To hunt down Jews?' He let out a weak laugh. 'Hell, no. Sure – some of my former colleagues loved that. But not me. I like what the Zionists are doing to the filthy Arabs. No . . . I'm here for you. Been following you . . . since Topkapı –'

'Topkapı? It was you. Why did you have to kill Fatih?'

'Didn't have to. Wanted to. Needed to know for sure what you'd been looking at. Suppose I could have found out without killing the stupid old fool . . . but where's the fun in that?' He sputtered. 'Strange coincidence . . . that I should be sent to follow you. Given the way our paths crossed in the past.'

Crossed paths? What the hell's he talking about? 'Who sent you? If you help me, I'll get you to a hospital.'

'Won't work. Haven't got long. Smell that shit in the air? Gut shot. But before I go . . . you *really* don't remember me? Shame. See, this is just a job. But Greeks and Turks – all Arabs. Dogs, every one. And killing them? That's fun. Like your wife . . .'

Ben froze. 'What the fuck are you talking about?'

'Your wife.' Schubert's face was grey with pain, but his thin lips opened in a lascivious smile. 'Karina? . . . Now, she never betrayed anyone. Not even you. Unusual. Couldn't help admiring that. And pretty, wasn't she? But stubborn . . . Even while my men fucked her . . . she screamed out your name. Shame. Had to kill her in the end. No use to us –'

White rage began to cloud Ben's mind. 'Shut. Up!'

'She fought, though.'

'I said – *shut the fuck up*!' Without thinking, Ben found the sharp-edged lump of glittering volcanic glass in his hand.

'But she did moan . . . in pain, mostly. But you never know with those Greek whores . . . maybe a bit of pleasure, too . . .'

Ben's mind went blank. As if from a great height, he saw his hand lift the obsidian and bring it smashing down onto Schubert's head, again and again. The German's eyes rolled back in their sockets as Ben beat the life out of him, the white bone of his skull gleaming through the sheets of blood pouring from the gashes on his head and cascading down his face. Ben didn't stop until Schubert's limbs had stopped twitching and his lifeless body had slumped into an unnatural position, held upright only by the javelin that pinned him to the door like a tangled marionette.

Hands sticky with blood, Ben stumbled over to where Ethan sat, the old man's eyes wide with shock. Once he was released from his bonds, Ethan collapsed back into the chair. Ben took a cloth from the desk and handed it to him to mop his wounds.

'Thank you, Ben.'

'But . . .' Ben gestured to the gruesome scene behind him. 'But, this . . . how will we explain this?'

'It'll be fixed. Don't worry about it. Go now – wash yourself in the bathroom down the hall. And return to your hotel. I'll call some people who can deal with this.'

Ben nodded. 'Thank you, Ethan.'

'There's one other thing you should know – I didn't tell you before because . . . well, just because. But before you came I had a call. From an American. Asking about you and why you were here. Of course I didn't tell him anything – not that I had anything to tell them then, anyway.'

Ben was confused. 'How did they know I was here?'

'I've no idea. But they do keep an eye on all the big hotels.'

Ben cursed himself for his stupidity. 'Of course they do. I'm an idiot – I should have known. I'll change hotels.'

'No point,' Ethan said. 'They know you're here now, and will find you no matter where you go in the city.'

Ben knew he had a point. 'But if they contact you again, Ethan – please. You mustn't –'

Ethan raised his hand in protest. 'Don't say another word, Benedict. I won't be telling them anything. America's no friend of Israel. Besides . . . well, I owe you my life. You'll always have a friend here.'

'I thought I already did.'

'You know what I mean. Now tomorrow, there'll be someone at your hotel who can take you into the Negev. If I was in any doubt before about how important this is, I'm not now. You have to find the tablet before anyone else. And I'll do whatever I can to help you. Now, go.'

THE TIMES
31 October 1956
UNITED NATIONS VETO AS BRITAIN AND FRANCE ISSUE ULTIMATUM

LONDON, Wednesday (Reuters)

In a shock development, France and Britain have vetoed a resolution calling for Israel to remove her troops from the Sinai.

News today of an airdrop of Israeli paratroopers near the Mitla Pass in the Sinai Peninsula was greeted with widespread international condemnation.

The Egyptian President, Colonel Nasser, declared it an act of war as allies in surrounding Moslem nations rallied to Egypt's defence.

Nasser also announced that an assault by four Israeli P-51 Mustang aeroplanes cut all telephone lines in the Sinai, causing severe disruption to Egyptian military command in the region.

Support for Nasser and the people of Egypt came in the form of a resolution proposed by the United States calling for Israel to remove her troops from Egyptian soil. The resolution was vetoed by both France and Britain, and then vetoed a second time after the same proposal had been re-submitted by Russia.

France and Britain have been vocal in their opposition to Egypt's seizure of the Suez Canal, and continue to voice their concern for the potential disruption of passage through the waterway, which both nations use as a crucial lifeline to their colonial possessions in the Indian and Pacific Oceans. France and Britain have sent ultimatums to Egypt and Israel warning that a failure to withdraw troops from the Canal Zone within twelve hours will result in a direct military response.

27

Jerusalem

Morning sunlight streamed into the foyer of the King David Hotel, setting aflame the gilded architectural fittings and reflecting off the blindingly polished Art Deco chandeliers suspended from the ornate ceiling.

Ben rested his head against the back of the chair and shut his eyes.

The events of the previous evening had shattered him. In the bathroom at the Hebrew University he'd rinsed away what he could of the gore covering his hands and spattered on his clothes, then jogged back to the hotel along darkened streets with nerves on edge in the expectation that he might be stopped by a patrol at any moment.

The impassive doorman barely glanced at Ben's dishevelled clothes and only acknowledged the drying spots of blood on his jacket cuffs with a slight twitch of his eyebrows, before dipping his head and opening the entrance to admit him to the hotel. Ilhan's greeting had been less temperate. Stretched

226

out on one of the twin beds in the room they were sharing, he had leapt to his feet as soon as he caught sight of Ben's face. Like a clucking grandmother, the Turk had checked Ben over for injuries and demanded a full account of his evening's activities.

'So,' Ben had concluded. 'It seems the next stop's the Negev Desert.'

Ilhan had shaken his head. 'This is going too far, Ben. You're risking your life and you don't even really know why. Let's go home.'

'No. Not now. But you should.'

'I should what?'

'Go home. You're right – it's too dangerous. And I don't want anything to happen to you. I've dragged you halfway across the Middle East. You've got nothing out of it –'

'I wouldn't say that,' interjected Ilhan. 'I was busy today. It's as I've always said: there's nowhere more profitable for a person in my line of work than a place at war. I've lined up a couple of new contacts, and arranged a shipment of local . . . ah, *souvenirs* . . . to be sent back to Istanbul. Mementoes from the Holy Land – the tourists in the bazaar won't be able to get enough of them. And I did very well out of our trip to Egypt.'

'Well, then I suggest you take your ill-gotten gains and find your way back north, my friend. There's nothing but trouble where I'm headed,' Ben had insisted.

Gazing out the window at Jerusalem's floodlit battlements, Ilhan had been pensive and silent. After a moment he spoke – so quietly Ben had to strain to hear him. 'I don't think you know how much I cherish our friendship, Benedict Hitchens. I admire your pragmatism and enjoy your company. If you're going to be in danger, then another pair of hands would surely be a help. I'm not going to leave you.'

Ben knew better than to try to discourage his friend, who was at least as stubborn as he himself could be – which was no small achievement.

Sleep hadn't come easily to Benedict Hitchens that night. The man he'd killed had torn open festering wounds from his past that Ben was now certain would never heal. He'd spent years trying to quash the hurt that made his heart constrict any time he thought of Karina. He had once hoped that to punish those who'd murdered her might help him forgive himself for not saving her. But the dried black blood under his nails from the smashed skull of one of her killers only made him feel hollow, where once he'd thought it might have cured him.

As he'd struggled to doze off, he'd listened to the sounds of the troubled city outside until the warm glow of the rising sun shone through the room's gauzy curtains. His mind was in turmoil; thoughts of Crete and of Karina tangled with vivid waking dreams of Schubert's dying eyes. Who'd sent the German after him was a more immediate concern; he was now certain he was being watched. And he didn't like it.

When light had filled the room, he'd resigned himself to the sleepless night that was and risen and showered, preparing himself for the journey ahead.

Bellhops and hotel staff scurried around the foyer as Ben sat with his feet propped on his duffel bag, waiting for the arrival of the Israeli escort promised by Ethan Cohn. He could see Ilhan's back in the telephone booth next to the reception desk as the Turk called the dealers he'd made contact with in Jerusalem. The soporific buzz of activity soothed Ben and he felt the approach of the sleep that had evaded him the night before.

In his imagination, the bleak but beautiful and pristine desert horizon stretched out before him into the white heat haze beyond. A warm surge of adrenalin rushed through his veins. He was on the hunt again. It was the one thing he knew he did well. It was also the only thing in his life that still gave him hope.

'Dr Hitchens?'

Ben started awake. 'Yes?'

Standing before him was a tall and lean figure clad in the light khaki uniform of the Israeli Defence Force. The man extended an arm taut with well-toned, ropey muscles and beamed down at Ben, his white teeth flashing against dark olive skin. 'Ari Fleishman, Dr Hitchens.'

Still disorientated, Ben staggered to his feet as the Jewish soldier seized his hand and pulled him into a bear hug. Ari kissed Ben twice on each cheek and slapped his shoulders affectionately.

'I'm sorry . . . you look surprised. It's perhaps too much for our first encounter,' the soldier said with a smile as he stepped back and gave Ben space to recover from the effusive greeting. 'Ethan Cohn – he's my uncle. I know what you did for him. And our family owes you a debt of gratitude. One I hope I can repay – in part, anyway.'

'Well, I owe your uncle a great deal as well,' Ben replied. 'Without him, I'd likely have no career.' Despite their falling out in the intervening years, it wasn't an exaggeration – as a mentor and teacher, Ethan had once been Ben's fiercest advocate.

From the corner of his eye, Ben saw Ilhan approaching. 'Ari . . .' With an outstretched arm, he indicated his friend. 'This is Ilhan Aslan. He'll be travelling with us. Ilhan, this is Ari Fleishman. His uncle is Ethan Cohn – the man I was telling you about last night.'

Ilhan's eyebrows shot up. 'Ah – I see. How is your uncle?' he asked.

'He's old. So he's sore, and a bit shocked. But he's also tough. A bowl or two of Esther's chicken soup and he'll be as good as new.' Ari laughed. He indicated the two duffel bags on the floor. 'That's all you're travelling with?' Ben nodded. 'Good. There's a bit of stuff in the back of the jeep. I've got the theodolite and tripod Ethan said you needed. And we can't go into the desert unprepared. Not a good idea to drive into a war zone without any weapons and a radio.'

'Weapons?' Ilhan looked startled. 'Is that really necessary?'

'We've been living here like we're at war for years. Even when we're supposedly at peace, I wouldn't go out there without a gun. Now? Not on your life. If you want to get there and back in one piece, we need to be able to protect ourselves.' Ari bent and picked up the two men's bags, hoisting them onto his shoulder as if they were filled with nothing more substantial than air. 'OK – if you're both ready, we should get going.'

The three men began to cross the foyer towards the front door.

'Mr Hitchens!'

A voice and the clack of hurried steps on the marble behind them made Ben spin around. Approaching them with hands clasped at his chest was the concierge they'd met when they'd arrived the day before.

'Mr Hitchens – before you leave, might I have a word with you?'

'Certainly.' *As long as it's got nothing to do with last night.*

The concierge dropped his voice. 'I thought it wise to let you know. The manager just informed me that some men were here last night asking about you.'

'Men?' *Christ – Ethan was right.* 'Who were they?'

230

'They didn't want to leave any details. But we have many important guests from around the world. Agents from the nations who have an interest in what's going on in Israel watch this hotel. And there's plenty of those. Daniel – the manager – thought they may have been Soviets.'

Ben looked around the foyer cautiously. It was still early and only a handful of people were around, most of them hotel staff. Those who appeared to be civilians were too elderly and too convincingly outfitted as Holy Land tourists to be Russian agents.

The concierge continued. 'I took the liberty of checking the front of the hotel. There are two men waiting out there in a car. Daniel recognised one of them from last night.'

'Show me.'

Through a window shielded from the street by a fan-leafed palm, Ben saw two men sitting in the front seat of a boxy grey sedan. The man in the driver's seat was hard to miss; atop his head was a fuzz of golden yellow curls. 'Is that the one?' he asked.

'Yes,' the concierge replied.

'Russians?' Ilhan piped up from behind Ben. 'They've followed us here from Cairo? Why?'

'Presume they're after the same thing everyone else is looking for,' answered Ben, cautious not to reveal too much.

'Excuse me,' interrupted Ari. 'You said you have many important guests staying at this hotel. They don't always want to be seen going to and from the building. Is that correct?'

The concierge smiled. 'Yes. Of course.'

'So you have a more inconspicuous entrance?'

'Yes. At the rear of the hotel. It leads through a tunnel beneath the garden and comes out at a gate on Paul-Émile Botta Street.'

The Israeli turned to Ben and Ilhan. 'You two leave the hotel that way. I'll pick you up from there. The gentlemen out the front won't know me, so I should be able to leave without attracting any attention. I hope.'

Ben's heart was pounding as he and Ilhan jogged along the narrow but sumptuously outfitted underground corridor leading away from the hotel.

'Makes sense,' Ilhan observed as he took in the crystal sconce lights illuminating the hallway. 'They're hardly going to shuttle visiting dignitaries' mistresses through an ordinary bunker, are they?'

A heavily barred gate blocked the way to the bright daylight outside, visible through an arched stone entranceway onto the street. 'That's it.' Ben grasped one of the uprights. The concierge had assured him the gate would open from the inside and lock automatically behind them. He held his breath and yanked. To his relief, it swung smoothly open and the two men were free to pass through to the city beyond.

'Steady, steady,' Ben cautioned Ilhan, forcing him to stay behind him as he checked the street from the archway. Ari had parked his jeep on the opposite kerb and stood beside the car's rear door. As far as Ben could see, there were no other people on the street.

'Quick! Run!' he commanded, bolting across the road. Ilhan's footsteps pounded after him as the two men ran for the jeep, jumping into the back seat.

'Inside! And stay down!' Ari said as he slammed the door shut behind them.

Ben and Ilhan crouched down below the level of the side windows as Ari started the engine. 'Got no choice. There are roadblocks up ahead – we'll have to drive back past the front of the hotel. So keep out of sight.'

He accelerated rapidly and rounded the corner. 'Just have to hope they've forgotten I was here,' he said. 'If they see me again, they may be smart enough to figure out what's happened.' As Ari approached the hotel he slowed to a sedate pace. 'Don't need to be drawing any unnecessary attention to myself. There they are!' he exclaimed.

'Think they see you?' Ben asked.

'I'm sure they will. Question is whether or not they think anything of it.' Ari assumed the guise of an Israeli soldier just out for a casual drive around town, his sleeves rolled up and elbow resting on the jeep's open window. 'Well, they're certainly having a good look at me,' he said under his breath as they drove past the grey sedan. 'Not much I can do about that. But the question is whether they'll decide I deserve a bit more attention.'

He picked up speed, peering in the rear-view mirror. 'Doesn't look like they're moving. Wait!' He paused. 'They're getting out of the car . . . crossing over to the hotel. Hold on . . . I'm going to head into the back streets. No good taking the main roads out of the city. If they find out you're gone, they'll be quick on our trail.'

'I think I greased the concierge's palm enough to buy me some discretion,' Ben said.

Ari laughed. 'You think so? Well, problem is, you're gone now. And that's the thing with anyone whose loyalty can be bought. There'll always be a higher bidder. Let's just hope we're long gone before the Russians find your friend's price.'

28

Mediterranean Ocean

Beneath Essie's feet, the metal deck of HMS *Theseus* bucked and rolled in the swell as the deafening roar of rotors turning assailed her senses. On the edge of the deck, the helicopter readied to take flight and the atmosphere seemed to pulsate as the machine's massive metal blades chopped through the air. Essie struggled to hear Captain Matthew Knight as he spoke. The officer handed her a pistol in a belt holster, his grim expression confirming his disapproval.

'Now, Mrs Peters, I've made my feelings clear.' Knight pursed his lips. 'I'm uncomfortable with you as a civilian – and a woman – having a weapon. There's a place for a lady, and the battlefield isn't it. But the powers that be –' he gestured over his shoulder to where Josef Garvé stood, stiff-backed and unmoving, '– insisted. Though heaven knows when we started taking orders from the Frogs,' he mumbled beneath his breath.

'Monsieur Garvé's just concerned for my wellbeing.'

'And the road to hell is paved with good intentions . . . Try to defend yourself with that, and you'll just as soon shoot yourself in the foot as anything else. So don't say I didn't warn you if anything goes wrong.'

'I can assure you, I know how to handle it,' Essie said.

'Anyway,' he said dubiously, 'it's a Colt M1911 . . . small enough to slip into your purse.'

'I'm not carrying a purse.' She unbuckled her belt and slipped the holster onto the webbing strap.

'Well, it won't weigh you down.' He considered her, sceptically. Whatever qualified as Captain Knight's ideal British woman, Mrs Essie Peters, in her military-issue khaki pants, shirt and heavy brown leather boots, her blonde hair scraped back and tucked beneath a cap, wasn't it. And she couldn't have cared less.

He glanced at his watch. 'Well, come on, then. Time to get out of here.'

Essie had been on board more aeroplanes than she could count. But the sensation of lifting vertically into the air from the deck of the *Theseus* in the Whirlwind helicopter was unlike anything she'd ever experienced. Her stomach dropped sickeningly as they pulled away from the aircraft carrier, its hull a metal precipice plunging into churning waters below. As the chopper banked out over the ocean, a rush of adrenalin made her heart pound and with bloodless fingers she gripped the edge of the metal bench seat.

Through the small window set in the chopper's fuselage she could see the Mediterranean's aquamarine and white-capped peaky waves rising and falling. In the far distance, they approached a thin, dull-brown line hazy beneath a fog of dust and heat. The Sinai Peninsula.

Knight's voice crackled through her headphones. 'We'll be over land soon. Need to keep our wits about us. The main helicopter assault isn't scheduled for a bit, so we're on our own. And that'll make us a target for the Egyptian Army. I'll likely have to make some defensive manoeuvres. So make sure you're buckled up.'

Essie hooked the webbing harness over her shoulders and clamped it round her waist. On the opposite side of the cabin, Garvé impassively checked his own belt. Not for the first time in their long association, Essie marvelled at the Frenchman's composure. One thing she couldn't understand was why he felt it necessary to accompany her on what was a dangerous mission when he could just as easily have stationed himself on the deck of his luxurious yacht anchored off Akrotiri, nursing a G&T and awaiting her return with the prize in hand. Most of all, she was mystified by the fact that he was travelling alone rather than with the bodyguards who seemed to accompany him everywhere. When she'd broached the subject with him, Garvé had cut her off abruptly, claiming that they could ill afford to include anyone else in the small circle of people who knew what they were doing and that without him, she'd be as good as on her own because he didn't trust Penney to be much help if things didn't go as planned.

Glancing at the third member of their party seated opposite Garvé, Essie shared the Frenchman's concern about Penney's likely lack of grace under fire. The Englishman sat rigidly on the metal bench with his eyes clamped shut, back pressed against the helicopter's fuselage while he clutched the nylon webbing lining the aircraft's interior. She now knew him to be a treacherous coward whose bluster evaporated like morning mist the instant he found himself anywhere other than a realm in which he could exercise the power and privilege he was born to but had done little to earn himself. Never in her life had she met anyone more likely to crumple under pressure.

'Right . . .' Knight's voice crackled to life again. 'Coastline approaching. Lean forward . . . away from the sides.'

Penney's eyes shot open. 'The sides? Why?'

'I'll be doing what I can to avoid shooters. But if they get a bead on us . . . the metal fuselage'll only help us so much.'

Penney stiffened, his face as white as a sheet. 'Great. Just great.'

'Still glad you signed on to continue your master's work, Adam?' Essie couldn't help herself. Adam said nothing but flashed her a look that somehow managed to combine abject terror and scorn. It was quite an achievement.

'Christ!' Knight exclaimed through the headphones. 'Anti-aircraft batteries . . . we're going to have to go in low . . . hold on!'

Essie braced herself as she heard the dull *whumpf* of the artillery on the ground firing at them. She felt the helicopter bank sharply and plummet down, its overtaxed engines screaming.

'Bloody hell! Shooters on the roof!' Knight cursed. He dragged the aircraft to the right and Essie felt the webbing of her harness constrict painfully across her chest as she was thrown forward. A sound like hail on a tin roof filled the cabin and a starburst of holes opened up in the floor as the helicopter was peppered with bullets.

'Shit!' Adam pulled his knees up to his chest. The pop of gunfire was suddenly interspersed with the sporadic metallic clangs of something hitting the fuselage. 'What the fuck's that?' he exclaimed.

'Grenades . . . hostiles on the roof of their houses – they're throwing grenades.'

'*Grenades!?*' yelled Penney.

'Don't worry, Adam,' said Garvé calmly. 'They don't stick. You've nothing to worry about with grenades unless those throwing them have impeccable timing, which few people do.'

'But the bullets?' Essie was feeling cruel. 'Well – if one of those hits the fuel tank, that'll be the end of us.'

Penney looked ill.

'Apologies, all,' said Knight. 'Out of choices – any higher and I'll put us in range of the anti-aircraft guns. But we'll be clear of Port Said in a minute.'

As quickly as it started, the clamour from outside dissipated and then stopped altogether. The helicopter levelled out and resumed a steady pace.

'Are we clear?' Essie asked.

'Should be,' Knight said. 'They know we're here now, but with what they've got descending on them soon, I doubt they'll worry too much about pursuing a single aircraft into the desert. And the Israelis have knocked out their communications. So even if there's a unit or two out here – and I'm certain there is – Egyptian command in Suez won't have any way of letting them know we're on the way. Should be fine from here on.'

Essie unbuckled her harness and moved to look out the window. In the distance, the glittering waters of the Suez Canal were a shimmering thread embroidered across the desert's golden sands. Beyond that, the emerald-green edge of the Nile River's delta spread like a satin sheet over the horizon. Towards the north, great plumes of deathly black smoke billowed into the sky.

'What's going on over there?' she asked.

'Got word of that before we took off. Bloody Nasser's sunk all the ships in the canal. Blocked the way through. There'll be a hell of a mess to clean up once this is all over.'

Let's just hope it's all worth it, thought Essie.

29

Negev Desert, Israel

Ari's authority and rank as *sgan aluf* – lieutenant colonel – in the Israeli Defence Force meant the jeep had gone unchallenged as they passed through the many military checkpoints on the road heading directly west out of Jerusalem and through the little wedge of Israeli land chiselled out of the territory on the bank of the Jordan River that the kingdom of Jordan had named West Bank.

Ben kept his eyes on the road behind them as they cleared the city, but there was no sign of pursuit. At the checkpoints they passed, Ari gave a description of the men and vehicle they'd managed to avoid at the King David Hotel, issuing instructions that they be taken into custody if they appeared, but Ben suspected they'd successfully evaded the Russians.

It may have been symptomatic of the heightened level of political tension, but the number of military vehicles on the road far outnumbered the scant civilian traffic of mule carts and tractors hauling hay and produce, though Ben couldn't recall it ever being any different when he'd been in Israel, or Palestine as it was known when he'd first come here.

While Ilhan took the front passenger seat, Ben had laid claim to the bench seat behind Ari in the hope he might be able to catch up on some sleep. He'd rolled up his canvas jacket to use as a pillow, but the jarring suspension made it impossible to avoid slipping to the floor, much less find a stable and comfortable position in which he could slumber. The prospect of sleep wasn't helped by the canvas cover stretched tautly over a flimsy metal framework serving as the jeep's roof, which flapped incessantly in the wind as Ari tackled the rough roads at breakneck speed.

Ben had surrendered to the inevitable and sat up again. They'd turned south once they'd passed through the rows of tents and prefabricated shacks of the settlement of Beit Shemesh, one of the many new towns the Israelis were building to house the exodus of Jewish settlers arriving in the land they believed God had promised them.

The three men travelled largely in silence past stands of eucalyptus trees and orange groves, Ben marvelling at the ceaseless labour of the kibbutzniks bent double as they cleared rubble-strewn and barren soil. In their wake he saw the fruits of their labour – nodding fields of maize and golden wheat crisscrossed with irrigation channels of reclaimed water, all part of neatly arranged, picturesque settlements that Ben knew to be the socialist collectives housing the Jewish migrants determined to build a nation.

Ilhan had been gazing at the landscape when he turned towards Ari, jaw clenched. 'What happened to the others who were here?'

The Israeli cocked his head quizzically. 'The others?'

'The others who were living here – in Palestine – before you arrived . . . the Arabs.'

'Ah.' Ari nodded. 'I see. You – you're an Arab?'

'A Turk.'

'Brothers, then. Well – this land – this "Palestine" – you know it was named for the Philistines? But after the Romans left it, it became a nameless place that passed between many hands . . . the Abbāsids, the Fātimids . . . the Crusaders. Then your people – the Ottomans. Only when the British arrived was it once again named Palestine. And, always, we were here. Not all of us, but enough to keep the flame burning. Even before the war, we were one-third of the population. We owned a seventh of the land. Those kibbutzniks . . .' He gestured to the labourers in the field. 'They're here because Jews from around the world bought this land from Arab owners who didn't live here and cared little for this soil until they realised what we were doing. Then, they began to care, but it was too late. This is our home. And we'll never leave it.'

'So you force the Arabs to wander as you've wandered for thousands of years. You do realise that it wasn't just the Jews that God said would inherit this land – it was all the children of Abraham. Including Muslims. And Christians.'

'We didn't force anyone to leave.'

Ilhan looked away. Ben could see his friend's fury expressed in the white line of his clenched jaw. 'What about the attack on Deir Yassin? You think the Arab women raped there – the children torn to pieces and the unarmed old men whose throats were slit – that wasn't done to send a message to the people who remained here? Little wonder so many of them left.' He shook his head in disgust.

Taking the beret off his head, Ari tossed it into Ilhan's lap. 'See that? The badge?' He pointed at the IDF insignia. 'A sword and an olive branch. Yes, we will fight if attacked. Most of us, though . . . we only want to live in peace. What the fighters of Irgun and Lehi did at Deir Yassin in the name of Israel was an abomination. But terrible things happen in war.'

Ilhan was silent for a moment. 'That's no excuse.'

'No,' Ari responded. 'No, it's not.'

From the town of Be'er Sheva they travelled south into the Negev along tracks cleared of boulders but littered with coarse rubble that had tumbled down from the looming escarpments of the ancient craters known as *makhtesh*. These seemed to have been sliced out of the landscape but Ben knew they had been formed when the ocean that once covered the Negev had retreated into what became the Mediterranean. As the jeep roared along narrow gorges eroded into the *makhtesh*, he saw the spiral forms of enormous ammonite fossils protruding from the cliff walls.

With the map Ethan had given him spread out on his lap and a compass Ari had loaned him, Ben kept them heading in the right direction, towards the tiny village of Mitzpe Ramon, the only settlement in the vast and forbidding landscape perched on the northernmost ridge of the Ramon *makhtesh*. Just south of the town, the track wound between towering tangerine and rose-coloured cliffs and continued on its meandering way towards the Gulf of Aqaba.

After their tense exchange, Ilhan and Ari seemed to have reached a détente of sorts, Ilhan acting as spotter to help negotiate the perilous and eroded track that skirted intimidating drops to riverbeds that hadn't seen water in many years. When they found their path blocked by the fly-blown carcass of an ibex, Ilhan helped Ben hoist the dead animal off the road by its massive, arching horns. The gassy and sweet smell of death made the men gag.

'If I thought we could bear the smell, I'd take those back with me,' said Ilhan regretfully, patting the horns. 'Do you have any idea how much I could sell them for in Istanbul?'

'There's not enough money in the world to make it worth putting up with that stench,' Ben responded.

'I don't know . . .' said Ilhan.

'No!' shouted Ben and Ari in unison.

Ben had identified the place on the map where they needed to strike west towards Har Karkom. Ahead was a dry riverbed hemmed in by steep walls that, if the chart was to be believed, would lead them to their destination.

He tapped Ari on the shoulder. 'This is it.'

The Israeli pulled the jeep over to the side of the track and the three men climbed out to stand beneath the blazing sun.

Ben was overwhelmed by doubt. 'So, to get to Mt Sinai, how far from here?'

Ari looked at him quizzically. 'Mt Sinai? Jebel Musa, you mean?'

'Yes.'

'From here we'd have to go south to Aqaba, then across the top of the gulf country and south into the Sinai. It's a long way. And I only came with enough supplies to get us to Har Karkom. Fuel . . . food . . . water – we'd be in trouble. But we could turn back to Mitzpe Ramon and try to find what we need for a longer journey if that's what you want to do.'

'And Mt Serbal?'

'Mt *Serbal*? Why would you want to go there?'

'There's a slim chance it's the place we're looking for.'

'Well, that's even trickier. It's further north and closer to the military action we're anticipating. But I suppose we could try . . .'

Ben took stock. He thought it highly likely Essie and Garvé were in the Sinai already. If that were the case, even if he managed to make it there, whatever was hidden away in the mountains would be long gone.

His theory about an alternative Mt Sinai had seemed so plausible up till now. But standing as he was at a literal and metaphysical crossroads, it had the bleak taint of wishful thinking rather than fact.

'I thought you were certain we were heading for the right place,' interjected Ilhan.

'I was,' Ben replied. 'Now, I'm not so sure.'

'Wait!' Ari exclaimed, reaching back into the jeep and fumbling around beneath his seat, his eyes fixed on the sky. 'There's something up there.' He grabbed a pair of binoculars and got out of the car, looping the strap about his neck. 'See there?' He pointed into the air.

Ben looked up. He didn't see a thing. 'What? What's wrong?'

Moving to his side, Ari grabbed his shoulder and directed his gaze. 'There! Right there! You can't miss it!'

A winged shadow spun in spirals against the indigo-blue sky. 'That? Yes, I see it. Isn't it just a bird?'

Ari pressed his binoculars to his eyes and beamed. 'Not "just" a bird. A Golden Eagle. *Aquila chrysaetos*. Wingspan over seven feet. The Roman legion that lay siege to Masada – the Golden Eagle was its symbol. They hunt hares and pigeons out here – and their speed . . . well – nothing like it. Seventy-five miles an hour when they strike. Phenomenal!' He dropped the binoculars so they hung from their strap and put his hands on his hips. 'Never seen one in the wild. What a day!' Ari looked apologetically towards Ben. 'Sorry . . . but I'm pretty keen on birds . . .'

'No kidding.' Ben laughed. 'Maybe it's a lucky omen.'

'It certainly wasn't lucky for the martyrs at Masada.'

'Yep. You could say that. But I'm grabbing on to anything I can at the moment. And I really hope I'm not leading us all on a wild-goose chase.' He watched the soaring bird silhouetted against a sky so blue it hurt to look at it. 'Right. Let's go.'

'South to Aqaba, or west to Har Karkom?' Ari asked.

'All or nothing.' Ben drew a deep breath. 'West.'

The men looked out across the daunting, rubble-strewn expanse, the golden rock of the cliffs blinding in the midday sun.

The Israeli slapped his hands together. 'Let's go then.'

30

Sinai Peninsula, Egypt

If ever I was to find God, it would be in a place like this, thought Essie as the helicopter banked low between the naked and weathered peaks that punched through the desert floor like bunches of fingers raised heavenward.

On the journey south, they'd flown over Bedouin camps in the oases that dotted the desert floor, the cacophony of the helicopter's passing causing herds of goats to scatter between the trunks of feathery palm trees dotted like gems around pools of sweet water. The men tending the flocks bolted out from the shelter of their goat-hair tents, waving ancient rifles that posed more danger to the people shooting them than they did to the airborne weapon of war that swooped above their heads like a metal raptor. But other than the nomadic tribesmen, they'd seen no human activity since leaving the outer reaches of Port Said.

Captain Knight's voice crackled to life in the headphones. 'There it is . . . off to the left.'

For those who placed stock in the stories of the Old Testament, the barren mountain that loomed ahead of them was the one upon which God had passed down the Ten Commandments to Moses. The folds and undulations of its worn contours were sensuous and flesh-like; the summit might have been a beast slumbering on the desert floor – a camel's back, or a leopard's flank. Any lingering vestiges of her religious upbringing had been extinguished years before, yet there was something about the mountain's quiet grandeur that moved Essie deeply.

'We'll set down to the north. I'll get you as close as I can to the monastery,' Knight said.

At the foot of Mt Sinai and its twin peak, Mt Catherine, nestled the religious community dedicated to the Alexandrian martyr who'd refused to denounce her faith and was beheaded by the Romans after the wheel intended for use to break her body fell apart at her touch. Her body was then transferred by angels to the peak of Mt Catherine, where monks from the monastery found her remains, uncorrupted and emanating a fragrant oil. *Or so the story goes*, Essie thought.

Despite her scepticism, there was no denying the intensity of the faith that had inspired the men who'd built one of the most remarkable Christian edifices in the world here in the sixth century AD, on the site where they believed God had spoken to Moses through the unlikely agency of a bush in flames. The sheer-sided, fortress-like structure housing the Sacred Monastery of the God-Trodden Mt Sinai hugged the foothills of the mountain that soared almost one and a half miles into the sky. Although she knew the defensive walls enclosing the main monastery buildings were over sixty feet high, from Essie's elevated perspective the mountain's imperious stature rendered them as insubstantial as a castle made of children's blocks.

The sight of their destination set Essie's heart pounding. *Not long now. Now we find out whether or not you know what you're doing.*

The stone walls, hewn one and a half thousand years ago from rocks that had once tumbled down the face of the mountain, towered over Essie's head as she stood at the unadorned arched entranceway to the monastery. Hanging back so the presence of a woman wouldn't upset the monks within, she watched as Josef Garvé lifted his hand and pounded at the heavy oak door set at the end of a corridor through walls that must have been at least ten feet thick.

She heard the shuffle of sandals on a stone-floored courtyard within. Bolts were unlatched and bars slid back, then the door creaked open, revealing a round-faced monk with a black beard speckled with grey which cascaded over his black cassock.

'Ευλογειτε,' he said in Greek, brow crinkled with curiosity at the new arrivals.

'Την ευχή σας,' responded Garvé, reverting fluently to the language he'd learnt on Crete during the war.

'Του κυρίου,' the monk replied. 'What brings you here?'

'We're here to warn you,' the Frenchman said. 'War is coming.'

The monk looked startled. 'War? Out here? Are you certain?'

'Yes. This man here,' Garvé said, indicating Penney who was fidgeting at his side, frustrated by the linguistic barrier that excluded him from the conversation. 'He's from the British Government. We've been sent to make sure you're safe.'

'And her?' The monk tilted his chin to indicate Essie standing in the shadows at the end of the corridor. She knew enough of Greek Orthodox traditions to understand that his reluctance to look at her wasn't borne of arrogance or animosity, but of a fervent wish to avoid temptation and preserve his modesty. The arrival of a strange woman in the cloistered confines of the monastery was an unsettling and disruptive event.

'She's Mr Penney's secretary. She's here to assist him with . . . administrative matters.'

The monk paused, gathering his thoughts. 'It's a matter for the abbot.' He stood back from the doorway. 'I'm Father Mathias. Please. Come with me.'

The searingly hot desert air burnt Essie's lungs as they passed through the tiny entranceway into the monastery where the community within the battlements functioned as a self-contained and self-sustaining village. She'd studied the layout of the monastery and knew it intimately. Beside the Italianate belltower of the basilica rose another tall, whitewashed structure, its summit capped with a dome and encircled by a narrow walkway; a minaret – not what might be expected within the grounds of a Christian sanctuary.

'Excuse me, Father Mathias,' Essie addressed their guide in Greek.

He glanced up, startled. 'Ah . . . yes?'

'The mosque – why is it here?'

'Ah . . . it's for the Bedouin. The men of the Jabaliya tribe.' His eyes darted frantically from side to side, desperately trying to find anything to look at other than her. 'When the Emperor Justinian decided to build the monastery here, he ordered two hundred men and their families from Alexandria and the Black Sea to relocate here to take care of the construction. Afterwards, they were to stay here to defend the monks. Even after the Bedouin converted to Islam in the seventh century, they remained loyal to the promises they'd made. They work here and help us with upkeep. We provide them with medicine and give them bread. In the desert, nobody survives alone – we may have different beliefs, but we need each other.'

Mathias ushered them forward towards a heavy door clad in bands of bronze held in place with massive metal studs. They passed through the entranceway into an alcove, the hot desert air suddenly chill within the space enclosed by the thick, stone walls. Facing them was a painted icon showing the Madonna with the infant Christ on her knee, suspended above a rendering of the monastery and flanked by two saints. Following the monk single file past black-clad ascetics sitting in silence, their mouths moving as they recited passages from tiny books of scripture, Essie, Garvé and Penney ducked their heads to avoid a low-slung archway leading into an enclosed courtyard where their footsteps rang out on cobblestones worn into grooves by the passage of thousands of feet over thousands of years.

'Wait here,' Mathias said, indicating a bench seat set at the bottom of a modest timber stairway leading to a second-floor balcony. 'I'll explain to the abbot why you're here.'

He trod up the stairs, the sound of his steps ringing out in a silence so absolute it was deafening.

'For over one thousand years, we've remained here undisturbed.' The abbot gazed at his visitors with gentle but inquisitive eyes, his white beard a soft halo against the pitch black of the veil draped from the flat-topped *kalimavkion* perched on his head. 'The greatest empire builders in history have left us in peace, even when the rest of the world was burning. This place was built by Byzantium ... Napoleon Bonaparte swore to defend our walls when he conquered Egypt. Even the man who is worshipped as the Prophet by the Muslims – Mohammed – he visited this hallowed place. In our library is the *Ahtiname* – a document he issued ordering that the monastery should be protected. And so it has always been. Why should it be different now?'

'Did you hear our arrival by air?' asked Garvé. Essie knew it was a rhetorical question; in a valley hemmed in by bare, stone escarpments and in a building with walls high enough to operate as an echo chamber, there was no way the monks could have missed hearing the helicopter's approach and cacophonous landing. 'The war that is coming will bring with it machines like the one we flew here in. And the weapons they carry with them are more powerful and more destructive than any that have been used in battle before. I doubt anybody would deliberately target your monastery, but what concerns the British and French governments is that missiles might hit you accidentally.'

The abbot leaned back in his ornately carved chair, elbows resting on the armrests and his wizened hands clasped at his chest. 'And why would the warriors who fight this battle be interested in a community of men whose only concern is to worship God?'

Garvé nodded, his head bowed. Essie marvelled at how obsequious he could be when he put his mind to it. 'Very reverend abbot,' he responded. 'I understand that it sounds unlikely to you. But these men are here to fight for possession of this land. We're here to ensure you're safe. With the radio we've brought with us, we'll communicate with the military to make sure they have the coordinates of your monastery recorded accurately and don't accidentally launch any missiles that might hit the building. But until we do, I must plead with you to order your brothers into the tunnels beneath the battlements. In there, you'll be protected.'

Shaking his head, the old man summoned Mathias to his side and murmured something beneath his breath. The monk nodded his head and scurried out of the room.

'Yes, we have stores down there. And water from the underground cistern. We can survive many weeks beneath the walls. We'll do as you ask.'

'Reverend, may I ask you a question?' Essie asked in Greek, her gaze averted modestly.

'Yes,' the abbot responded, grabbing at a string of amber κομπολόι beads on his desk and flicking them anxiously between his fingers. 'Yes, you may.'

'Have you had any other unexpected visitors here recently? Other than ourselves?'

The old man frowned. 'No. Some pilgrims. But that's not unusual. Or unexpected.'

'Any Americans?'

'Americans? No. Armenians, yes. Also some Greeks and Russians. But no Americans. Why?'

'No reason. Just curious,' Essie responded.

The abbot shrugged. 'You mentioned you need to use your radio. Can you do that in here?' he asked Garvé.

'No – we need to be outdoors. We were thinking the monastery garden would be suitable.'

'I'll ask Mathias to escort you there.'

Garvé shook his head. 'That won't be necessary. We studied the floor plan of the building before we arrived.'

'Oh, you did, did you?' the abbot said, looking at the three interlopers curiously. If he was planning to pursue the question further, he was interrupted by the mournful pealing of the bells in the church tower echoing through the labyrinth of stone buildings and corridors. The abbot stood and walked towards the door. 'My brothers will be concerned. If you'll excuse me, I must join them and explain why we're doing this.' He ushered his three visitors out. 'You'll tell us when we're safe?'

'Of course,' Garvé assured him.

'The Mother of God be with you.' The abbot made the sign of the cross with his hand as Essie, Garvé and Penney found their way back down the stairs.

'Why are you worried about Americans, Essie?' Penney asked.

'Just checking nobody has a head start on us,' she responded.

'Any Americans in particular?' The Englishman sounded panicked.

'No. Nobody specific. It's nothing. Don't worry about it.' At the bottom of the stairs she stopped and opened the satchel she'd slung over her shoulder. Taking out her notebook, she opened it to the page where she'd copied a map of the monastery from an account written by a traveller in the nineteenth century that she'd found in the British Library. She oriented herself by the belltower and the looming peak of Mt Sinai. She pointed to an archway. 'That way.'

'Good. I've had enough of this place. It smells bad. Musty. Like a cellar that needs a good airing. Or a wet dog,' Penney whinged, heading for the door.

Garvé moved alongside Essie. 'You really don't have to worry about him, you know,' he murmured quietly.

'Who?'

'You know who. Hitchens. He's miles away.'

'How can you be so certain?'

'Trust me. If he's planning to catch up with us, he has some work to do.'

The three unlikely confederates walked outside into the blazing sun.

Wish I shared your optimism, Essie thought.

31

Negev Desert, Israel

This must be what it feels like to be on the moon, Ben thought as he braced himself against the bone-jarring passage of the jeep across the ancient, dry riverbed. The first few miles they'd travelled across the open desert had been tortuous, with impassable boulders that had tumbled down from the cliffs over centuries blocking their way and forcing Ari to take a circuitous route west. But just when it seemed it was going to take days to travel a distance that should have taken no more than a few hours, the path ahead opened up and it seemed to Ben that they were following what might have been, at some time in the distant past, a caravan route through the desert. Although the path was still rough, it was clear of major obstacles and seemed to be heading in the direction they needed it to.

The people who'd passed through here before had left their mark. On the edge of the riverbed, in the lee of the staggeringly sheer cliffs that hemmed in the *makhtesh*, Ben saw rough circles of stones that showed where nomads had erected their tents. Charred patches on the cliff walls were all that remained of the hearths where they'd cooked their meals and warmed themselves against the Negev's night chill.

Something caught his eye on an escarpment. 'Hold on! Stop!' Ben shouted, slapping Ari's shoulder.

'Wait, Ben!' the Israeli exclaimed as the archaeologist flung the jeep's door open and jumped out before the vehicle had even come to a halt. He scrambled up the steep hill of scree hemming the mountain's base up to the point where it met the cliff's flat face. Carved into the eroded surface were masses of lines of the sinuous script Ben recognised as Nabataean. Each character was the size of his palm, and the ancient graffiti stretched from ground level to above his head, and as far as he could see along the cliff wall. Though he recognised the alphabet used by the people who'd carved the city of Petra from the rock walls of Jebel Al-Madbah in Jordan, that knowledge was useless – the Nabatean alphabet had evolved into modern Arabic, but nobody had worked out how to decipher the ancient language. *Another one for my bucket list of academic ambitions.*

Ben knew the desolate landscape they were driving through had been home to the civilisation that controlled the trade in incense and spices from the lands at the southern-most tip of the Arabian Peninsula that the Romans had called *Arabia felix* – blessed Arabia. But he was still surprised to find such irrefutable evidence of the Nabataean presence here, far to the east of the well-worn route used by the caravans of camels that carried frankincense, myrrh and cinnamon across the desert from the Gulf of Aden through Petra to ports in the Mediterranean. He ran his finger along the rock. The inscription was pitted and weathered, and covered with a glossy mineral accretion that would have taken thousands of years to accumulate in the intricately carved whorls making up the script. Whoever had chiselled the letters out of the stone had done so many, many years before Ben's arrival.

'Ben?' called Ilhan, who'd exited the jeep and now stood at the base of the slope, shielding his eyes from the blinding sun with a raised hand. 'What's up there?'

'Nothing!' he responded. 'At least – nothing that has any bearing on what we're looking for … I don't *think*.' He scooted back down to the jeep and took the map on which he'd been marking their passage as they travelled through the desert. Pointing to their location, he checked the compass. 'As far as I can tell, we're here. If my calculations are correct, the twin peaks of Har Karkom should be nearby.'

'So,' exclaimed Ari, banging on the outside of the driver's door with an open palm. 'Stop wasting time! Come on!'

In the labyrinth of steep-sided canyons that carried them towards their destination, Ben was concerned he'd struggle to identify which mountain, exactly, was the one Ethan had identified as Mt Sinai. But the instant the jeep skidded around a corner and exploded in a cloud of dust and gravel out of the ravine and onto an open plain, he knew he'd worried for nothing.

In the distance, across a lunar-like landscape of sand and coarse rubble, two flat-topped summits tilted up out of the desert floor, their ancient faces eroded into ripples and folds and glowing a rosy pink. Although Har Karkom wasn't a particularly tall mountain, in the arid landscape it appeared monumental. 'There,' Ben said unnecessarily, pointing through the windscreen. He had no doubt it was the place they were looking for, but whether or not it was also the spot Balinas had chosen to hide the Emerald Tablet remained to be seen. A sickening lurch of doubt made him flinch, even as he realised it was too late to change his mind and turn around.

The men drove in silence on the approach to Har Karkom's foothills. The horizontal bands of rock that made up the ancient massif had been worn down over many millions of years, some withstanding the elements better than others and leading to a geological effect that left its slopes looking like the layers of a cake. But what set Ben's heart pounding were the countless tumuli dotted across the plain surrounding the mountain. Some were small – their summits no higher than a couple of feet. Others were larger; one they passed would have been at least twenty feet tall by Ben's estimation. Elsewhere, flat slabs of stone stood upright in rings like miniature versions of Britain's Stonehenge, in close proximity to man-made platforms of rubble that Ben guessed would once have been plastered. And, everywhere, Ben saw petroglyphs – although none exactly like the ones Ethan had shown him in his office. But countless others, geometric forms depicting animals including ibex, leopards and camels, as well as human figures and features – eyes and hands – were scratched into stone surfaces in apparently random patterns.

Ari took the jeep to a point at the base of the mountain beyond which the vehicle could no longer safely progress, just at the foot of a low escarpment presided over by the ruins of what once would have been a fortress tower, although only a dozen courses of its walls of roughly worked stones remained intact.

Ben jumped out of the car with his two companions, his attention immediately switching to what was on the ground. The petroglyphs were literally everywhere. Like the one Ethan had given Ben, some were inscribed on stones that fitted in the palm of his hand. Others were random agglomerations of meaningless symbols carved into flat boulders the size of the jeep's bonnet. But they carpeted the ground.

He walked towards a low ring of stones at the foot of the mountain. Ilhan and Ari followed him as he clambered into its centre and kicked purposefully at the dirt.

'There ... there it is.' Ben murmured, dropping to his knees and sweeping aside the pale dust with his hand.

'What?' Ilhan asked.

He pointed at a circular depression in the hard-packed earth. 'A tent pole went here. I'd say this is Bronze Age. So thousands of years ago, a nomadic family unpacked the pole they'd have been carrying with them. Timber was a scarce commodity – the tent pole would have been a priceless heirloom, passed down from generation to generation. They'd have propped it up in the hole, laid the skin tent over the top, and hemmed it in with a circle of stones ... And here,' he kicked at a massive piece of fine-grained granite, its top surface worn down into a smooth concave depression, 'one half of a grindstone. The same people who set up the tent would have used it to grind down the grain they carried with them to make flour. As for this ...' Stepping outside the stone circle, he picked up a ceramic sherd. 'Whoever made it over three and a half thousand years ago dipped the vessel into a liquid terracotta slip and then burnished the surface to a shine using a pebble ...' Realising he was rambling and that Ilhan and Ari were looking perplexed, he pulled himself up short.

The truth was, Ben was overwhelmed by the density of archaeological remains at Har Karkom. Everywhere he looked he could see something – wall stubs, stone pillars and depressions in the ground that hinted at something buried beneath the soil. And with each step, he crushed a carpet of stone tools and pottery sherds beneath his feet. The evidence of humankind's intensive engagement with this vast, arid and unpopulated space was mind-boggling.

The three men recoiled and looked skyward as they heard the banshee-like wail of Spitfire aircraft approaching. If Ben needed a reminder of the urgency of the mission they were on, that was it.

'This petroglyph,' Ben said as he slapped the stone Ethan had given him onto the jeep's bonnet. 'This is what we're looking for.' The churning excitement in his gut told him he was on the right track. When he was in the field, Ben's unerring ability to sniff out treasures had earned him the grudging admiration of his peers; so much so that in some quarters he'd become known as the 'water diviner'. As he felt the scorching sun of the Negev Desert burning the back of his neck, he welcomed the prickling sense of second sight he knew so well.

'"Petroglyph"?' Ari said as he picked up the stone and turned it in his hand. 'What does it mean?'

'"Petro-" from the Ancient Greek for "stone", and "-glyph" meaning "carving".'

Ari kicked at the stones scattered at their feet. 'But these are all over the place.'

'No – we're looking only for stones with these symbols, specifically,' Ben said, pointing at the abstract marks engraved on its surface. 'A crescent, a serpent, a horned staff and a circle. They're alchemical symbols. And I hope they're going to lead us to the cave we're looking for.'

He stood with his hands on his hips, surveying the landscape. 'Ilhan, you and I will inspect the tumuli – we'll go together, moving out from the base of the mountain.

I presume what we're looking for won't be too far from here. I hope, anyway. And Ari . . .?'

'Yes?' The Israeli beamed at Ben, clearly enjoying himself.

'You're in the armed forces. Can I assume you're in pretty good shape?'

Ari shrugged and flexed his biceps. 'Sure. Of course.'

'Right. Then I need you to hike to the top of the two summits of the mountain and see what's there. Focus your search on this side – the map indicates that we'll find what we're looking for by aligning ourselves with Orion's Belt . . . and that will rise tonight in the southern part of the sky. So what we're looking for should be in the northern quadrant. But if the cave's already been exposed over the years, I want to know about it before I waste too much of my time down here.' He pointed at a ravine running between the two peaks. 'There's a track there – should get you to the top pretty quickly. If you find anything, just shout out. With the canyons about here, and nothing much else, we should be able to hear you. OK?'

'Done!' Ari gave Ben a mock salute and jogged towards the path, a canteen of water clanking at his side.

Ben and Ilhan stood silently beside each other and scanned the innumerable man-made stone hillocks dotted across the plain.

'Are you sure about this?' Ilhan asked.

Despite his excitement at the archaeological wealth around him, there was no ignoring the doubt that clouded Ben's mind. 'As sure as I can be,' he responded, hoping he sounded convincing as he broke away and headed for the nearest *gal`ed*.

'I'm not sure you always realise the potential complications of some of the situations you get yourself in,' Ilhan shouted.

'Oh, believe me, I know exactly how much trouble I'm getting myself into.' Ben bent and picked up one of the petroglyphs that made up the first stone mound. *Ibex*, he thought and tossed it away, scanning the pile of stones. *Not the one we're looking for.* 'Enough with the life advice, anyway. I need your help.'

Ilhan trudged to the neighbouring *gal`ed* as Ben moved on to the next.

He picked up another stone. Nothing. *He's right*, he thought. *This is going to be a big job.*

The next tumulus yielded nothing, nor the one after that. The two men crisscrossed the desert floor from one mound of stones to the next. As the sun sank lower in the sky, Ben was overcome by misgivings. *It is* ridiculous. *What are the chances this is the right place? Seriously, why didn't I just head straight for the Sinai instead of running off on this wild-goose chase? Why was I so certain it wasn't the Mt Sinai everyone else knows . . .? Why the hell do I always have to be so goddamned contrary?*

Just as he thought this, there was a shout from Ilhan. 'Ben! Here!'

He jogged over to where his friend stood beside a tumulus that was about six feet in height. He held out a stone and pressed it into Ben's hand. 'Were you looking for something a little like this?' he asked.

Ben looked down. A horned staff, a crescent, a circle and a serpent. He let out a cry of delight. 'Yes!' Scrambling up onto the tumulus' sloped side, he grabbed at the other small, engraved stones that made up its bulk. Every single one of them had been engraved with the same symbols. Any doubt he'd had about whether or not this was the monument they'd been searching for was put firmly to rest when Ben saw what was at its summit: a black stone carved into the form of a raven.

He scrabbled in his satchel for his notebook.

'So, do you think this is it?' Ilhan asked.

Ben opened the book to the page where he'd copied the map from the Topkapı document. With a forefinger shaking with excitement, he tapped the illustration of the black bird perched on top of the pile of stones. 'Yes!' he said. 'You found it. This is it!' He smacked Ilhan affectionately on the back before bolting back to the base of the mountain to summon Ari.

'Well. I suppose that's a good thing, then, isn't it?' said Ilhan quietly to Ben's retreating form.

32

Sinai Peninsula, Egypt

The trees growing outside the monastery's battlement walls in the merciless desert sun were among the few varieties that could survive the Sinai's harsh conditions. After centuries of care and using precious water drawn from the monastery's underground cisterns, gnarled olive trees, date palms and pencil-thin black cypress pines had grown between meandering paved paths in the gardens that provided the only sustenance the monks could coax from the desert. An orchard of pomegranate, citrus and nut trees bore testament to the back-breaking labour and unshakable faith of the men who'd carved an existence in the wilderness.

Essie consulted her map and led her two companions towards a simple two-storeyed building standing at the centre of the garden. They passed a single file of Bedouin men dutifully responding to the summons pealing from the belltower in the main monastery building. The Arabs wore blindingly white *thobes* topped with striped sleeveless coats and *kufeya* held in place on their heads by camel wool *igal* twined about their headdresses. They stared unapologetically at the three visitors as they passed, the fiercest scrutiny reserved for the woman who dared wear pants that displayed the outline of her legs and – worst of all – the most intimate parts of her body.

'Hmm,' leered Adam. 'They like what they see, Mrs Peters. Can't say I blame them.'

Essie was disappointed to see that the anxiety that had kept him silent on the flight to the monastery had evaporated and he was back to his most obnoxious self. She ignored him while suppressing a shudder and kept walking towards the lower level of the chapel, where a freshly whitewashed arched entranceway was gated by a grille of metal bars with a simple Greek cross set into the lintel. 'Here we are.'

Pushing the gate open, she led Penney and Garvé into a low-ceilinged space lined with arched entranceways opening into small alcoves illuminated by dim, indirect light that came through windows set high in the walls. As their eyes adjusted to the dark, shapes began to take form.

'Are they . . .?' Penney said, leaning closer to the alcoves and peering at the contents. 'Oh, Christ!' he exclaimed, jumping back.

'Yes. Bones. I'm surprised you're so squeamish, Adam,' Essie took great delight in his discomfort. 'It's a matter of practicality. Out here, there's virtually no good soil – it's next to impossible to chip graves from the rock, and sand shifts too much to be any good for tombs. It's the same on the Greek islands. So the monks have six graves out there in the garden where they bury those who die. Once their bones are bare – it takes five years or so – they're interred here, in the ossuary.' Enjoying herself, she directed him to a crucifix-topped glass case further along the passageway. 'A salient reminder for you, Adam – beauty, strength and power mean nothing. Life is nothing but a dream . . . a shadow. At the end, we're all just bones – ashes to ashes, and all that. *Memento mori* – remember death. Have a look in there. The Righteous Stephanus in person.'

Penney edged cautiously towards the cabinet, flinching when he saw what was within. 'How absolutely revolting,' Penney exclaimed, peering at the mummified figure dressed in religious vestments. 'Thank God for the good old C of E.'

'Strange sentiment coming from one of Aleister Crowley's disciples,' Essie snapped.

'Just saying,' said Penney defensively, arms crossed at his chest.

'So,' interrupted Garvé. 'Where do we begin?'

'I need to find something. Just give me a moment,' Essie replied.

When she'd first uncovered the hidden map in Topkapı, most of the clues were totally obscure to her. She'd always loved a good puzzle, but the problem was that even with the help of the hints preserved in Aleister Crowley's account and her extensive knowledge of ancient history, identifying an exact location for the tomb was next to impossible. She recognised Orion's Belt, of course, and knew it would be the pointer in the heavens that would direct her to the cave. She could see that the keystone referred to by Crowley was hidden beneath a pyramidal stack of what looked like round stones, but she didn't know where to start looking no matter how many ways she attempted to interpret the clues.

She'd thought she'd exhausted all options until she found a rough sketch of a statue in Crowley's notes and, in desperation, had decided to take a trip to Cairo to examine it. It was there that she'd identified the same alchemical symbol she'd seen stamped in the front of the book in Topkapı. As soon as she'd interpreted the hieroglyphic inscription that mentioned Mt Sinai, it all made sense. She knew of the monastery's famed charnel-house and had seen photographs of the morbid piles of skulls and bones. The *caput mortuum*, the death's head, above the summit of the mountain, confirmed she was on the right path. All she needed then was plausible cover to get inside the monastery. Colonel Nasser had obliged with his action in the Suez Canal, not that he'd ever know the real reason behind Great Britain's irrational rush to attack the Sinai.

Essie worked her way along the corridor. In each alcove, the bones were arranged neatly and stacked like with like: legs with legs and arms with arms. If she was right, she'd find what she was looking for in one of the alcoves containing the skulls.

Essie had learnt what she could about the charnel-house associated with the Sacred Monastery of the God-Trodden Mt Sinai, but she hadn't anticipated how many dead monks had accumulated over the one and a half thousand years the monastery had been operating. There were far more piles of skulls than she'd imagined there might be.

How the hell am I going to know which is the right one? she wondered. *Please tell me I'm not going to have to dismantle all of these . . . I feel bad enough doing this as it is, without having to destroy them all.*

As she was grappling with her already compromised conscience, she saw it. 'Thank Christ!' she exclaimed beneath her breath. 'Here!' she called out. 'It's over here!'

The two men joined her. 'How do you know?' Garvé asked.

She pointed. As they'd seen elsewhere in the monastery, a fresco depicting the Virgin and Christ child had been painted onto the wall at the back of the alcove. But it was the inclusion of some atypical details in the composition that had caught Essie's eye.

'What?' Garvé couldn't see it.

Essie flipped her notebook to the page where she'd copied down the diagram from the archive in Topkapı Palace and pointed at the pile of stones with a black raven perched on its summit, and the death's head hovering in the sky above the cave on the mountaintop. 'There! Do you see now?'

Garvé looked from the notebook to the fresco. A pile of skulls sat beneath the Virgin's throne while above, a black raven lifted the topmost skull from the stack into the sky. 'Yes. I do believe you're right.' His face creased into an uncharacteristic smile. 'Well done.'

'So, what do we do now?' Penney asked.

'You're not going to like it,' Essie answered, enjoying every minute.

Dust rose in clouds and Essie was forced to confront the realisation that they were inhaling the dead. It wasn't that she hadn't seen more than her fair share of skeletons over the years – she'd lost count of the number of ancient tombs she'd opened and desecrated, stripping the dead of precious things they no longer needed. But this seemed different, somehow; more immediate and personal for some reason. As they dismantled the bier that housed the skulls of monks who'd, in most cases, been dead for many hundreds of years, Essie couldn't help but think that the hollow-eyed sockets were contemplating them with a collective look of disapproval.

Refusing to use his bare hands, Adam had pulled the sleeves of his shirt over his fingers and grasped the bones through the fabric, holding them at arm's length to deposit them gingerly on the growing pile in the passageway. In contrast, Garvé seemed to be enjoying himself, grabbing the skulls in handfuls with his fingers hooked through the eye sockets, and flinging them contemptuously onto the stone floor outside. Essie winced as those he tossed with more vigour than others smashed into the wall and shattered. For her part, she treated the mortal remains of the monastery's monks with more reverence, carefully lifting them from the stack and placing them gently with their fellows.

Other than the clatter of bone on the stone floor, the silence was deafening. As they worked, the light coming through the high windows began to dim and take on a pale mauve cast as the sun approached the horizon.

It was as they were reaching the end of the interminable pile of skulls that Essie caught a glimpse of something that was pure, crystalline white between the bones. Her heartbeat quickened as she gently pushed the last skulls aside.

'Have you found it?' asked Garvé, who'd noticed her change of pace.

Sitting on the stone floor was a piece of glittering quartz that had been shaped into a sharp-ended crescent. Essie picked it up, feeling its cold weight in her palm. 'Yes.' She could scarcely believe it herself.

'That?' Penney asked incredulously, peering over her shoulder. 'That's what we're looking for?'

'Yes,' she replied. 'That's to say, it's the key we need to get us into the cave.'

'Hmm,' the Englishman mumbled with eyebrows raised, clearly unimpressed.

'So, what now?' Garvé asked.

Essie looked up at the softening sky outside. 'Now? We wait.'

33

Negev Desert, Israel

'So,' said Ilhan, hands on hips. 'What do we do now that we've found this? Is the tablet going to be in there, somewhere?'

'Not the tablet,' Ben replied. 'Something else.'

'What?'

'We'll know it when we see it,' he said. 'I hope. Now, let's get these stones out of the way.'

Fact was, Ben had no clue. He'd interpreted the symbols on the map to mean there was something hidden beneath the pile of stones that he needed to access Balinas' tomb. But what that might be, other than something shaped like a crescent moon, he had no idea. All he could do was hope that it would become clear once he found it. As always, he was flying by the seat of his very shabby pants.

Even before Ari had arrived back down on ground level, skidding and leaping nimbly down the sheer slope like a mountain goat, Ben and Ilhan had cleared away almost a

270

third of the stones piled on top of the tumulus. Each one of them was engraved with the four symbols.

Breathing heavily, Ari hailed Ben as he ran up towards where the two men were working. 'Ben! Ben! Something . . . Up there! . . . I found . . .!' He squatted down and dropped his head between his knees as Ben jogged over to him.

'You OK, Ari?' he asked.

Ari gave him a thumbs-up. 'Yes . . . Fine. Thank you. Long way up . . . Long way down. And . . . it's hot . . . *too* damned hot.'

'No kidding.' Ben wiped the sweat from his own brow. 'So – what've you found? Is it the cave?' He clenched his jaw, anticipating disappointment. If the Emerald Tablet's hiding place was already exposed, they were too late.

'On one mountain, nothing . . . Or nothing I could see.' He took a deep breath and composed himself. 'But on the other – well, this might sound crazy. I don't think I was imagining it. Still, the heat . . .'

'What? Tell me,' Ben said impatiently.

'It's a column. A tall rock. But it's been carved into a shape. A shape like a . . . ah . . .' He hesitated. 'A man's . . .' Ari pointed coyly at his groin.

'A phallus?' Ben asked.

'A what?'

'Phallus. Penis.'

'Yes, yes,' the Israeli said, blushing. 'One of those.'

Ben grabbed his satchel from where it sat on a rock and pulled out his notebook. 'Like this?' he asked, pointing at the drawing he'd made of the hidden map in the Topkapı manuscript. On the right, beneath the stylised stars and death's head was the vulva-like cave. On the left, an upright phallus.

'Yes!' Ari exclaimed, pointing at the erection on the mountaintop. 'That's exactly it!'

'If the phallus is on the eastern summit, then we should find the cave on the western peak.' Ben smiled. Each new thing they found fuelled a glimmer of hope. He was beginning to allow himself to believe they were on the right path.

With Ari's assistance, they picked up pace, and within a relatively short period of time, Ben found himself standing on a circular platform made up of the small stones and measuring about a foot high and twelve feet in circumference. Around its perimeter was a chaotic scatter of stones that lay where the three men had tossed them.

And somewhere beneath this, Ben thought, his heart pounding as much from excitement as from the labour expended, *is something we need to find the tablet.*

Ari and Ilhan were concentrating on the outer edges of the mound, and Ben focused on its centre. As he bent down and continued to shift the petroglyphs from the pile, he felt the sun burning his skin through his shirt, which was stuck to his back with a muddy paste of dust and sweat. Perspiration dripped from his brow into his eyes and ran down his nose to spatter in black drops on the stones, only to evaporate instantly in the scorching heat.

His hands were red raw from handling the rocks; not even the callouses earned from years of excavation were enough to protect his skin from the abrading heat stored in the stones. He shifted another handful aside and glimpsed bare earth beneath. He stood up and put his hands on his hips. 'I've bottomed out here,' he said to the other two men. 'Nothing yet. But I'll keep clearing from the centre, outward.'

He stood on the patch of dirt and squatted down, tossing the stones aside a handful at a time. As the petroglyphs were cleared and the bare space at the centre of the circle began to expand with nothing to show for it, Ben's excitement began to mutate into a black dread.

'Ari,' he called as he continued to clear the rocks. 'How long would it take for us to drive to Mt Sinai . . . I mean, the *other* Mt Sinai, Jebel Musa?'

The Israeli stood up. 'Jebel Musa? As I told you before, that will be difficult, Ben. From here, we'd have to go back to the track we were on before, then swing south and approach the mountain from there. And we'd be crossing the Egyptian border into the Sinai.' He shook his head. 'It would take a long time, even if things were normal. But there's going to be military action around the border tomorrow . . . it may have started already. It'd be very dangerous. Particularly for me. I'm an Israeli officer. The Egyptians will shoot me on sight.'

Christ, Ben cursed. He shifted forward onto his knees. That was when he felt it.

Where before he'd been kneeling on packed, gravelly sand, he now felt a different surface beneath his knees. He scuttled back and brushed at the earth with the side of his hand.

There . . . Bloody hell! he thought, scarcely believing what he was seeing.

Embedded in the soil was a perfectly formed crescent carved from a white stone whose crystalline matrix reflected glittering light back at him.

'Here! Here!' he called out. 'I've got it!'

The other two men dropped the stones they'd been holding and ran to where Ben knelt in the dirt.

Ben took his trowel out of his back pocket and scraped the packed soil away from the crescent's edges, avoiding the temptation to lever it out of its resting place until he'd loosened the dirt around it. Despite the excitement that gnawed away at his insides, he'd seen enough damage caused to fragile artefacts over the years from overenthusiastic and impatient excavation to risk doing the same thing himself. Whatever it was that the stone was supposed to do, he doubted it would work if it was broken.

At last, he felt it ease free of the soil. He coaxed it out of the ground with his fingers. It was a beautiful object; cold and heavy in his hand with its edges ground down into a perfect arc.

There was no doubt at all that it had been placed there deliberately.

As the three men waited for night to fall, they shared an unpalatable meal of reconstituted army rations washed down with tepid water.

The hazy, mauve glow of dusk washed over the horizon as Ben set up the surveying equipment on the spot where he'd uncovered the white stone. Night fell and overhead the desert sky was an immense, midnight-blue cupola punctured by a billion pinpricks of light. Ari tossed Ben a rough woollen blanket to throw about his shoulders and ward off the night's chilly air as he waited for the constellation of Orion to rise above the horizon.

As Ben watched the outstretched arms and bow of the hunter appear above Har Karkom, a distant sound made him flinch. 'Was that thunder?'

'Out here? At this time of year? No,' responded Ari. 'Sounded like an explosion.'

'Really? We've got to be a hundred miles from Suez.'

'Nothing else around to stop the sound.' By the light of the gasoline lantern, Ari set up the radio. 'I'll check.'

A harried conversation in Hebrew followed – none of which Ben understood. When Ari ended the call, he explained. 'It's Nasser. The British air force attacked, and he's been sinking the ships in the canal.'

'Jesus!' Ben exclaimed. 'What a bloody mess.'

Ari laughed. 'Welcome to the Middle East.'

Ari and Ilhan were fast asleep, curled up in the foetal position under their blankets and huddled around the coals of the fire when Ben saw the three stars of Orion's Belt align in a position perpendicular to the horizon. Ben peered through the theodolite at the three gleaming astral bodies – Alnitak, Alnilam and Mintaka. The Three Sisters.

Against the glittering night sky, the summit of Har Karkom loomed like a spill of Indian ink on blotting paper. With a torch clamped beneath his chin, Ben adjusted the theodolite and recorded the linear measurement that would exist if he were to draw a line through the three stars until it met the earth.

Somewhere there. That's where you are.

As his two companions snored and mumbled to themselves in their sleep, Ben dared to hope.

34

Sinai Peninsula, Egypt

After finding the keystone buried beneath the pile of skulls in the monastery's ossuary, Essie, Garvé and Penney had returned to the helicopter to get the equipment they needed for the next stage of the search. When they arrived there, they found that Captain Knight had gathered brush and started a small campfire at a safe distance from the aircraft. With the rapid approach of what Essie knew would be a bone-chilling desert night, she was glad to see its flickering flames.

Knight had refused to leave the aircraft when they'd first landed and he saw the gathering of curious Bedouin who'd assembled at the sound of the helicopter's approach. Initially keeping their distance, the Arab men had gradually overcome their fear and ducked reflexively as they stepped beneath the now stationary rotors to inspect the strange new arrival in the valley. Running their hands over the fuselage, they'd rapped at the metal and tugged at the door handles, ignoring Knight's entreaties that they leave it alone.

Knight explained to his passengers that he had seen how quickly curiosity morphed into covetousness when people living in primitive conditions encountered high-technology military equipment. And because the group's retreat from the desert required a functional vehicle, he'd decided to stay with it to make sure the Bedouin didn't begin dismantling it to souvenir its working parts.

Dusk darkened to night as Adam stretched out on the floor of the helicopter in an attempt to sleep, with a blanket rolled up beneath his head as a pillow, and Garvé made use of the radio Captain Knight had set up to contact military headquarters.

Garvé had offered to assist Essie to retrieve the surveying equipment and take it back into the ossuary in preparation for the anticipated appearance of Orion's Belt in the sky above Mt Sinai. Desperate to hijack a moment of solitude, she declined his offer.

Hefting the equipment onto her back, she returned to the monastery, where she set it up on the spot where she'd found the white stone. The light of the kerosene lamp cast long shadows in the deathly quiet charnel-house and flickered on the jumble of skulls they'd tossed onto the floor. Essie attempted to stifle her guilt at the thought of the monks emerging from the tunnels only to find that this sacred place had been desecrated.

A sudden sound from outside made her start – the hollow clash of rock on rock. *Calm, girl. Calm*, she reassured herself. *You know what that is . . . it's nothing . . . just a rockfall.* Still, it made her feel uneasy. She liked to think she didn't have a superstitious bone in her body, but her heart was racing and her breath came in raggedy gasps as she finished setting up the theodolite. It took a supreme effort to stop herself running out of the chapel. She knew she had to return later to make her measurements, most likely in the loneliest hours just after midnight, and she didn't relish the thought one little bit.

'Did y'hear that?' asked Knight as Essie returned to the fire where he was stirring baked beans in a small saucepan. 'Rock slide. Common around these parts, I'd imagine.'

'Where's Garvé?'

'Still playing with that damned radio. With everything we've got going on in Port Said, the frequencies'll be pretty jammed up.'

A movement in the shadows caught Essie's eye.

'Speaking of common,' Knight said, looking up.

A Bedouin woman dressed in a striped robe hanging to the ground approached them tentatively. A black headdress fell over her shoulders like a bride in mourning, and the lower part of her face below her eyes was also covered in a veil embroidered with colourful thread and small silver coins that jangled as she walked. In her hands, she held a battered metal dish over which sat a large round of unleavened bread. She sidled up to Essie and, eyes averted, handed her the tray.

'*Shukran*,' Essie said. '*Teslam iidak*. Health be on your hands.'

The woman's eyes widened in surprise that the strange woman knew Arabic. '*Wa-iidak*,' she responded, before turning and disappearing back into the night.

'Speak wog, do you?' scoffed Knight. 'You're quite the bundle of surprises, aren't you?'

Penney, who'd roused from his slumber, wandered over and joined the other two at the fire. 'So, what have you got there, Mrs Peters?'

Essie lifted the still-warm disc of bread and inhaled the fragrant steam, shutting her eyes as the smell carried her back to her own childhood. An indeterminate red meat – either goat or camel, she guessed – had been cooked slowly over charcoal till the meat fell off the bones, then scattered on a bed of *pilav* rice with chopped almonds and lentils stirred through it.

'Meat and rice,' she answered. 'Smells delicious. Do you want some?'

'Me?' Penney asked incredulously. 'Eat that muck? You can't be serious! It's likely to give me the raging trots, if it doesn't kill me first!'

Essie tore off a piece of bread and used it to scoop up some of the meat. It was, as she'd anticipated, absolutely delicious. 'Are you sure? It really is very good. What about you, Captain Knight?'

'Not on your life, missy!' He raised the unappetising pannikin of orange beans. 'Good old English grub'll suit me just fine. Hate to think where the hands have been that made that. Damned if I'm letting it anywhere near these chompers!'

'Enough beans to share with me, captain?' Penney asked.

'More than enough,' he replied.

Essie scooped up another handful of the Bedouin *pilav*. 'Your loss,' she said, secretly pleased that she could keep it all to herself.

In the heavy silence of the night as the three men slept by the warmth of the fire, Essie lit the kerosene lamp and found her way across the desert floor to the stone walls that surrounded the monastery's garden. Her footsteps echoed off the mountain's naked rocks and her passage was marked by the small pool of light shining from the hissing lantern. Beneath the vast dome of the night sky, she felt utterly insignificant. For some reason, she liked it.

Inside the ossuary, shafts of moonlight shining through the small windows cast a chequerboard pattern of pale blue light on the paving stones. She found her way to the alcove where they'd uncovered the keystone. The theodolite now stood an alien sentinel at the centre of the small space. She looked up to where the nearest window was set high in the wall. It took her a moment to believe what she was seeing. Visible against the velvety black night sky were the three stars of Orion's Belt running in a row that was perpendicular to the earth's surface.

Her heart began to beat faster. *This is it. This really is happening.*

THE TIMES
1 November 1956
BRITISH AND FRENCH TROOPS ATTACK AS NASSER BLOCKADES SUEZ CANAL

LONDON, Thursday (Reuters)

An Israeli Government representative announced today that an Israeli plane has been shot down over the Sinai as troops cross the peninsula and British and French bombers launch an airborne operation against the Egyptian air force.

In an unequivocal response to British, French and Israeli action in Egypt, President Nasser ordered the sinking of the forty ships currently at anchor in the Suez Canal.

British Government sources have stated that the damage done to international shipping will have serious repercussions for the economies of all European nations whose trade relies upon access to the Indian Ocean through the canal.

Nasser claimed the orders were provoked by the appearance of British Valiant bombers over the skies of Cairo. It is thought the aeroplanes, which are stationed on the Mediterranean island of Malta, were destined for the city's airport where the Egyptian air force is based. But upon hearing of the evacuation of American civilians through Cairo airport, orders were revised and the British planes instead attacked the Almaza air base on the outskirts of the city.

Meanwhile, an official army spokesman said that Israeli forces had overrun Egyptian frontier posts and crossed the desert to occupy positions within eighteen miles of the canal. Their actions came in response to Egyptian land and sea attacks on Israeli communications. An Israeli Army

Meaghan Wilson Anastasios

spokesman has said that Israeli units in the Negev and Sinai Deserts were machine-gunned by Egyptian planes.

Israel's military assault – which signalled the end of an unsettled seven years' truce between the two countries – has caused great shock around the world. Egypt announced that by launching a full-scale military invasion, Israel had, in effect, signed its own death warrant.

There has been no statement as yet about military or civilian loss of life.

35

Negev Desert, Israel

After scribbling the information he needed in his notebook, Ben had joined his companions in the deafeningly quiet still of night by the coals of the fire and slept as if dead, feeling neither the frosty air nor the sharp stones that formed his bed.

He woke from a sleep untroubled by dreams as the horizon blushed tangerine at the approach of the sun. Gathering desiccated saltbush and tumbleweeds, he stoked the fire and boiled water for tea before waking his bleary-eyed companions.

'Two sugars for me,' Ilhan mumbled through lips cracked and puffy from sun exposure the day before.

'Good idea. Me too,' said Ari.

Ben handed them a mug each. 'Well, in case you were worrying –'

'Couldn't *sleep* for worrying,' quipped Ari, who'd snored without break through the night. If they'd needed any proof, it showed that he'd spent a lifetime surviving in conditions far worse than these.

'As I was saying,' Ben continued, 'everything happened as expected. The three stars of Orion's Belt aligned right over the mountain . . . if we follow that line, we'll find Balinas' cave. I hope.' He took a sip of his own tea, the syrupy jolt shocking him awake.

The sun's gleaming disc was just appearing on the horizon, shooting blinding beams across the desert sands. Suddenly, a humming so low that it was almost felt rather than heard made the air vibrate. Ben peered at the dawn sky. 'You see anything?' he asked Ilhan and Ari, who'd sensed the same thing and stood up, scanning the heavens.

'Planes,' Ari said, 'bombers.' He raised his binoculars to his eyes. 'But nothing I can see.'

'So those things come in handy for tasks other than watching birds?' Ben asked, attempting to lighten the mood. The Israeli didn't reply.

The vibrations increased in intensity then began to fade away to nothing. It seemed to Ben as if the world was holding its breath. When the sound of explosions came from beyond the horizon, his muscles clenched reflexively.

'That was closer than last night,' Ari said, all humour gone from his voice. He went back to the jeep and cranked up the radio.

'You *do* know this isn't your war, don't you, Ben?' asked Ilhan, as the two men looked towards the rising sun.

With a renewed sense of urgency, Ben keyed the coordinates he'd established the night before into the theodolite and identified geographical markers along the line that had been defined by the three stars of Orion's Belt.

Scanning the projected search area, he spotted three vertical rock faces that might plausibly accommodate the entrance to a cave or cavern. Although there was a chance that over time erosion had caused the entrance to the cave to be covered by a cascade of rock so substantial that it had merged with one of the many gentle slopes that made up the plateau on Har Karkom's summit, it seemed unlikely. And if life had taught Ben anything, it was that it was better to dismiss the easiest options first before facing the more complex alternatives.

The three men gathered their equipment and began the hike up the canyon to get to the plateau on Har Karkom's western summit. Although it was still early and the sun was low in the sky, the transition from bitterly cold night to scalding day was well progressed, and as Ben approached the first of the rock faces he'd identified, he felt sweat beginning to form on his back.

'Right,' he said as Ilhan and Ari joined him. He indicated the vertical surface that rose above their heads, reaching a maximum height of about twenty feet. A low tumble of rubble had accumulated at its base, but there was no immediate sign of there being a cave, or anything like it.

'We're going to divide this cliff face into three. Ari, you take that end. Ilhan, take the other. I'll start in the middle. What I need you to do is to examine the rock very, very carefully.'

'What are we looking for?' asked Ari.

'To be honest, I'm not entirely sure,' said Ben. 'But it'll be something that looks out of place.' He grabbed a fist-sized rock from the ground, walked over to the cliff and rapped it with the stone in his hand. It made a dull, thudding sound. 'Hear that?' he asked. The two men nodded. 'That's solid rock. If there's a cavern behind any part of this, it'll make a hollow sound – you'll hear an echo.'

Ari and Ilhan picked up stones of their own and went to work.

The search of the first cliff face took less time than Ben had anticipated but yielded nothing. On the approach to the second location, he was struggling to contain his frustration when he noticed something on the otherwise featureless surface that caused his heartbeat to quicken. He picked up his pace.

'Ben? What is it?' asked Ilhan, who was following, with Ari in his wake.

Yes! Ben thought as he got closer to the cliff. *That's more like it!*

A narrow cleft – not much broader than Ben's shoulders at its maximum width, but twice his height – bisected the rock. A drift of rubble lay in front of it, but the gap in the stone was otherwise clear.

'Here! Look at this!' he shouted as he reached the crevasse. Flicking on the torch he carried clipped to his belt, Ben shone it into the pitch-black space beyond the entrance.

'What can you see?' asked Ari, peering over Ben's shoulder.

The light shone a beam along a rough-edged stone corridor. Ben couldn't be certain, but it looked like it opened out into a cavern beyond.

'Something . . . not sure,' he said. 'I'm going in.'

'I'm coming with you,' said Ilhan.

'No – you two stay out here. There's a risk of rockfall, and if something goes wrong, I don't want you stuck in there with me. You're more use to me out here if I end up entombed in there.'

Ben sidled into the stone passage. After the heat of the desert sun, the air in the rock chasm was cool and close. He'd scarcely made it four metres in before there was a shout from outside.

'Ben! Come!' It was Ari.

Frustrated, Ben edged back out of the corridor. 'What is it?'

Ari didn't respond. He was standing on the edge of the escarpment, binoculars held up to his eyes.

'Not another bloody bird, I hope!'

'No.' The Israeli raised his hand and pointed at the horizon. 'Something else.'

In the far distance, a trail of dust spiralled into the air. 'What is it?' Ben asked. 'Troops?'

'Not ours,' Ari replied. 'Jeeps. Two of them. When I spoke with headquarters last night, they said we were still a long way clear of the battlefront here, and there was no intention to expand south into the Negev yet . . . their focus is on the Sinai Peninsula. The Egyptians will be defending their border – there's no advantage to them coming down here. If they're looking for the war, the people in those jeeps are going in the wrong direction. They're here for us.'

'Friend or foe?' Ben asked, feeling a clinical detachment wash over him – a sensation he recalled all too well from his years fighting the Germans in Crete.

'Russians.'

'How do you know?'

'They've a dancing bear in the passenger seat.'

'Really?' Ilhan interrupted.

Ari looked at him sideways. 'No. Not really. It's a GAZ-69. Russian jeep.'

'Russians? That can't be good,' said Ben.

'Exactly what I was thinking. Thought we'd managed to shake them in Jerusalem. I was wrong.'

'You said you brought weapons?'

'Yes. And it looks like they've taken off the windscreens. Better for desert travel.'

'Good. But any advantages we might have will soon be gone. Let's get down there and put out a welcome mat for Ivan.'

36

Negev Desert, Israel

A s the silhouettes of the two vehicles approached in the distance, the three men retreated behind an outcrop at the base of the rough path that led up to Har Karkom's flat-topped summit. They'd made use of what little time they had to set snares on the tracks made in the sand by their own vehicle, on the assumption the Russians would follow the same route. But with little time to finesse the ambush, Ben was concerned the new arrivals would have no trouble seeing the traps they'd laid for them.

There was only one way he could see of improving their odds of success. 'Ilhan?'

'Yes, Benedict.'

'This may be an unfair assumption to make. If so, I'm sorry. But I don't think you've had much experience with hand-to-hand combat. Is that fair?'

'If you don't count fighting with the old women at Eminönü to get my hands on some *hamsi* in the fish markets, then yes. You're right.'

'We have a problem. And you can help. We don't want them looking too closely at the road as they approach. So here's what I need you to do. Get up to the escarpment and move about purposefully so they're looking up at you rather than down at the ground. Use the binoculars to direct flashes of light from the sun in their direction . . . kick rocks around so you're raising some dust into the air. Really get active once they're close – that way they'll be distracted. And take the radio – if you see we're in trouble, call Israeli headquarters –'

'They won't help us,' Ari interrupted.

'Call them anyway,' said Ben.

Ilhan retreated to the plateau as Ben and Ari scoped about to find a good vantage point from which to target the approaching vehicles.

They identified two of the higher tumuli flanking the track. 'Best we attack from two sides,' Ari said. 'Split their defence.'

'Absolutely,' Ben agreed. 'We'll already be outnumbered – can't give them a single focus to draw fire. So . . . we start shooting after they've passed through our traps. Never know – maybe we won't need to fire. Perhaps we've done such a good job, we'll knock them off in one fell swoop.'

'Ha!' Ari laughed. 'We should be so lucky.' He opened his khaki backpack and pulled out two submachine guns. 'You know this? MAT-49. It's got a double trigger – semi or fully automatic . . . whichever suits you best.' He tossed Ben some extra magazines.

'Yes. I know it,' Ben replied. 'So – French weapons, then. That *is* where you've been getting them.'

Ari shrugged. 'We must defend ourselves. And we take weapons from whoever'll sell them to us. Besides – they're good guns.'

Ben checked the magazine and extended the retractable stock. 'They are. This'll do nicely.'

It's disturbing how quickly we revert to our basest instincts, Ben thought as he marvelled at the speed and ease with which he'd assumed the clinical mindset that had allowed him to evolve into a feared killer on the island of Crete during the war.

There'd been a time when he'd doubted his capacity to do violence, and questioned the moral and ethical dimensions of war. But after Karina had been taken from him, he'd lost any qualms he might have had about killing.

As he kept his eye on the vehicles he knew contained men who intended to do him harm, he didn't think twice about what he was about to do. His breathing was measured and calm as he lined his sights on the men in the second jeep; he assumed the Russians in the first vehicle would be neutralised – temporarily, at least – by the booby traps they'd set for them. That meant the men in the second jeep posed the greatest immediate threat.

The cars were approaching at speed towards two stunted acacia trees that stood on either side of the track. Each vehicle contained two men seated in the front, with another three on the bench seat behind. *Ten*, Ben thought. *Ten of them, three of us . . . well, two-and-a-quarter, if I'm honest . . . sorry, Ilhan. This won't be easy.*

Whatever it was that Ilhan was doing up on the ridge was working – all the men in the jeep were peering up, shielding their eyes from the sun. Even the drivers were glancing up as they drove, confident there was nothing on the road that posed a hazard to their progress.

He steeled himself as the jeeps neared the trees. The first indication he had that the trap they'd set had worked was when the leading jeep's wheels kicked a spray of gravel into the air and jerked suddenly when the driver's foot dropped onto the brake. It was a reflexive reaction, and too late to stop what happened next. Both men in the front were propelled backwards, and geysers of lurid red spurted into the air from their necks as their heads were removed from their trunks by the razor-sharp wire Ben and Ari had strung across the road.

Whether or not the three men in the rear seats escaped with their heads was academic as the jeep rolled forward and hit the second of the traps they'd set for the Russians. A landmine exploded with a shattering boom that made the ground shake and quiver. The body of the car was thrown off its axle and its occupants tossed into the air like rag dolls. With a deafening *whoosh* that seemed to suck all the oxygen out of the air, the jeep's fuel tank ignited, shooting a column of black smoke and hellish fire hundreds of feet into the air.

The driver of the second vehicle reacted quickly, slamming his foot onto the brake. Ben steadied himself and lined up the bead of his sight with the man's head. As he pulled the trigger and the driver's head jerked back violently, the jeep veered off its path and accelerated towards the hillock Ari had been perched behind. The Israeli had obviously seen the jeep careening towards the tumulus because he broke cover, raising his machine gun to take aim at the oncoming vehicle. A burst of gunfire took out the other Russian in the front seat as Ben put another round into one of the men in the back seat.

The two surviving men vaulted out of the back of the vehicle while it was still in motion and before its front wheels hit the slope of the hillock. The metal chassis became airborne as it was tipped off balance at speed, flipping over and landing with a tearing crunch on top of the three men who'd been shot and so remained in the vehicle. If they hadn't been dead before, Ben thought to himself, they certainly were now.

The two Russians who'd escaped the bloodbath hadn't seen Ben, but they locked their sights on Ari, who was now exposed on the summit of the stone mound. Ari dropped and rolled down the slope as the two men ran towards him, cocking their guns. There was nowhere to hide as he raised his own weapon to return fire.

Ben took a deep breath and steadied himself as he locked his sights on the man who was closest to Ari. He pulled the trigger. The man dropped like a stone. The second man disappeared from Ben's sights behind the tumulus.

C'mon, Ari! Ben urged silently as he stumbled down the side of his own hiding place. Head down, he approached the other Russian from behind. Billowing black smoke from the burning jeep blocked his view. *What the hell's going on? Take him out!*

As he rounded the other side of the hillock, he realised what had happened. He arrived just in time to see Ari smashing at a gun that must have misfired. The Russian was already too close as Ben raised his weapon and took aim, felling him, but not before the Russian had shot Ari in the throat.

'Fuck! No!' Ben howled as he ran to the Israeli's side.

It was too late.

Ari lay in sand now sodden with his blood, feebly attempting to ebb the arterial flow from the gaping wound in his neck. Ben tore off his own shirt and rolled it into a pad that he pressed against the dying man's throat. It was dripping red in moments. Ben knew it was futile; although it was possible to manually clamp the carotid artery, Ari would need immediate surgery once that was done, and they were too far from medical help for it to be any use. He'd seen enough men die during the war to know that prolonging Ari's suffering would just be cruel.

The Israeli made no sound, opening and shutting his mouth like a landed fish, his eyes darting desperately about as he, too, realised the hopelessness of his situation. As his movements grew weaker, Ben took Ari's bloodied hand and held it tightly.

'Don't worry, Ari. I'll make sure they know what you did here. And I'll tell Ethan where to find you. They'll take you home to your family. You'll be buried by the people who love you in friendly soil.'

Ari's muscles spasmed, then his body relaxed as his last breath left his lungs. His head lolled back and his lids half dropped over his eyes as his face found repose in a strangely peaceful expression.

'What happened?' There was the sound of a scrabble of rock as Ilhan skidded up behind them. 'Oh.'

Ben wiped the tears from his eyes with the back of his hand.

'We have to bury him.'

The gaping crater the landmine had left in the sand became Ari's grave. Ben and Ilhan had wrapped his body in a spare canvas sheet and used the shovels from the back of the jeep to backfill the hole. When they were done, they took the tyres off the overturned Russian vehicle and put them in a pile to mark the spot where they'd buried the Israeli so the army could come and retrieve his remains.

Cleaning himself up as best he could afterwards, Ben slipped on his one spare shirt and turned to Ilhan. 'You know the thing I really hate about this?' he said.

'What's that?'

'It means the Americans were right. The Russians were listening in to everything I said in Cairo. The conversation I had on the phone with Raphael . . . my plans to go to Jerusalem.' He sighed. 'And I can't stand Americans being right.'

'But, Benedict. You're –'

'I'm American? Yeah . . . unfortunately. We're a revoltingly smug race; it's one of our least endearing characteristics. Anyway, what I don't understand is how the hell the Russians worked out we were coming to Har Karkom. I didn't say anything about that on any of my calls – Ari and Ethan are the only other people who knew. And considering how it's worked out for Ari, I can't believe it was either of them who put the Reds onto us.'

Ilhan said nothing as he gazed down at the body of the man who'd shot their friend. The Russian's angelic golden curls ruffled in the hot wind blowing across the desert, an accumulation of sand and grit already gathering in the sockets of the man's dead eyes and in his gaping mouth. The Turk's features were contorted as he prodded the Russian with the tip of his boot. 'This is wrong. Ari didn't deserve this. What are we going to do with these bastards?' he asked.

'Them?' Ben said. 'They came to kill us. We don't owe them anything.'

Overhead, the burning fuel had sent a pall of black smoke into the air that had started to bleed across the sky in a long, and very distinctive, trail.

'And thanks to that,' he pointed up, 'we don't have any time to waste. It may as well be a neon sign in the sky signalling where we are. If anyone else is trying to find us, it's going to make their job that much easier.'

Ben felt the weight of the keystone in his backpack as he edged through the corridor leading into the mountain. He'd convinced Ilhan to wait outside in case something went wrong.

The walls seemed to press in on him. He tried to keep his breathing under control; if there was one thing in particular that bothered him, it was confined spaces. That, alone, was the reason his archaeological interests had veered away from the ancient history of Egypt; he couldn't bear the thought of pursuing a career that required navigation of the cramped tunnels and shafts that were, more often than not, the only access points to the tombs carved out of the Egyptian landscape. He could keep his natural responses in check for a short amount of time, but to do it for extended periods would have made his mind snap.

He suspected it was only his imagination, but with just the feeble light of his torch to see by it seemed the height of the roof was dropping as he moved through the dark. The other, unhelpful, function of the artificial light was to create long and rather ominous shadows on the uneven walls. Ben knew it was nothing, but it put his nerves further on edge. Adrenalin surged in his blood, an irrational quavering at the back of his mind telling him to turn and head back out to the open air. But he forced himself to push forward.

Ahead, he dared to hope he saw the torchlight diffusing in open space. He gritted his teeth and rushed through the last few feet of the tunnel, stumbling into an open cavern.

'Ben? Are you all right?' called Ilhan.

Looking back, Ben could see his friend silhouetted against the sky. 'Yes! Everything's fine! You can follow me in . . . and bring the lantern!'

Heart pounding, Ben spun slowly around, raking the light of his torch across the walls of the cavern. A long stone bench had been chipped out of the wall, and there was the remains of a hearth. *A hermit found his way here – perhaps an early Christian monk,* he thought. *There'll be water in wells about the base of the mountain. No reason someone shouldn't survive out here in the wilderness by himself for a while.* 'Forty days and forty nights, even,' he murmured. He still wasn't allowing himself to entertain the thought that he might well have found the last resting place of the alchemist, Balinas, and his Emerald Tablet.

As Ilhan progressed along the tunnel, the brighter light of the kerosene lamp began to wash into the cavern. Ben saw scattered sherds of broken pottery and finely worked stone tools on the ground, but nothing resembling a dead alchemist, or his treasure.

It was only when Ilhan entered the cave and illuminated the enclosed space properly that Ben saw it. Chiselled into the wall immediately ahead of him were the four symbols. A horned staff. A serpent. A circle. And a crescent moon.

But it was the crescent that made his heart leap. Unlike the other shapes, which had been made by carving the outlines of the abstract forms into the wall, the entire crescent had been chipped out of the stone.

He could scarcely believe what he was seeing. Taking off his backpack, he removed the keystone.

This is it, he thought.

'Is that what we're looking for, Ben?' Ilhan asked.

'Could be,' he replied, his voice shaking. He held the white stone up to the void in the wall. It was exactly the same size and exactly the same shape. He ran his fingers across the surface. 'Ilhan – bring the lantern here, would you?'

Something was wrong. Ben bent and picked up one of the stone tools lying on the floor and scraped its sharp edge along what he'd at first assumed to be one of the four stone walls of the cavern.

'Christ!' he exclaimed.

'What?' Ilhan asked.

'Clay. This is clay. Not stone. Look!' He picked up a larger stone and smashed it against the wall. A large chunk broke off. Ben picked it up and crumbled it between his fingers. 'Clay. This surface has been made out of clay. It's an artificial wall.'

And, Ben thought, heart pounding, *the only reason to build a false wall is if you want to hide something behind it.*

As the Turk held the light closer, Ben saw that what he'd thought at first was just a natural fissure in the surface was, in fact, something else. Two narrow, parallel breaches ran vertically upwards from the ground to join in an arch overhead, enclosing the engraved shapes.

Ben bent forward and blew a stream of air into the crack. An ancient accumulation of dust was dislodged, and the breach became even more obvious. 'This is a door!'

'What? Where?' asked Ilhan incredulously. 'I don't see anything!'

Ben could hardly believe it himself. 'I'm sure it is. And I think I know how to open it.'

He took the white stone crescent and gently slid it into the void that appeared to be made to measure.

There was a slight resistance as Ben fitted the keystone into the slot. He pushed on it gently. The cavern was filled with the gratingly loud sound of two hard surfaces grinding together, followed by a muffled thump.

'What on earth was that?' shouted Ilhan, alarmed.

'A latch. I think.' Ben pressed his shoulder into the stone and pushed, his boots skidding on the gravelly floor. He felt it begin to give way. 'Give me a hand!'

'Are you sure you know what you're doing?' Ilhan asked nervously as he joined Ben.

'Yes. Kind of. I think so. Here . . . help me push.'

The two men grunted as they laid into the door. It shifted imperceptibly. 'I don't think we can do this on our own,' Ilhan said.

'Yes! Yes we can!' Ben cried. 'Again!'

Once more they pushed with all their might, and once again it moved, but only a frustratingly small amount.

'OK. Different approach!' Ben put his back to the door and braced his feet against the floor. Ilhan followed his lead. 'Now, PUSH!'

He bellowed as he shoved backwards with all the strength of his legs, his thigh muscles burning. The rough surface dug into his back and the tendons in his neck strained as he kept up the pressure. Legs quaking, Ben thought he was going to have to give up when he felt it begin to yield. 'Quick!' he shouted, grabbing Ilhan's arm. 'It's giving way! Get back!'

The two men tumbled towards the back wall of the cavern as the clay door swung open, revealing the hidden room beyond. Ben and Ilhan buried their faces in the crooks of their arms as the cavern filled with a dense cloud of fine dust.

As the haze began to dissipate, Ben looked up.

37

Sinai Peninsula, Egypt

As soon as the ink-black night began to lighten with the pearly grey of early dawn, Essie rose from the cocoon she'd made for herself under a pile of canvas sheeting she'd found folded in the corner of the helicopter's cabin. The sub-zero temperatures of the desert at night had turned the metal fuselage into an icebox, and although she knew it would have been much more comfortable – and warmer – if she'd slept by the fire, minor discomfort was preferable to a night spent in close proximity to Adam.

She stoked the fire and brewed herself a cup of tea as the three men roused themselves.

'Did you get what we need?' asked Garvé, his eyes bleary with sleep.

'Yes – I think so,' she replied. 'Won't know until we get up there. Captain Knight?'

'Ma'am?' the airman responded jocularly.

'Are you planning to stay here to guard the helicopter again today?'

'Actually,' Garvé interjected, casting a sharp glance in Essie's direction. 'I *insist* you stay. We can't risk losing our only way out of this place.'

'Quite right,' Knight said. 'I'll stay put here. You can call out if you need me. It's so still and quiet, my guess is we could have a conversation from one side of this valley to the other without raising our voices.'

'Fine. Then, Josef, I'll need to ask you and Adam to please help bring the excavation equipment up the mountain. I'll take what I can. But once you're done with breakfast, meet me at the chapel. I'm going back there now to take some elevations and see if I can spot the cave.'

'So you think we'll need to dig for it?'

'I don't know. But I'd rather be prepared than not.' She stood and hoisted a khaki backpack onto her shoulders.

'Not staying for breakfast?' Knight raised the pot he was stirring on the fire. 'More baked beans!'

'Not for me, thanks,' said Essie. She held up what remained of the unleavened bread the Bedouin woman had brought her the night before. It was a bit dry and rubbery, but still delicious. 'This'll do me fine.'

He shrugged. 'Your funeral!'

Endowed as she was with a generally sceptical outlook on most things in life, the ease with which Essie spotted the entrance to the cave through the theodolite's viewfinder planted a seed of doubt in her mind.

It had aligned perfectly with the measurements she'd taken of the three stars in Orion's Belt the night before. But it was so clearly visible, even to the naked eye, that she couldn't believe that Balinas would have chosen a hiding place that could be so readily found.

The reason she didn't dismiss it outright was that she knew the mountains around the monastery were riddled with caves and retreats used for millennia by hermits and ascetics. As far as anyone else was concerned, the one she'd identified had nothing to distinguish it from the hundreds of other caverns on the mountain.

But as she trudged up the slope, the nagging voice in her head bothered her. The massive peak of Mt Sinai had been attracting pilgrims for thousands of years and many of the holy people who'd sought refuge in the Sinai had been canonised. If the cavern she'd identified had been home to one of these now venerated Christians, there would have been the remote region's equivalent of tour groups arriving regularly to worship there. Any remains left behind by Balinas would be long gone.

As they grew closer, her optimism was buoyed by the fact that there was no obvious path leading to the cave; if it had been visited over the years, it hadn't been done with a regularity that had left a mark on the mountain slope, unlike the route snaking up Mt Sinai to the small chapel at its summit, which was significant enough to be visible from where Essie was – at least half a mile away.

She reached the entrance to the cavern long before her two companions, who were trudging up the mountain in her wake.

Essie peered inside. Beyond the narrow entrance, the cavern opened out into a high-ceilinged space that was roughly circular, with the exception of a single, flat-faced aspect immediately opposite the entrance. Along one wall was a rough bench hewn out of the rock, with a charred patch on the wall beside it that would have been deposited by a small cooking fire. Although the light in the cave was dim, in places she could see that the walls had been painted with

Greek script and naive depictions of Biblical stories; no doubt the work of the holy men or women who'd chosen this place as a sanctuary.

'Anything there?' puffed Garvé from further back down the slope.

There was nothing to indicate the cave had also, at one point or another, accommodated an ancient alchemist. 'Nothing yet,' she shouted over her shoulder as she ventured further into the cave.

She put the kerosene lamp down on the floor and struck a match to light it. As the wick caught the flame, the cave was illuminated with a warm light.

That's odd.

The flat wall facing the entrance was intersected by a large crack running from the ceiling to the floor. That wasn't what caught her eye, though. It wasn't unusual to see fissures in stone. But the edges of the opening she was looking at were crumbly, like stale cake, and the wall's surface appeared strangely powdery.

She touched it with her fingertips. *That's not stone*, she thought. *It's clay!*

She held up the lantern and inspected the wall in more detail. There was something else that was peculiar – something she hadn't noticed when she'd first entered the cavern. A collection of abstract shapes had been carved into the clay. She recognised them immediately – the circle, staff, serpent and crescent she'd been pursuing since Topkapı. Of the four, three were rendered in outline only. Just the crescent shape had been chiselled out in its entirety.

She heard laboured breathing behind her as Garvé and Penney entered the cave. 'Is that it?' the Frenchman asked.

'Possibly,' Essie responded. Although she didn't want to sound too hopeful, her heart was racing.

With shaking hands, she took the keystone out of her backpack and pressed it into the inscribed shape. It was a perfect fit. She pushed a little harder, and with a grinding sound, the clay wall moved.

Garvé and Penney joined her. 'Come on, help me push! One, two, three . . .' she said. They pushed together and the panel crashed and tumbled into the room beyond.

Coughing, Essie covered her mouth and nose with her sleeve and stumbled across the fallen rubble.

The air cleared, and she saw what lay in the hidden room beyond.

38

Sinai Peninsula, Egypt

She wasn't sure what, exactly, she'd been expecting. But it certainly hadn't been this.

Nothing.

No dead alchemist. And, most importantly, no Emerald Tablet.

Essie's head was spinning. She felt as if she was going to faint.

'What? What's in there?' gabbled Penney. 'Tell me!'

'Not a thing,' replied Garvé, who was standing at Essie's shoulder.

'No! That can't be right!' the Englishman howled, stumbling into the open space. 'There's *got* to be something. What about that?' he asked, pointing at the back wall of the hidden room.

The rough stone had been ground down to a flat surface engraved with a neatly carved inscription in Greek text.

'What does it say? Quickly!' Penney snapped.

Essie gathered herself, the shock transforming into a spinning ball of anxiety in her gut. *Stay calm. He's right. Perhaps it points us somewhere else. It's not hopeless. Yet.* 'Judging by the letter forms, it's Byzantine,' she said. She ran her finger across the symbols, her lips moving as she translated the text in her head.

When she reached the end, she released the breath she'd been holding in with an explosive sigh. 'Well, I'm afraid that's it. It's not here.'

'What? No! That *can't* be right!' whined Penney.

'What does it say?' asked Garvé in a chill monotone.

'We've been deceived. Or, I should say, I've been deceived.' She translated the inscription aloud.

By the grace of thrice great Hermes,
and those who seek to learn from the seat of knowledge,
Balinas, master of the wise and foremost of the prophets,
was blessed with a greater gift of God and of Wisdom
than all those who came after Hermes.
Those true disciples who seek that gift will find truth.
But those who seek with eyes that are blinded by earthly desires
here will find only an empty tomb.
By the orders of Justinian the Great, the vessel was drained,
its blessings carried by angels to the one, true, holy mountain.

The two men were silent. 'So, that's it,' she said. 'If it ever was here, it's long gone.'

Penney's eyes bulged out of their sockets as his rage fought to find an outlet. He rounded on Essie. 'You *STUPID BITCH*!' he shrieked.

'Adam! That's enough!' Garvé ordered.

'I'm ruined! My uncle only backed me on this because he thought you knew what you were doing! Now it's all fucked!

And all because we put our fate in the hands of a jumped-up secretary!'

'I said, that's *enough*!'

'I didn't do anything wrong,' said Essie quietly. 'I didn't make any mistakes. I just followed the leads that were left to send us in the wrong direction.'

It didn't make her feel any better, but as she sifted through what had happened, it began to make sense. Justinian had been Emperor of Byzantium, and it was on his orders that the monastery had been built at the foot of Jebel Musa. That ensured the mountain would forever be identified with the Biblical Mt Sinai. As the capital of Byzantium was Constantinople and Topkapı his palace, Justinian would have known of Balinas and his secrets. And as a vigorous defender of the Christian faith, he believed alchemy to be a threat to the orthodox beliefs he championed. In 529 AD he abolished the study of all the ancient sciences and embarked on a campaign of persecution of all faiths other than Nicaean Christianity. Essie could imagine him agreeing to cooperate with a plot to hide Balinas and his legacy.

I guess I can take some small comfort in the knowledge that I'm the first person since then to crack the code and take it far enough to find the red herring Justinian left here. Operative word there being 'small', she thought. But there was no way of sugar-coating it – Essie's failure made her feel ill. 'Unfortunately it leaves us at a dead end.'

'Not necessarily,' said Garvé. 'Essie – you've known me long enough now that you should know I rarely embark on something like this without a backup plan.'

39

Negev Desert, Israel

B en couldn't believe what he was seeing.
The room glowed green as if cast in light shining
through a stained-glass window.

'Is that him?' Ilhan asked unnecessarily.

Propped up against the centre of the wall at the back of
the room, a figure sat, cross-legged. Time, and the arid desert
conditions, had sapped Balinas' flesh of the fluids that had once
surged through his body, drawing his skin taut over brittle
bundles of bones and dehydrated muscles. Even under those
brutal physiological conditions, the expression on the long-dead
alchemist's face was somehow serene. The sharp lines of his
cheekbones and jaw curved arabesques into the darkened
leather of his skin. His lips were parted slightly, showing a
glimpse of starkly white teeth, while hooded eyelids feathered
with dark lashes dipped gently over long-empty eye sockets.

The Emerald Tablet rested in what once would have
been his lap, angled back against a ribcage delineated starkly

beneath mummified skin. The tablet's iridescent glow seemed to come from within, gleaming with a peculiar intensity that was as ominous as it was mesmerising.

There's something about it that feels not quite right, Ben thought. He'd never been a superstitious man, but if he'd believed in such things, he would have said that there was an aura that emanated from it that was both humbling and terrifying.

Transfixed, Ben moved closer. There was, as he'd expected, an inscription on the tablet; but rather than being incised into the hard surface, the letters were raised, as if the strange substance had been liquified at an extreme heat then poured into a mould when molten and allowed to harden.

Ilhan stood by his side. 'What is it, Ben? Why does it shine like that?'

'I've no idea. I can guess, but that's all it would be – a guess. I assume it's been irradiated somehow or another.'

'Radiation?' Ilhan exclaimed, alarmed. 'Is it safe?'

'I honestly can't say. But I'm not going to take any more risks than we already have. I don't think I even want to touch it with my bare hands, to be honest.'

He looked around the room, every corner of which was well lit by the unearthly green glow. There was nothing there, other than the mummified alchemist and the tablet.

His mind was racing. 'C'mon!' he summoned Ilhan. 'We've got that canvas sheeting down at the jeep. And the jerry cans . . . I'll cut a hole partway into one of those. We can wrap this thing up in the canvas and slip it inside. We need to cover it in as much material as we can to absorb the radiation . . . if that's what it is. Might fashion some sandbags to throw over it as well till we get it back to the city.'

As he spoke, Ben had turned and was walking swiftly back towards daylight, barely noticing the narrow passage that had caused him so much discomfort on the way into the cave. 'Your contacts in Jerusalem – do you think they'll be able to give us a well-insulated trunk? We'll need something pretty solid to get it back to Istanbul safely.'

'I'm sure they can, Ben.' Ilhan sounded dubious. 'But what are you going to do with it once you get it there?'

'Haven't decided yet,' he responded. 'You know me. Never one to plan too far ahead.'

'Right. Have you got everything ready to go?' Ben asked Ilhan, who stood nervously behind him.

They'd carted everything they could think of up to the cave to wrap the tablet, and Ben had contrived a casket to hide it in. He had two reasons for doing so: he wanted to make sure it was well hidden in case they attracted the interest of a military patrol or two between the Negev and Jerusalem; and he also wanted to do what he could to protect Ilhan and himself from any radiation that might have been leaching into the air around the peculiar object. He'd used Ari's hunting knife to saw three edges of a square out of the side of one of the empty metal jerry cans, then levered it open like a sardine can. They'd used duffel bags to fashion sandbags that were now packed into the jeep's tray in readiness for their departure, and Ilhan had also cut strips from the canvas he'd reclaimed from the Russian jeep that had escaped incineration and strapped them round Ben's hands to form makeshift mitts. With his fists bound up in layer upon layer of canvas, Ben now looked like a very nervous professional boxer.

'Do you think that's going to be enough?' Ilhan asked.

Ben hesitated. 'Well, it takes a while for low-level radiation to do any damage. So get back to me in ten years or so and ask then.'

'That doesn't make me feel any better, Ben.'

'Sorry.' He took a deep breath and moved towards the back wall where Balinas' cadaver sat nursing the Emerald Tablet. Heart pounding, he reached for it, the poisonous light reflecting onto his bound hands and shining in beams into his eyes. As he touched the slab gingerly, he felt his muscles tense. He was bracing himself, but for what, he wasn't exactly sure. However, the air seemed to crackle with an electric tension like the moment before a lightning bolt strikes the earth.

Ben held his breath. He shifted the tablet slightly, leaning it away from where it had slumped into Balinas' torso after almost two thousand years of mortal decay. A shift, a crack. Ben flinched. But he held the tablet tightly.

The symbiotic relationship between the long-dead alchemist and his treasure was broken. Ben lifted it away. He knew it was ridiculous, but for a moment he thought Balinas' spidery fingers might suddenly spring to life and grasp at the thing he'd gone to such lengths to keep at his side. But – nothing.

'Ilhan . . . quickly! Bring me the canvas . . . and the jerry can.' Ben didn't want to hold on to the uncanny stone any longer than he had to. He'd later think he'd been imagining it, but as it rested in his canvas-swathed hands, it seemed to vibrate with an unearthly resonance.

After Ilhan had laid the canvas out on the ground, Ben placed the tablet in the centre of the sheet and wrapped it tightly, then jammed it into the metal case and levered the roughly cut lid shut.

'Toss me the other sheets!' Ben said as he frantically unwound the binding from around his hands.

The two men parcelled the jerry can between multiple layers of canvas until it resembled a badly wrapped, and very large, birthday gift.

'Well, that's the best we can do, I suppose,' said Ben. He tried to lift it. 'Can't do this on my own, I'm sorry, Ilhan.'

With a sigh, the Turk took the other side. 'Fine.'

Manoeuvring the unwieldy – and now fairly heavy – object through the narrow corridor was a challenge. When Ben and Ilhan finally made it to the entrance, they were both puffing from the exertion and had broken out in a sweat.

The transition from the still, chilly air in the cave to the scorching heat outside was a shock. It took a moment for Ben's eyes to adjust to the blinding white light.

'Let's take a breather before we take it down,' he said.

'No arguments from me, I can assure you,' said Ilhan, panting.

'Water?' Ben offered his canteen to his friend.

'Yes. Thank you.' Ilhan took it gratefully.

The two men sat in the meagre shade of the overhang at the entrance to the cave.

Suddenly, Ben heard something. He raised his hand. 'Shh!' he said. 'What's that?'

'What?' asked Ilhan nervously.

A low throbbing sound filled the air.

'That. Can't you hear it?'

'I can't hear anything. Are you sure? It's probably just like the other night – bombers on their way to Suez.'

'No – it's different this time. And it's getting closer. Here.' Ben held out his hand. 'Give me the binoculars.'

Ilhan handed them over reluctantly. 'There's nothing there, Ben. You're imagining things.'

'I just want to make sure. Can't blame me for feeling a little jumpy.'

Ben scanned the horizon. He was right. Just above the desert sand, a black silhouette loomed and grew larger. 'There! It's coming from the south. Fast.' He handed the binoculars back to Ilhan.

'Is that a helicopter?'

'Must be.'

'Maybe they'll pass us by.'

'Maybe they will. But we've got something worth taking now.' Ben stood and began to lope towards the path leading down to the desert floor. 'And if they decide to drop in, I want to make sure we're ready for them.'

40

Negev Desert, Israel

Ben had set himself up a sniper's nest behind a rocky outcrop overlooking the wreckage of the two Russian jeeps they'd left where they were, figuring that if the approaching helicopter was to land and the people inside it were looking for them, its pilot would choose a place where they'd left their footprints – literally and figuratively. Ben had more than enough ammunition to pick off any fighters that stepped off the aircraft, and from his elevated position, he'd be well defended from an assault on the ground. He'd only be exposed if they decided to take to the air again. Even then, he and Ilhan could seek refuge in Balinas' cave.

'This isn't necessary, Ben,' Ilhan said. 'Perhaps they're here because they've seen the smoke from the jeep and think there's been an accident down there . . . They're not necessarily here for us. Or the tablet.'

'You're right,' said Ben, shifting the rifle butt from where it nestled into his shoulder and checking the sights. 'And if that's the case, they'll have a poke around down there and then take off again. Don't worry. I'm not going to just start shooting. Not till I know for certain they're coming after us. I promise.'

As the helicopter approached the wrecked vehicles, it hovered, then slowly descended, its rotors kicking up a spiralling cloud of sand that quickly obscured the aircraft.

'Right. Now we see what we're dealing with,' Ben said.

The rotors slowed and the whirling dust began to settle.

Ben took a deep breath and steadied himself. Although he was well hidden from below, there was no protection from the blazing sun that burned overhead. He felt the sweat on his forehead begin to bead and run towards his eyes. With a dusty hand, he wiped it away.

Once the rotors were spinning as slowly as a ceiling fan in the tropics, Ben saw movement within the aircraft's metal chassis. A side door slammed open, and three figures stepped out.

'No!' Ben murmured, disbelieving, as his breath caught in his chest.

'What?' asked Ilhan as he raised the binoculars to his eyes. 'Oh. Is that . . .?'

'Yes.'

There was something about her – the way she moved, the way she held her head.

You know you'll never be over her, don't you? a treacherous voice in his head declared.

His heart was pounding as he watched her walk assuredly across the sand, echoing his moves of the day before as she bent to inspect the broken pottery sherds and ancient stone tools that carpeted the ground.

Always such a damned professional, he thought with grudging admiration.

He snatched the binoculars out of Ilhan's hands. She may have made some superficial changes to her appearance, but there was no denying it was her. And as much as he hated himself for it, he was paralysed again by the primal desire that washed over him every time he was near her.

Get a grip! he berated himself.

Ben felt another jolt of recognition when he turned his attention to the figure standing behind Essie.

'Garvé,' he snarled.

'The Frenchman?' Ilhan asked.

'Yes.' Ben was shocked. 'This is no accident. How did they know we were here? They haven't just stumbled on us – this is by design . . . how the *fuck* did they know?! No way that woman worked it out by herself. She's good, but she's not *that* good!'

Pounding blood buzzed in his eardrums as he lined the bead of his sights on Garvé's forehead. 'Well, there's an unexpected upside to all this, anyway.' Ben chambered a round and readied to shoot.

'No! Ben, stop!' Ilhan grabbed his friend's forearm. 'Think about it. They've got a helicopter. If you shoot the Frenchman, they'll attack us from the air. There'll be no escaping them!'

Ben clenched his jaw and, through the telescopic sight, watched the face he still knew intimately from the nightmares that woke him in the dead of night. At that moment, there was nothing he wanted more than to see Garvé's features disintegrate in a hail of bullets. But Ben also knew Ilhan was right. He'd have to shoot the Frenchman's companions as well. And with the woman he'd known as Eris down there, even though he wanted to see her suffer, he knew he'd never be able to kill her.

'*Why* does she have to fucking well be with him?' he cursed.

She cared nothing for you . . . tried to destroy you. Why would you give her even a moment's thought? he asked himself.

But he already knew the answer. *Because it's her.*

'Fuck it. You're right,' Ben said. 'So – change of plans. No shooting . . . unless they decide to be difficult. And even then . . . flesh wounds only. Now, they're still playing around down there – I need you to give them something to chase. Same tactic we used with the Russians. Get yourself somewhere they can see you, and let them follow you to the cavern. Make it look like you've seen them and are trying to run for cover. Lead them into the hidden room, but hide in a corner of the first chamber. When they get in there, all they'll be interested in doing is seeing what's in the hidden room. Hopefully they'll be distracted enough by our old friend Balinas that they won't see you behind them. Meantime, I'll come up behind you, herd them into the tomb if they're not already in there, and lock the door behind them. We hijack their pilot and get the tablet out of here, and he can fly back to retrieve them once we're clear. Sound good to you?' Even as he said it, Ben knew there was only the slimmest of chances it would work. There were just too many moving parts to the operation. But he couldn't see any other alternatives.

'I suppose so,' Ilhan said dubiously. 'I should go now?'

'May as well. But try not to make it look like you're leading them into a trap.'

'But I am.'

'Yes. But we don't want them to know that.'

Ilhan took a deep breath and bolted out onto the plateau, kicking dust into the air as he had earlier in the day.

From his hidden vantage point, Ben saw Garvé look up as he caught sight of Ilhan moving about.

That's it, you motherfucker . . . take the bait.

When he'd seen Garvé and Essie moving towards the pathway leading up to the plateau, Ben knew he had time to reposition himself closer to the cavern so he was ready to spring the trap once Ilhan had led them inside. He'd moved so he was now hidden behind a mound of boulders near the crevice in the cliff face where they'd also stashed the makeshift crate containing the Emerald Tablet.

He'd been relieved to see that the helicopter pilot had decided to stay with the aircraft. Although he couldn't know who was at the controls, its markings told Ben it was from the British Air Force, so he assumed the uniformed pilot was a military man. Ilhan wasn't going to be any use to him if he was forced to fight, and if Garvé and Essie had been accompanied by an experienced fighter, he would have been in trouble.

There was a third person in the group on the ground. But with the finicky way the spindly-framed stranger moved about the landscape, fanning himself with his straw hat, Ben knew immediately he wasn't a physical threat. He had no intention of underestimating Josef Garvé, though. Or Mrs Essie Peters, for that matter.

The three figures crossed the plateau quickly, heading straight for the pitch-black gash in the rock.

As they neared the entrance, Ben held his breath, transfixed by the woman who led them. He was no more than thirty feet from her. A sudden blast of hot desert wind scoured the flat top of the mountain, carrying with it grit and sand and the smell of her. Ben squinted against the dust and watched her shield her own nose and eyes from the choking assault of airborne particles. As quickly as it appeared, it died away, and she dropped her hand back to her side.

Now that he was this close to her, he could see her expression. The tightness around her eyes and the set line of her mouth belied the confidence and composure in her body language.

Is it me you're thinking of? he wondered. *How do you feel, knowing you're about to confront the man you betrayed? You put up a good show of it . . . but how cold-blooded are you, really?*

'The American – I didn't see him. Where is he?' Garvé's voice was as repellent as he remembered it.

Don't worry, you fucking demon, Ben thought. *You'll be seeing me soon enough.*

'He'll be inside.' Her voice. It carried the same husky undertones, though rather than the Greek accent she'd adopted when she'd been playing the part of Eris Patras, she now spoke with the refined cadence of a well-brought-up woman more at home in Knightsbridge than in a desert at the ends of the earth. Even in the crucifyingly hot desert air, a chill shiver of desire made him flinch. *Who the hell* are *you?*

Ben forced himself to focus on the matter at hand. *Garvé won't have come up here unarmed. Nor will she.* Sure enough, Essie had a holster at her waist. If Garvé was carrying a weapon, it was concealed somewhere else. *So, when I go in, I have to assume there'll be at least two weapons.*

'So,' the Frenchman said. 'Would you like to take the lead, Adam?'

'Me? Why me?' whinged the third member of their party.

'You'd rather a woman goes into danger before you?' Garvé said.

'Why not you?'

Garvé said nothing.

'Fine.' The Englishman sighed. 'But you'd better back me up!'

'We will. I promise.'

The man Ben now knew by the name Adam entered the chasm tentatively. Essie and Garvé followed. Neither had their weapons drawn.

Amateur move, Ben thought with relief. *I'll make you regret that.*

He waited, counting down two minutes on his watch – more than enough time for them to make it into the hidden cavern.

Standing, he slung the rifle over his back from its strap and drew his own revolver, chambering a round so he was ready.

Heart pounding, he crept along the rough wall until he was standing right beside the edge of the cleft. He held his breath and strained to hear if there was any noise coming from within. Nothing.

Careful to keep from whacking his rifle on the walls of the corridor, he moved stealthily into the dark, treading like a cat at night so the sound of his footsteps didn't signal his approach to those inside the cavern. A dim pool of light – the kerosene lantern – was visible just a dozen or so feet ahead of him. His muscles tensed and every nerve in his body was on alert as he readied to burst into the room, gun held in an outstretched hand.

They won't be expecting you, but you'll have to move as fast as lightning, he thought.

He edged further towards the cavern.

There are three of them. Go for Garvé first. Line him up. Make him hand over his gun . . .

The horizon line of the light shining in the cave was barely an arm's span away from him.

. . . Then her. Can't underestimate her. Not again. Not this time.

Through the narrow entrance to the cave, he could only see a sliver of the room. Nobody was within sight. And he couldn't hear a thing. Nothing.

Ilhan . . . where is he?

Something was wrong. But he was already committed.

No pulling out now.

He held his breath.

One, two, three . . . He burst into the open space.

41

Negev Desert, Israel

'I'm sorry, Benedict.' It was Ilhan. 'I didn't know what to do.'

His friend was kneeling in the dust at Garvé's feet with a gun to his head.

'*He* may be sorry,' the Frenchman said, a grim smile contorting his face. His eyes were exactly as Ben remembered them – black and pitiless, like a shark sizing up its prey. 'But I'm not. Benedict, it's been *far* too long.'

Ben's mind was racing. *What can I do? What can I do?* His eyes darted around the room, trying to find a solution. *The prick's no hand-to-hand fighter. I could tackle him ... take his gun. Or Essie – no way she could defend herself from me if I went after her pistol.* But he knew it was hopeless. One move, and Garvé would pull the trigger.

'Before you do anything foolish, pause for a moment to consider the value of your friend's life. He's nothing to me ... less than nothing. If you force me to pull the trigger, I shan't

322

lose a minute's sleep over it. But you, on the other hand . . . I'd have thought you had enough ghosts haunting your dreams already without adding another to their number. Am I right? Now, lower your weapon, please.'

'You fucking ghoul,' Ben said, his voice shaking with fury. He bent and put his pistol on the floor.

'And the other one.'

Ben swung the rifle off his shoulder and slid it across the dirt towards Garvé.

'Now,' the Frenchman said in a conversational tone of voice. 'The Emerald Tablet. Judging by the rather singular corpse in there, I assume you found it. Where is it now?'

'I'm not telling you.'

Garvé sighed and shoved the barrel of his gun into Ilhan's brow, hard enough that the Turk stumbled backwards and almost toppled over. 'I don't feel like explaining again . . .'

Essie stepped towards Ben, her hand outstretched. 'Ben . . . please . . .' she said.

'You?' Ben couldn't even bring himself to look at her. 'You can shut the fuck up!'

Out of the corner of his eye, he saw her flinch.

He knew he had no choice. 'It's outside. There's a tumble of boulders just outside the entrance. It's packed in a jerry can.'

'A jerry can? Clever. Well, I can't say I'm surprised. A lack of ingenuity was never one of your failings. Isn't that right, Essie, my dear?'

She said nothing.

Garvé shrugged. 'Up you get then,' he said to Ilhan. 'You played your part well. Thank you.'

Ilhan looked at Ben with mournful eyes as he stood up, but made no move to join him.

What . . .? Ben was confused.

'Oh dear,' Garvé said. 'You really didn't suspect anything? Now, that *is* one of your failings, Dr Hitchens. Blind faith doesn't seem to serve you well.'

'Ilhan . . .?' *No. I can't believe it.*

The features Ben knew so well were contorted with remorse and confirmed the worst.

Ilhan refused to look at Ben.

A cold fury began to burn in Ben's chest. 'It makes no sense. Ilhan? Why would he . . .?'

'Why? You'll have to ask him,' said Garvé. 'And, fancy that – we've two people in this godforsaken place who have first-hand experience of betraying you. Seems you're able to bring out the very worst in people, Benedict. I'd leave Essie here with you to join in the conversation – I'm sure she'd bring quite a unique perspective –' Ben saw her glance up sharply. 'But she's proven to be too valuable over the years. So, unfortunately for you, she'll be coming along with me.'

'What are you going to do with it?'

'The tablet?'

'Of course the tablet. What else would I mean?'

'No need to be churlish, Benedict. And it's none of your concern. Even my dear associates here are partially in the dark . . . Essie, Adam, on that subject – I should warn you. There's been a change of plan.'

42

Negev Desert, Israel

'Change of plan?' Essie was wearing another accent, but Ben knew her well enough to recognise the anxiety in her tone.

'Yes,' Garvé answered. 'Under other circumstances, I'd rather not discuss it here. But I'll need your cooperation for this – it's going to involve telling a white lie or two to Captain Knight.'

'Lie? About what?' The reedy-necked man in the corner who'd been silent till now piped up.

'About our destination after we leave, Adam. We won't be going directly back to the ship. I'm taking the tablet to the Israelis.'

'Fucking Ethan!' Ben exclaimed.

'Who?' Garvé asked.

'Ethan. He's behind this, isn't he?'

'I've no idea who you're referring to.'

'Ethan. Ethan Cohn. The archaeologist. You hooked into him in Crete during the war.'

'Him? The old man? Please! This plan is operating at the highest levels of government. He wouldn't have a clue.'

'The Israelis?' Essie asked, her face blanching. 'Why didn't you tell me?'

'I know your past, dear lady. And I feared you'd be reluctant to help if you knew the ultimate destination of our find. But you mustn't concern yourself – there's no change to our agreement. You'll still get the same percentage of the sale price. Only this way, you'll get more. Much more. There were multiple buyers – the Americans, the Russians ... and our British patrons, of course. Though the Israelis were willing to pay through the nose for Balinas' discovery. They plan to use it to accelerate the nuclear program they're not supposed to have.'

There was a startled bellow from the corner. '*WHAT?!*' Penney's face was as purple as an overripe plum, his eyes bulging out of their sockets and mouth hanging open. 'You're going to give it to the *FUCKING JEWS?! OVER MY DEAD BODY YOU WILL!*'

'Don't tempt me, Adam,' Garvé said ominously.

'That tablet ... it's mine! By right, it's mine! Without me, you wouldn't even know it existed! You wouldn't even be *here*! And the Master ... Crowley ... he entrusted its secret to *ME*! Not you ... *ME!*'

'I don't deny that, Adam. But it doesn't make any difference at all to me. And it doesn't change the fact that I've sold it to the Israelis.'

'You had *NO RIGHT*! No right at all! It wasn't yours to sell! It's mine! It's my pathway to another plane of existence ... through it I'll find enlightenment. And all you're thinking about is gold!'

'It's not about gold, Adam. Or enlightenment. Your uncle knows that. Everybody wants this because it's the future ... the tablet is the key to unimaginable power. And you can't have it. Not for your foolish and deluded endeavours. No matter how much you wish it.'

'You can't take it from me! You can't!' Penney stamped his feet and slapped his palms on his thighs. 'This is my pathway to eternal life!'

'You? Find eternal life? Well, we can't have that, can we?' Garvé said. He cocked his gun and pointed it at the centre of Adam's forehead.

'What . . .? No! Get that thing out of my face!' Adam's fury evaporated. 'You . . . you can't! . . . My uncle . . . Uncle Bill . . . He won't let you get away with this!'

'How is he going to know what really happened here? I'll be able to come up with some plausible story.' He used his other hand to point at Ben. 'Useful scapegoat right here, for a start! You're no use to me anymore. And the truth is, your uncle won't miss you. Nobody will, if we're honest. Isn't that right, dear lady?' Garvé said, glancing at Essie.

'Essie . . .' Adam turned his attention to her. 'Please! You can't let him do this!'

She stood with her hands crossed at her chest and, by her silence, condemned him.

But her reaction when Garvé pulled the trigger and sent a bullet spinning into Adam Penney's skull showed she hadn't been expecting the Frenchman to follow through with his threat. Essie's eyes were black with shock and her mouth gaped as Adam Penney's lifeless body slumped to the floor.

Although Ben recoiled from the sound of the gunfire that reverberated around the room, he knew Garvé better. He would never question the Frenchman's resolve.

'Well, no great loss there,' Garvé said.

'. . . but . . .' Essie interjected.

Garvé peered at her through eyes narrowed to slits. 'After what he did to you, I thought you'd be pleased.'

'You knew?'

'Of course. Did you really think someone that undisciplined would keep his sexual escapades secret?'

'You didn't say anything.'

'It was none of my business. I don't care what you do in your private life. And I didn't think it was something you'd have been particularly proud of. So I thought it best to keep it to myself. This –' he waved his hand towards Penney's corpse, '– had nothing to do with you. I'd tired of him. And he's a loose end we're better off without.'

Garvé turned to Ben with his gun raised. 'Speaking about loose ends . . .' He took aim, Ben squarely in his sights.

Ben felt a peculiar detachment as he looked down the barrel of the pistol held in Garvé's steady hand. He shifted his gaze to the Frenchman's face. *Watch for that momentary flinch – the tell that'll show when he's about to pull the trigger. Then drop and roll – take his legs out.* He had no intention of dying, least of all at the hands of the person he despised more than any other.

'No!' interjected Essie. 'Please. That's enough – nobody was supposed to be killed!'

'That's often the case, Essie. We start with the noblest of intentions. Yet people die anyway. Collateral damage, it's called.'

Ilhan, who'd been silently watching the events unfold, now stepped forward with both hands raised. 'You've got what you wanted. You said you'd just take the tablet and let Ben go.'

Garvé grinned grimly, exposing his peculiarly small but very white teeth. 'I lied.' He licked his thin lips.

There – that's the tell.

Ben watched as the Frenchman squeezed the trigger.

43

Negev Desert, Israel

Before the hammer had even engaged the firing pin, Ben had dropped down and launched himself towards Garvé. At the same time, Essie ran at the Frenchman and grabbed his arm as Ilhan dived forward to put himself between Ben and the gun.

There was a deafening explosion followed by a wet thud and a grunt; the expulsion of air from lungs as the bullet hit flesh. A body hit the earth with a sound like a bag of wet sand being dropped.

Ben checked himself. Whoever had been hit, it wasn't him. Essie was still standing. That left only one other person.

'Ilhan!' Ben turned and rushed to his friend's side. The Turk's olive skin had taken on a greenish tinge as the blood rushed to his vital organs in response to the shock to his system. His eyes were black pools and his lips were white and agape as he looked down at his leg in disbelief.

The bullet had torn a hole in his thigh. Blood streamed through the tear in his pants, seeping into the dust on the floor and staining it black. Essie stood to one side, aghast, as Garvé took in his handiwork dispassionately.

'Your scarf!' Ben screamed at Essie. 'Give it to me! Quickly!'

Startled, she unwound the red and white cotton wrap from around her neck and shoved it into Ben's outstretched hand. He ripped it in two, twisting one half into a tourniquet which he fastened above the wound. The other he used to staunch the bleeding. He gingerly felt the back of Ilhan's leg. Judging by the broken skin he felt there, he knew the bullet had passed through the muscle and exited the leg, which was good news, and although blood was still flowing from the wound, it wasn't gushing at a rate he'd expect if an artery had been damaged.

'Ben, I'm ... I'm sorry ...' Ilhan whispered through parched lips.

'Shut up.'

'... but I ...'

'Seriously, Ilhan, you need to stop talking. Whatever you've got to say ... just shut up. Don't want to hear it.'

Garvé stood above the two men. 'Where to from here?' he said. He gripped the pistol in his right hand and tapped his chin pensively as he spoke. 'Everything's just become terribly messy. Oh, well.' He cocked his gun and pointed it at Ben. 'Your turn.'

'No!' Essie shrieked, grabbing Garvé's arm. 'That's enough, Josef! We've got the tablet. Just leave them. Please? I don't want this on my conscience.'

'Conscience? Still have one of those, do you?' The Frenchman giggled. 'I disposed of mine many years ago. I highly recommend it. It makes life so much easier. It is interesting to see you're still nursing some affection for your American, though.'

Essie blushed, her eyes downcast. 'It's not that. I just don't want anybody else to die.'

'Fine. It won't be by my hand, then. Though you know, you're consigning them to a far less merciful end by leaving them alive out here. But, so be it.' Garvé lined Ben up in his sights once more. 'You! Help your friend into the tomb.'

'No! He's in pain,' Ben exclaimed. 'Just leave him here. He's going to die anyway.'

'You're probably right. But do it all the same.' Garvé wagged the gun in Ben's face. 'And don't think that just because your girlfriend has won you a reprieve, that I won't shoot you anyway. Her advocacy won't count for anything if you push me too far.'

'You fucking animal!' Ben cursed. Lowering his voice, he bent and hooked an arm beneath Ilhan's shoulders. 'Here – lean into me,' he said as he flexed the muscles in his legs and hoisted the Turk up onto his one good leg. Ilhan groaned, his eyes rolling back in his head. 'Steady,' Ben said as he helped him walk slowly towards the cavern's inner room. In one corner was a pile of off-cuts from the canvas sheeting they'd used to wrap the tablet; Ben guided Ilhan towards what was the only vaguely comfortable place in the cave and helped him lower his injured body down into a prone position.

'Thirsty ... water ...' Ilhan said in a voice cracking with pain.

In the main cavern, Ben knew he'd left his backpack leaning against the wall. 'Over there ... Eris, Essie – whatever your name is – there's a canteen. Get it for me.'

He heard the sound of footsteps. She entered the hidden cavern holding the water and lantern.

'I don't know why you're bothering, Essie,' said Garvé from the other room. 'It'll just prolong the inevitable.'

Essie said nothing, just passed the canteen to Ben and placed the lantern on the floor. She turned and walked out.

'What? No goodbyes?' Ben said bitterly. 'You know we'll die in here.'

'Yes. That's the plan,' said Garvé, and he hefted the door shut.

44

Negev Desert, Israel

Light from the kerosene lantern flickered on the walls and illuminated the deathly pallor on Ilhan's face. Ben was relieved to see that the wound was now just seeping, rather than streaming, blood, but the trauma of the injury had caused the Turk to go into shock. His breathing was shallow and rasping, and his blood-deprived extremities were shuddering with cold.

What have I done? Why did I have to push this? I could've – no, should've – stayed in Istanbul. Everything was going along perfectly well. Why won't I ever learn to just be happy with the status quo? Ben berated himself. He looked down at his friend shivering at his feet. *And why did you betray me?* he wondered as he did what he could to cover Ilhan with the scant supply of canvas sheeting. *I'd have expected it from that bloody woman, but not you.* In the chilly air of the cave, it was next to impossible to warm him up. Ilhan's survival depended upon getting out, and getting out quickly.

If we're going to be stuck in here for good, there's no point worrying about it. And if we do – by some miracle – manage to find a way out, there'll be plenty of time to talk about it later. Got to work on that door, he thought. He ran his fingers around the door's edges, hoping to find a breach of some sort he could use to get a handhold and drag the panel open.

Nothing.

Set high up in the door was the butt-end of a stone cylinder that had been set in the clay; it was about the same point in the wall where Ben had inserted the keystone to gain access to the room, and he assumed that whatever function the cylinder had, it related to the locking mechanism that had held the door closed for close to two thousand years. He pushed at it and tried to jiggle it loose in the hope it might trigger the latch. When that failed, he decided to give brute force a go. Even though he knew the chances of making an impact on it were slim, Ben began to pound the door with his shoulder, hoping he could shift it off its hinges. But given how much difficulty it had posed even when there had been two of them trying to push it inward, he suspected it was going to be futile. After five minutes of hammering, all he had to show for it was a bruised and battered shoulder.

Although he hadn't noticed any signs of another way out when he'd been in the room before, there'd been no reason to look for one. With that in mind, Ben picked up the lantern and worked his way around the walls, inspecting every crack and crevice to see whether it might offer access to another space beyond. He knew there wasn't much chance he'd find anything, so it was no surprise when he drew a blank.

As he saw it, there was only one possible breach in the otherwise impenetrable prison they found themselves in; the point where the thick clay wall met the cave's rock face. He studied the seam closely. Although every effort had been made to ensure the wet clay had been pressed into every ridge and groove on the stone surface, in places it had pulled away from the rock as it had dried.

Balinas' mummified visage contemplated the scene with calm resignation. Ben knew what he had to do. He picked up one of the stones that covered the floor and began to work at the breach, chipping away tiny fragments of clay, most of them no bigger than a match-head.

This is going to take a while.

If his watch was to be believed, he'd been working away at the wall for over three hours, and the only impact he'd managed to make was a depression not much bigger than a cereal bowl. As time passed, he was becoming increasingly desperate; if it had been just him in the room, he would have been less concerned. With the water in the canteen, he knew he could survive without food long enough to eventually break through the wall. But Ilhan didn't have the luxury of time. The wound in his leg would become septic and the infection would kill him, if blood loss didn't end his life first.

Ben was relieved that the symptoms of shock appeared to be wearing off. Ilhan's skin had acquired a healthier blush, and his breathing – which had been shallow and coarse – seemed to be finding a more regular cadence.

With a rattling sigh, the Turk filled his lungs and expelled the air in a blast. 'Ben?' he said.

'Yeah?' Despite his lingering anger, Ben was relieved to hear his voice. 'Do you need anything? Actually, water's all I've got to offer.'

'Thank you. Yes.' He sounded drained but lucid. *That's a good thing*, Ben thought.

He handed Ilhan the canteen. 'Here. But don't drink it all. We need to make it last. I'm not looking forward to drinking our own piss, which might be the only alternative if I can't find a more effective way of digging into this wall.'

Ilhan's face was grim, his mouth turned down at the corners. 'Ben . . . what the Frenchman said –'

'Don't want to talk about that now,' Ben interjected.

'But I want to. I need to explain.'

'Well, that's fine for you. But I don't want to hear what you've got to say. Right now, it doesn't matter.'

'To me, it does. If I die here –'

'You're the luckiest bastard I know. If anyone can make it out of here alive, it'll be you.'

'But if I don't . . . it's important you know why.'

Sighing, Ben sat down in the dust, his back against the cold, stone wall. 'People have died because of you, Ilhan. Good people.'

'I know. That wasn't meant to happen . . . *This* wasn't meant to happen.'

'And yet, it did. That man's a soulless leech. Death follows him.'

'I wasn't to know. He promised nobody would be hurt . . . I believed him.'

'More fool you.'

'Garvé telephoned me. After we'd been to Topkapı. The man who killed the archivist. Ricard, his name was. He found out we'd been there and that you'd seen Balinas' book . . . he was working for Garvé . . . had been since the war. The Frenchman then told me to go with you and tell him what you found . . . and where we were going. The phone calls I've been making – they've been to him. I think the Russians must have been listening to the calls I made from the hotel in Jerusalem – that's how they would have found out we were coming here. That morning, while we were waiting for Ari, I called the Frenchman . . . told him we were coming here – to Har Karkom. I told him . . . Told him everything.'

'So you've got Ari's blood on your hands as well. Nice work.' Ben felt sick to the stomach. 'Why?' he asked, his voice tight with grief. 'How much did your loyalty cost him?'

'It wasn't that. It wasn't money. No amount would have been enough. But he knew things about me that I needed to keep secret . . .'

Ben snorted. 'You didn't do this to keep your bloody antiquities smuggling business quiet, did you? Or the fakes you peddle through your shop? Because that's hardly a secret!'

'No. Not that. You know me – I'm not ashamed of that. Perhaps I should be, but I'm not. No – this is something else. Something much more sinful.'

'Sinful? For Christ's sake, Ilhan. Enough with the riddles.'

'Truly, Benedict. If my family were to find out about this . . . my mother – it would kill her.'

'Given how difficult she makes your life, wouldn't that be a good thing?'

'I'm serious. It would bring great shame to my family. And I'm afraid when I tell you, you'll think less of me.'

'Well, my opinion of you right now is at an all-time low. So I wouldn't worry about that. Besides, we've done plenty of shady things together. I can't think of anything that would shock me.'

'This is different.'

'Well, how about you let me make that decision myself?'

'It's something that only happens occasionally. When I'm at the *hamam* – the bathhouse. There are times when . . .' Ilhan paused and drew a deep breath. 'I have intimate relationships with men. I don't know how Garvé found out . . . he must have had me followed. But he knew. He said he had evidence . . . photographs. Men who would tell stories about our time together. That's why I couldn't let you kill him before, although, God knows, he deserved it. He said if anything happened to him, a package would be sent to my mother. And if she – if anyone – ever found out, that'd be the end for me.'

Ben couldn't believe what he was hearing. 'But . . . what? You don't like women, then? You've been – I mean, I *thought* you'd been – with so many over the years. How . . .?'

'It's not that simple. It's not that I don't like women. It's just that I sometimes like men as well. And now, with everything that's happened, I feel so stupid. I should have done what I know was the right thing . . . tell that man I'd never betray my friend. But I'm weak. That's all I can say. I'm sorry, Ben. This is all my fault.'

'No,' said Ben. 'If I hadn't decided to go chasing after that damned woman again, we'd be warming a couple of chairs in a *meyhane* in Beyoğlu instead of stuck here. Besides . . . I think you've been punished enough.'

'Now that you know this about me, I'll understand if you can no longer be my friend,' Ilhan said quietly.

'At this rate, we're going to die here and I'd rather it be by the side of a friend than not. So to fire you from that position now would be a little premature. You should know that who you choose to mess around with makes no difference to me. I'd rather not know the gory details, to be honest. Don't need those pictures in my head – whether it's with a woman or with another man. Besides, if we ever make it out of here, I don't have the luxury of dumping you as a friend – you're the only one I've got left.'

The two men fell silent, the cave deathly still apart from the sound of their breathing.

'So now I know this big secret of yours, I've got one question for you,' Ben said. 'What about me? You say you fancy men. But you've never propositioned me. Should I be insulted?'

Ilhan laughed weakly. 'You're not my type.'

'Don't be ridiculous!' Ben guffawed. 'I'm *everybody's* type!'

After their conversation, Ilhan had fallen into a troubled sleep, grunting and mumbling unintelligibly while Ben resumed his slow-moving attack on the wall.

This is hopeless, he thought. Making a large enough hole in the clay was going to take much more time than they had, and Ben knew that even if they did get out, it was a long drive back to civilisation and the medical care Ilhan desperately needed. And that was assuming that the Frenchman had left them the jeep. *I've got to try something else.*

The depression he'd managed to chip out of the wall was larger now, though he knew from the depth of the doorway that he had to make it through at least a foot of clay to get to the other side. *I'll try kicking at it.* It would be risky – even if he did manage to break through, it was just as likely he'd be crushed by falling chunks of solid clay as get clear. But Ben knew there weren't any alternatives.

To maximise the amount of pressure he could exert, he lay on his back in front of the dip in the wall. Drawing his knees back, he slammed the soles of his work boots into the wall. He was disappointed but not surprised to see that it had no discernible effect at all. He did it again. Nothing. And again. Still nothing. But on the fourth try, he was sure he felt something give way. Heart pounding from the exertion, he crashed his feet into the wall again. There was a sound – a grinding crack. *Once more*, he urged himself. Then, he'd scurry back against the far wall – he didn't want to end up buried beneath what was coming.

With all his might, he battered the solid clay then scooted back to crouch beside Ilhan, ready to shield his friend in case the wall came tumbling down.

The sound of something giving way filled the room. It was deafening. Ben covered his ears with his hands and half closed his eyes in anticipation of a cloud of debris filling the enclosed space. Through his lashes he saw a blinding beam of light – but not where he was expecting it. It wasn't where he'd been attempting to make a breach. It was right in the centre of the wall. Right where he knew the door to be.

45

Negev Desert, Israel

'Here – he needs this.'
Essie Peters stepped through the doorway and threw Ben a first aid kit. 'There's dressings and antiseptic. And morphine.'

There was no mistaking her silhouette, or her husky voice. But for a moment, Ben thought he was hallucinating. 'But . . . you're . . .'

She gestured towards Ilhan impatiently. 'Don't talk! Help him!'

Mind whirling, Ben called on his memories of military field trauma procedures. First, he snapped off the glass bulb at the top of the morphine ampoule and took the tiny round of protective cork from the tip of the needle. He swabbed the crook of Ilhan's elbow and slipped the needle under his skin, sending the morphine coursing through his bloodstream. Using the iodine, Ben cleaned the gunshot wound as best he could. As he was struggling to raise Ilhan's leaden limb to get

341

to the exit wound on the back of his leg, he became aware of Essie's presence at his side.

'Can I help?'

'Yes. Lift this. Carefully. Hold it up so I can get a dressing onto it.'

As she slipped her hands beneath his knee to elevate his thigh, Ilhan groaned, his face contorted with pain.

'Don't worry, buddy. In a minute or two, that stuff'll kick in and you won't feel a thing, I promise. It's so potent, I've been sorely tempted to indulge in it myself at times as an alternative to gallons of liquor.'

Essie had dropped to her knees beside him and rested Ilhan's lower leg on her thighs while Ben wrapped a clean bandage around the wound, which was now packed in sterile dressings. As he expertly turned the edge of the compress and secured it with a pin, the back of his forearm brushed hers. Their eyes met at the physical contact. Essie held his gaze for a moment then looked away, colour rising in her cheeks.

'I've brought a stretcher as well,' she said. 'It won't be easy, but I'll be able to help you get him outside. We don't have to get down to the desert floor – I've got the helicopter up here on the plateau . . . I'll go and get the stretcher now.'

Ben grabbed her arm. 'No. First you have to tell me why you're here.'

'Why?' she answered. 'Well. That's not an easy question to answer. Isn't it enough that I regret what's happened to the two of you, and that I wanted to do what I could to fix things?'

'I saw your face when that fucking animal said he was giving the tablet to the Israelis. And he mentioned your history – by that, I assume he meant your *real* personal history; not the bucket of hog-swill you sold me.'

She winced. 'It's a long story that will take more time than we have,' she said, glancing at Ilhan. 'He needs to be in a

342

hospital . . . soon. And if you still want to stop Garvé, you don't have long. We flew back to Jerusalem – from there, he was taking a private plane to Istanbul. That's where the deal's being finalised.'

'You said he was selling it to the Israelis – why wouldn't he just do the handover in Jerusalem?'

'Because he doesn't trust them. He wants it to be on neutral territory.'

'Why would you care who gets it, anyway? I thought you only cared about money.'

'Not always. Believe it or not, I do have one or two guiding principles. One of which is that I'd rather people didn't die during the course of one of my operations.' Essie pointed at Ilhan. 'So can we get him moving? Please?'

'First you need to tell me what the hell you're planning to do. How on earth is this going to work? You're trying to tell me that Garvé let you bring the helicopter back here?'

'No. Not exactly. He let me take it so I could fly back to my family in Cairo –'

'Your family in Cairo?'

'As I said. It's a long story. But I pulled a gun on the pilot and forced him to fly me here. I've contacts in Jerusalem who can fly us to Istanbul – I figure we can follow Josef and you can retrieve the tablet.'

'So, judging by that, your business arrangement with Monsieur Garvé is formally at an end.'

'Yes.' She laughed ruefully. 'I'd say that's a fair assumption to make. Though, hopefully, it will be some time before he works that out. Otherwise we'll never catch him.'

'And why would you think the pilot's still out there waiting for you?'

'Because I didn't give him any choice. He's been . . . restrained.'

'I see. So when we get to Istanbul, you'll know where to find your former partner?'

'I know the people he works with in the city – he was organising the meeting with the Israelis through them. As long as he doesn't find out what I've done here before we arrive, his friends in Istanbul won't have any reason not to believe I'm still working with him . . . I hope. But it's the only chance we have.'

'Will you be able to pass through customs? Won't the police be watching for you on the border? You're not the type of tourist they're trying to attract to Turkey.'

'I've been in and out of the country three times over the past eighteen months as Estelle Peters. I've never had any trouble with my British passport –'

'British . . .?'

'Fake, of course. But good enough that nobody ever stops me. And there'll be no reason for them to think there's anything wrong when I arrive at the airport this time. Josef certainly won't have told the authorities what he's planning to do. And now,' she said as she took his arm gently, 'we really should go.'

Ben looked into her upturned face, the skin at the corner of her almond-shaped eyes creased with anxiety and her full lips set in a grim line. His inclination had been never to trust her again. But at this moment, he was plum out of choices.

'All right. Let's do it.'

She paused. 'There's one other thing I need you to do. It's going to sound peculiar, but it's for your own good. I promise.'

Essie's logic had been impeccable, and in the rush to get Ilhan out of the cave it had seemed to make sense. But as she secured

Ben's hands and legs to the metal uprights of the bench seats in the helicopter's fuselage, he'd begun to question his decision. *You've done it again, Benedict Hitchens,* he cursed himself. She'd always shown a remarkable capacity to convince him to do things that always seemed to end badly . . . for him.

She is right, though, he thought. *She's a ghost – and can just disappear once this is all over. But me and Ilhan – if this pilot thinks we've cooperated with her, we'll be tracked down and charged with hijacking a British military vehicle. This is the only way we won't be held accountable.*

Ilhan, who was comatose on the stretcher, posed no threat, so she'd decided it wasn't necessary to restrain him to maintain the façade and convince the pilot she was transporting them under duress.

'So,' he murmured. 'I've had an idea about how we can slow that bastard down. When we get to Jerusalem and you're arranging our transport, I'll need to make a phone call.'

'Who are you planning to call?' she whispered.

'Never mind.'

'Someone who can help?'

'Yes. I think so.'

'You don't sound too certain.'

'He's someone I've had some issues with in the past.'

'Well, if he can help, it's worth a try.' She smirked as she wound the rope about his limbs. 'Don't forget, you need to make a fuss,' she murmured. 'I'm forcing you to do this against your will.'

'That's not entirely untrue.'

'Good – then sound convincing!' she responded.

'Ouch!' he cried as she yanked the rope tight.

'Steady on down there, woman!' shouted the pilot. 'No need to be rough! By the looks of them, they've been through enough already!'

Good, Ben thought. *Sounds like he's bought her story, anyway.* Now he just had to hope she planned to carry through with what she'd promised.

She was leaning across his chest, reaching for the webbing secured to the body of the helicopter to loop the rope through it. Her breasts pressed against his upper arm, and tendrils of her hair that had fallen loose from her ponytail brushed his cheek. Despite himself, he was aroused by her proximity as she bound his limbs efficiently.

'Too tight?' she asked beneath her breath.

'No. I'm fine.'

'Right!' she yelled forcefully, winking at Ben as she stood upright. 'You watch yourself, OK? I'm going back up to the cockpit – we'll be taking off to Jerusalem in a minute. After that, I'll be using you as bargaining chips back in Turkey!'

'You'd be lucky to find anyone willing to exchange even a stale *simit* for my life,' Ben responded. It wasn't an exaggeration.

THE TIMES
2 November 1956
BRITISH, FRENCH COMMENCE
BOMBARDMENT OF SUEZ

LONDON, Friday (Reuters)

Silence from Westminster, but Paris Press declares: 'We have landed.'

Unconfirmed reports say British and French forces have landed in the Suez Canal Zone. Although there is an official news blackout in force until the British Prime Minister, Sir Anthony Eden, speaks, it was reported in the French evening newspaper, *France Soir*, that the landing operation began at dawn.

Although no official confirmation has been issued by the British Government, in tacit acknowledgement of the report, the Foreign Secretary, Mr Selwyn Lloyd, has said: 'There comes a time when men and government have to decide to act, and not to talk.' Such action is justified by Britain as promoting the cause of peace in the region.

If troops have entered the Canal Zone, it's expected they will storm ashore over the next twenty-four hours to secure the cities of Port Suez, Ismailia and Port Said. French reports state that three thousand paratroopers have been dropped into Egyptian territory in advance of a full-scale amphibious landing.

These airborne troops were met with fierce Egyptian resistance from tank, mortar and machine-gun fire. Cairo Radio claimed, 'The entire population is taking part in the national resistance.' Despite this, the Anglo-French forces were reportedly able to seize control of the Port Said airport and two strategically important bridges spanning the backwaters of the canal.

In advance of the attacks, Colonel Anwar el-Sadat, managing editor of the semi-official Egyptian newspaper *Al Gomhuryia*, had warned Britain and France that the consequences of landing troops in the Suez Canal Zone would mean 'there will be war to the last drop of our blood'.

Retaliation from the Moslem nations has been swift. Saudi Arabia has cut all ties with Britain and France, and has ceased the supply of oil to their tankers. In Syria, army units demolished British oil pipelines. The British Government has declared that it holds the Syrian Government directly responsible for 'these acts of sabotage and for causing the flow of oil to cease'.

Britain's allies quickly jumped to her defence. From Australia, the Minister for External Affairs, Mr Casey, branded Egypt as the true aggressor and said that Israel was the instigator 'only in a technical sense' and that the current Israeli attack on Egypt was a 'completely understandable kickback' by Israel after many years of provocation.

It's been claimed that British and French action in Suez will stop the inevitable march of war across the region and unmask Soviet military penetration into the Middle East. From Moscow, Russia cautioned Britain and France that the conflict would lead to World War III, saying she fully intended to 'crush aggression' and to re-establish Middle East peace. A Russian spokesman declared the government would not hesitate to use military force if necessary. The Soviet Premier, Marshal Bulganin, wrote to President Eisenhower, calling upon the U.S.A. to join the U.S.S.R. in a united military intervention to keep the peace.

This occurs as the United Nations (U.N.) struggles to resolve the conflict. Despite nearly one hundred U.N. Security Council meetings to solve disputes between Israel and her Arab neighbours, there has been no lasting solution.

This situation deteriorated further when, the British and French claim, Russia began sending arms to Egypt. 'The plain fact is that the Middle East was becoming a forward base for the Soviet Union,' said one source in the British Foreign Office.

Egypt's response to the U.N.'s inaction has been to threaten to leave the organisation because of what it describes as 'its clear failure when confronted with the ambitions of the big imperialistic Powers'.

Meanwhile, it is clear that the United States will not bail out Britain and France. It is widely acknowledged that relations between the U.S. and its chief European allies have fallen into a parlous state of disunity and conflict. This echoes global sentiment, which asserts that the Anglo-French move in the Sinai is completely illegal.

The U.S., which has been attempting to establish stronger ties with the government of Colonel Nasser, objects to any action that will disrupt the delicate balance of power in the region. The U.S. has warned Britain and France in no uncertain terms that the military path they have taken could ignite a major war.

President Eisenhower and John Foster Dulles, Secretary of State, are reported to be deeply angered at reports of the Allied move on the Canal Zone. They fear the action will galvanise the Moslem world and inflame a 'holy war' against Britain and France stretching from the shores of the Atlantic to the Persian Gulf.

46

Istanbul

Ben's instructions to the cab driver after they'd passed through customs at Atatürk airport had been unambiguous. 'Police headquarters – quickly!'

Seated at the opposite end of the bench seat in the back of the car, Essie's brow was furrowed with concern as she toyed with her hands in her lap, her knuckles white as she flexed and intertwined her fingers. 'Will we get there in time?'

'I don't know. I hope so. Hasan said he was going to follow him from the airport after he landed. But there's no way of knowing whether or not things went to plan.'

'If Garvé's already met with them –'

'Yes,' Ben snapped. 'Then the Israelis have the tablet. And there's nothing we can do about it.'

The flight from Jerusalem to Istanbul had been fraught and they'd landed in Turkey with their nerves in tatters. Not only was time running out if they were to intercept Garvé

before he made the exchange, but as Ben had anticipated, Ilhan had succumbed to a raging fever as infection took hold. With only the most rudimentary medications and basic first aid equipment, there had been little Ben could do but watch his friend writhe in pain while poison flooded his veins and sweat ran off his body in sheets. He'd nursed Ilhan's head in his lap and mopped his fevered brow while offering up prayers using whatever flimsy remnants of belief in a higher power he still retained.

The pilot of the small plane Essie had arranged in Jerusalem radioed ahead and an ambulance was waiting for them as they taxied into Atatürk airport. Ben had felt a surge of relief when the doctor who'd examined his friend voiced no concerns about his prospects for recovery and promised that after an operation to repair the damage to his leg all he'd need was bed rest, fluids and an industrial-strength course of antibiotics. The peace of mind that came with knowing Ilhan would recover meant Ben could turn his attention to the next stage of their operation.

Golden light streamed in through the cab's window. The monumental double arches of the Valens Aqueduct framed the hills of Beyoğlu as they approached the steep descent to the bridge across the Golden Horn, its waters glittering in the morning sunlight.

Despite his anxiety, it was comforting to see the peaked silhouette of the Galata Tower standing proud against the gentle mauve horizon. *Home*, he thought. He caught sight of Essie's profile backlit against the sky and forced himself to look away.

'So,' he said in a matter-of-fact tone. 'We need to work out what to do next. Now, you're not the most popular person with the Istanbul police force.'

She smiled ruefully. 'No kidding.'

'So when we get to the station, you won't be able to come in with me,' he said.

'You're not planning to go there with them, are you – to get the tablet back from him?'

'Sure. I want to look that bastard in the eye when I take it.'

Essie locked eyes with him. 'Do you really think that's a good idea? Isn't it best to let the police do it? Do you *really* want him knowing you're involved in this?'

'Yes. I do,' he replied. Ben's heart pounded with ferocious joy at the thought of confronting Josef Garvé and stealing something that meant so much to him, as the Frenchman had done to him so many times before. 'But you can't come with me. There's a *lokanta* opposite police headquarters. You can wait for me there. Understand?'

She nodded silently in agreement.

The hint of crispness in the autumn air warned of the approach of winter, but the humidity that settled on their skin was still warm and cloying. Essie had rolled the sleeves of her linen shirt above her elbows, and her hands were linked in her lap. Although she and Ben had been studiously avoiding any physical contact, as the cab jolted its way down Atatürk Boulevard, the motion of the vehicle made them sway from side to side. The car swerved to avoid a pothole, sending Essie sliding along the bench seat until her hip pressed hard against Ben's and her bare skin grazed his forearm.

'Sorry,' Essie mumbled, blushing, as she shifted herself back to the opposite end of the seat.

Ben said nothing. Fighting the most primal of urges, he clenched his hands into fists and tried to distract himself from the burning hunger that was eroding his will.

The cab passed beneath the broad arches of the aqueduct that the Byzantine Emperor Valens had built in the sixth century to carry water for the populace from the mountains to the immense cisterns beneath the city's streets. The ancient metropolis embraced the curves of the steep hills that were rent in three by the two bodies of water intersecting Istanbul – the Golden Horn that split the European half of the city in two, and the Bosphorus, which ran from the Black Sea to the Sea of Marmara and divided Istanbul between the continents of Europe and Asia. With the potent magnetism of the woman seated at his side making his senses short-circuit, Ben wished there was the equivalent of a Bosphorus between them.

Not long now, he assured himself. *Almost done, and then you can send her on her way.*

Ben wished he had any certainty that he'd find the resolve to do just that when the time came to farewell her.

'Garvé has his yacht here. It's anchored just off Tophane. He went straight there after he landed. Sugar?' Superintendent Hasan Demir offered Ben a small silver bowl and a teaspoon.

Ben tapped his foot impatiently. 'If he's here already, Hasan . . . with all due respect, shouldn't we be arresting him rather than sitting here drinking tea?'

'Benedict Hitchens, you've been in this country long enough to know the importance of these rituals,' Hasan said as he considered his guest critically. 'Besides. I have men watching the yacht. They'll radio as soon as they see any movement. Almond?' The police officer indicated a dish of chilled almonds on the tray.

'I don't want any bloody nuts, Hasan! I want to stop Garvé! How do you know the trade hasn't already been done?'

'I don't,' Hasan said patiently. 'But what I do know is that he took a launch out to his yacht after his arrival. And loaded into the back of that launch was a metal case that looked a little like a large suitcase. Neither Josef Garvé nor the case has been seen leaving the boat. So I think it's safe to assume they're both still on board.'

'What if they're sailing somewhere – maybe they're going to do the deal somewhere else?'

'If they weigh anchor, I'll call on the assistance of the navy to follow him.' Hasan sighed and placed his gilt-edged glass of tea down in its saucer, interlinking his hands on the desk before him. 'Ben – believe it or not, I *do* know how to do my job. This is out of your control now. Please. Trust me.'

The radio set on the bench behind Hasan's desk crackled to life. Eyes cool, he spun in his chair and grabbed the handset.

'What is it?' As he listened, Hasan's mouth set into a grim line. 'Yes . . . yes. I see . . . Fine.'

He ended the call. 'He's moving. Came ashore five minutes ago. Looks like he's headed for Sultanahmet.'

Ben leapt to his feet. 'Come on, then!'

'No,' Hasan said sternly. 'I think it's best that you stay here.'

'And miss the chance to let him know I'm the one who's done this to him?' Ben shook his head. 'Not a chance.'

'If you come, you must stay out of sight. This is a major police operation. We can't be seen to be pursuing a personal agenda.'

'I'll be on my best behaviour. I promise.'

Even as he said it, Ben knew it was a lie. The chances of him being able to control himself when he laid eyes on Garvé weren't great.

47

Istanbul

'Have a guess which of these gentlemen he's meeting?'
Hasan asked. It was a rhetorical question.

Three men in unseasonably heavy suits were perched
self-consciously in a row on a park bench in the shadow of the
Blue Mosque's ethereal dome. All three were wearing dark
sunglasses. By the kerb, a black sedan idled, its driver's eyes
darting from side to side as he scrutinised the people passing
by in the heavily populated square.

'Where is he?' Ben fidgeted in the passenger seat of
Hasan's car.

'Close . . .' Hasan sat forward in his seat, squinting. 'Wait . . .
black Chrysler Crown Imperial. This is him.' He opened the
glove box and selected two of the weapons stored in there –
one he slipped into a holster on his ankle, the other in one on
his shoulder. He reached for the door handle and stepped
out onto the pavement, straightening his jacket over the
bulge of the gun hidden beneath it. 'You . . .' Hasan bent to

address Ben through the open window. 'Remember what you promised? Stay here.'

Ben nodded tightly.

His insides were churning as he watched the gleaming car pull up behind the second vehicle. A chauffeur wearing a peaked cap leapt out and opened the rear door. Out stepped a heavily built man in a black suit who moved as if his limbs were made of jointed steel. Behind him Ben could see the slight frame and distinctive orange hair of the man he would quite happily see dead. A second man as physically intimidating as the first stepped out of the vehicle and stood beside his companion, creating a wall of impenetrable hired flesh at Josef Garvé's back.

Fury at the mere sight of him made Ben's blood curdle. His ears were ringing as he tried to still his breathing and resist leaping out of the car to pound Garvé's face into the pavement. More times than he could count over the years, he'd awoken at night, sweating and with an animal's scream caught in his throat from a dream in which his hands were wrapped about the Frenchman's throat as he crushed his larynx and watched the light drain from his eyes. But this was neither the time nor the place. Fantasies had to wait. Hasan was right, and Ben knew it.

Ben watched as Hasan's officers, who'd fanned out and positioned themselves on the perimeter of the large square leading to the Blue Mosque's northern flank, began to tighten the noose on the gathering of men at its centre.

Looking for all the world like a successful middle-aged businessman, Hasan sauntered casually towards where Garvé was introducing himself to the three Israeli agents.

Once he was within ten feet of the group, Hasan gave a rapid hand movement. The massing police broke into a run and drew their weapons, surrounding the six men.

Garvé's two bodyguards noticed first. Even before the police were in position, they'd drawn handguns from their holsters and were shielding their ward with their not insubstantial bulk.

'Police!' Hasan shouted, his own weapon at the ready. 'Put your guns down, and lie down on the ground!'

The three Israelis raised their hands and dropped to their knees. Ben could see Garvé's lips moving. His two bodyguards glanced at each other and then opened fire at the advancing phalanx of police.

As they did, Garvé bolted, just as his two escorts were felled by bullets from Hasan's gun.

Responding to the shots, the Turkish police converged on the fallen men. Taking advantage of the confusion, Garvé was gone, disappearing into a crowd of shocked onlookers.

Fuck that! Ben reached for the glove box and grabbed one of Hasan's handguns.

'Get out of the way! Out of the way!' Ben screamed in Turkish as he tried to push through the crowd of bystanders.

'Ben! No!' Hasan shouted as the American ran towards the expansive plaza that had, in millennia past, hosted chariot races.

The paving stones rang beneath his leather-soled boots as Ben pounded towards the fleeing figure of Josef Garvé. *Christ!* he thought. *Pretty fast for an old man.*

What Garvé might have lacked in physical strength, he made up for in mobility. *Slippery, like the fucking rat he is*, Ben cursed as he struggled to keep pace with the nimble figure ahead of him, the tails of the Frenchman's dark linen suit flapping behind him like bat wings.

He heard the sound of footsteps behind him. *Hasan. Got to keep away from him.* Ben had no intention of letting Garvé escape, and if Hasan caught up with him, he knew he'd force him to give up the chase. *No way he gets away with this*, Ben thought grimly. *No way.*

Ahead, a series of narrow alleys branched off the hippodrome, passing between teetering three-storeyed wooden homes with garlands of washing hanging from the windows. Ben knew the streets beyond were a maze. *If the bastard gets in there, I'll lose him.*

He arrived at the intersection just in time to see Garvé take a left and quick right. *Divan Yolu. That's where you're headed, isn't it?*

Ben kept up the pursuit. Sure enough, he saw Garvé bolt across the wide boulevard, leaping over the metal tram tracks intersecting the road. Legs burning, Ben chased him past the creeping shadow of Çemberlitaş – Constantine's Burnt Column – towards the dome of the Nuruosmaniye Mosque. *Really? You fucking idiot. The bazaar . . . You've picked the one place I'm damned sure I know a whole lot better than you do.*

Ben skidded down the cobbles outside the pointed arch of the Grand Bazaar's Nuruosmaniye Gate and belted into the wide arcade that transected the covered market. It took a beat for his eyes to adjust after the sudden transition from the bright light of day to the dim atmosphere inside, and he was momentarily blinded by the brightly lit displays of shimmering gold in the windows of the jewellery shops lining both sides of the main street bisecting the bazaar.

The arcade curved slightly and sloped upwards from the gate. Ben could see Garvé ahead, weaving through the slow-moving crowds of shoppers perusing the gilded treasures on offer. The Frenchman glanced over his shoulder, slowing for a moment until he caught sight of Ben on his tail. Even from that distance, Ben could see his eyes widen with surprise when he saw that he hadn't managed to shake his pursuer.

That's right, you bastard. There's no escape!

Instincts from many years past kicked into gear. A rush of adrenalin pushed Ben forward, his muscles burning.

The Frenchman skidded around a corner, turning right and heading into the heart of the bazaar's maze of lanes. *Think you'll lose me in there, do you?* Ben smiled grimly. *Not on your bloody life.* One street back from the intersection Garvé had taken, Ben turned right, barrelling down a laneway lined with stores bedecked with leather goods and cobblers' wares. Ahead was an ornate marble fountain that sat at the centre of what Ben knew was a junction with another arcade that would take him to the street Garvé had followed.

He tore around the corner. Sure enough, ahead he saw the Frenchman turn onto the same street, checking as he did to make sure Ben wasn't still following him.

Get out of sight, Ben thought. *Let him think he's free. Let him relax.* He ducked behind the fountain and waited until he was sure Garvé would have moved on. *I'll find you anyway.*

Once he knew he was clear, Ben resumed his pursuit. He could trace the Frenchman's frantic passage through the bazaar by the wake he'd left behind him – shopkeepers huddled together, gesticulating and chattering.

When he reached the terminal point of the lane he'd been following, he stopped. *Left or right?* he wondered.

An old man sat on a low, rush-bottomed stool outside a shop on the corner of the two streets, its interior stacked high with neatly folded kilims and carpets.

'Excuse me, sir?'

'You're Turk?' the man asked, incredulously.

'No. American. Could you please tell me – has someone passed here in a hurry? A foreigner with red hair – wearing a blue suit.'

The old man nodded. 'Yes. He came this way.'

'Where did he go?' Ben asked impatiently.

'Passed by, then he went in there.' He extended an arthritic finger towards a door set in the wall between two shops. 'Don't know what he wants in there, though. Nothing to buy. No shops.'

I know exactly what's in there, Ben thought. *And given there's only one way in and one way out, I'll wager you don't, you fucking prick.*

48

Istanbul

Ben took the timber steps leading up to the bazaar's roof carefully. Three flights up, the stairwell terminated at a metal door which was usually secured with a sliding bolt, but now stood ajar. He approached the doorway cautiously.

If the bastard's on the other side, and shoves the door, I'm done. He looked back down the steep flight of rickety stairs. The next thing to stop his fall would be the marble floor.

Ben crouched and reached for the lower corner of the door, which hung open above the uppermost steps. Slowly, slowly, he inched it open, bracing himself for the moment Garvé would shove the door back towards him, expecting it to make an impact and send Ben tumbling backwards.

Nothing. He released the breath he'd been holding and crawled up the rest of the stairs on hands and knees. Keeping his head as low as possible, he peeked over the door's lower sill.

On the other side, a short flight of stairs led to a narrow walkway that crossed the myriad small domes that covered the bazaar. Put in place so workmen could repair the ancient roof when it succumbed to damage caused by earthquakes, floods and fire, the walkway mirrored the chaotic map of the arcades in the market below. Except that here, all the paths were cul-de-sacs.

Searching for another doorway that would lead him back down to ground level, Josef Garvé had found himself at one of those dead ends.

'Dead' being the operative word, Ben thought.

He stood, no longer concerned about being seen. In a single movement, he took the pistol from his pocket.

'Garvé!' Ben shouted, aiming the gun at the Frenchman's head.

Garvé flinched, hand reaching for what Ben assumed was a weapon beneath his jacket. 'Don't you fucking dare!' Ben shouted as he jogged along the walkway towards him.

'Or what, Benedict?' Garvé scoffed. 'What are you going to do?'

Ben's peripheral vision was fading to grey as fury made his mind spin. With a fist calloused by years of manual work, he grabbed Garvé's collar and crushed it between fingers white with rage, pressing the muzzle of his gun into the Frenchman's temple.

Behind Garvé, the path ended abruptly and beyond that, the bazaar's domed roof plunged steeply towards the street below. Unsummoned, a vision of his dead wife Karina came into Ben's mind, and he pushed the Frenchman backwards so the heels of his shoes were tipping over the edge of the walkway as he teetered on the brink of a dizzying fall.

I want to see you spinning . . . spiralling through the air. Think you can fly, Frenchman? Ben shoved him again, dragging him back at the last moment.

Garvé stumbled, glancing backwards. Despite the peril, his voice was steady. 'As I said, Benedict, what are you going to do? These moments of personal crisis – it's always interesting to see how people react.'

Ben's throat constricted and the words that came out were hoarse and spoken through clenched teeth. 'Imagine . . . you're me . . . what would you do?'

Garvé attempted to laugh. 'Me? Be you? Don't be ridiculous.'

'Wrong answer.' Ben drew back the pistol and smashed it into the Frenchman's mouth.

Garvé's lips were shredded, sandwiched between teeth and metal. Blood cascaded down his chin, along with white chips of the teeth Ben had shattered. He spat, covering Ben's shirt in a filthy shower of blood and gore.

Through tattered lips, Garvé spoke, his words thick. 'You see how easy it is for me? I took your friend . . . your lover . . . and most of all, your beautiful wife. The German, Ricard? You know it was me who told him where to find your wife, don't you? You see, there's nothing I can't do . . . nobody who's out of my reach.'

'Yeah. You're right,' said Ben, lifting the gun, now sticky with Garvé's blood. 'Which makes this easy . . .' He drew back the hammer.

'Ben! No!' Footsteps behind him.

'Help!' Garvé shrieked. 'Officer! This man has attacked me!'

'You, shut up!' Hasan shouted. 'I know exactly who you are and what you've done! Ben?'

Ben could hear Hasan's laboured breathing behind him. 'Stop right there, Hasan!'

'You know, if you kill him, I won't be able to protect you. A foreigner murdered – and a wealthy one, at that. There's no hiding that.'

'Then walk away. Leave.'

'Too many people have seen you, Benedict. How do you think I found you?'

Ben's heart was hammering in his chest. 'I don't care anymore. I want this to stop.'

He looked at the man in front of him, the lower part of his face destroyed with gory bubbles of air bursting as he tried to breath in and then out through his shattered mouth. But above that, lifeless black eyes considered his captor clinically and Ben knew that if Josef Garvé were to survive this, he would never be free of him.

As the Frenchman leant away from Ben, his weight was approaching a point of critical mass where gravity meant his body would break free of Ben's grip and tumble over the edge.

Just let go, he thought. *Let him go. For Karina.*

Then he thought of her. Essie.

A soothing voice was at his shoulder. 'Let me take him, Ben. He's going to be in jail for years. Trying to smuggle nuclear material, and collaborating with the Israelis? He's finished.' Hasan rested a hand gently on Ben's back. 'Please, Ben.'

Essie. Although he knew there was much about her he didn't know, she was real. And she was waiting for him.

Ben dragged Garvé away from the precipice and flung him down onto the concrete walkway.

'Thank you, Benedict.' Hasan hoisted Garvé to his feet. 'You've done the right thing.'

'You think so?'

As the Turkish officer led the Frenchman away, Ben sat on the edge of the path, his legs hanging over the iron rooftops of the bazaar below. He buried his face in his hands and wept.

49

Istanbul

'He's not happy,' said Hasan, lighting a cigarette clamped between manicured fingers.

'Well, he wouldn't be, would he?' Ben replied. 'Can I have one?'

After the confrontation on the rooftop, Ben was deflated. He struck a match and lit up, inhaling the burning smoke deep into his lungs.

The two men stood side by side and watched as a pair of uniformed officers transferred a locked metal crate from the tray of an open-backed truck to a small delivery van.

'What excuse did you use for seizing his property?'

'Excuse?' Hasan tilted his head back and gazed at Ben archly, black brows lifting over his golden-brown eyes. 'If what you told me about the contents of that box is true, then I don't need one. Attempting to transport something across the border that poses such a threat to the health and safety of the people of Turkey is a very serious crime. Besides, now it's evidence.'

'Thank you, Hasan. I hope handing it over to me doesn't cause you too much trouble.'

The Turk shrugged. 'It's nothing.' He drew deeply on his cigarette, holding the smoke in his lungs before releasing it to dissipate into the air.

'Won't you need it to prosecute him?'

'We ran the Geiger counter over it. Sent it off the dial. And we documented the readings so we don't need the actual object. It should be enough to keep the Frenchman locked up in a cell for a while so we can find a way of charging him with the death of the people he had killed in Topkapı and Niğde . . .'

Ben's blood ran cold. 'Niğde?'

'You knew him, I think. He used to work at Eskitepe. Cem Yıldız – the curator at the Akmedresi.'

'Ah, shit!' Ben exclaimed.

'A man was seen leaving the museum washing blood from his hands,' Hasan continued. 'Stocky. Dark hair. When they found Cem, the investigators knew from his wounds it was the same attacker who'd killed Fatih in the archives. And with the testimony of the witnesses, they knew it wasn't you who did it. You're clear of any suspicion.'

'Cem . . . was he . . . ?'

'Yes. The local officers had never seen so much blood. Whoever killed him was a butcher.'

'Schubert was his name. Ricard Schubert. And, yes, he killed Fatih in Topkapı.'

'Any proof of that?'

'From the horse's mouth. But you'll find that horse doesn't have much to say for himself anymore. He met a pretty nasty end.'

Hasan scrutinised Ben intently. 'At your hands?'

Ben said nothing.

'Ah. I see. Added to what I saw of you today . . . well, it seems there are always new things to learn about you, Benedict Hitchens.' Hasan inhaled a deep draught of cigarette smoke. 'I'm pleased to hear that's the last we'll see of him, anyway. I thought he must have been working his way through our population of librarians. Can't afford to lose them all.'

'Cem was a curator. Not a librarian.'

The Turk waved his hand dismissively. 'Same thing.'

'And the woman?' Ben could barely bring himself to ask. 'There was a woman – Sebile. In Tyana . . . Kemerhisar. Did the bastard follow us there as well?'

Hasan looked confused. 'Who?'

'A woman who lived in the town.'

'Not that I heard. Would her death have been noticed?'

Ben thought about Sebile's largely solitary existence. 'She lived alone.'

'Nothing's been reported yet,' he replied. 'Maybe she escaped.'

'If that animal was after her, I wouldn't be too sure of that,' Ben said.

Hasan walked over to the van and opened the driver's door. 'Here,' he said, tossing Ben the keys. 'It's a vehicle we seized from a smuggler. Nobody will miss it. Keep it as long as you like and bring it back when you're done.'

Ben checked that the crate was well secured in the back. 'Did you open it?' he asked.

'After what you told me? Not on your life.'

'What are you going to tell Garvé about where it went?'

'It's evidence, so usually it would be sent to our storage facility on the outskirts of the city.'

'With his contacts, even if he's in prison he'll be able to pressure for its return.'

Hasan laughed. 'You've obviously never been to our warehouses. The men who oversee them are well-meaning, but utterly overwhelmed by the scale of their responsibilities. Documentation is – ah, what's a polite way of putting it? – fairly relaxed. I'd estimate that ninety per cent of what's there isn't recorded properly. And you'll note I said "warehouses" – plural. There are literally millions of objects stored there. When they can't find it, the administrators will just attribute its absence to carelessness and sloppy handling.'

'If you're keeping an eye on illegal movements of stolen antiquities, why are you happy to let this one go?'

'Well, it was brought *into* the country, wasn't it? Now, if you were trying to take it out – that would be something else altogether.' He took another drag of his cigarette. 'What do you plan to do with it?'

'Haven't decided yet. But don't worry. It'll be safe.' A plan was formulating in Ben's mind, but he knew better than to share it. He trusted Hasan, but he also knew that the fewer people who knew about the tablet's destination the better.

'I suppose I should thank you for helping me foil an act of international terrorism on Turkish soil, shouldn't I?' Hasan turned and looked out through the high, wrought-iron fence that encircled the police headquarters towards the *lokanta* on the opposite side of the street. His eyes narrowed. 'So. That's her, is it?'

Ben was silent. Barely visible in the back corner of the crowded restaurant was an identifiably foreign woman with blonde hair tied back in a ponytail, her head bowed over a bowl as she ate.

Christ! Ben cursed. *Of course he knows what she looks like now, you idiot! He was the one who showed you the recent photo of her. That's what started this whole damned thing.*

'You know,' Hasan continued, 'there's still an outstanding warrant for her arrest . . . *multiple* warrants.' He paused a moment as he dropped his cigarette onto the paving stones and ground it beneath his heel. 'If you were planning to offer her a bed for the night, I'd be compelled to come to your home and take her into custody . . . say, tomorrow morning.'

Is he saying what I think he's saying? Ben wondered.

'I should let you know, though,' Hasan said. 'In light of the seriousness of her many . . . *many* . . . crimes, and her demonstrated ability to elude capture, tomorrow I'd be obliged to blockade the road to your *yalı*. But manpower at the moment is stretched . . . I regret to say that I couldn't call on my colleagues in the naval police to cover your home from the sea. So if she were to decide to depart the city along the Bosphorus . . . well, that might make things very difficult for me. And it would be a *terrible* shame if she were to slip through my fingers yet again. Wouldn't it?'

50

Istanbul

A blue haze from the charcoal grills burning on board the boats docked at Karaköy drifted over the row of vehicles waiting for the ferry's arrival. Ben's stomach growled, his appetite suddenly roused after hours of dormancy by the enticing smell of grilled fish being prepared for the ubiquitous Istanbul snack of *balık ekmek*.

'I'm starving,' he said without looking at Essie. 'The ferry's not leaving for a bit. D'you want one?'

'I'm fine, thank you,' she replied. 'Still full from the beans and rice at the *lokanta*.'

'Suit yourself.'

As a bow-legged fisherman miraculously kept his balance on the deck of his swaying boat and sliced open a crusty loaf of freshly baked bread to cram it full of lettuce, onion, tomato and fillets of charred fish, Ben watched Essie out of the corner of his eye. He became a walking cliché at the sight of her — his breath accelerated, his heart pounded and blood rushed

370

to his head. No matter how determined he was to remain unaffected by her, it was impossible. His desire was a blight that gnawed at his insides with jagged teeth.

Ever since Hasan had all but promised him an undisturbed night to spend with her, Ben's mind had been whirring. For a start, he had no idea what plans she had for herself. He'd driven down to the docks, but hadn't extended an invitation to her to join him on the ferry to the Asian side of the city. Yet, she was still by his side. Even if she did elect to come with him, he had no idea what he'd do once they reached his home. There was no denying the physical hold she had over him. But he was still humiliated and angry after the two-act betrayal that had plunged his life into disarray. Finding a way to forgive that wouldn't be easy.

Then again, she did save your life, he reminded himself. *That has to count for something.*

The journey from the Negev had been so frantic, they'd scarcely had the chance to speak, and certainly not about the things that had occurred between them in the past. He hadn't even had a straight answer from her about why she'd risked so much to come back and rescue them. Even if Josef Garvé never did work out that she'd been directly involved in the events that led to his arrest, the pilot of the helicopter she'd hijacked would surely let him know that she'd re-routed the flight back to the desert to retrieve the two men the Frenchman had left there to die. And given what Ben had just done to Garvé, knowing she was responsible for setting him free would be the nail in her coffin. Although he knew from personal experience that she was an accomplished and very convincing liar, there didn't seem to be any plausible way to fudge her way out of that one. All she could hope was that Hasan was right and Garvé would be behind bars for a very, very long time.

He bit into the sandwich as he walked back to the line of vehicles. *Christ, I needed that*, he thought as he savoured the salty tang of the crunchy fish and the soft white bread.

She was resting against the bonnet of the van, gazing out at the chaotic traffic negotiating the crowded waterway. 'I've never been able to understand why there aren't more collisions,' she said as he joined her.

'It's like couples on a crowded dance floor. Or a flock of starlings in flight. Looks anarchic to spectators, but there's an underlying order to it all.' He wiped the crumbs from his chin with the back of his hand. 'Like life.'

Essie nodded.

'So,' he continued. 'What're you planning to do next?'

'Uncharacteristically, I haven't given it much thought. There are some urgent things I need to take care of in London before news gets back to Josef about what I've done. Then I'll disappear again. Even in jail, his reach is formidable. I doubt I'll ever be able to consider myself safe. What about you?'

'Back to work for me. I've got the excavation at Mt Ida occupying most of my time these days.'

'And the tablet? Are you going to sell it?'

'Haven't decided yet,' he said. *One thing I do know, though – you're one of the last people on the planet I'd tell*.

She gazed towards the hills of Sultanahmet and the ethereal domes of Hagia Sophia and the Blue Mosque. 'Just do me a favour – whatever you decide, please don't give it to the Israelis.'

'Why would you care?'

She paused a moment, then drew a deep breath. 'You've asked me about my past. My *real* past. My mother and father . . . they were Arabs from Palestine. That was where I was born. When the Jewish settlers began to arrive, my father resisted their moves to occupy our homeland. The *al-nakbah* – the catastrophe . . . it's why the story I told you about the life I'd imagined for myself in Smyrna came so close to the truth. In Palestine we had our own "catastrophe", as did the Greeks in Smyrna. My mother and sisters were murdered . . .' Her voice began to waver.

Ben glanced up at her face. Fat tears were forming along her lower eyelids and her bottom lip was quivering. Despite his determination to limit physical contact with her, he reached out and took one of the hands she had knotted together in her lap.

Essie turned her face towards him. 'My father – he saved me. We moved to Cairo. He married again – my stepmother and half-sister are still there. He could never accept Israel, and so he kept fighting – until the British captured him and executed him. After that, I became someone else. And that's why my past shouldn't matter to you. But it's also why I don't want to give Israel anything that might help them crush people like my family.'

'You know what the Jews suffered during the war – you can't blame them for wanting to find a place they could be safe.'

'No. But it didn't have to be the way it is. We could have lived peacefully together.'

'You said your father was fighting them –'

'Stop!' she spat. 'You don't . . . you *couldn't* . . . understand!' Essie took a deep breath. 'I think it's best that we don't talk about it.'

'Fine with me.'

From across the turgid, black waters of the Bosphorus, the Kadiköy ferry sounded a mournful cry as it approached the docks. The white light of day was dimming as the sun prepared to plunge below Istanbul's proud minaret and dome-dotted horizon.

'It's getting late,' he said, releasing her hand. 'Whatever you're intending to do next, it will have to wait until tomorrow. Do you have somewhere to stay?'

She wiped the tears from her cheeks with the back of her hand. 'I could probably get a room at the Pera Palace.'

'Yes. I'm sure you could.' *There's that damned pounding heart and surging blood again.* 'Or, you could stay with me.'

She looked up at him through thick, black lashes. 'Are you sure?'

Not really, he thought as every cell in his body said the opposite.

'Yes.'

51

Istanbul

Essie and Ben fell into each other's arms the moment they were through the unlocked front door of his darkened home. Moonlight painted a blue tapestry on the scuffed floorboards as it shone in beams through the window panes and the front door they'd left open.

They shed their clothes in a scatter along the hall, stumbling naked towards the long flight of stairs that led to the first floor. They kissed each other deeply, tongues probing between lips wet and swollen with hunger. Ben pressed up against Essie's soft olive skin, the hair on his chest brushing against her nipples and making them harden and ache. His belly was flat and firm against hers as she dug her nails into the muscles that rose like a column from the dip of his back at the base of his spine to the span of his broad shoulders.

He groaned as she leant against him, feeling his hardness pulsing and hot between them. With one hand Ben reached up to cup her full breast while entwining his other in her hair – now blonde, but still as strong and silken as he remembered it. He responded to the pressure of her body on his, sliding against her and slipping his hand down between her legs.

Essie's legs buckled as he began to stroke her with a featherlight touch. Her heels hit the bottom step and she lost her balance. Ben caught her by her waist as she stumbled and guided her down to lie on the flight of wooden stairs. She dropped her knees apart and Ben lowered himself between them, supporting his weight on his hands and entering her in a single stroke. Essie cried out as he slipped inside her. She hooked her feet between the bannisters and pushed back against Ben's grinding hips as she opened her legs as far as she could, wanting to feel every inch of him.

Ben grabbed the handrail to brace himself as he plunged inside her. His knees were trembling as he struggled to contain himself. The sensation of being in her – on her – and the feeling of her satiny skin and yielding wetness was utterly overwhelming. As she began to reach climax, Essie arched her back, wrapping her arms around his neck and clamping him between her thighs as she found a rhythm. Ben's body responded, driving him over the abyss, his mind awash with pure white light.

Ben and Essie did eventually find their way to his featherbed, which was perched unceremoniously in the centre of his bedroom at the rear of the house, where it overlooked the slow-moving waters of the Bosphorus and the constant stream of cargo ships and freighters that plied its waters. They made love again without any of the urgency and desperation of their past couplings.

When they finally fell back onto the pillows, Essie surrendered to a dreamless sleep, her breath coming in deep and measured waves. Ben lay at her side, relishing the euphoric catharsis that overwhelmed him. His body ached and he was paralysed by a weariness he felt down to his bones. The dust of the desert still clung to his skin and his legs stung from the day's exertion. The warm bloom of sated desire made Ben's limbs heavy and he turned on his side to gaze at the face of the woman he seemed unable to resist. She slept with her eyes slightly open, giving the uncanny impression that she was watching him. Her full lips were parted as she breathed in and out, and Ben reached over to stroke her cheek. She smiled gently in her sleep and rolled across the white sheets, turning her back to him and resting her head on his bicep, nestling against him so their two bodies felt locked together. He bent and kissed her head.

Outside his bedroom's French windows, the glittering lights of the sea traffic merged with the blinding stars shimmering in the velvety black night sky. From the mosque on the opposite shore, the muezzin called the faithful to prayer. Ben thought of the last time he'd fallen into a deep slumber at the side of this woman as the same song had echoed around their bed chamber. It had only been four years, but it felt like a lifetime ago and in many ways, it was. So much had changed since. She now claimed to be telling him the truth about who she was and what she wanted. But the tangle of lies she'd caught him up in meant he'd never be able to trust her again.

As sleep took hold, a kernel of doubt wedged itself between his ribs and gifted him troubled dreams where dreadful things long forgotten clawed at his heels.

52

Istanbul

Ben awoke to the screams of gulls and terns in determined pursuit of the fishing fleet returning to the markets of Istanbul, their nets brimming with the shimmering marine plunder they'd scooped from the depths of the Black Sea.

He turned, reaching across the bed with a sickly feeling rising in his gut. He knew before he even looked. She was gone.

With an ominous sense of déjà vu, Ben untangled himself from the sheets and pulled on his undershorts.

You idiot, he berated himself. *She's bloody gone and done it to you again.*

Fury began to boil inside him as he walked down the corridor towards the stairs. *It's İzmir all over again. Stupefy me with a night of lovemaking. Then take off while I'm asleep.*

Then he remembered. *The tablet!* In his rush to get inside, he'd left the keys in the ignition of the van.

Fucking fool! He punched the wall then picked up pace, taking the stairs two at a time.

He skidded around the corner into the sunroom that doubled as his kitchen, which also happened to have the best view of the driveway.

Still there. Thank Christ!

The rusty white van was still parked beside the house, exactly where he'd left it. He let out a sigh of relief.

There was a crash from the pantry.

'Do you have any eggs? I was going to make us omelettes.'

He heard her voice, but couldn't quite bring himself to believe it.

Essie stepped through the doorway wearing one of Ben's shirts, its tails dangling almost to her knees. 'Ben? What's wrong? Are you all right?'

'I thought you'd left.'

'Why?' She looked puzzled. 'Why would I do that?'

He just looked at her.

'Ah, yes. I see.' Her eyes were downcast. 'It's different this time.'

'How?' Ben's anxiety boiled over. 'How on earth is anything different? Christ! Nothing's changed! I don't even know your real name!'

'It's so long since anyone used my birth name, it doesn't feel like it belongs to me anymore. Names are just labels we give things.'

'Labels? Yeah, I guess you're right. But, let's be honest – they're fairly important ones.'

'Hardly anyone knows my name . . . my stepmother. My sister . . .'

'Garvé?'

She said nothing.

'Yeah. That's what I figured. Of course he does. So it's fine for him to know it, but not me. I get it.'

A wave of nostalgia smashed into him and he drew in a shuddering breath. Outside, the sun was rising above the hills on the European side of the city, casting the overgrown garden in a golden light. A path snaked from the back door down to the ramshackle jetty where Ben's boat bobbed about in the relentless currents flowing through the Bosphorus.

'Anyway . . . none of that changes the fact that the rising sun out there means our time's up,' he said. 'The omelettes will have to wait till next time,' he said. 'Some olives and bread on the run will do us for breakfast. Hasan warned me he'd be coming in the morning. No idea what time he meant. But if we're going to get out of here safely, we need to leave quickly. Do you have any plans?' He laughed wryly. 'Why do I even ask? You always have one of those, don't you? Just tell me where you need me to take you.'

Essie looked crestfallen. 'I thought the train would be the best way to get out of the city. They'll be watching the airports here so that's where I think I'll stand a better chance. From Sofia or Bucharest, I should be able to arrange a flight to London. The best place for me to leave would be Sirkeci Station. If it looks like the police are there, I can take a ferry to the Dardanelles and island-hop to Athens.'

'Fine. I'll take you across to Eminönü. Sirkeci's nearby. And the ferries for Çanakkale leave from there, too.'

'I know.' She reached out and took Ben's hand. 'Ben – I'm sorry for everything that's happened. I really am.'

'Seriously . . . don't worry about it,' he said, not meaning a word of it. He shook his hand free. 'Water under the bridge.'

Ben's tiny boat dipped and lurched in the waves and wake of larger vessels as it crossed from the Asian side of the city to Seraglio Point on the European shore and the turrets and towers of the palace from which the Ottoman sultans had ruled over one of the world's greatest and most enduring empires. For once, his seasickness didn't bother him.

They'd barely spoken a word to each other since they'd taken the weed-strewn path from Ben's house to the jetty, where he'd pulled the boat alongside and offered her a hand to steady herself as she stepped down onto its deck. She refused his assistance, leaping nimbly onto the bucking boards and taking a seat on the half-rotten bench at the boat's bow, eyes looking into the distance across the white-painted prow as Ben kicked the motor into action.

As Ben had hoped and expected, there'd been no last-minute intrusion from the Turkish police, and they'd pulled away from the dock with relative ease, the only soundtrack to their passage the wheezing chug of an engine Ben knew was long overdue for an oil change.

The chaotic docks at Eminönü loomed ahead. Ben's heart was pounding. A voice buried deep within screamed at him to reach out to her, to take her in his arms, and beg her to stay with him forever. But the wounds she'd carved into his most tender parts still ached, and another side of him begged for a circumspect outcome that would save his sanity. That kept him silent, even as Ben came to the burning realisation that this would most likely be the last time he'd ever see her.

He threw the boat's rope up to a dock worker who tied the mooring line to a bollard and lowered a ladder so they could clamber up to shore. Ben watched her scale the rungs as if she'd been born on board a ship and tried to convince himself it would all be for the best.

He stood on the dock's worn timbers and looked down into her eyes as men and women jostled past them, scurrying to make it to one ferry or another as the captains tugged their steam whistles impatiently.

'Sirkeci Station,' he said, attempting to maintain a matter-of-fact tone. 'It's over there.'

'Yes. Thank you. I know,' Essie said. 'Oh! I almost forgot.' Reaching into the small bag hanging from her shoulder, she took out a parcel wrapped in brown paper and handed it to Ben. 'Here. It's the book from Topkapı. Garvé gave it to me after that animal stole it.'

Ben was dumbfounded. 'You're not planning to sell it? Even with the page I tore out of it missing, it'd still be tremendously valuable on the black market.'

'No. Not this time. I've caused enough damage already. I'd rather it goes back to where it came from. Might as well do one thing right. Will you be able to put the missing page back into it and give it to Hasan, please?'

'Sure. Yes. If that's what you want.'

'It is.' She looked up at him. 'You know, all the time we've been apart, you've always been with me. Your eyes ... it's always been your eyes. I've never been allowed to forget them. Green. Like the sea when a storm's approaching.' She placed one hand on his shoulder and the other at his waist as she stood on her toes and kissed his lips, lingering and pressing her body against his.

He didn't know what to say, and even if he had, he wasn't sure he would have said it anyway. Ben drew a deep breath and held it in, struggling to maintain his balance.

'Goodbye, Benedict Hitchens.' For the briefest of moments, she held him tightly in her arms, then stepped back, smiling sadly before she turned to join the surging crowd moving towards the station. Mid-stride, she stopped and turned back to face him.

'. . . Noor,' she said.

382

'What?'

'The name my parents gave me when I was born. It's Noor.'

Without another word she disappeared into the crowd of commuters.

THE TIMES
9 November 1956
CEASEFIRE IN EGYPT: ALLIED TROOPS
OCCUPY SUEZ CANAL ZONE

LONDON, Friday (Reuters)

The month's events in the Sinai have led to what is described by former allies as 'an irrevocable loss of prestige on the part of the British and the French governments'.

Just before midnight yesterday, Egyptian radio announced that President Nasser had accepted a ceasefire on condition that all foreign troops were withdrawn from Egypt.

British Prime Minister, Anthony Eden, has been under increasing pressure at home and abroad over a conflict that has been condemned by many of his countrymen and allies. He remains unrepentant, declaring there will be no apology for British action in Egypt.

The Prime Minister has maintained that the invasion was necessary to secure freedom of passage through the Suez Canal after Egypt's nationalisation of the waterway in July of this year. Those in Britain who opposed the military action claim that the effective operation of the canal since Egypt took over the shipping channel negates Eden's claim.

Meanwhile, President Nasser's standing in the Moslem world has never been higher. It is perceived that through military defeat he has managed to secure a political victory. The popularity of his staunch resistance to the British, French and Israeli attack on sovereign Egyptian soil has assured his position among his countrymen. The other members of the Arab League have also pledged to support him in any further conflict in the region.

It is hoped the intervention of elder statesman, Winston Churchill, who has written to President Eisenhower, will go some way towards healing the rift between the British and the United States governments. 'I do believe with unfaltering conviction that the theme of the Anglo-American alliance is more important today than at any time since the war,' the former Prime Minister wrote. 'Whatever the arguments adduced here and in the United States for or against the Prime Minister's action in Egypt, to let events in the Middle East become a gulf between us would be an act of folly on which our whole civilisation may founder. The skies will darken indeed and it is the Soviet Union that will ride the storm.'

In Israel, military authorities announced their intention to launch a 'peace offensive' after their decisive victories, expressing their hope that they might negotiate an amicable settlement with their Arab neighbours.

The conflict in the Suez Canal Zone is certain to have broader political repercussions in Britain. In a letter published in this newspaper, influential Liberal Party member, Lady Violet Bonham Carter, wrote: 'Never in my lifetime has our name stood so low in the eyes of the world. Never have we stood so ingloriously alone.'

53

Kemerhisar, Turkey

Ben squinted through the sandy haze thrown up into the air as the decrepit van bumped and jarred along a path better suited to the passage of mules and goats than motorised vehicles.

A troupe of barefoot village boys, their eyes black and mouths gaping in masks of chalky dust, belted along in a ramshackle procession behind what was sure to be the most exciting thing that was likely to arrive in Kemerhisar that week – a blond-haired foreigner driving a white van.

As he'd left the outer suburbs of Istanbul, Ben had known he had an excruciatingly long journey ahead of him. With the cargo he was carrying in the back of his vehicle, he knew the wisest decision would have been to take the most direct route into central Anatolia through the nation's capital, Ankara. But as he'd entered the outskirts of the town of Adapazarı and crossed the stone bridge built by the Emperor Justinian in the sixth century AD, he'd made a decision to

386

turn south towards Kütahya instead and, beyond that, his old stamping grounds in Konya. It was a road less travelled, and, crossing as it did the craggy peaks leading to the sweeping plains of the central Anatolian plateau, Ben knew it was risky. He doubted that the loaned van had the stamina to make it out of Istanbul, much less travel halfway across the country along roads that were hardly more than shepherd's tracks. He'd justified it to himself with the thought that if anyone were following him, they wouldn't be able to keep their presence hidden on a route that few sane motorists would choose voluntarily.

In reality it was unlikely anyone was on his tail. The real reason he'd taken the southerly route was that his brief and emotionally fraught encounter with the woman he'd known as Eris, whose real name he now knew to be Noor, had triggered in him a peculiar sense of nostalgia. He hadn't been back to the excavation at Eskitepe for years – not since he'd been banished from his position by the director of the British Institute of Archaeology when he'd heard rumours of Ben's arrangement selling minor finds to Ilhan so that he could afford to expand the excavation. Ben knew it would be awkward if he were to turn up unannounced, and he didn't intend to visit the actual site as he drove through town. But he still felt a burning need to see it again, if only from a distance, which he did, stopping by the road to watch the workers scuttling like ants across the flat-topped hill.

Despite his fears, luck had been on his side; although the van's mechanical performance hadn't improved on the journey, it didn't deteriorate either. He'd arrived at the Sefer Hotel in Konya late in the day. It had been his base during the excavation season, and when he approached the reception desk he'd been welcomed by the proprietor as an old friend and offered a shot of Bowmore single malt from the bottle he'd bought for Ben and kept under the bar waiting for what turned out to be a much-delayed return to the city. The next morning, as he'd pulled out of the hotel's parking lot, Ben felt as if he'd somehow closed a door on something that had been bothering him for many years.

When the sign for Kemerhisar appeared on the road ahead many hours later, Ben's fear that the van would break down and leave him and his precious cargo stranded dissipated, leaving in its place dread at what he might find when he arrived at Sebile's cave house.

The hillock of white tuff with its neat, wooden door appeared, hemmed in by a crop of late maize and Sebile's orchard of fruit trees, their leaves edged with autumn gold. Ben pulled alongside the stone fence that encircled the tiny home.

'My name is? My name is?' A bouquet of cheeky, dusty faces filled his window as the village children parroted the only English phrases they knew. 'Mister, mister? My name is? What time is it? What time is it? My name is?'

'Move, little ones,' Ben said in Turkish as he pushed the door open and waved them away.

That shut them up! he thought as he watched their eyes widen when they heard the foreigner speaking their language.

'Now,' he said, drawing a coin from his pocket and holding it in front of them. 'Who'd like to earn some money?' One eager-eyed boy who looked like the little hellion who'd caused Sebile such trouble when he and Ilhan had first visited the village grabbed it from Ben's palm. 'Me! I do! What do I have to do?'

'What's your name?'

'My name is Bahadır.'

'And my name is Ben,' he said. 'Now, Bahadır. This is my car. Nobody is to go near it, and *nobody* is to open any of the doors. I need you to protect it as if it were your sister's virtue.' The boys stifled giggles behind raised hands. 'And the rest of you,' Ben continued. 'If you help him, I'll give you all coins as well. Understand?'

'Yes, sir!' they shouted.

Ben turned towards Sebile's front gate.

'Why are you going in there, Mr Ben?' Bahadır called out. 'Are you looking for the old woman?'

'Yes,' Ben replied. 'I am.'

'She's gone,' they chorused.

'Did you see her leave?' he asked.

'No,' Bahadır answered. 'We didn't see her leave, sir. But we haven't seen her for many days. So she must have gone.' His voice dropped. 'Or maybe she's dead,' he said solemnly. 'She's old, and old people die, you know.'

'I hope not,' said Ben.

'If she is dead,' said Bahadır, 'can we see? I've never seen anyone dead before.'

'Let's not get ahead of ourselves,' said Ben. 'For now – you just worry about making sure my car's safe. OK?'

Bahadır gave Ben a mock salute. 'Yes, sir!'

The door into Sebile's home was unlocked. Ben steeled himself for what he expected to find within.

The neatly arranged room he and Ilhan had visited was thrown into disarray. The stacks of books that had once lined the walls had been thrown haphazardly across the floor, pages torn out and bindings bent back. The few pieces of furniture that had been set against the walls were now in a chaotic stack at the centre of the room, and the straw mattress from Sebile's bed had been slashed open, its stuffing spread in a golden carpet across the stone pavers.

Ricard Schubert – because Ben could only assume he was the one who'd torn Sebile's house to pieces – had certainly been thorough in his dismantling of the old woman's possessions. But the one thing it seemed he hadn't found – in here, at least – was Sebile herself. There was no sign of her.

Maybe he caught her outside, Ben thought.

He opened the door to search her small garden.

'Hey, sir, Mr Ben?' shouted Bahadır. 'Is the old woman there? Is she dead?'

'No!' he answered. 'Don't you worry about what I'm doing – you just focus on your job!'

'Yes, sir!' Bahadır cried.

There weren't many places in the small orchard where a body might be hidden from sight. *The maize*, he thought as he looked at the densely packed stand of yellowing plants.

His muscles tensed when he saw a worn slipper protruding from between the corn stalks.

Christ, no. He bent over and parted the dried stems.

It was a slipper, but without a body attached to it. Ben exhaled heavily.

There's one other place you might be, he thought. *Was Schubert smart enough – or patient enough – to look there? And, more to the point, did you have time to get down there? Only one way to find out.*

Schubert had managed to throw all Sebile's furniture on top of the entrance to the underground city that lay beneath the old woman's floor. That made Ben suspect that her attacker hadn't found the trapdoor.

He threw aside the shattered bed frame and the table and chairs. The kilim beneath, though rumpled, was still in place over the hidden entrance.

Ben pulled the carpet back and grabbed the metal ring set into the timber frame, yanking the trapdoor open. He peered down into the darkness.

Nothing.

'Sebile? Are you down there?' he called out.

Silence.

He looked about the detritus of her kitchen and found the stub of a beeswax candle. Ben trod gingerly down the ladder that led to the labyrinth carved out of the volcanic rock. When he reached the floor below, he fished about in his pocket and retrieved his matches to light the candle.

The flame took hold and the room was gradually washed in a dim light.

'Ah. It *is* you,' said a voice from the corridor that led into the pitch-black darkness beyond.

Ben started. 'Christ! Sebile!'

'What's got you so jumpy?' she asked as she stepped into the pool of light, and turned the wick up on the kerosene lantern she'd dimmed.

'I thought you were dead.'

'Me?' She laughed wryly. 'Not likely. Though if you hadn't chosen to drop by, I might have been in a spot of bother. I always keep a supply of food and water down here – never know when you might need to make yourself scarce for a bit. But I haven't been able to open the trapdoor.'

'That would be because most of your possessions were piled on top of it.'

'Is that so? Well, that would explain it.'

'What happened?'

'A man arrived. I saw him coming down the road from the garden. Didn't like the look of him. Not one bit. I was weeding between the cornrows. He didn't see me as I ran. Lost one of my slippers –'

'I found it.'

'You did? Good. I'd hate to have to make a new pair.'

'Why did you run?'

She paused, eyes locked on Ben. 'I know people. And I could tell he was someone I'd rather not meet.'

'You're a very good judge of character, then.'

'You knew him?'

'Enough to know he was no good.'

'You said "was".'

'That's right. He's dead.'

'I see.' Sebile nodded. 'You killed him?'

'Yes. I did. He murdered my wife during the war.'

The old woman took his hand and patted it. 'Then you've corrected the balance. You mustn't let it bother you. Now – can I offer you some tea?'

'That would be lovely. But first, there's something I need to show you.'

54

Kemerhisar, Turkey

The pockmarked volcanic stone walls of Sebile's home gleamed with the same poisonous green light Ben remembered from the cave in the Negev Desert where he'd found the Emerald Tablet nestling in Balinas' lap.

Tears streamed down Sebile's weatherworn cheeks, her pale eyes reflecting the viridian glow that flooded the room. She was transfixed. 'You found it! I knew you would. And . . . him? You saw him?'

Ben nodded. 'Yes.'

Sebile advanced towards the open crate, hands extended as if she were paying the ancient artefact homage.

He gently took hold of her forearm. 'I don't think it's safe to touch it, Sebile.'

'No – I know. It's not,' she said. 'That's what killed him, of course. The radiation. But to finally see it after studying it for so long, protecting its secrets . . .' She reached out and closed the lid reluctantly. 'But you're right. It's best not to be exposed any longer than necessary.'

Something didn't add up for Ben. 'Sebile, you seem to know a lot about this. When you told me about the tablet and Balinas, you said you learnt about it as someone who moved in esoteric circles in Paris . . .'

'That's not entirely accurate.' With a heavy sigh, she righted one of her chairs and moved it towards the window where she sat down. 'You know, when I spoke about the spiritual aspects of alchemy, I told you of the pursuit of the Great Work – the Philosopher's Stone . . . the ability to transmute matter that leads to the transformation of the alchemist's soul and, if he or she masters the art, the physical body as well. I was . . . I am . . . an alchemist. Once, I was known as Fulcanelli.'

'What?' Ben couldn't fathom it. 'You're a man?'

'I was. But now, I'm me. An old woman named Sebile living in a small village in the middle of Turkey. If you master the Great Work, you see, you learn that everything material is fluid. Form . . . shape . . . matter – it's all just about perception.'

'OK. So . . . you're a man dressed as a woman?'

Sebile smiled indulgently. 'Think of it however you wish, Benedict. But the fact remains that after the war, I needed to hide, and the best way to do that was to adopt a new form. When the Nazis – and the Americans, even the Soviets – were pursuing me and I'd lost my adept to that hateful man, Crowley, I was the only remaining link to this gift and to Balinas' legacy. So I did the only thing I could to preserve the sacred knowledge – I became the divine androgyne and chose to assume the form of a woman.'

'If you're Fulcanelli – which, to be completely honest, I'm finding a little hard to understand or believe – then didn't you know the location of Balinas' tomb yourself? Why did you send me off on that damned chase? And, more to the point, if you were so worried about somebody else finding it, why didn't you just go and retrieve it yourself?'

'I would have liked nothing more.' She smiled sadly. 'But it wasn't that easy . . . it couldn't be. We were sworn to protect Balinas' secret, and that meant none of us ever knew exactly where the tomb was. From master to adept through the ages, we passed on the location of the clues so that one day, if it became necessary, somebody could uncover and interpret the trail Balinas left behind. As for why I didn't go and find it myself?' Sebile spread her arms. 'Look at me. My mind may be strong, but nothing changes the fact that I'm old and, much as I hate to admit it, fairly frail.'

'What about the scarab you gave me – Psamtik's heart scarab?'

'One of the clues we've preserved. It was, as you worked out, a pointer to the statue in Cairo. The trail of clues has changed over the years. But the destination has always remained the same.'

'You told me the scarab was buried next to the marble piece I saw at the museum in Niğde . . . so that was a lie?'

'No – it *was* buried there. By me. I just didn't tell you how it got there. Now, you've had your questions. It's my turn. You could have sold this for more money than you'd ever need in a single lifetime. At the very least, if you'd given it over to one of the great archaeological collections of the world, you'd have been famous – more famous than you are now. Yet you brought it to me. Why?'

Ben gathered his thoughts before responding. It was a question he'd asked himself many times since he'd resolved to bring the Emerald Tablet back to the same place Balinas had found it almost two thousand years before. 'The truth is, I'm not entirely sure. It just felt that it was the only thing to do. The possibility of it being in the hands of people who don't understand it – well, let's just say there wasn't anything I saw in the behaviour of those who were chasing it that made me feel confident that it would be handled with the awe and dread it seems to deserve. Balinas was right. Humankind hasn't earnt the right to have this yet.'

Sebile gazed at him. 'Could it be that this has been a journey of transformation for you too, Benedict Hitchens? Don't tell me the tablet's somehow managed to make you a better man?'

He laughed. 'There's no alchemical magic that powerful, Sebile.'

'Why don't you stay here? Learn from me. You know, the things you've dedicated your life to finding – all those things you discover beneath the soil. It's all just refuse: the shed skin and detritus left on earth after the spirit of life sloughs off its material form and returns to the firmament. You can pursue a much higher purpose, you know – one that will clear the rubble of your past from the path that lies ahead.'

'The thing is, I do have a life,' he said gently.

'Ah. I see. Is it a life that brings you fulfilment?'

'Yes. Sometimes.' Ben thought of the woman he'd just farewelled and the empty mansion that awaited him by the Bosphorus. 'It might not be much,' he said, smiling. 'But I'm beginning to let myself hope it might be on the improve.'

THE TIMES
19 November 1956
BRITISH ECONOMY FALTERS AS ATTEMPTS MADE TO REPAIR ALLIANCE

LONDON, Monday (Reuters)

Crippling petroleum price hikes and plummeting sovereign reserves strike the British Government as it works to repair the damage to its relationship with the United States in the wake of the Suez fiasco.

The economic future of Great Britain hangs in the balance as the nation struggles to absorb the devastating effect on oil supplies directly attributable to Britain's invasion of Egypt.

This crisis has led to the imposition of fuel rationing for the first time since the end of the Second World War. In response, gold reserves in Britain have plunged, causing a financial crisis that threatens to cripple the nation.

Although it remains largely unsaid in Conservative circles, there has been some concern voiced about the health of the British Prime Minister, Anthony Eden. Labour politicians have been less circumspect, with Aneurin Bevan recently saying of the Prime Minister's state of mind: 'I have not seen from him in the last four or five months evidence of the sagacity and skill he should have acquired in so many years in the Foreign Office. I have been astonished by the amateurishness of his performance. There is something the matter with him.'

There is mounting concern in the West about growing Russian influence in the Middle East. Canada's External Affairs Minister, Mr Lester Pearson, urged the United Nations to give its Middle East police force the power to act in Syria if it was required to 'deal with worsening problems' there. Mr Pearson also said: 'There are reports that Russian penetration is going on in Syria to an alarming extent and that there are moves inside Syria which might result in the control of the country domestically by a group which seems quite willing to work with the Soviets. For the interest of global peace, this cannot be allowed to occur.'

Meantime, Israel has indicated it will be willing to withdraw its troops from the Sinai Peninsula. But it is likely to maintain control of the Gaza Strip and the strategic port city of Sharm el-Sheikh at the mouth of the Gulf of Aqaba.

Epilogue

London

As the black cab crawled through the interminable procession of London traffic, she sat on the rear seat, clenching and unclenching her fists and fighting the leaden veil of dread that had been threatening to descend upon her ever since her departure from Istanbul. It was a sensation that was as unfamiliar as it was unwelcome.

Much of her life had been spent fabricating a web of artifice that protected her from those who would like to peel away the carefully layered lies to find the woman who lay beneath. For the last few years, her home in London had been the one place she knew she could find sanctuary, and until her rash decision to return to the Negev Desert, she'd defended it with a single-minded ferocity. But by releasing Benedict Hitchens from the cave that Josef Garvé had intended to be his tomb, she'd acquired herself a formidable enemy. Even if the Frenchman languished in a Turkish prison for years, she knew without any doubt that he'd find a way to get to her.

He knew many of her weaknesses; secrets that could be used to hurt her. His retribution, when it came, would be cataclysmic.

And so she found herself in a race for her life. But it was no longer as straightforward as it had once been for her to vanish. It used to be simply a matter of packing her bags, changing her hairstyle and assuming a new name. She had enough money to begin life again with a new identity elsewhere and knew hidden corners of the world where she'd have a good chance of remaining safe. In the past, she would never have risked returning to London. The possessions and mementoes she'd accumulated were all things she'd shed without a moment's hesitation.

But things were different now. This time there was something she could never leave behind.

The cab pulled up at the front of her home, and as she waited for the driver to hand her the change, she looked up at the terrace's façade with the indifference born of the knowledge that she was about to leave it forever. It was a beautiful house, and one she'd enjoyed living in. But the money from its sale would go some way towards filling the hole in her finances left by the income she'd imagined was coming her way from the sale of the Emerald Tablet. If she wanted to disappear, she needed to make sure she did so with a war chest that would cover her living expenses for as long as she wanted to stay hidden from sight.

Inside, she could see a light burning in the hallway, and her heart began to pound with excitement. Anticipation pushed dread to one side as adrenalin kicked in.

It hasn't been long, but it feels like an eternity, she thought. *I wonder how he'll be when he sees me?*

Hands shaking, she fumbled in her purse for the key as she walked up the tiled pathway to the front door. Slipping it into the lock, she turned the latch and pushed it open. All was silent. Then, she heard him.

Footsteps rang along the hallway – first hesitant as he questioned the evidence of his own eyes, then frantic as he ran towards her, arms outstretched.

She wrapped him in her arms and squeezed him tightly, tears springing into her eyes as he kissed her cheeks and pressed her face between his soft hands.

More footsteps followed as a heavy-set woman appeared in the hallway, a broad smile on her lips. 'He missed you . . . but then, he always does.'

She looked down into the upturned face of her angelic child and kissed him where his soft baby hair touched his forehead. 'Was he a good boy?'

'He always is,' said his nanny.

Her son looked up at her with the expression of immaculate love that she now knew to be the exclusive domain of young children and their mothers.

His eyes shone – green. *Like the sea when a storm's approaching*, she thought. *Just like your father's.*

Acknowledgements

If only because it's always made me laugh for being so phenomenally lazy, I'd love to go the Oscars acceptance speech: 'Thanks to all of you who made this possible. You know who you are!' But as much as I hope that the people I'd like to thank already know how grateful I am to them, given how modest they are – well, most of them, anyway – they mightn't realise I was referring to them. So, I won't be taking any chances.

Firstly, to the booksellers, readers and reviewers who joined me on Benedict Hitchens' first adventure in *The Honourable Thief*, thank you for sharing the journey. Without you, there is no book industry. Thank you for your passion and enthusiasm for the written word.

Of course, books don't come into print without a formidable team in the engine room. For that, I'm indebted to the advocacy and advice offered by my agent, Clare Forster, of Curtis Brown Australia, and the mentorship and support of my publisher, Cate Paterson. I'd be lost without the two of them. Sincere thanks to my editor, Alex Lloyd – well, we did amazing things (no, not *that* Alex Lloyd). After he took off to the bright lights of London, the brilliant Brianne Collins stepped in, helping me trim the luxurious locks of hair I seemed determined to insert on every page. One of the things this book taught me – I have a real thing for hair. Who knew? Thanks also to

Dan Lazar, of Writers House (US), and Gordon Wise of Curtis Brown UK for their representation.

My time working on excavations in Greece and Turkey provided the fabric of the world depicted in my novels. For that, I owe a debt of gratitude to the archaeology department of the University of Melbourne which gave me an education and, under the tutelage of the late, great, Tony Sagona, more good times than I can count. Thanks also to my dear friends in Turkey; Hasan, Metin, Cansin, Chris, Bahadir, Jane and Belma. I'll always be grateful to you for making your home, my home.

Speaking of friends, writing is a solitary pursuit. Which is where good ones come in – friends who are happy to listen to you bellyache, and drag you out to lunch or dinner when you're at risk of becoming a shut-in. Thanks, always, to Jo, Kaz, Mimi, Sophie, Sandra, Andy and Senta, and Andrew and Banu (yes – there are far too many Andrews in my life). You helped me keep my sanity. The same is true of my beautiful family. My two sisters, Victoria and Phoebe, are my guiding lights, and without my inspirational mother, Loretta, Jim, Dianne, Adrian, Andrew (see what I mean?), Stella, Jane, Phil, Sue, John, Katherine, Ariana, Sophia, and the late, great WFW, my life would be very beige indeed.

And then there's my family of the nuclear variety. Roman and Cleopatra – my two (not-so) little angels. You're extraordinary human beings, and not a day goes by when I don't give thanks to whatever powers-that-be directed you into my life – even those days when you leave your plates out of the dishwasher. Thank you for the humour, life and love you bring into my world.

Last, but not least by any measure of the word, Andrew. Without you, none of this would be, and my life would be a pale shadow of what it is. Sure, I wanted Indiana Jones. But you were the best I could get. Insert ironic smiley-face emoji here. Thank you, husband. Here we go again.